CROOKED
LITTLE LIES

CROOKED LITTLE LIES

BARBARA TAYLOR SISSEL

LAKE UNION
PUBLISHING

Published by Lake Union Publishing, Seattle

www.apub.com

Amazon, the Amazon logo, and Lake Union Publishing are trademarks of Amazon.com, Inc., or its affiliates.

ISBN-13: 9781503944848
ISBN-10: 1503944840

Cover design by Mumtaz Mustafa

Printed in the United States of America

For David, aka Buddha Boy, whose shining light never fails to illumine my path, and for Jo, a sister of the heart and a kindred spirit.

1

Lauren didn't know on that Friday in October, when she saw him walking alongside the road's edge, that he would soon vanish, or that in the wake of his disappearance, dozens of people would feel compelled to search for him.

When she spotted him that morning, it was in nearly the same instant she realized she'd turned the wrong way on the interstate feeder, and a fraction of a second later, there he was, mere inches from her bumper, so close her heart stalled. Her glance shot to the rearview mirror once she passed him, half-afraid of what she'd see. His outrage at the least. But his pace was unbroken, as if he were oblivious of how close he'd come to being struck down. Still shaken, she pulled onto the road's shoulder, keeping an eye on him. She'd seen him walking around town before. In fact, her sightings of him were regular enough that if she were to go more than a few days without one, she would wonder about him, even worry a bit for his well-being. But she had never seen him here, where the traffic was constant and fierce.

He was youngish, twentysomething, Lauren thought. Young enough that she could have been his mother. Young enough that watching him now, she felt pangs of distress. Who was he? Why was he on foot? The questions cut across her mind. He didn't look as if he were a homeless person or a vagrant or a homicidal maniac. She felt his situation was something other than that. But what really scared her was how easily he could be killed. She could see it in her mind's eye—his single misstep, the car coming on too fast, clipping him, knocking him hundreds of feet.

On the following Wednesday, when the police questioned her in the wake of his disappearance, she would say it was her fear for him that caused her to stop that morning. But truthfully, she didn't know. Maybe she'd stopped because she'd come so near to harming him herself, or maybe her own recent brush with death had heightened her sense of the fragility of life. Or maybe it was the mother in her. What if he were one of her children? She kept her glance on his reflected image. He seemed . . . not lost but isolated, solitary in a way that made her heart ache. He held himself with his torso awkwardly canted to the right, and the crookedness caused a hitch in his step, yet his pace was dogged, as if he were on a mission. And somehow it was the suggestion of commitment, of fidelity to purpose that hurt her heart worst of all. Did anyone know he was out here? Did anyone care? It was crazy, but when he was within feet of her car, she opened the door and got out.

He stopped abruptly, his head coming erect on his neck, eyes widening, nostrils flared. He might have been an animal on alert, scenting air that was laden with car exhaust and carried a fainter underscore of fried food from the McDonald's that was a little north of where they stood. Lauren closed the distance between them slowly, not wanting to frighten him, and lifted her voice above the sound of the traffic. "Are you okay?"

He didn't meet her gaze, looking past her instead at some point in the distance. He was an inch or two taller than she was, and slender, and his features were finely drawn. His eyes were dark and deep set, and his hair was rumpled and curled over his collar as if it hadn't been cut in a while. But his clothes were clean and pressed. He wore a blue-plaid cotton shirt buttoned to the neck, over gray chinos. He looked cared for, Lauren thought.

She introduced herself. "I'm Lauren Wilder," she said. "I live here, in Hardys Walk. Do you live here, too?"

He nodded and met her glance but only for a moment. Still, there was nothing in his demeanor that caused her to worry for her safety. What she felt, and she would say this to the police, was concern for him. She would tell them she would have stopped for a stray dog. She would say sometimes people and animals get lost and need rescuing. They need help to find their way home. She wouldn't tell that she knew this from her own experience. The police would quickly learn of her accident though, and given the nature of her injuries and their lingering effects, they would question her regarding the accuracy of her memory, whereupon she would insist her recollection of the incident was as good as ever, as if insisting made it so. But what else was there to count on in this world other than your life and your mind and the rational way the two things worked together?

The light changed, and the passing stream of traffic created a warm, oily wind that buffeted the legs of Lauren's jeans, the loose hem of her shirt. She looked back at the boy. Man, really. Her son and daughter, Drew and Mackenzie, were fourteen and eleven respectively, but in a short handful of years, they would be in their twenties and considered adults. Her awareness that this stranger before her was no child gave her pause. Still, she asked for his name, then as quickly, she apologized. It wasn't any of her business, and if she was using him as a distraction to forget her own woes, that was despicable.

"My name is Bo Laughlin." He answered her readily, still looking over her shoulder. "I live in a white house, yes, a white house. I have a big dog named Freckles. My sister's name is Annie. Annie

Beauchamp. I'm going to buy candy for her. I have enough. See?"
He pulled out a roll of cash held together by a rubber band, showing it to Lauren.

"Oh, you should put that away." Her heart contracted with
misgiving. Something was wrong, but exactly what wasn't obvious
to her. His speech was precise and clipped, and while he didn't quite
meet her gaze, his eyes were clear, and she saw intelligence behind
them.

He said, "I should go now."

"Does Annie know where you are?"

He didn't answer Lauren, only blinked rapidly at something,
real or imagined.

She captured his gaze again. "Could I call her for you?"

"There." He gestured to the convenience store some fifty feet
beyond where they were standing. "Going there for candy, thank
you. Good-bye," he said formally, and then he brushed by her.

Lauren turned, watching him go, and she felt helpless and
confused in equal measure. Unlike her, he seemed so sure of his
objective and so completely unaware of his limitations. Given her
recently lamentable track record, who was she to judge what those
limitations were? And yet once he disappeared inside the store,
she got into her car, took her cell phone out of her purse and sat
staring at it for a moment. She should do something about him,
shouldn't she? But calling 911 didn't feel right. It wasn't that sort of
an emergency.

She dialed Tara's cell number, leaving a message when her
younger sister didn't answer, and then, keeping the phone in her
hand, she considered calling Jeff. Not that long ago, she wouldn't
have thought twice about it. But it was different now. Jeff was wary
of her. Cautious. He claimed to have forgiven her, but even if that
was true, he hadn't forgotten, and he didn't trust her. Why should
he? Most people were careful around addicts, even recovering ones.

Lauren didn't blame them. She watched herself; she had to, after the way she'd slipped up. Panic was her constant companion, and it was as rough as a prizefighter who kept throwing punches long after the bell had rung. Even now, she felt the wild swing of its clutched fist battering her ribs and bit down hard against it. She couldn't allow it, couldn't believe in fear that was groundless. It would take her sanity and run, if it had not already.

Searching the Internet, she found the nonemergency number for the Lincoln County Sheriff's Office and entered it. The woman who answered identified herself as Marilyn Wingate, and when she asked how she could help, Lauren described Bo Laughlin and her concern.

"What's your location?" Marilyn asked.

Lauren told her she was on the northbound feeder of I-45 just north of Bayberry, the intersection that bisected Hardys Walk, near the town's center. "I would never have seen him at all if I hadn't turned the wrong way. Too much on my mind, I guess." Glancing at herself in the rearview, she thought what an understatement that was.

"We'll send a patrol car, if there's one in the area," Marilyn said. "The trouble is he's likely to be gone by the time a deputy can get there."

"Other people must have seen him. I know I've spotted him any number of times at different places around town. Maybe there isn't any cause for concern. He doesn't seem mentally challenged, really." Lauren was remembering the concise manner of Bo's speech, his neat appearance. Was she interfering, then? Indulging in some delusional fantasy? That's what Jeff would say. He'd assume she was on something, probably tear up the house, hunting for her stash. It sickened her to think of it, that this was what they had come to. This was the place where they lived, on the dark, unraveling edges of doubt and lost faith, love that was uncertain.

5

"I don't recall other reports, but that doesn't mean there haven't been any," Marilyn said.

Lauren mentioned the cash Bo had shown her.

"Was it a lot?"

"I don't know, but people have been killed over a dollar, less even."

Marilyn asked for contact information, and when Lauren said she and Jeff owned Wilder and Tate Commercial and Architectural Salvage, there was a bit of a pause before Marilyn said, "Really?" in a tone Lauren recognized, the knowing one that caused her to steel herself for the inevitable questions. *I heard about your accident,* Marilyn would say. *I can't imagine what you've been through, how you survived.* Hardys Walk was small enough that when Lauren had fallen thirty-seven feet down the shaft of a church bell tower and lived to tell about it, it had briefly made the local news. Her own terrible fifteen minutes of fame . . .

But Marilyn only said, "Can you hang on? Just for a sec. While I give this information to dispatch, okay?"

Relieved, Lauren answered, "Fine," even though she had a laundry list of errands to run. She kept an eye on the store while she waited. Bo had gone inside, but so far, she hadn't seen him come out.

Marilyn came back on the line. "They'll try and find an officer in the vicinity who can do a welfare check."

It wasn't a priority. Lauren could tell by the way Marilyn sounded. She would tell the police that, too, when they questioned her Wednesday about her sighting of Bo—what would turn out to be the second-to-last-known sighting of him. Lauren would say that if an officer had come when she'd called, Bo wouldn't have disappeared.

"Wilder and Tate, huh? My husband and I have bought vintage windows from you for our bungalow. We were told they came out of an old farmhouse you took down. I can't even imagine how you do that, deconstruct an old building."

Ah. Here it is, Lauren thought. Marilyn was taking the back way in. Rather than coming across as nosy, she managed to sound somehow reverent and wary.

"There aren't many women doing that sort of work, are there? It must be so difficult."

Lauren said it could be, that the jobs were often tedious, hot, and dirty. She might spend entire afternoons doing nothing but yanking nails out of a pile of hundred-year-old siding or beadboard. Being a woman made her an oddity, too. The men in the trade had trouble believing she could do as good a job. But she was stronger than she looked, or she had been, and her slighter frame allowed her to work in tighter places, like church bell tower shafts. She said, "I mainly work the smaller jobs." Lauren was drawn to the salvage end of the business, the preservation of historical treasures. "My husband works the big commercial jobs. He's into heavy equipment and dynamite."

Marilyn laughed. "Just like a man." She paused, then said something about needing a door.

She meant a vintage door, Lauren realized. "We have several," she said. "Actually more than several." She laughed, thinking of the rows of old doors stacked like soldiers at the warehouse. It would take a person days to get through all of them.

"Maybe my husband and I will come take a look this weekend. Will you be open? It would be fun to meet you."

"We're open, but I'll be out of town over the weekend, unfortunately."

Marilyn expressed regret.

"I don't guess you know anyone who wants to buy a house on eighty acres in the country?" Lauren didn't know why she asked—as if there could be any chance it would be so easy.

"Whereabouts?"

"About an hour's drive north. It's my grandparents' farm near Lufkin. Between Lufkin and Nacogdoches."

"Beautiful country," Marilyn said. "Seems as if it should sell quickly."

"I hope so," Lauren said because that was the expected response, the one everyone—especially Jeff and Tara—wanted. They didn't need more trouble from her, more argument and unhappiness. They were fed up with all that. Lauren would feel the same way, she guessed. Still, the idea of strangers living in her grandparents' beloved house was so foreign, so beyond comprehension—like selling your arm or your heart, your family's legacy. So much of their childhood was framed by that house—its porch posts and sun-warmed floorboards, the hidden nooks that only they knew. Who else would love it as much? Who else would hear the echo of their laughter around every corner?

"I'll check into this young man's situation a bit more, see if I can follow up with the sister. Annie Beauchamp, right?" Marilyn asked.

Lauren thanked Marilyn, stowed her phone, then pulled onto the feeder and took a quick right into the convenience store parking lot. That's when she caught sight of Bo again, what would turn out to be her last glimpse of him, coming out of the store and climbing into a car, a sedan. Was it a Cadillac? Lauren wasn't good with cars. Something black and sleek. She drove a Navigator, not because she wanted to drive a vehicle that was huge and gas guzzling but because she was always hauling something. She slowed as she passed the car, long enough to see that a woman was driving it, an older, white-haired woman, and that Bo was in the front passenger seat, laughing. Clearly, he was fine, perfectly fine.

Lauren slowed even further, openly staring, taking in Bo's smiling face, the woman's white, white hair, done in a French twist.

She gave off an air of elegance, of the sort other women envy. She was the kind of woman who made you feel you wouldn't mind getting old so much if you could do it like her, with her sort of grace. Lauren bet she would be wise, too. Too wise to do anything so foolish as to waylay a young man who was a stranger and then call the police on him.

A horn honked. Lauren's glance jerked to the rearview mirror, and her eyes collided with the driver of a blue pickup behind her, then lifted to travel the line of vehicles snaked behind him, all of them waiting on her. She set her foot down on the accelerator harder than she meant to, making the Navigator leap forward, adding to her agitation. This was the sort of thing Jeff meant when he said her mind wasn't all there yet. Six weeks after she'd been discharged from the hospital, Dr. Bettinger had cleared her for driving on the condition that she keep the distances short and the routes familiar, but even with Bettinger's okay, Jeff thought it was too soon. Sometimes when she looked at him across a room or when they were out shopping or on a job, he'd tap his temple. *Think.* He wanted her to think, to be aware, to be reasonable. He wanted her to be herself again. So did Lauren, in the worst way.

She got packing boxes at the U-Haul store and, before leaving there, contacted the sheriff's department again, hoping to reach Marilyn, to say never mind about Bo Laughlin. *I overreacted,* she would say. She wasn't prepared for it when an answering machine picked up and stumbled through an awkwardly worded apology. She tried to forget about the incident after that, but she couldn't, not entirely. She didn't know why, and when she learned the following week that Bo Laughlin was missing, she was shocked yet she also felt vindicated. Maybe she wasn't crazy after all. It would seem sensible then to contact county law enforcement and remind them of her encounter with Bo. Jeff would argue she should leave it alone, that she didn't need more stress. He would say the moment she saw Bo get into the car—which turned out to be a Lincoln, not a Cadillac—it was too late to save him.

But in Lauren's estimation, *too late* wasn't so easily defined; it wasn't a place you could point to and say, *there, that's the one*—the exact moment when ordinary life ended and the nightmare began. In hindsight, as hard as she would search for it, Lauren would never find that precise moment, the one where, if only she'd realized the nature of the calamity that was taking shape, she might have done something, acted in some way to prevent it, a way that would have kept them all safe.

2

The trouble with life, as far as Annie Beauchamp was concerned, was that it never gave you a clue about what was coming. When a terrible thing happened, life just charged at you, running full out, clobbering you, usually from behind. You were down then. You were left sick in your stomach and broken in your heart, trying to pick up your wits, your scattered pieces, and when you looked back, you saw that you didn't have a clue, not one inkling.

That's how it was when her dad walked out on her and her mom, when Annie was three, and that's how it was when her mom died late on a Saturday night in April two years ago, in a car accident, and that's how it was on that Friday morning in October, when she went to Madeleine's, the café where she worked as a waitress, only she didn't know it yet.

Anne didn't suffer a single pang of prescience when Madeleine came out of the kitchen after the lunch rush to ask about Bo— would Annie call and see if he could come in and work the dinner shift? Madeleine often employed Bo to bus tables and wash dishes. Plus he was a pretty good prep chef when he was on his meds.

Annie said she'd try to find him, and setting down the sugar shaker she was refilling, she pulled her cell phone out of her apron pocket, thinking, as she always did, of how kind Madeleine was. Thinking Bo better have his phone on—he often didn't—and agree to come in and help Madeleine out or she'd kill him. But he didn't answer, and when she called his dad, who was her stepdad, although she'd never called him anything other than JT, JT said he hadn't seen or heard from Bo in a week.

"So, how are you? What have you been up to?" Annie asked. JT hadn't set eyes on her in more than a month, but she didn't expect him to comment on it or to ask how she was. They'd drifted apart after her mom died.

"Oh, you know, the usual," JT answered, which meant work, home, beer, frozen dinner in front of the TV, and bed, in that order. Get up tomorrow, do it all over again. Once Annie had asked her mom what she saw in JT, and her mom had said he was regular, as regular as the six o'clock news. She could count on him to work, to bring home his pay, to have dinner with her at home and stay there, plus he was kind. Unlike Annie's dad, she meant. Who knew where that guy was?

Annie told JT maybe he and Bo could come to the café and have dinner one day soon, get the family together, such as it was. That was how good she was at predicting the future, how good she was at planning for it.

"Yeah," JT said. "Sure thing, kiddo. We'll do that, maybe next week."

Annie hung up. He hadn't expressed any concern about Bo. But she almost never worried about her stepbrother, either. She knew his ways and his places and how he could get distracted. She ducked her head into the kitchen and told Madeleine she hadn't found him yet, but she'd keep trying. Madeleine nodded, as unperturbed as Annie.

She said, "You'll be here early tomorrow, do your baking."

It was a command, but after a year and a half working at the café, Annie was used to the older woman's brusque manner. In fact, she'd come to appreciate it. There was never any doubt where you stood with Madeleine, and underneath, her heart was softer than warm butter on a summer day anyway. Who else would keep a job open for Bo? He was in high school when Madeleine first hired him, more reliable and less crazy acting, but every year since then, he'd lost a little more ground to some world he conjured in his head.

Annie handled his money when he would let her have it. She paid his bills, and like JT, she kept a bedroom for him in her house, although he preferred living on the street. Living free, he called it. Living close to nature. He only carried the cell phone she'd given him, because she insisted. He didn't want electronic gadgets, not even a TV; he couldn't watch it. The moving pictures and voices alarmed him. He didn't need a bed, either. He didn't sleep that much. Mostly, he walked. And walked. And wrote things down in a small notepad he kept in his shirt pocket. He was like Thoreau, he'd say. *You ever heard of him?* he'd ask. Annie didn't know why he walked so much. Not exactly. But when he did, he was determined. At twenty-three, he appeared more certain of his direction in life than she was at twenty-seven. Annie told herself that in his time, people had said Thoreau was nuts, too, and a fanatic.

There were days Bo showed up out of the blue on her front porch at dawn, or at noon or two in the morning, holding a fistful of bedraggled flowers, weeds he'd pulled up roots and all from the roadside, or a wilted bouquet he'd found in someone's trash. There were other days more recently when he'd passed her on the street as if he didn't know her. Annie fed him and kept track of him as best she could, when he allowed it. It's what her mother had done, even though Bo wasn't hers; she had watched over him for the seventeen years she'd been married to Bo's dad. Annie thought her mom had cared more for Bo's well-being than JT did. Not that JT's neglect was intentional. It was just that as Bo drifted further into his own world, JT seemed less able to relate to him, to be with him and look after him. So Annie had assumed the responsibility because someone had to. Someone should care.

She left the café by the back door and headed to her car, a battered 1983 BMW that had belonged to her mom, that her mom had bought used, that, as of right this minute, had some 322,000 miles on the odometer. Every day, Annie wondered how much longer it could last. She hated how much she relied on the car and how grateful she was for a thing she had only because her mom had died.

Annie unlocked the BMW's door, and while she waited for the heat to disperse, Carol Fisher pulled her truck into the adjacent space. Carol's truck was possibly older and more battered than Annie's car. Plus it didn't have a lick of paint on it. But Carol couldn't care less. She waited tables at Madeleine's, too, and she'd laugh if anyone—one of their regular diners, say—made a joke about it. "Hey, it's paid for, asshole," she'd joke.

Annie loved her; she loved the way Carol went through life as if it were a joy, a big adventure. She and her husband, Leonard—Len, Carol called him—and four grown sons, who with one exception had stayed in Hardys Walk, owned Fisher and Sons Organic Farm, where they raised livestock, vegetables, and feed crops, all of it grown the natural, organic way. Madeleine bought from the Fishers, a lot of people did. Sometimes the very same people who'd say there wasn't any money in farming, especially farming like the Fishers did it. If Carol heard them, she'd laugh her big, infectious laugh and agree they were right, there sure wasn't much money in it. Just one hell of a lot of satisfaction, she'd say. Satisfaction and contentment. Annie envied that.

How do you get there? she would ask. She wanted so badly to know. But no one could tell her, not even Carol. *You just do it,* she said. *It's easy,* she said. *Honey, you can get happy in the same shoes you get sad in,* she said. *Trust me.*

The truck door slammed, and Annie waited for Carol to come into view. Ordinarily, Monday through Thursday, Carol arrived before the lunch crowd and worked through dinner until closing, but today, she'd had a doctor's appointment.

"Hey," Annie said as Carol rounded the tailgate.

"Hey, yourself." Carol stowed her keys in her purse. "You on your way out to the farm? Len's got your order. I told him to set some pumpkins aside."

"The Small Sugars?" It was the only variety Annie would use in her pumpkin muffins, which had made her semifamous. She wasn't sure how it happened that she'd become the café's designated baker. Madeleine and Carol—everyone, actually—assumed Annie loved it, but Annie didn't know that she did. She would only go so far as to say she didn't mind baking, any of it, except the hours, which were horrible. Annie was at work, up to her elbows in flour before the birds sang a single note, every morning except Sunday when the café was closed. Madeleine was old-school. She said the Lord was on to something good when he'd declared Sunday a day of rest. Madeleine said just because you can do a thing like stay open and work seven days a week doesn't mean you should.

Madeleine also said baking gave Annie's life purpose and direction, but Annie wasn't so sure of that, either. She looked at Carol. "You didn't happen to see Bo on your way here, did you?"

"No, is he MIA again?"

"Off on one of his treks, I guess. Or maybe at the library." Annie remembered the time a year or so ago when the library had been closed and locked with Bo inside it all night. He hadn't even noticed. They'd found him the next morning, asleep in the aisle between books on philosophy and astrology, with something by Carl Sagan in his hand. He'd repeated passages from it for weeks afterward, so frequently Annie had thought she would go insane. She could still, if called on, repeat them herself. *"If you wish to make an apple pie from scratch, you must first invent the universe."* If Bo said it once, he'd said it a thousand times. Annie wasn't sure of the meaning, even after he tried explaining it. She remembered him saying the quote reminded him of her, of her love of baking.

"But I don't know if I love baking," she argued.

"You'll learn to," he said, "if you do it long enough. You need something in your life to love." *Someone,* he had added. He meant not only her mother. That was impossible, though. No one else would ever be as constant or as tender as her mother. No one would ever care so much about her. Annie had thought when her mom died, long before Annie was ready to let her go, that she would die, too. But she hadn't.

She met Carol's gaze now. "I'll go by the library on my way out to the farm. He's probably buried in the stacks."

"Driving everyone nuts," Carol said.

"Yeah," Annie said. There were folks in town who went out of their way to avoid Bo. They ignored him, pretending he was invisible, and there were others who tolerated and looked out for him, but they also got exasperated with him, the way he would pace and talk incessantly or not answer them at all. At the library, he could make a pest of himself, given the way he would wander the aisles, repeating himself, quoting whole passages from memory hour after hour. He pulled books off the shelves, too, but the librarians had somehow managed to train him to put them back. Otherwise, Annie was certain they would bar him from the premises.

"You called JT?" Carol asked.

"He hasn't seen him." Annie settled into the BMW, slammed the door, started the engine, and a part of her brain did register a funny hiccup, one she'd not heard before, but she ignored it. Lowering her window, she said, "I'll see you later."

Carol waved. "Call me if you find Bo."

Annie said she would. She didn't give it a second thought, that Carol had said *if* and not *when*.

3

"Hey, you."

Lauren felt Jeff sit beside her on the edge of the bed. She felt his palm, cool on her cheek, felt him tuck strands of her hair behind her ear, and his tenderness surprised her. He hadn't touched her, not in days, perhaps weeks. She couldn't pinpoint exactly when the shift away from her had taken place. It was possible she imagined it, his aloofness and the increasing strain between them. It seemed to her that her thoughts, the impressions her mind seized on were like sand castles, built and destroyed at the whim of some mental tide that seemed beyond her control, even her understanding. But his closeness now opened an ache inside her, as if her body recognized some nurturing touch it had been missing.

"How's your head?" he asked. "Still hurting?"

"I'm really sorry," she said as if the pain were her fault. The headaches were part of the raft of symptoms that continued to plague her in the wake of the accident. They weren't migraines, per se. She didn't have the visual anomalies that often went along with those, nor did she suffer from nausea, but they still packed a punch that could level her.

"What have you taken?"

Of course Jeff wanted to know. It was only natural, given her history.

"Just what Dr. Bettinger gave me." Lauren couldn't remember the name of it. She did remember that when she'd voiced her concern, he informed her he was fully aware of her situation and what he was prescribing was non-narcotic. He'd given her an affronted look. Maybe it was ridiculous to think a doctor would prescribe addictive drugs to a recovering addict. Still, she didn't like Dr. Bettinger much. His demeanor was as cold as his hands.

Lauren missed Margaret. Her hands when she examined Lauren had always been warm. Even when Lauren was a tiny girl, Margaret had run warm water over the disk of her stethoscope before putting it on Lauren's chest. But Margaret had been more than Lauren's doctor; she had also been her godmother and the one who kept Lauren together and functioning when her parents died suddenly, before Lauren finished college. Margaret had often said in the days following the accident that Lauren was brave. Holding Lauren through the hours of pain, she had whispered into Lauren's ear, *I think you are so very brave.*

It wasn't true, but when Margaret said it, Lauren had almost believed it.

Jeff left the bed, went into the bathroom, and came back with a cloth dampened with cold water. She settled it over her eyes. "If this keeps on, I don't think I'll be much use at the farm."

"I doubt you could stand the ride in the shape you're in."

Lauren heard the sound of drawers opening, and lifting the cloth from her eyes, she saw that he was stuffing a canvas bag with socks and underwear, his shaving kit. "You're going?" She had hoped he wouldn't, that her headache would serve to delay the whole process.

He zipped the tote. "We've got to get the property on the market. You know that."

"So you keep telling me, but I don't know why you won't at least consider selling this house. It's worth more. We could buy a smaller house or a condo. We'd save so much more than just the mortgage payment—all the fees and just trying to keep up the yard and—"

"How can you want to coop us up like that? Do you really want to listen to the neighbors flush their toilets? Do you want to fight some jerk next door when his TV's on too loud?"

"Then why not live at the farm? It's only until we're back on our feet."

"Lauren, for Christ's sake, we've discussed this a hundred times. You want me to drive a hundred sixty miles a day to work? You want the kids in some Podunk school? The academics in those country-school systems suck, and don't even get me started on their athletic programs."

"C'mon, Jeff. You don't know anything about the schools up there." Lauren rose on an elbow, wincing at the pain that arced across her brain.

"I know what it takes to get recognition, to make a name for yourself, to earn respect. I know college athletic scouts don't generally mess with 3A programs."

"That's assuming Drew wants to be scouted, that he's good enough at football to be given a scholarship."

"Oh, that's nice, Lauren. I love how you have faith in him."

"He's not you, and you aren't your dad. You aren't going to make news fodder out of your life or Drew's the way your dad did with all that 'Wilder the Wildman' foolishness, and I thank God for that. You're a good dad, Jeff, a better dad."

He sighed. "Look, Drew's a good player on his own. He deserves whatever chance I can give him."

"Assuming his grades come up enough for him to play again."

"He's already brought them up, and now that you're better and things are getting back to normal, I know they'll stay that way."

"But even so, he's not the big football hero, the star quarterback you were. He doesn't crave playing like you did. I've heard you say it, that he doesn't have the same fire in his belly." Lauren lay back. It was an old argument, one she had less and less energy for.

"How's he going to go to a decent college without a scholarship? It's only four years until he graduates. What do you think I'm going to do, pull the money out of a fucking hat?" Jeff sounded more perplexed than angry.

Still, Lauren was annoyed. "There are grants, loans we can apply for."

The silence that came was battered yet familiar, a recurrent injury that, unlike her physical injuries, didn't seem inclined to heal.

"It's not shameful to need help, Jeff. It doesn't make you a failure."

He broke their gaze, wiping his hands down his face, blowing out his breath.

"Jeff?"

"You just don't know."

"Well, if I don't, it's because you won't tell me. I'm not an invalid or incompetent. I'm your partner. We're equal, and that means I take my share of whatever load of bad news it is that you're carrying."

The look he shot her was resigned. "Let's not do this, okay? We're both under a lot of pressure. Let's just get the farm sold, then we can talk about what's next."

"I don't understand the rush."

"The decision's been made. What's the point of waiting?"

She shifted her glance.

"C'mon, babe. Let me handle it, and I'm not saying that because I don't feel you're competent. I just want the life we had. I want it to be good again. Like it was."

Before the accident, he meant. *BTA*.

"I'm damned if I'll give up. I've worked too hard."

"I would have been content with something smaller. I've always said that."

"What is the point of bringing that up now?"

"I know why living in this neighborhood means so much to you, but, Jeff, your dad is old now. He's lost most of his mind. Whatever it is you're looking for from him—his approval, respect, I don't know—he can't give it. And as for what other people think of us—"

"It's got nothing to do with Pop. I've built a name and a reputation in this community. I've got connections, people I do business with. The kids have good friends. We've put down roots. I'm not tearing all that up."

She might have said it was already torn up, but he knew that.

"We'll be fine." He came to the bedside and bent to kiss her temple, her mouth. "We'll get back on our feet. You'll see. We're getting some decent work now—taking down the old Waller-Land building is going to make our fourth quarter."

"Yes." She paused. Had they won the contract, then? She searched her foggy brain. Oh, but now, here it was. She did remember, and she smiled at Jeff. "I picked up the permits."

"Yes, you did," he said. "Thank you." He smiled as pleased as she was that the memory had returned to her.

"But you still think we should sell the farm."

"I don't see another way. I'm sorry."

"I should go with you, then, since you're so determined," Lauren said, although she wondered how she would stand it, packing away her grandparents' belongings, watching as the house became an empty shell. How would she close the door for the last time? How could she walk away?

"No. Stay. When do you ever get a weekend like this without me and the kids and a hundred things to do?"

That might have been a legitimate question back in their old life, when she would have been thrilled by the prospect of oodles of time with no one to cook for or clean up after. It had been a rare occurrence then for Jeff and Lauren to have a weekend to themselves. Having lived in the neighborhood for all of the sixteen years they'd been married, they had a network of friends who had shared childcare along with birthday and holiday celebrations, backyard cookouts, carpool duties. But things were different now. They didn't fit into the circle the way they once had, and Lauren didn't know how to go back, how to make amends—if it was justified or even possible. Step nine of the twelve cautioned you should not attempt to ask forgiveness if doing so would only cause further harm. She didn't know if it would or not.

"Give it time," Jeff said, reading her thoughts.

"A person makes one mistake . . ." she said and wondered why she was defending herself, how she could even imagine there was a defense.

"I know."

"It wasn't on purpose." That was her refuge—her lack of intent, shabby as it was.

"I know that, too."

Do you? The query sat in her mouth. Asking it would start them arguing again. She would only feel worse, more angry, more ashamed. She had thought she was so much better and stronger than she'd turned out to be. *Brave?* What a joke. "I feel so useless, lying here."

"You don't want to push it, though, get dizzy and fall again, right? Just concentrate on getting well."

"I am well."

"You know what I mean."

Unfortunately, she did. He was referring to the little lapses, the tiny glitches and misfires that still occurred in her brain. Like this morning when, instead of turning right, she'd turned left and nearly hit Bo Laughlin. It overcame her anew, the panic at how close she'd come. She would tell Jeff, but it would only underscore his opinion that she ought not to be driving, period. He might try to push it, take her car keys, say, or insist she have someone with her when she drove. She'd lose every shred of her independence then, every step of the ground she'd worked so hard to regain.

"You're picking the kids up at school?" she asked.

"Gabe's dad said he's got all their camping and fishing gear packed. He wants to pick up the guys and head straight to the lake. I told Drew to call me when they get there."

"I know you wish you were going with them." Fishing was a favorite pastime of Jeff's, one he and Drew shared.

"Next time," Jeff said.

"What about Kenzie?"

Jeff answered she had a ride, too, with Amanda, her best friend.

Kenzie was spending the weekend with her. Suzanne, Amanda's mom, had gotten tickets to see the Houston Ballet perform *Sleeping Beauty* for Amanda's birthday. Last year, Lauren and Suzanne had taken the girls to a performance of *Giselle*. It was tradition, the four of them seeing a ballet two or three times a year and dining afterward, fashionably late. Lauren had only learned to love the ballet when Kenzie, at age three, conceived a passion for it. She and Amanda had taken classes together since then. It was how Suzanne and Lauren had become close, ferrying the girls to and from lessons and each other's houses, gathering embellishments for costumes, sharing the endless grind of rehearsals, the thrill of an opening-night performance. But it was awkward now. Suzanne had seemed relieved when Lauren told her she couldn't accompany them to the ballet, that she would be away this weekend. Jeff said it was her imagination, and it would be so easy to think so, but even Lauren, with her injured brain, couldn't be that deluded. Whatever was left of her friendship with Suzanne didn't amount to more than the pretense they kept in place for their girls' sake.

"Can I get you anything before I go?" Jeff asked.

"A new head?"

"Babe, I can fix a lot of shit, but I think that's a little beyond my expertise."

Lauren heard the smile in his voice, and her heart eased.

"Did you call Tara?" he asked.

"I tried; she didn't answer. I left a message. You realize she and Greg might cancel."

Greg Honey was Tara's current boyfriend, the latest in a long line, and as much as Lauren liked him, as much as she wished her little sister would find someone to make a life with, she would break them up if she could find a way, and not think twice.

Jeff shrugged into his jacket. "If they do, I'll pack and load what I can by myself. Maybe I can get Greg to meet me at the warehouse on Sunday and help unload. That's where you and Tara want the stuff, right?"

Lauren said it was.

Jeff bent to kiss her again, and while his touch was brief, his mouth on hers was warm and tender and conveyed his concern for her. When he straightened, she caught his hand, looking into his eyes. She wanted badly to reassure him, to tell him she was fine, that he could count on her as he once had. Words to that effect flooded her mouth, but she bit down on them and released him. She was lucky he was standing by her, given the way she'd disgraced him and their children. Some husbands—lesser men than Jeff—would have walked out.

25

Lauren slept for a while after he left, and when she woke the room was cool and filled with muddy shadows, and the ache in her head had subsided; her mind felt clearer.

"I'm much better. I think I should come," she said later when Jeff called. "There's so much to do."

But he only repeated what he'd said earlier, that she should rest, take advantage of a weekend to herself. "I'll call you later tonight, see how you're doing."

Ending the call, she wondered, and she wasn't proud of herself for it, if his checking on her was more out of suspicion than concern for her well-being. Even though she'd been clean and narcotic-free for almost a year, he still watched her. He looked into her eyes, not out of love, not in the name of romance. No. He was examining the size of her pupils. It made her furious. It made her angry enough that sometimes she almost hated him, and she regretted that, too. But she regretted her weakness that had led her to get hooked in the first place even more. Gloria, her sponsor, said Lauren's emotions were normal. She said it would be helpful if Jeff would attend meetings, too, but so far, he refused.

He wasn't the addict, he said. Why should he? Or else he said he had too much work.

Both things were true.

He wasn't an addict. But she didn't feel like one, either. It wasn't as if she'd gone looking to get high like some reckless party girl. She hadn't willfully chosen to take drugs any more than she'd chosen to fall from the bell tower of the old church they'd been deconstructing. She'd cracked herself up to a point nearly beyond repair, collapsing her lungs and smashing her pelvis. There'd been internal bleeding. All of that in addition to slamming her brain against the walls of her skull. Once she stabilized and began the long road to recovery, she'd suffered bouts of pain so excruciating that at times not even the doctor-prescribed OxyContin could touch it.

It was only recently that she'd been able to look back and take comfort and a degree of satisfaction from how far she'd come in the twenty-two months since the accident. At first, she'd been unable to speak properly or do simple things like tie her shoes. She'd finally learned to walk again, but she was warned she would always need a walker. When she tossed that contraption out the door, the doctors and her physical therapist said she'd use a cane the rest of her life. She'd proven them all wrong. She'd recovered her speech and her motor skills. Everyone had been in awe of her willingness to work. They said she was lucky. Like Margaret, they believed she was brave. They didn't know about the narcotics she took by the handful, the ones she got on the sly. How had she learned the ways?

Her memory of that time was so hazy, even she didn't know, not really. One day, she'd been an ordinary wife and mother, a businesswoman, someone who walked the straight and narrow, and the next, she'd been swallowing dope like candy. It scared her, thinking how easily she'd become hooked. But the worst part for her was the mortification that came from knowing she had been stoned, doped to the max in front of her children and others, their friends and neighbors. She'd made a spectacle of herself.

Done to Jeff what his father had done. Made a mockery of him. Made him look like a fool by association. Coach Wilder, the Wildman, had been known for his explosive temper and outrageous antics both on and off the collegiate football field. It might have been easier growing up if Jeff could have out-and-out hated his dad, but they'd been trapped together by their mutual love of football, the impossible dream of the Wildman's expectation that Jeff would go pro, and Jeff's struggle to fulfill it. Maybe if he'd lacked talent, if the scouts hadn't come wooing, if the media hadn't made such a thing of it—Wilder and his Wild Old Man. The jokes, rendered in headline format, had gone on through four years of high school and three years of college. It wasn't until Jeff's junior year, when he sustained a gruesome hit to his knee, tearing every ligament, that his career ended, and the press, along with the Wildman, gave up. Without football, Jeff nearly ceased to exist in his dad's mind. Jeff was still battling feelings of failure and abandonment when Lauren met him. In their early days together, when they were falling in love, he'd credited her with restoring his confidence and the will to find a way other than football to achieve success in his life, which in his mind then had been the same as proving himself to his dad.

But even that had faded now, Lauren thought, with age, with the onset of the Wildman's Alzheimer's. Jeff had eventually come to view the injury as a mixed blessing. It had ended his football career, but at least the notoriety had ended, too.

Until now.

Now he had his druggie wife's antics to deal with, to excuse and explain—to live over.

She'd made him the object of gossip and whispered speculation, made them outcasts, and the reality of what she'd done to him and to their children was the thinnest of blades slipped between her ribs. No matter which way she turned, it hurt. And in one small, frightened corner of her mind, she was still waiting for the day when he would act on the ultimatum he'd given her months earlier, that she get off dope or he would be forced to take Drew and Kenzie and leave her. She had been so angry at him, and at Tara when she took his side. The two of them had aligned themselves against her. For her own good, they said. Out of love, they said. You won't stop yourself, so we're doing it for you, they said. Dope or your kids: you choose. It had infuriated her all the more because, down deep, she knew they were right and it shamed her. She honestly didn't know if she would have stopped without their interference, their threats.

It haunted her now, that they might still be plotting to take her children and toss her into an institution. It was ridiculous; she knew it was. Yet she was afraid. She doubted them, and she was aggravated by them, and resentful, and sorry for them and herself, and she didn't know what to do about any of it. And that was the hardest part.

Lauren was dozing when Tara called her back, worried for her, asking what she could do, and when her sister said, "Remember the little bed tray Mama used when we were sick, the blue one she painted the bouquet of daisies on?" Lauren's heart constricted; she felt the burn of tears. She guessed it was the pain making her weak, and the affection in Tara's voice, her obvious concern. How could she doubt Tara's allegiance, her own sister?

Lauren said, "She brought us chicken soup with those little alphabet noodles."

"And cups of shaved ice flavored with grape juice when we had strep throat."

"I still miss her sometimes, TeeRee, so much."

"I know. Me, too."

"I thought Jeff would cancel."

"Well, we really need to get this done, you know?"

"But he seems so—"

"So what?"

"I know he doesn't tell me everything."

"He doesn't want you to worry."

"But why can't he see that not knowing only makes me worry more?"

The note of vexation was there in the beat of silence before Tara spoke, before she said, "You have to stop doing this to yourself."

Lauren groaned. "Please don't lecture me, TeeRee."

"But we've been over this. You make this stuff up in your head, that Jeff's conspiring against you, that he's going to divorce you and take the kids away, and it's so not true. The man has done every-thing he can to get you well. He's killing himself, working, trying to keep you guys solvent."

"I know," Lauren said, although she wondered sometimes if, in part, killing himself wasn't a ploy, a way to make himself look like a good guy, a heroic guy, one who was keeping it together in spite of his loony wife. Or maybe the long hours were a way to avoid her. She'd thought that, too.

"Look, this isn't you doing this. It's your brain. It gets ideas, bad ones, and runs away with you." Love mixed with exasperation shone in Tara's voice. She'd given the speech before, so many times they were both tired of it.

Tara had sat in on a few of Lauren's sessions with Dr. Bettinger. She knew the potential for aftereffects in the wake of Lauren's head injury—everything from hallucinations to bouts of paranoia, extreme fatigue, emotional outbursts, even the onset of psychosis—as well as Lauren. Tara had heard Bettinger say some or all of whatever symptoms Lauren might endure would go away, eventually. Or not. Who knew? Not Bettinger. The neurologist only said not to expect recovery to unfold in a straight line, that it was often two steps forward and three back. He cautioned Lauren might never mend in a way that would make her seem entirely familiar to herself or to her family. He repeatedly told her she was lucky, that others with a less traumatic injury than hers were disabled for life.

He had said she hadn't made it easier, getting hooked on Oxy.

Lauren sat up, closing her eyes when her head swam. "I really think I should be there. I mean if you all are so determined to get this done—"

"No," Tara said. "Jeff's right. Think of it as a little mini vacation and rest."

"You talked to him?"

"Texted."

"Huh." Lauren picked at the coverlet. Was it the post-addiction paranoia that made her think Tara and Jeff seemed to be in touch with one another more than they had been before the accident? Or was that thought, when it blinked off and on in her brain, the product of real intuition, one she should pay attention to?

"He said you got groceries."

"I did, everything except wine."

"We can pick that up at Scarlett's." Tara named the country store that carried everything from duck liver pâté to cowboy boots.

"Maybe you should skip it."

"The wine? Why?"

"Well, because drinking around Greg . . . It might be hard for him to not join in."

"Why shouldn't he? You drink wine sometimes. What is up with you two, anyway?"

"I don't know what you mean." But Lauren did know very well, and she wished she hadn't mentioned Greg now. She wished she had bitten off her tongue instead.

"It's just lately you've been acting as if you think he's dangerous or something. Why? What's changed between you two? You had such a mutual-admiration thing going."

"Have you asked him?"

"He acted like you, as if he didn't know what I was talking about. But I know better."

There was a lot Lauren could have said. The trouble was she didn't know if she had the right. She bit her lip.

"It can't be because he used drugs. I mean you knew that. We all knew it. He's always been up front about it."

Lauren's mind seized on this. "Well, still, it's hard for me to feel comfortable about my little sister dating a guy who was on heroin."

"All right, but honestly—and don't get mad when I say this, but you used drugs. They may have started out as prescription, but is that really better? So I don't see how you can judge him."

"Oh, Tee, you know me better than that. I do admire Greg. He's like a—a mentor, you know?" It was true, a fact that only served to complicate Lauren's sense of the situation, of the danger Tara might be in from Greg, the very same Greg who'd been there when Lauren crossed the line and went from using to abusing OxyContin. Greg had recognized what was happening before anyone had, least of all Lauren herself. He'd understood in the way only another addict could how it had happened; he knew the hell it was to quit and what it cost Lauren every day to stay away from it. She deeply appreciated him for his support, his kindness and acceptance. But there were other things, aspects of his character, that bothered her, and some of these went beyond the disturbing piece of Greg's history, the thing she knew about him now that she was forced to keep from Tara.

Because telling would violate the privacy that 12-step members relied on when they shared their stories at meetings. But what of Tara's right to know? What about her safety? What about Lauren's obligation to Tara? What if Greg slipped and went back on heroin? It had happened before, and by his own admission, he became a different person, a kind of monster. Someone without remorse or conscience.

She would kill him, Lauren thought, if he ever did anything to harm her sister.

"It's not personal." She said the only true thing she could.

"Then what?"

"You should be careful, that's all."

"Well, it isn't as if we're together a lot these days, anyway, I'm working so much overtime. I'm too tired to be fun. But I don't want to talk about that, either." Her job, Tara meant. The one with no particular future.

You could quit, Lauren wanted to say. You could be anything you want to be; there's still time. She could have said that, too. But it was useless to remind Tara of how she'd gotten to the place where she was, serving as an executive assistant to a public relations manager in the oil-field industry. The thing was, Tara should be the manager. She should have her own company. She was smart and articulate, outgoing and vivacious. She loved people. She had planned to go to college, had talked of earning a degree in public relations or in marketing, and she would have—if she hadn't gotten pregnant and married right out of high school. Lauren never liked reminding Tara of that, but there were times when she did it anyway, although today wasn't one of them. She only said she wished Tara were happier.

"What about the message you left me earlier?" Tara scooted past it. "The kid you saw walking on the feeder road. Did something happen to him?"

"Almost," Lauren said. "I came really close to hitting him, so close it scared me. Do you know who I'm talking about? Have you seen him? Out walking, I mean?"

"All the time, and it's a wonder to me that someone hasn't knocked him in the head or run over him."

"I stopped and talked to him."

"What? Are you crazy? He could be a maniac, for all you know."

"He isn't. No way. His name is Bo." Lauren went on, describing him, the determination in his step, his single-minded focus. She mentioned Bo's sister, Annie Beauchamp, and his dog, Freckles. "A psycho wouldn't name his dog Freckles," she said.

"Well, he might just to fool you."

"I don't think he's violent." Lauren paused, remembering. "I couldn't drive by him this time, you know? It's what people do. We drive by anything and anyone who gives off the least whiff of trouble."

"Yes, but sometimes *certain* people—and I'm not naming names here, okay? But certain people take offense if you interfere."

Lauren smoothed her hand over the duvet cover. Tara was alluding to the time when her family, and Margaret, and Greg, whom she'd scarcely known at the time—had conducted the intervention, when they'd told her how badly she was hurting herself and hurting them. Lauren had accused them of treating her like a child. It still galled her, the way they'd acted, the way she'd behaved—shrieking at them like a madwoman. She cringed every time she recalled the scene, one more on the infamous list of scenes that her children had witnessed. "I thought about that," she said now, "how much I resented it when you confronted me. I probably should have left Bo alone."

"It's hard to know the right thing to do," Tara said.

Lauren thought how often, after they lost their parents, she'd tried to guide Tara, telling her what to do, how to live, whom to date, blah-blah, only to watch her go off and do the very thing she'd been warned against. But you couldn't stop people from making mistakes, not even when you loved them, not even when they were your own flesh and blood and you'd shared everything, including the air you breathed, from childhood forward. She and Tara had slept in beds pulled so close together they could have held hands, and if one of them got scared, they climbed into the other one's bed.

They had called themselves the Forever Sisters.

And in the years after their parents were killed, their bond had only grown stronger, but then Tara got pregnant and married too young, and Lauren was overwhelmed running a business and taking night classes to finish college, and life happened, the years went by, and they weren't so close anymore.

Was that it? Was it simply the passage of time that had created the wedge?

Lauren's bewilderment at the loss, the sudden ache of it, pierced her skull anew. She could have whimpered. She could have said I love you, but she didn't do that, either. When Tara said she was home and that Greg was there, packing the Jeep, Lauren only said, "I labeled the box with the sheets in it."

"Great," Tara said. "Just what I want to do after a ten-hour day at the office, put sheets on the beds. The house'll have to be aired out, too. Plus I've got a stupid safety report to write that'll take me half the night."

"I'm sorry, Tee, truly." It was all Lauren could think of to say. Then, "Make Greg and Jeff do the sheets."

Tara laughed at that, and Lauren did, too, and she would remember it later, their shared laughter, but she wouldn't be able to recall the exact sound.

· · ·

Lauren slept again, and her dreams were disjointed, a series of misaligned images, vivid and disturbing. In one sequence, she was driving in downtown Houston near the bus station, on a side street she vaguely recognized. When she stopped her car in the middle of the block, a man approached, and she rolled down her window a little way, mere inches, a space wide enough to allow in the road stench and a furtive meeting of their hands. When she woke in her bedroom later, it was completely dark, and she was sweating and afraid. She sat up slowly, still caught in the dream—more than caught, feeling it, actually. The city grit was lodged in her pores. It sanded the surfaces of her clenched teeth. She dragged her fingertips through her hair, reassuring herself that it hadn't happened. She had not driven her car into Houston to buy drugs.

But later, after her shower, when she went into the study to find a book to read, her attention snagged on a basket filled with old auction catalogues. Why did she keep them? Jeff wasn't much for going to auctions, and although Lauren and Tara loved them, they hadn't gone to a single one since before the accident. Pulling the basket off the shelf, she began leafing through the stack. And that was how she found it. The small plastic bag, no more than two inches square, had adhered to the glossy cover of a fourteen-month-old brochure announcing the sale of an assortment of vintage farm implements. She ran her fingernail underneath it, lifting it, eyeing the depression it had left behind on the brochure's cover, which pictured a 1930s-era red Farmall tractor. The color where the packet had lain was faded. She set it on her open palm, remembering the man in her dream who had handed it to her in exchange for the cash she'd given him. But this was no dream; it was real.

Real, she thought, and her heart slammed against the wall of her chest even as her brain betrayed her, leaping as it did with anticipation. She closed the packet in her fist, and when she opened it again, it was still there. As real as the round yellow tablets it contained.

Lauren didn't need to examine them to know that each one was carved on one side with "OC" for OxyContin and on the other with "40," indicating the milligrams. She set the packet on the bookshelf, keeping her eye on it. The old craving was alive inside her, biting and harsh, almost but not quite eclipsing her panic, her wonder. How had she come to have these? Was it possible that her drive into Houston hadn't been a dream? Was she hallucinating? Dreaming still? Was her mind truly going, as Bettinger had predicted it might?

Taking the packet into her hand again, scarcely breathing, she spilled the tablets into her palm and touched each one with her fingertip. There were six, a half dozen. A six-pack. Back when she'd used the drug, she could have made six 40s last almost two days. It was nearly the amount of time she had to herself right now, the rest of tonight, all day tomorrow. Closing the tablets in her fist again, she left the study and went into the bathroom and looked at herself in the mirror; she wasn't really aware of her image so much as she was of the thought that no one was here to see anything she did, and they wouldn't be, not until late on Sunday afternoon.

4

On her way out to Fishers' farm to pick up the pumpkins and the rest of Madeleine's order on Friday afternoon, Annie stopped by the library and asked about Bo, but no one there had seen him in several days. Annie tried his cell phone again, and when she got his voice mail, she left him another message, a brief, frustrated, "Call me." She was fuming as she headed out of town. He was such a child sometimes, an irresponsible child. She wasn't his mother. She wasn't even his sister, not really. Searching the roadsides for him, she thought how she had no family. She thought how much she wanted her mother.

Her head was so filled with her mental rant that she didn't consciously register the BMW's shimmy or the clatter the engine made. Only when it quit right in the middle of the farm-to-market road she was traveling on did it get her full attention. Still, she was in disbelief, pushing the accelerator to the floor, bending forward, urging the car onward as if it were a horse, thinking, *Please*. Thinking, *This can't be happening*. But it was and with the engine dead, the power steering was gone, too. She yanked hard on the steering wheel, managing to get the car off the road and onto the grass that verged on its tarred edge. "Shit," she muttered, shoving the gearshift into

Park. She pounded the dashboard with the heel of her hand and said it again, louder: "Shit! Shit!"

A cow that could have passed for the Borden Dairy cow, Elsie, ambled over to the fence as if Annie had summoned her, and hanging her head over the rail, she stared balefully at Annie. "I should leave this piece of shit here," Annie said to the cow. "I'll ride you where I need to go from now on. How about it?"

The cow lifted her huge head and mooed.

"Hah!" Annie dug her cell phone out of her purse, but of course there were no bars. Not this far out of town. "Perfect," she said softly. "Just perfect." The only saving grace was that she'd left the car windows down, and stowing her phone, she sat for a moment, listening to the useless engine tick as it cooled. Listening to "Elsie" chew. She heard a pair of mourning doves calling, a softer chirr of crickets. A welcome breeze fanned her cheeks. In spite of herself, her troubles, her eyelids grew heavy, and curling her hands around the steering wheel, she rested her head on them. She'd been up since four, going like a house on fire, as her mother used to say. It wasn't the life Annie had envisioned, although if anyone had asked, she couldn't have told them her plan. She didn't have one.

Bo said love was all about persistence.

How could he be so wise and so goofed up all at once? How could she miss him so much? He drove her crazy, but he was nearly her only friend, the closest thing she had left to a relative.

She didn't hear the tow truck pull in behind her or the door when it slammed or the man's footsteps when he approached. And when he said "Miss?" she jumped, violently, blinking, trying to clear her vision.

He peered in at her, concern radiating from his expression. The sort of concern that appeared genuine. A radius of fine white lines cornered his eyes and seemed to suggest he either squinted or laughed, a lot. She thought he was older than she was, past thirty, maybe. But she glanced away too quickly to be sure, concerned about her appearance, that the wetness on her cheek was drool. She put a hand there.

"Are you all right?" he asked, and now he sounded wary. It occurred to her he might think she was drunk or on drugs.

She straightened, swiping at her face. "I'm fine," she said. "It's this stupid car. It just quit. It was shaking and making this noise—like a cough—and then it died."

The man took a step back, running his glance from the hood to the trunk. "A cough, huh?"

She looked at him again and couldn't decide if he was mocking her.

"How long have you been sitting here? Have you tried starting it again?" he asked.

"No," she said and felt ridiculous. Why hadn't she?

"Want to give it a whirl?"

He twirled his finger, and then she was certain he was mocking her. Her cheeks warmed, and she felt betrayed when the car's engine caught, but the noise it made, the loud knocking, had him shouting at her to shut it off.

"That doesn't sound good at all," he said. "Pop the hood for me?"

She glanced in the rearview mirror at the truck parked behind her. "You drive a tow truck?"

"Um, yeah. Is that a problem?"

She looked at him. "There's a dog inside."

"That's Rufus, rhymes with doofus, which he mostly is."

She looked forward, through the windshield, and saw her cow friend meandering down the fence line.

"I'm not a maniac, if that's what's got you worried. My name is Cooper, Cooper Gant." He pulled out a wallet, a well-used brown leather wallet, and handed her a business card.

"It says you're a welder for Gant Oilfield Servicing." She noticed the same company name was stitched on the pocket of the brown T-shirt he wore.

"It's my dad's and my uncle's company. I work for them."

"But you're driving a tow truck."

"The truck's a side business," Cooper answered patiently. She liked his voice. It was low and calm, with a bit of a drawl, but not so he sounded hokey. "My dad and uncle have a lot of that going on. Side businesses, I mean. According to my mom and my aunt, it keeps them out of trouble."

Annie didn't say anything.

"You want to pop that hood now, or maybe you want to walk back to town?" He smiled.

She did as he asked, and while he lifted the hood, she got out of the car and, leaning against the front fender, looked where he was looking, at the snarl of machine parts and belts. Not that she could make any sense of what she saw. Changing the oil and the tires was about the extent of her car smarts.

Cooper wiggled this and that and mumbled that it might be her harmonic balancer, as if Annie would know what that was. She imagined an orchestra conductor, his raised baton.

"I don't know much about BMWs," Cooper said. "My dad's the mechanic in the family. I could tow you, or do you have someone you'd rather call?"

She didn't, she said. "This is all I need. Stupid car." She kicked the tire, felt childish, and kicked it again anyway.

"Maybe it won't take too long," Cooper said kindly.

But it wasn't just the time; it was the money, too. She never had enough of either one. "How am I going to get to Fishers'?" She was looking at the tarred-over pavement when she asked, unaware that she'd spoken aloud until Cooper offered to drive her.

"You're talking about the farm, right?" he asked.

"You know it?"

"Who doesn't?" Cooper pulled a rag from his back pocket, wiped his fingers, and said he'd gone to school with the oldest of the Fisher sons. "We graduated in the same class, in 2000."

"You went to Hardys Walk High?" Annie asked. "I graduated in 2003. I don't remember you."

"I was an art nerd," he said without a trace of regret.

She met his gaze. His eyes were shades of gray, the color of the sky before a storm, but his expression was quiet. In fact, his entire manner seemed peaceful, and yet she would swear that at any moment, he might burst out laughing. She felt drawn to him. She liked standing here with him. She wasn't afraid.

She said, "Where would you tow the car so your dad could look at it? Into town?"

"No, lucky for you, the garage is on the way to Fishers'. We can drop it off, and I can run you out there."

She looked at him.

"You did make it seem as if you really needed to get there."

Annie explained where she worked and what she was after, essentially the makings for breakfast at the café tomorrow. She mentioned the muffins. "I wanted to get the pumpkin cooked tonight."

"Well, then, let's get to it." Cooper went to the tow truck, climbed in, and pulled it in front of the BMW. In a matter of minutes, it seemed, he had it loaded. It turned out he knew Madeleine, too. He said he'd eaten at the café dozens of times, that he'd seen Annie there, that she'd waited on him. Annie almost didn't believe him, but why would he lie? He didn't strike her as the lying kind. But who knew? People could fool you.

She waited for Cooper to mention Bo, to question her about him. If he'd dined at the café at all, he must know about Bo and wonder about him. Almost everyone did. She'd had people ask her straight out what was wrong with him. She wondered at their nerve, their lack of respect, of compassion. *Obviously, he's smarter than you are.* That was one answer she gave them.

Cooper opened the passenger door of the tow truck and told Rufus to get in the backseat, which was more a shelf covered with an old tarp and some other stuff, a tool box and assorted, tattered-looking manuals. Rufus obeyed, sitting tall on the tarp, tail wagging.

"He's an Irish setter, right? He's gorgeous." Annie took the hand Cooper offered her, letting him boost her onto the high seat, and leaning around it, she let Rufus get a look at her. "You are a hand-some boy," she said in a silly voice, the one she reserved for dogs and other four-legged creatures. "Such a good doggie."

Cooper got into the driver's seat and switched on the ignition. "You'll be hard to live with now, won't you, buddy? Got a pretty girl giving you attention."

Annie scratched Rufus's head between his ears and around them, and when he practically swooned, she laughed, delighted.

"You like dogs." Cooper sounded pleased.

"I do, very much." She fastened her seat belt. "I like cats, too, and just about any animal."

Cooper pulled onto the road, and she asked him how far they had to go.

"About eight miles," he answered. "Fishers' is maybe fifteen miles farther on."

Annie nodded, and watching the countryside pass, she wondered if she should take him up on his offer to drive her there, if she should impose. She would owe him then, and she really didn't like that. But if she didn't get to the farm, Madeleine would have to go, and that would mean leaving Carol on her own at the café. Stifling a groan, Annie asked Cooper about his art. "What do you paint?"

He met her glance, brows raised.

"You said you were an art nerd. I assumed you were a painter."

"No. I'm a welder."

Now Annie raised her brows.

"Between the oil field–service work and the car-repair gig, there's always a lot of scrap metal lying around. I make stuff out of it."

"Really." Annie didn't know what else to say.

"Yeah." He glanced at her, then back at the road. "It just came over me one day," he went on as if she'd asked. "I was looking around at all the pipe and odd pieces of sheet metal and scrap, and I started fooling around with it. Next thing you know, I built my mom an arbor for her garden, then a gazebo. After that, the neighbors started asking for stuff. Now I'm in business. I've got orders and customers from all over, more than I can keep up with."

"Sounds cool," she said, because it did. She liked that he'd begun by building something for his mother. She wondered if he would say he'd found his life's purpose.

He said, "I tried painting. You know, landscapes, even portraits, but it turned out I was pretty bad. I like working with my hands better."

They turned down a gravel road, and Annie saw a metal building and a sign painted in fresh-looking green, white, and brown lettering that read "Gant and Sons." She'd been by the place before, she realized, passing it every time she went to Fishers'. As they got closer, she saw the garage had three bays, only one of which was empty. There were other cars and trucks, too, parked around the area along with an assortment of heavy-duty machinery. In an adjacent field, dozens of pallets were stacked with pipe of every type, length, and diameter, more than she'd ever seen in one place. The pallets were set apart the width of a riding mower, and the grassy aisles between them were neatly cropped, giving the property an air of orderliness and prosperity.

The sun was hot on her shoulders after she climbed down out of the tow truck, Rufus at her heels. A man came out of the middle auto bay. Tall, broad-shouldered, and dark-haired like Cooper, he walked toward them, his gaze flashing from Annie to the car and back to Annie.

"She got you stranded?" he asked, and Annie realized he meant the BMW.

Cooper made the introductions. "Annie, meet my dad, Patrick Gant. Dad, this is Annie Beauchamp. She works at—"

"Madeleine's, in town." Patrick took Annie's hand in his warm, rough-palmed clasp. "I know this young lady, or rather, I know her pumpkin muffins. It's that time of year again, isn't it?"

Annie said it was.

"The café serves the best food in town." Patrick winked at Cooper. "Other than your mother's."

Annie smiled and thanked him. She said Madeleine did most of the cooking. Unlike Cooper, she remembered Pat Gant. He came into the café fairly often, every couple of weeks, for breakfast, mostly.

Cooper and his dad got the BMW unloaded and into the middle bay. Pat lifted the hood, and when he gave a sign, Cooper turned the key in the ignition. The engine clattered to life. Annie covered her ears. Rufus bolted. Annie lost sight of him and then, moments later, saw him drinking from a nearby water bowl. When Rufus came back after Cooper cut off the engine, he was holding a scruffy chew toy in his mouth, that resembled a frog with warts. He offered it to Annie, and the look in his golden eyes was somewhere between a taunt and a plea. She took hold of it, wrestling with him, playing his game.

She and Bo had found a dog once when they were kids, some kind of bird-dog mix. He'd had three brown patches on his cream-colored torso and a smattering of tiny brown specks dotting his muzzle. Not so originally, they'd named him Freckles. He'd belonged to Bo more than anyone else. They'd been inseparable, and when Freckles died, Bo, who was seventeen at the time, was hit hardest. He began isolating himself after that. He seemed to live more and more in his head. He'd started walking then, too. The family blamed Freckles's death, but it would have happened anyway. That was the nature of Bo's disease, the awful evidence of the loosening connections in his brain.

The ones that were even looser now in the two years since her mother died, Annie thought. She let Rufus have the frog, running her hands over his head, absently scratching his silky ears. Somehow, despite his symptoms, Bo had managed to graduate high school and work for Madeleine. It was only since her mom's death that his walking had totally taken over, that his existence had become almost marginal. He didn't see it that way. He was fine, perfectly fine, in his own eyes. Even when he got confused and thought her mom or Freckles was still alive, it didn't register that anything was wrong. Sometimes Annie thought they were the reason why Bo walked; he was looking for them.

Pat ducked out from under the hood and declared she did indeed have a bad harmonic balancer.

"What is that?" Annie asked.

"Well, without getting too technical, it keeps the engine, in particular the crankshaft, working smoothly. But over time, it can get loose, or the rubber wears out, and the engine will run rough and make a lot of noise, or it'll quit altogether."

"Is it expensive to fix?"

"Depends. If it's just the balancer, you're looking at maybe a couple hundred, but if there's belt damage or damage to the crankshaft, it'll run more. Thing is, I don't have the right parts here to fix it. I'd have to order them out of Houston. I don't see that many BMWs, especially vintage BMWs." He smiled.

Annie thought it was kind of him not to call the car what it was, a beater. She wanted to kick the tire again but refrained.

He said, "Might take a day or two. To get the parts, I mean."

"Oh, no," she said.

"I can take you to Fishers'," Cooper said, "and back to town . . . and wherever." He shrugged.

She glanced sidelong at him, unable to imagine he was as eager as he sounded to become her chauffeur. She thought how uncomfortable it would make her, riding alongside him, taking up his time, being in his debt. But what choice did she have? She thanked him and thanked his dad. She offered Cooper gas money, too, even though she had no idea where it would come from, but he refused.

He said he needed to go to Fishers' anyway, and when his dad shot him a glance, he said, "What? Mom told me she wanted a pumpkin. I'm going to get her one."

"Really? Don't you think you're a little old for a jack-o'-lantern?"

"Geeze, Dad. Pie. She wants it for pie."

"Oh, yeah, right." Pat winked at Annie, and she ducked her head, feeling charmed, feeling the heat from the pleasure she took in their bantering color her cheeks.

"Are you sure it's no trouble?" Annie asked when she and Cooper were under way. They'd left the tow truck and were in Cooper's pickup. Rufus poked his nose into the space between the seats, and she gave it a scratch.

Cooper said it was no problem. He said, "I was serious about Mom wanting a pumpkin."

"Oh, of course. I know that."

They rode in silence the rest of the way, and after a few minutes, Cooper pulled in through the farm's entrance, slowing more than was necessary, saying to Annie, "You asked about my art. I made this gate."

"It's amazing," she said, meaning it. The image, rendered in metal, was of a cow and its calf, peering out from beneath the stylized, wide-spreading canopy of a live oak. Across the top of the gate, a row of scrolling letters spelled "Fisher and Sons Organic Farm."

"The detail is so precise. It's steel, isn't it? How do you cut steel into those tiny leaves, into the shape of a cow?"

"You'll have to come by my studio sometime, and I'll show you."

Annie didn't answer. They stopped in front of the farm store just as Len Fisher came across the drive, and she was glad for the distraction. The men backslapped one another and agreed it had been too long.

"I didn't know you knew each other," Len said, looking from Cooper to Annie.

Cooper explained about the car. Annie said she'd come for Madeleine's order and the bushel basket of Small Sugars that Len had set aside for her.

Pretty soon, they had everything loaded in the back of Cooper's truck, and Annie started to climb inside, but then she stopped, looking across the hood at Len. "You haven't seen Bo in the last day or two, have you?"

He thought a second. "Nah. Last time was maybe a week, ten days ago. He was walking the overpass near Woodridge and Pike."

Annie made a face and said what she knew Len was thinking. "He's going to get killed."

"I started to pull over and get him. At least to tell him—" Len broke off. He and Annie both knew that neither action would have done any good. Bo went his own way; he did what he wanted to do.

Cooper was looking between them. "Who's Bo?" he asked.

Annie's surprise at Cooper's ignorance was weighted with dismay. She didn't like having to explain any better than she liked answering nosy questions. It wasn't that she was ashamed of Bo as much as she hated that once she told people, they backed away. They didn't want to hear the medical terms, the host of psychological jargon Bo had been saddled with, most of it within the past five years. It angered Annie, too, because there were still periods of time when he was pretty normal, an ordinary person with an extreme amount of intelligence and a few quirks. Who didn't have a few quirks?

"He's Annie's brother," Len began.

"Stepbrother." She corrected him automatically. "He has some issues—" Breaking off, she looked at Cooper, but there was nothing to do but say it. "If you've ever seen the guy who walks the roads around town, that's Bo. That's my stepbrother."

"I have seen him." Cooper's gaze on hers was steady. "In fact, I saw him earlier today."

"Where?" Annie asked.

"In the convenience store, the one on Bayberry where it crosses I-45. I'm pretty sure he got into a car there, a black Lincoln, a Town Car. A woman was driving it."

"We don't know anyone who drives a Town Car," Annie said. She and Len exchanged a glance.

Cooper looked nonplussed.

"Bo wouldn't get in the car with a stranger," Annie said. "It's one of his rules. He's fanatical about it."

5

All Lauren could think about were the Oxy tablets. Where had they come from? How had they happened to be buried in that basket? *Did Jeff know about them?* That was the question that left her cold. When he called on Saturday morning, she waited with breath held while he talked about sorting through her granddad's tools, and an old Hoosier cabinet he'd found in the barn. But Lauren was listening so hard for the other—an accusation about the drugs—she didn't really register what he said or even how she responded. What if he was waiting for her to say something about the Oxy? What if this was a test? The notion crashed into her brain. She imagined his response if she were to try to defend herself, if she were to tell him how near dawn, after doing little more than dozing all night, she'd bolted upright, tossed aside the covers, gone into the bathroom, and swept the tablets into the toilet, flushing it before she could stop herself.

At first, she was horrified—what had she done?—and then almost immediately, she felt ridiculously righteous and celebratory, but she was no closer to figuring out how she'd come to have the drugs in her possession, and even if she could explain it, Jeff would never believe her. He'd get that look on his face. She could picture it: the faint curl of his lip, the way he had of rolling his eyes.

After Jeff let her go, Lauren called her sponsor.

"Maybe I was hallucinating," she said. "I've done it before."

"While you were still in the hospital, you mean," Gloria said.

"Yes, but I've done it since I got home, too. Once. I woke up from a nap convinced I'd been to the grocery store and bought stuff for dinner, a chicken, potatoes, even a Caesar salad. I mean, I could feel it in my hand. You know how those salad bags are cool and kind of moist? But later, when I looked for the chicken, it wasn't in the fridge. None of what I could have sworn I bought was there. Crazy, huh?" Lauren laughed shakily, but the memory still frightened her.

"I had vivid dreams, too, getting off booze," Gloria said, "and I remember once after I stopped, about a year later, my husband found a half-empty fifth of bourbon above the ceiling in the garage. I must have hidden it there, but I had no recollection of it. Maybe that's what happened with you. Maybe the effect is even more intense because you hurt your head."

Lauren considered the idea. "The dream, though . . . finding the Oxy like that, right after—I don't know. It just seems . . ."

Is there a more logical explanation?

The silence filled up with the question.

Lauren would celebrate her first year of sobriety next month, while Gloria was an old hand at recovery, twenty-three years down the road. She was calm and reassuring. She said Lauren was doing great. "But maybe you should call your doctor."

Lauren said she would if it happened again, but even that was a stretch. Bettinger would order tests, all kinds of scans. He'd pull out his trusty pad and write out a script for some medication. She wasn't going back to that. She wasn't living that life anymore. She couldn't bear to listen to his warning that there might be increasingly more terrible symptoms lurking in her future than the ones she had already experienced. Seizures, for instance, or going totally bonkers. If she wasn't already.

"Put it behind you for now, then," Gloria advised.

And Lauren tried. By Saturday afternoon, when her headache was completely gone, she drove out to the warehouse. Jeff had left the store in the charge of the two part-timers for the weekend, who in addition to being students at the University of Houston were also the sons of neighbors. She let them go, shooing them away when they protested, thinking they were around the same age as Bo Laughlin. She didn't know why, but his situation weighed on her. He was like a loose bolt, an odd part, rattling around the streets. She worried for him; she worried for herself.

Had she hidden those Oxy tablets the way Gloria had hidden her bourbon? Suppose there were more in the house and Jeff or one of the kids found them?

Going into the office at the back of the warehouse, she sat down at Jeff's desk, intending to check their e-mail, but instead, when she woke the computer, her attention caught on the screen saver Jeff had created using a montage of photos from past deconstruction projects. There were a few of the old dairy barn they'd taken down five years ago and a couple of the two circa-1900 Craftsman bungalows that had been in the same tiny town, even on the same block. The town's name slipped her memory now. There was one taken in Houston of a 1970s-era, ranch-style house, where of all things, they'd recovered a thirty-six-inch Wolf gas range in near pristine condition. There were several shots of Jeff and a crew that included Lauren and Tara in hard hats, holding pry bars, filthy and grinning at day's end, standing in front of the goods they'd salvaged: piles of lumber, vintage windows and doors, light fixtures, cast-iron sinks, a claw-foot tub, hand-turned porch posts, ornately carved cornice trim, ceiling medallions, all kinds of hardware—a veritable treasure trove of times gone by, that once it was cleaned up could be repurposed to become a beloved part of someone else's history.

That was the heart of it for Lauren, what she loved most about the work and where she derived the most satisfaction. A couple of the nurses, even Dr. Bettinger, had asked her how she could do it, why she would do such hard, dirty work, as if the salvage business was no place for women. But there was a lot a woman could do, from taking down chandeliers to unscrewing cabinet door fronts to gently prying vintage beadboard from lath walls. But where she often made a difference was in her size. She was five seven, slim and lithe, where Jeff was big, broad shouldered, and tall at six and a half feet.

The day they met, Jeff's size was the first thing Lauren noticed about him. It was three years after her parents died, and Lauren had taken over running their antiques shop. Named for her father, Freddie Tate's was in the Rice Village then and catered to clientele who preferred higher-end, handpicked European furnishings with a decidedly French flair. Lauren had kept up that inventory, and the shop was crammed with a collection of Louis XV armoires and buffets, assorted chairs and tables. The day Jeff walked in, Lauren glanced up to see this enormous man, standing in the doorway, staring at the crowded collection of period furniture and locked, glass-fronted display cases loaded with priceless china, and the what-am-I-doing-here look on his face was so comical, it made her laugh.

"Are you lost?" she said.

"Well, if I am, I don't mind," he said, wending his way through the crowded store toward her. He was down from Dallas, he told her, killing time, waiting to talk to a guy at a nearby restaurant about a local demolition job. It turned out knocking down buildings and hauling the remains to the city dump was his line of work. He'd gotten into it without much thought after leaving his dream of a pro football career and a good chunk of his heart in a Dallas hospital ER. Lauren was the one who asked him if he'd ever thought of trying to salvage the stuff, the brick and lumber, tile flooring, granite and marble vanity tops, rather than trash it. No one then, in the early to midnineties, was talking much about the economics of reusing building material versus tossing it into a landfill. But Jeff was interested, and while he continued to take on the big commercial salvage jobs, their early dates were spent driving the countryside between Dallas and Houston, appraising smaller buildings—not only old houses but dilapidated sheds and barns with the roofs half-gone. Once they deconstructed an old grain silo. Turned out a lot of folks were agreeable to having an abandoned building on their property removed in exchange for the material Jeff and Lauren and their crew hauled off for free.

Neither she nor Jeff had wanted to live in the city, so Jeff bought acreage on the outskirts of Hardys Walk, more than enough land to accommodate his heavy equipment and his warehouse along with the inventory from Freddy Tate's. Lauren had wanted to build a house, something small and cozy, on their business property, but Jeff wanted to live in town, in the posh, gated community of Northbend, and she'd let herself be talked into it. After all the other expenses, there was little cash leftover for a huge wedding, so they were married in a quiet civil ceremony. Tara had been difficult. She hadn't liked Jeff, but Lauren was too happy to pay much attention. Her thought, if she'd had one, had been that Jeff and Tara would work it out. Now Lauren touched the tip of her finger to the computer screen, to a photo of herself brandishing a pry bar. Jeff was grinning down at her. It was from right after they married.

From the days when he'd thanked her for saving him, calling her his little toughie.

Because she was strong for her size and didn't mind hard work. And because she could get into tight places like old-country-church bell towers, where no reasonably sized man, much less a man Jeff's size, could go. She hadn't thought twice about climbing into the belfry two years ago to have a look at what it would take to get the bell safely down, and it was dumb—really dumb—but she hadn't considered the possibility of bats, either—that as she climbed the ladder, flashlight in hand, one might swoop at her. When one did, she was so startled, she lost her grip and her footing.

And her joy in her work.

She had yet to recover that. She tired easily now, and often her hip hurt, not in the sharp, lacerating way it had when her injuries were still new; it was more a dull throbbing, an ache so deep in the joint not even therapeutic massage reached it. No one could say how much better it might get or even if she would improve at all from the place where she was. It was up to her, what happened from here. She should get back into the gym; she should sign up for yoga. She had yet to do either.

Some days, it was hard finding the will to get out of bed.

Lauren clicked on the e-mail tab and scrolled through the messages, scanning the list quickly, but then one from Cornerstone Bank, with a subject line that read *New & improved sign-in process*, caught her eye. But they didn't bank at Cornerstone. That's what she was thinking when her cell phone rang.

She tugged it out of her purse, eyes still on the screen.

It was Jeff, asking about her head.

"It's better," she told him, but her attention was fixed on the bank notice, catching on random phrases: *happy to have you . . . if you have any questions . . . to set up an online account . . .* Had they switched banks? She waited, but no recollection of doing that surfaced. Jeff asked where she was. "The office," she said. "There's an e-mail here—" Lauren stopped, not wanting to hear it, that she'd forgotten. It would only worry Jeff, and anyway, if she gave it time, the memory would come back. It was how her brain worked now, like a light with a faulty switch.

"What e-mail?" he prodded.

"Never mind. How are things going there?" Lauren went to the window that looked out on a field fenced in rusty chain link. There was a scruffy patch of woods in one far corner. She could hear the traffic on the nearby interstate, the insistent percussion of tires pounding pavement.

"Tara's acting like she doesn't want to sell," Jeff said. "Maybe you're right. Maybe we should hold off. The place means a lot to you two."

Lauren was taken aback. "Really? But you were so—you said it was the only way."

"Yeah. It's not like she doesn't need the money, too."

He meant Tara, whose financial judgment was as impaired as her relationship judgment.

"You do realize when we sell, she'll blow every dime."

"We can't let her," Lauren said, and she knew how pointless it sounded, but still she persisted. "She's got to invest it. Talk to her; she'll listen to you. Just not around Greg."

"Why not?"

"Because, he's not family. It's not his business." It was more than that, but Lauren wasn't up for a discussion that was liable to get heated. It was hard enough on a good day to keep a coherent track of her thoughts, of all that was said, and on a bad day, when something happened to undermine her confidence—like finding that bank e-mail—it was impossible. The words would come, only to scatter like a flock of small birds. "Will you just talk to her?" Lauren left the window.

"Okay. But honestly? How she spends her money is none of our business, either."

"Maybe not, but she ought to be on her knees, praying we don't die first."

When Jeff laughed, the sound was easy, and Lauren laughed, too. She asked if he would need help unloading on Sunday, and he said Greg had offered, sounding surprised. Jeff thought Greg was a lightweight, a party boy. He was always saying he didn't trust Greg's commitment to stay off heroin. What Lauren thought Jeff was really saying was that he didn't trust her. Sometimes she had an unruly urge to call him on it, too, to say how do you know? But that was only pride goading her, and like Jeff, what she wanted more than anything was to be past it, to have her family back the way they'd been. She wanted so badly to be restored in their eyes, to be worthy again of their love and trust. No one could know what the loss of that had cost her.

No one except another addict—like Greg. Where Jeff doubted him, she rooted for him. She wanted him to succeed. She relied on him. They were friends on a level only they understood, and it was frustrating—their association with 12-step—the private things she knew about him complicated everything.

Lauren shouldered her purse. "He's a good guy, Jeff. His heart's in the right place."

"But you don't want him around Tara. I don't get it." Jeff was bemused, rightfully.

"Even you've said he's too young for her." Lauren parroted Jeff's complaint about Greg back at him. At thirty-seven, Tara was six years older than Greg.

But that was the least of Lauren's worries. Leaving the office, walking through the warehouse, she wondered if she could keep it up, her pledge to keep Greg's history to herself. She wondered what Jeff would do if he knew. She thought he might physically manhandle Greg out of Tara's life, even out of Lauren's own life. He might ask her to stop attending 12-step meetings with Greg. She hadn't thought of that before, and it made her heart sink.

Jeff started to say something, but she asked him to hold on. "I need to lock up." She turned the key, gave the knob a jiggle.

"Your sister's going to do what she wants," he said when Lauren came back on the line, and she knew more from his tone than his words that he was through talking about Tara.

Lauren might have been annoyed at him. She might have ignored his obvious dismissal and pushed the subject. But more discussion meant taking the chance that she'd blurt out something she shouldn't. Jeff wasn't long on patience when it came to Tara's issues anyway. He thought Lauren tended to put Tara and her needs ahead of his and their children's—even her own needs. It was a perennial complaint, a bone of contention they fought over on occasion. But Jeff hadn't been in the picture when her mother and father were killed in a car accident in France, where they went annually to buy inventory for the shop. Lauren had come of age by then, but Tara had still been a minor and at risk of being farmed out, a ward of the state.

It still scared Lauren all these years later to think how close she'd come to losing Tara. Even though she'd dropped out of TCU, where she was pursuing a degree in fine arts, and returned home, demonstrating her commitment, her maturity, and her willingness to shoulder the responsibility of caring for her little sister, it hadn't been enough to satisfy Child Protective Services. Not until Margaret stepped in as Lauren's advocate. She talked to a family-court judge, one whose wife she'd saved, and she used that on the judge, twisting his legal arm without apology. After that, once the papers were signed and Lauren was given guardianship, with Margaret's continued moral support and advice, Lauren had finished raising Tara the best she could.

And here was something else that Lauren knew that Jeff didn't seem aware of: when it came to parenting, guilt was part of the package. And whether Jeff agreed or approved of it, Lauren felt she was as much Tara's mother as she was her sister. She felt responsible for Tara's shortcomings; she felt it was her fault in some way that Tara couldn't form a lasting relationship and couldn't handle her money. And the thing was, she didn't know how to stop, how to unfeel those feelings that only seemed to grow thicker, becoming even more stubbornly entrenched as time went on.

She started the Navigator.

Jeff asked what her plans were, and she said she was going home, adding that she was tired.

"Why are you there anyway, wearing yourself out?" he asked. "You didn't need to go in at all this weekend. I told you I had it covered."

Lauren felt a jolt of surprise. He sounded almost angry, the way he had in the early days following her release from the hospital when he'd followed her around, hovering and clucking like a mother hen. A psychologist she'd seen while in rehab had said it was normal behavior for a primary caregiver, especially one like Jeff, who took his responsibility so seriously. That mood had passed, though, once Lauren was stable again and more her old self. "I'm fine, Jeff. Everyone gets tired."

The noise he made suggested she wasn't everyone. "Go home, okay?" he said. "Get some rest."

She said she would and then drove to Cornerstone Bank instead. It was after-hours, and the suburban business center where the bank was located was nearly deserted when she pulled into a space in front of the building. She sat a moment, studying the image of her SUV in the plate-glass window, trying to picture the office inside and the face of the bank official she and Jeff would have spoken to about opening an account. Nothing came.

But maybe that was because she'd never been inside. The bank could have sent the message by mistake. Or someone using their name could have opened the account. Lauren straightened, mind leaping. She should have realized—considered the possibility of identity theft. Didn't it happen all the time?

She drove home, only subliminally aware of the sky and landscape as they receded into dusk and of the oncoming headlights that flashed by her like small moons. Leaving the SUV in the driveway, she walked quickly through the house, flipping on lights as she went, to dispel the evening gloom. In the study, she sat at the desk, waking the computer, and after she found the e-mail from Cornerstone Bank, she clicked on the link it offered, where she was prompted for a password. *Carter2000*. She typed in Drew's middle name and birth year, their standard password, and received an error message. Her breath hitched. She tried Kenzie's middle name and birth year and then her own, with the same result. None of the alternatives worked. So—

Sitting back, she thought for a moment, then found her way to the bank's main web page. She would call them, get to the bottom of this. By now, her pulse was tapping so quickly and loudly, she could hear it in her ears. Thoughts collided in her head: that it was unnerving to discover someone had stolen your name, that Jeff would be so pissed. There was a mounting excitement, too, as she dialed customer service, that she could handle this crisis, that she *was* handling it. Her call went through, the line rang, and that's when she saw it—the folder on the desk, with a page poking out, one that had the Cornerstone Bank logo on it. She'd set her purse down on the file, she realized, ending the call. Looking through the thin sheaf of documents, copies of the originals, she saw that she and Jeff had, indeed, opened an account there. In mid-September, around six weeks ago, according to the date. There was her signature.

Lauren returned the papers to the folder and nudged it to the far corner. Tears threatened, and she pressed her fingertips to her eyes, stopping them. She wouldn't cry, wouldn't beat herself up. *It'll get better. You're on the right track. Recovery is never a straight line.* Everything her physical therapist and half a dozen nurses had said to encourage her ran through her mind. *Relax*, they'd said . . .

Who knew? Maybe now that she'd seen the paperwork, if she could relax, the memory would come back to her, hopefully by the time Jeff mentioned it. If it didn't, she could fake that she knew. She'd done that before, feeling terrible for it. Feeling more scared and separated from her family than ever. But when she told them how her brain blinked off and on, or when she couldn't manage to hide it, Jeff, the kids, and Tara—they all looked at her with such pity. They looked at her as if she were a ticking bomb and they were just waiting to see when and how horribly she would go off.

It was dark and she was exhausted by the time she ate the leftover mac and cheese she found in the refrigerator, heating it up in the microwave, standing at the sink. She took a hot shower, hoping she would sleep, craving it. But it didn't happen, and toward midnight, she got up, and going into the bathroom, she flung open the medicine cabinet, pattered her fingers along the shelves, scattering the collection of bottles, a thermometer, the Band-Aids, hunting for it, the small plastic sleeve that contained the six Oxy tablets. Of course they were gone; she knew it. What an idiot she'd been to toss them. Jesus Christ, what had she been thinking?

She searched the bookshelves in the study, took things out of the cabinets in the kitchen; she hunted through drawers, but it was useless. If she'd hidden more Oxy, she didn't know where it could be. Back in the bedroom, she sat on the bed's edge, head in her hands, trying to sort out what was worse: imagining you'd done a thing you hadn't, or doing a thing and not remembering? After a while, she lay back, crooked her elbow over her eyes, and surprisingly, she slept.

The next morning, on waking, she was glad for whatever it was, act of bravery or stupidity, that had prompted her to flush the dope she'd stumbled across. She felt pleased with herself for once, as if she'd won a contest or gotten something over on herself. She ate the toast she made, tossing the crumbs outside to the birds when she finished, then went into the study to look again at the bank forms.

Her mood wavered, but no. She wouldn't sit here and brood. Instead, she drove out to Fishers', where she bought Swiss chard, sweet potatoes, Brussels sprouts, pears and apples, and the first of the fall tomatoes plus three pumpkins to carve into jack-o'-lanterns, and on the way home, she told herself she was fine. All she had to do was to hold on to this, her sense of routine, of what was usual and ordinary. All she had to do was stop scaring herself.

• • •

Drew was home first that Sunday, and when he lifted the lid of a red-handled foam cooler to show her the body of the five-pound smallmouth bass he'd caught early that morning, she looked into its fishy eye, and she was glad for it, for the project she and Drew would undertake together in getting it to the dinner table. She didn't even object to the fishy, river smell rising off the slick iridescence of its scales. She got out the big cutting board and found the boning knife. Drew filled a bowl with ice water to drop the fillets into once they were cut, and they took everything outside.

"I tried to call Dad, to tell him." About catching the fish, Drew meant. He set down the bowl of water and knelt beside Lauren on the deck. "He'll freak when he hears." He took a bite out of the apple he'd pulled out of the sack Lauren had left on the kitchen counter. "I even tried Aunt Tara, but she didn't pick up, either."

"Huh." Lauren had tried calling Tara, too, and she'd texted her without success. They hadn't been in touch since early Saturday.

Her silence was vaguely disquieting. Lauren had sent her a message to that effect early this morning: *Hey, just give me a word so I know ur ok. Jeff said u might be having 2nd thoughts???* She made a deep cut behind the fish's gills. "Do you see how I'm doing this?" she asked Drew.

"Let me do it." He set down his apple core.

She looked at him. "Can you?"

He took the knife. "Sure. Who do you think cleans the fish me and Dad catch?" He flashed a look at her, and then he said, "I guess you weren't around when I learned. You were still out of it probably."

She looked away. Did Drew mean out-of-it hurt or out-of-it doped? But what difference did it make? The thing was, for whatever period of time it had taken her to come back to some semblance of normalcy, the better part of a year at least, she'd been absent—first physically, then mentally, and in that time, her children and her husband had done things together, shared experiences she'd never know about. She listened to their talk about them, like now, and she felt hurt, ashamed, and resentful. Some twisted combination. It was wrong. She knew they'd gone through hell, too. Drew had told her that back in September, in a hard, unforgiving voice. Six weeks into the school year, when his grades kept him from playing football for the high school JV team, to his and Jeff's everlasting embarrassment, he'd blamed Lauren for it. It was her fault, the chaos she'd caused in their lives. How was he supposed to concentrate with all the drama going on?

He made a slit along the fish's dorsal fin, then slid his fingers into the opening, feeling for the backbone. Intent on his work, he said, "Man, I wish Dad could have been there when I hooked this baby."

She shifted her glance, afraid if she continued to watch, she'd caution him about cutting himself. "He'll be sorry when he hears."

"We didn't catch shit—sorry, I mean squat—the last time we went out." His sideways grin was quick, abashed.

And so endearing Lauren wanted to ruffle his hair, cup his cheek, but the moment felt so fragile to her—that sudden grin, his apparent ease rocketed her back to the days before the accident when they'd been close. She couldn't bear it if he flinched.

A half hour later, Drew was upstairs, hopefully finishing his homework, when Kenzie came home. Hearing the car, Lauren left the laundry room, where she was folding clothes, and went out onto the porch. The girls climbed out of the backseat, and after they hugged, Amanda got into the front beside her mom. Suzanne waved and Lauren did, too, and their eyes connected, but the moment was brief and wary. Lauren ought to be used to it by now, the loss of Suzanne's friendship, but every time their paths crossed, it cut her heart open. They'd shared so much, helped each other out so often; they'd laughed and cried and celebrated together . . . but what good was it, grieving for what was so clearly lost?

"Hi, Mommy." Kenzie came up the steps, smiling. Her smile was beautiful, or it would be when the braces came off. Jeff was only half kidding every time he said by the time that happened, they'd have sunk enough money into Kenzie's mouth that they should be able to slap four wheels on it and take it for a drive. The orthodontia was just one more huge expense on the list that was growing as quickly as the kids.

Lauren took Kenzie's pink tote from her and slung it over her shoulder, smoothing her daughter's silky dark hair back from her face. "Did you have fun? How was the ballet?"

"Sublime." Kenzie's second love, after ballet, was language. In school, vocabulary was a favorite subject. "I want to dance like that."

"It's hard work." Lauren led the way into the house.

"I know. I have to want it more than anything else." Kenzie repeated what Lauren had said so many times.

She wasn't sure she liked the idea of Kenzie loving something that much. Passion was never easy; it wasn't a joy every moment. She'd thought when Kenzie asked for ballet lessons in first grade, it was only because Amanda wanted them, but when Amanda quit to join the pep squad, Kenzie stayed with it. She attended classes three times a week now, and they had recently bought her first pair of toe shoes. Kenzie was over the moon.

"I went to Fishers' and got pumpkins," Lauren said.

"Really? For jack-o'-lanterns? Can we carve them now?"

Lauren smiled, all at once feeling light with gratitude that her headache was gone, the Oxy was gone, her children were home safe, a fish was filleted, and the laundry was done, all the small things. "Sure. Unless you have homework," she answered Kenzie.

"No. I finished it Friday in study hall."

"Put your things away, then, and tell your brother if he's finished his homework to come and help if he wants to. We'll take the pumpkins outside on the picnic table."

Kenzie headed up the stairs and then paused. "Mom?" she asked, turning slowly around. "Is Daddy still mad at you?"

"I don't think so." Lauren was puzzled. "Why?"

"Because, you know, last week, when you didn't charge enough for that job when Daddy took down the Anderson barn? He said you made him lose, like, a ton of money, and how was he supposed to make it up?"

Lauren's heart sank. It was dumb, really dumb, but she'd so hoped Kenzie would forget about it, the ugly argument she'd witnessed, her mom and dad shouting at each other at the top of their lungs—worse than kids. Worse than any performance Kenzie and Drew put on when they got into it. It still rankled. It was true; they had lost several thousand on that job because of her mistake. She'd transposed the numbers on the contract, and no one caught it until the job was done and signed off on at an amount way below what it had cost to get the barn down. They'd been counting on the income, had needed it to make their month.

The day Jeff discovered the discrepancy, Lauren and Kenzie were just coming into the warehouse when he barreled out of his office, yelling something about Lauren screwing up, intimating that she must be back under the influence. It was a moment before she realized he was blaming her as if he wasn't equally responsible. He'd taken the contract to be signed. He should have checked it over, seen her error. That was why it was called a partnership.

Almost instantly, she felt on fire, just lit up. She yelled back at him—things like if he was going to accuse her of being back on OxyContin every time she forgot something or made a mistake, why should she bother with recovery? Where was the end of his suspicion? When would he consider her debt paid and let her out of guilt jail? Poor Kenzie was flattened against the wall, dark eyes huge with alarm. Yelling was taboo in their family, like hitting and saying *shut up*. Lauren and Jeff pointed to themselves as examples. They didn't do these things, therefore Drew and Kenzie shouldn't, either.

But those rules only made sense when applied to the family they'd once been, before Lauren tumbled from the church bell tower, smashed her head and her pelvis, and plummeted down the OxyContin rabbit hole. She looked at Kenzie. "Your dad should have—" Lauren began, but then she stopped, biting down on the influx of her panic and aggravation. Kenzie didn't need excuses. What she needed was reassurance. "He's not mad anymore, okay? He said he was sorry, remember? It's fine. Everything is fine."

"You and Daddy are really stressed out." Kenzie came down one step.

"Well, honey, things are kind of difficult right now, you know? But we'll get through it, I promise." Lauren smiled, holding Kenzie's gaze, and when she came down the rest of the way and circled Lauren's waist hard with her thin arms, Lauren pulled her close, bending her cheek to the top of Kenzie's head, inhaling her sweetness, drawing it deeply into herself through the cold, bruised shade of her sorrow. Their embrace lasted only moments before Kenzie turned and flew up the steps, shouting for Drew, telling him something about whoever got into the backyard first got to carve the biggest pumpkin.

Lauren watched her daughter disappear into her room through a prism of tears. Sometimes she thought she couldn't bear it, the weight of her daughter's forgiveness and her love.

• • •

The moment Jeff got home, Drew brought out the bowl filled with fillets to show him. He launched into his fish story. Gabe and his dad hadn't caught anything big enough to keep, he said. No one fishing at the lake that day hooked a fish as big. Jeff listened to Drew as if nothing else mattered. Watching them, Lauren wanted to shush Drew. She wanted to say *Your father's exhausted.* She wanted to smooth her hand over Jeff's brow, wipe away the dark smudges under his eyes. He looked so old and haggard, as if he'd aged overnight. Or had she not been paying attention? It jolted her somehow, how much she still seemed to miss, as if her mind were elsewhere without her permission.

"I tried to call you, Dad," Drew said.

"Huh? What?" Jeff was admiring the fish. "How do you want to cook this bad boy?" he asked.

"Grill. We should definitely grill it, right?"

"I could sauté it," Lauren said, thinking she would save Jeff the trouble of supervising Drew outside, but he said no.

"A bass that size has got to be grilled. Right, champ?"

Lauren passed Jeff a beer. "Are you okay?"

"Sure. Why wouldn't I be?"

"It's a mess at the farm, isn't it? More work than you thought."

"Yeah."

A look crossed his face. Was it regret? Could he be like Tara? Were they both having second thoughts? Lauren started to ask; she might have reopened the whole subject then, but he pinched the bridge of his nose, and when he looked at her again, when he said, "It'll probably take a couple more weekends" and "I'll have to figure out when," something in his tone, like impatience or aggravation, some weariness—she didn't know—stopped her, and she only nodded.

Jeff looked at the bottle of beer in his hand, drank some, gave her a quick glance. "Maybe when we go back, it should just be the two of us. Tara and Greg may not want to go. They weren't that much help anyway."

"What happened?"

"Nothing."

"The money—you talked to Tara about her money, investing with Greg, and she didn't take it well."

"Something like that."

"Greg knows?"

"Yeah, maybe. Guy's a loser. I told Tara she needs to get away from him."

She wouldn't have taken that piece of advice well, either, Lauren thought, and Greg would be angry at her now, too. He'd suspect her of talking to Jeff about him.

They'd made another enemy.

Great.

After dinner, when the kids had gone upstairs, Lauren followed Jeff outside. They sat in adjacent chaise longues on the deck and looked at the moon, hanging like a fat, misshapen pearl in the dark throat of the sky, and Lauren again considered it, taking up the whole thorny matter of selling the farm. But then Jeff took her hand, and reveling in his touch, she didn't want the moment spoiled if she was wrong in assuming he might be softening, yielding to her way of thinking that the farm shouldn't be allowed to pass out of their family.

They would find another way.

File bankruptcy, if Jeff could stand the blow to his pride. It might allow them to keep this house, possibly even protect the business and the farm somehow, too. Maybe that was a lot to hope for.

But they could look into it. They had options, Lauren thought.

Even Jeff might have thought of a plan. That could be the reason for opening the account at Cornerstone Bank. She turned to him to ask about it, holding the question in her mouth. But the night was so lovely and quiet, and his grasp was so warm. He was always warm, and she loved that about him, and later, in bed, when he pulled her into his embrace, she welcomed the heat of his kisses, the touch of his fingertips as he teased a path from the hollow of her neck, to her breast and lower, to outline the curve of her hip. She looked into his eyes when he entered her, and she wondered if it was a trick of the light or were they shining from tears?

"Jeff?" she whispered, touching his face, encountering the damp evidence.

He paused, locking her gaze, and it was only for a moment, but his expression seemed so intense, so desperate and filled with longing, that she pulled him to her, pulled him more deeply inside her, giving herself to him. Providing him with shelter. Because sometimes, that was all you could offer, and after the way he had sheltered her, it was the least she could do.

• • •

The next morning, they were in the bathroom, in the midst of their usual routine, and she felt normal and ordinary and rejoiced in it.

Something had shifted between them last night; in their lovemaking, she and Jeff had rounded some awful corner. *He had cried!* The thought blazed in her mind. She was filled with hope. They would be all right. She glanced sidelong at him. "This will sound crazy."

"What?"

"I don't remember opening an account at Cornerstone Bank."

"We were there last month. We talked to Paul Thibideaux, my buddy from Dallas? He's the VP."

Lauren saw her own hope mirrored in Jeff's eyes, that any minute now, the details he was feeding her would raise the memory from the dead zone in her mind. She shook her head, touched her brow.

"You signed the papers," he said. His tenderness, if there was any left from last night, was tinged with a degree of impatience.

She turned to lean against the vanity countertop, saying she'd seen them. "On the desk in the study."

Jeff spit toothpaste into the sink. He rinsed his mouth, wiped his face with a towel. "You were sick of Diane sticking her nose into everything we do. We both were."

Lauren made a face. Diane Taggert was a teller at First State, where she and Jeff had banked for years. She was also a neighbor and nosy, just as Jeff said. *How are you, dear?* She'd ask every time she saw Lauren, and it wasn't out of genuine caring. The question and the stare that accompanied it were more pointed, like daggers. *Are you still sober?* That's what Diane really wanted to know. *Taking care of your poor kids? Walking the straight and narrow?* Lauren thought Diane felt entitled to meddle. She'd earned the right, given all she'd done for the Wilders in the wake of the accident—organizing an entire team of neighbors who, through the long weeks of Lauren's hospital stay made sure the refrigerator was stocked with groceries, the house was cleaned, and the kids were ferried to ballet lessons and football practice. None of their neighbors in those early weeks had seemed able to do enough, but that changed. People didn't bring casseroles to the family of a dope fiend.

"It's a relief, right?" Jeff asked.

"I don't know. I guess. It's just—"

"What?" He bent his head, wanting her gaze.

She thought of the Oxy she'd found, that he might know about it and be waiting in vain for her confession. She was failing him again. Failing to be honest, to show courage. *Tell him*, she ordered herself. But she couldn't; she was too afraid of losing him and her children, not to mention her mind.

"It's nothing." She went into her closet to escape his scrutiny. If only there were someone she could talk to. Someone safe.

But there wasn't. Not since Margaret died.

6

Bo was wearing red earmuffs the day Annie met him for the first time, and Batman pajama bottoms with a green T-shirt turned wrong side out. He was six and she was ten, and she'd been dragged to McDonald's by her mother to have dinner with Bo and his dad. Annie's mom said she and Bo's dad, JT, were friends, but Annie was no dummy. She knew JT was more than a friend. She saw them kiss. She saw how her mom smiled at JT and at Bo, all moon-eyed and sugary, and it infuriated her. She got madder still, on that summer evening at McDonald's, when her mom took her off to one side and whispered to stop the pouting and be nice. "Bo's been through a lot."

She jiggled Annie's elbow. "A lot," she repeated with emphasis.

Annie wondered what *a lot* meant but not enough to ask. Under duress, she took Bo out to the play area with the big colored tubes you could slide around in, even though she was too old to go there.

"C'mon," she said when he hung back, "and take off those stupid earmuffs."

"They help me," he told her gravely.

"How? It's a hundred degrees outside. You look like a moron."

"When I have them on, the noise goes away, and I can hear my mommy singing."

Annie frowned.

"She's in heaven. She's an angel."

"She's dead?" Annie couldn't imagine it, not having her mama.

He nodded, still solemn, and Annie's heart melted.

"My dog died," she said. "She was old, but I had her since I was two."

"What was her name?" Bo asked.

"Cassie," Annie said. "I still miss her."

Bo took off his earmuffs and held them out to Annie. "You can wear these, and maybe you'll hear her the way I hear my mom."

He let the earmuffs be packed away a year later, after JT and Annie's mom got married, when they became a family. Annie put stuff away, too, the way kids do—her dolls and the squishy blue doggie her mom had made for her out of an old towel when she was a baby. She didn't think about Bo's earmuffs again until her mother was killed in the car accident. Annie guessed Bo went into the attic and got them, because he'd been wearing them the day after the funeral when he'd found her outside on the back steps crying. Sitting beside her, he took them off and pulled them over her ears. He circled her shoulders with his arm and held on to her, and she leaned against him, finding comfort in his presence. He was her brother, and she loved him even when he acted crazy.

Even when he walked for miles on end like someone possessed. There were other indications, too, that his brain was wonky, periods of time when he talked too fast or not at all. Times when he forgot to eat or bathe or sleep. He couldn't concentrate. But then, a patch of days or even weeks would pass and he'd behave almost normally, almost like his old sweet, quirky self. *We're all oddballs.* Annie's mom had said that. But while she was alive, she never stopped searching for answers, for ways to help Bo. He was tested and scanned, counseled and medicated. Labels were tossed around like confetti, but the general consensus was that he suffered from schizoaffective disorder topped with bipolar and autistic tendencies—and earmuffs. That was the one constant with Bo. He wore his earmuffs, religiously.

Red ones—always red—worn so frequently that Annie got to the place where she thought she might not recognize him without them, and that was why, on Sunday evening, when she found them discarded on his bed at JT's, it scared her.

She'd been worried since Friday when she was at Fishers' with Cooper and he said he'd seen Bo get into a car earlier that day, a Lincoln Town Car, driven by a woman. *What woman?* Annie had asked Cooper, but of course, he didn't know. Why would he?

Annie scooped Bo's earmuffs off his bed, thinking two things: One, he never rode with strangers. And two, he always wore his earmuffs.

She brought them into the den, where JT was watching football on ESPN, and held them up. "He left these here. Did you know?" She lifted her voice over the sound of the game announcer.

JT looked at her, then back at the television, half shrugging.

"Something's wrong. He never goes anywhere without these." Annie walked over to the TV and switched it off.

JT sighed, rubbing his eyes. "Almost never."

"He was seen on Friday getting into a car with some woman, probably a stranger. He never does that. You know it's one of his rules, JT."

"About the time you figure out his rules, he changes them. Where did you hear this anyway?"

Annie told him about Cooper's sighting of Bo at the convenience store.

"He's the guy who towed your car, right? You think he knows Bo well enough to say for sure it was him?"

Annie rolled her eyes. "Everyone in this town knows Bo."

JT picked up the remote and turned the TV back on, muting the sound. "He's probably at the library or down at the rail yard, camping out in one of the boxcars."

Bo loved the old switchyard. He went there as often as he did the library, but Annie had looked there. She and Madeleine had spent the better part of Saturday looking for Bo in every one of his usual places, and Annie said so now to JT. "There's no sign of him. No one's seen him all weekend."

"What about your car? You get it fixed?"

"Cooper brought it to me this morning." Annie sat on the edge of the ottoman, where she'd sat so often when her mom was alive. Often enough that the rose-colored piping was worn. Annie traced the cording with the tip of her finger. They were going to re-cover the ottoman and the matching chair. They'd even figured the yardage it would take and talked about fabric, something soft, the color of moss, they'd thought. Maybe chenille. *Oh, Mama . . .* Annie's throat closed against the bite of her tears. Would it never go away? The ache of missing her? The need to talk to her, to ask her advice?

Annie didn't know how to feel about Cooper and his dad. When she asked Cooper how much she owed for the car repairs, he'd given her an invoice for $123.52, and that included the part, the harmonic balancer, and the labor. She was no mechanic, but even she knew it should have been more, a ton more, maybe as much as three or four or five hundred dollars more.

Not that she could give Cooper the amount on the invoice. She'd had to admit to him she didn't have it and ask if she could pay it off, twenty dollars a week. It was the most she could afford. He said it was fine, that they trusted her; he made it easy. Too easy. She hated owing him, hated being treated as if she were a charity case. She had wanted to tell him he could keep the car. She didn't need it or him. She ended up thanking him instead. But she hadn't invited him in, and it shamed her to remember. She'd declined his invitation to accompany him and Rufus to the lake, too. She realized it was perverse, and she deplored it, the way she'd cut off her nose to spite her face.

"Bo wouldn't go with a stranger," she insisted now to JT. "He wouldn't go this long without answering his cell phone, either." Annie studied Bo's earmuffs in her lap, passing her hand absently over one red-furred earpiece, smoothing it.

"I tried a while ago, before you came, to get hold of him. His voice mail's full."

"Of my messages," Annie said. "I think we should call the police."

"Oh, now, I think that's kind of drastic," JT said quickly. "Let's give it another night."

"Why? Do you know of any place else he might be, another place he might have gone to?" Something in JT's expression made Annie ask.

He didn't answer. He kept his gaze from hers, too, and it seemed deliberate.

"The woman Cooper saw Bo with, do you know who she is?"

JT said he didn't.

"Well, there must be some reason why you aren't worried."

"I'm worried. Just not as much as you. Did you check the shop?"

JT meant Shear Heaven, the hair salon where Annie's mom had worked as a stylist. "I called," Annie said. "They haven't seen him."

The silence filled up with the mystery of everything JT wasn't saying, and it went on long enough that he picked up the remote, but before he could restore the volume, Annie said, "When did you see him last?"

JT lowered the remote. "I don't know, a couple days ago, maybe. I've been working a job down in Houston and one out here. The days are kind of tangled up." JT was a telephone-system installer, a whiz with anything electronic. He'd often said that if he could, he'd rewire Bo's brain. It was always there in JT's eyes, how much he hurt for his son's deficiencies. He didn't show it, but Annie knew he'd give anything to have Bo be right, to keep him safe, to see him happy. JT would give his last dollar, maybe his own life.

Annie put on Bo's earmuffs, waiting to hear Bo speak to her, listening in her mind as if he might tell her where he was, but what came was fear, spilling through her, a river of ice.

She didn't sleep well that night, and the following day, Monday, when Cooper came into Madeleine's at the tail end of the lunch rush, her nerves were frayed and raw. She didn't want to see him, to take his order, to speak to him at all. She didn't return his smile or his wave, and it was rude. He'd been nothing but kind to her.

But why? What did he want? She couldn't imagine he was interested in her, and even if he were, she was too tired and too broke and, now, too panicked over Bo to think of romance. She watched Cooper take a stool at the near-empty counter and looked around for help from Carol, but she was working two booths and a table near the door. Minding the tables closer to the kitchen and the counter was Annie's chore. Reluctantly, she walked over to Cooper, said hello, and asked what she could get for him.

"Nothing, thanks," he said. "I came in to see if you've heard anything."

She shook her head, and the fear in her stomach pushed its fist into her throat.

"Don't you think you should let the sheriff know?"

"That's what I've been telling her." Madeleine came out of the kitchen. "Well, look. There's Hollis now."

Annie followed Madeleine's glance to the front of the café, where a tall, silver-haired man wearing a sheriff's uniform was coming through the door. "You called him?"

"He's come for his lunch," Madeleine answered, but she wouldn't meet Annie's eyes.

Cooper raised his hand. "Sheriff Audi."

Annie's heart faltered. She recognized him. She had waited on him many times, but she didn't know him other than he made her nervous. It wasn't personal. Hollis Audi had never given her any reason to be anxious. Something about police in general had that effect on her. She didn't know why. It wasn't as if she'd ever had any dealings with them, not so much as a speeding ticket.

"He'll be wanting his sandwich," Madeleine said, and she went into the kitchen.

Sheriff Audi came over. "Hey, Coop." The men shook hands. Then, as if he registered a disturbance, he divided his glance between Annie and Cooper. "What's up?"

"Her brother's missing," Cooper said.

"He's not my real brother," Annie said and wondered why. Because Bo was related to her in every sense that mattered.

"Bo? We're talking about Bo Laughlin?" Audi asked.

"You know him." Cooper was matter-of-fact.

"Sure, everyone in town knows Bo." Hollis Audi said the same thing Annie had said last night to JT. "He's missing? Since when?"

"Friday." Cooper answered again, because Annie seemed incapable. "Really, before that, I guess." He looked to her for confirmation.

She said, "I haven't seen him for nearly a week. No one I know of has, except Cooper, and I've checked everywhere I can think of."

"When did you last see him? What day?" the sheriff asked.

"Last Wednesday," Annie answered. "He came here. We had tea." She looked over at the booth nearest the door, where Bo liked to sit. *So he could get away quickly? So he could see out?* Annie wasn't sure, but he always chose that spot. If it was occupied, he'd wait for it or he'd leave altogether.

Last Wednesday when he came into the café, the booth was empty, and Annie had sat with him, watching while he sugared the already-sweetened tea and stuffed down two of the carrot-and-cinnamon muffins that were leftovers from the batch she'd made and served to that morning's breakfast crowd. She remembered nagging him about eating so much sugar; she remembered he'd been agitated and jumpy. *I could tell you something.* He'd said that to her more than once. But she'd been focused on the sweets, determined to get her point across by basically venting her disgust over his diet.

Why hadn't she asked him what was wrong? Why hadn't she slid in beside him and put her arms around him? She bit her lip. How many times in that single afternoon, after she'd spoken to him in her brittle, authoritarian voice, had he told her he was sorry; he would do better, he promised. *But just listen,* he'd said, *I heard talking . . .*

She looked at Bo in her mind; he'd been wearing his earmuffs. She was certain of it, and if that was true, then at some point after leaving the café, he'd gone to JT's and left again without them. The fact that he'd forgotten them worried her even more now. Clearly he'd been upset; his mind had been in more than its usual turmoil. *I heard talking . . .*

What had he meant? Had he heard voices in his head? Real voices? Why couldn't she have shut up for five seconds and let him tell her?

"Bo wouldn't go this long without touching base." Madeleine had rejoined them and was answering some question the sheriff had posed that Annie had missed. "A couple of days is his limit, wouldn't you say, Annie?"

Madeleine sounded so definite that Annie agreed even as she searched her mind for an exception, and not finding one, she said, "I can't think when he's ever gone this long without at least calling or texting me."

"Something else," Madeleine said. "I paid him last week, in cash like I always do. He showed me some other money he had then, wrapped up with a rubber band around it. He wouldn't say where he got it."

Sheriff Audi looked from Madeleine to Annie.

"It isn't stolen, Sheriff. Bo's not a thief," Annie said.

"Is he using, dealing drugs again? Because you know we've run him in for that."

"Not lately; not in a long time. He's not on anything." Annie crossed her arms tightly around her middle, hoping she was right, praying she was.

"You're sure." Sheriff Audi wasn't. Annie could tell by the way he sounded.

"I'd know," she said, flatly, although that wasn't true. Under the weight of Cooper's glance, she felt pushed to explain. "He hears voices in his head sometimes, and when they get really loud, when they shout—" Annie's throat closed around the threat of tears.

She felt Cooper cup her elbow in his palm to steady her. "It's okay," he murmured, and it wasn't, but Annie was somehow reassured anyway.

"He self-medicates," she said. "He won't take the doctor-prescribed meds, but he'll take the stuff a stranger, a—a dope dealer on the street hands him—or he did. But not lately. Not in nearly a year now. I'd know," she reiterated.

"People have been known to take advantage of him," Madeleine said, and Annie heard her reluctance, shades of her hovering fear.

"Yeah," Sheriff Audi said, and he blew out a sigh as if the thought of such cruelty depressed him.

Annie said, "Bo was working other places besides here. He did odd jobs for JT, for the neighbors. They could have paid him. That might be where he got the extra cash."

"I told him not to go showing it around," Madeleine said. "I said to him that very morning showing off that money would invite nothing but trouble." Her voice shook. "What are you going to do about this, Hollis?"

"Put out a BOLO," Sheriff Audi answered, and when Madeleine frowned, he interpreted for her. "It means 'be on the lookout.'"

"Ah," Madeleine said. "Sounds very Hollywood. But this isn't the movies, is it? It's real life."

"Yes, ma'am, that it is." The sheriff was respectful. But everyone treated Madeleine with courtesy. You didn't dare do otherwise. Sometimes Annie thought she might be the only one in town who was aware of the softness that formed the center of Madeleine's heart.

She said she'd made Sheriff Audi his usual lunch, ham and Swiss on rye toast.

"Can you sack it up for me?" he asked.

Madeleine said she would.

"You want to sit there?" The sheriff addressed Annie. He indicated an empty booth. "I can work up a description."

Annie hesitated. To accompany this man, to help him with his report, would make it real; it would confirm there was good reason to be afraid, and she didn't want to believe it. Even though she knew better.

She had called JT on her way to work this morning and told him if she didn't hear from Bo by the end of her shift, she was going to the police. In a way, she'd meant it as a test. She couldn't shake her sense that JT knew something about where Bo was, and after she warned JT of her intention, she thought for sure he'd tell her not to bother, that involving law enforcement wasn't necessary. But he didn't say anything, didn't respond at all, and fear came, jolting up Annie's spine, ringing in her ears so loudly, she had to pull off the road.

"You really don't know where he is?" she demanded.

"No. My God! Don't you think I would have told you?"

Doubt hardened the silence. The very air had felt consumed by it and by their mutual foreboding. Annie didn't remember now if they said good-bye.

"Go on."

Annie glanced at Madeleine.

"Carol and I can finish up," she said. "Cooper, stay with her, okay?"

Annie wanted to say she didn't need Cooper, but it wasn't true. She was glad for his presence when he slid into the booth next to her.

The sheriff got out a notebook, and when he asked, Annie told him everything she remembered about the last time she saw Bo. She described what he was wearing, a blue-plaid cotton shirt and gray chinos, and said she had no reason to believe he would have changed his clothes. "He'll only shower at my house or at JT's." She didn't add that Bo often complained the water in other places was infested with alien microbes. It would only add to the sheriff's suspicion of drug use. She did tell Sheriff Audi about Bo's earmuffs, that he'd been wearing them when he came to the café on Wednesday, but he wasn't wearing them now.

"So he must have gone to his dad's house at some point after you saw him on Wednesday and taken them off, is that right?" The sheriff looked at Annie. "He could have changed clothes then, too, couldn't he? Did you look? Would you know?"

"I'm not sure, but I can check," Annie said.

"Also, if you have a recent photograph, that would help, too." Sheriff Audi glanced up from his notepad, in anticipation of her answer.

As if he thought she should whip out a photo on the spot. "I can probably find one. I just don't know how recent it will be.

I'm sorry." Annie wondered why she was apologizing. Because they weren't the all-American family? Or any sort of family? Because they didn't take pictures? They had been better at those family sorts of things before her mother died. Her mom had been the tie that bound them.

Sheriff Audi said they would use whatever she could find. "Is it possible JT saw Bo later in the week than you, that he could confirm what Bo was wearing?"

Annie said she doubted it. "I don't think he pays much attention to Bo's clothes."

Until JT married her mom, he pretty much dressed Bo in whatever he could find at the Goodwill store. Bo was thrilled when Annie's mom took him to JCPenney. *Brand-new clothes*, he kept saying. Shirts and pants no one else had worn. Annie remembered the care he'd shown afterward, folding them carefully when he took them off. Sometimes he'd slept in his favorites. Annie had rolled her eyes. She'd made fun of him and called him a dork. Why?

Cooper said, "I'm pretty sure when I saw Bo on Friday he was wearing what Annie described."

"Gray pants, blue-plaid shirt." The sheriff leaned back. "You say the car he got into was a Lincoln?"

"Yeah. Town Car, maybe 2010, 2011. Black. I didn't pay attention to the license plate, but the woman driving it was older. At least her hair was really white. I didn't get any sense it was a dangerous situation, though. Bo got into the front passenger seat under his own power. He was talking a blue streak. You know how he goes on."

Sheriff Audi nodded.

Annie's cheeks warmed. The understanding of Bo that Cooper and the sheriff seemed to share seemed almost intimate. It made her want to defend Bo, to say *You don't know anything about him*, even though it was clear there was nothing to defend, that they were only sorting through the facts, trying to find a direction, a way to help.

"He and the woman were laughing," Cooper said, "as if Bo was telling her jokes."

"Bo doesn't joke," Annie said.

Both men looked at her.

She thought of what JT had said, that as soon as you worked out Bo's rules, he changed them. But Bo didn't laugh easily or show much emotion, except when an animal or a person was hurt. When that happened, he felt it, too. She remembered the time Freckles was sick with some virus. Bo stayed up all night, holding him. She remembered when she had tonsillitis, he walked nearly a mile each way to the Baskin-Robbins because she loved their French-vanilla ice cream with chocolate syrup the best. By the time he got home, the ice cream had softened, but that only made it better; all that melty, chocolate-swirled ice cream had felt so soothing and cool against her raw throat. She could still taste it, could still see how Bo sat on her bed beside her, how he cared that she hurt. It brought her to tears, remembering these things about him. She pressed her fingertips to her eyes.

"What about a cell phone?" the sheriff asked. "Does Bo have one?"

Annie lowered her hands and said he did, giving the sheriff the number. "Can you find him that way?" Her heart seized on this possibility, relating it to movies and shows she'd watched on television.

"It's possible, if the phone is on, or even if it isn't, as long as—" The sheriff broke off.

"As long as—" Annie prompted.

"I think the battery has to be good, right?" Cooper asked.

"Yeah. That's why the sooner we get going, the better."

But that wasn't the only reason. Annie could see by Sheriff Audi's and Cooper's expressions that it wasn't. "You think someone might have done something to Bo; they might have taken his phone—" she began.

The sheriff interrupted her. "We don't know anything at this point, Annie."

"Do you have someone in mind?"

"Can you think of anyone who might want to hurt him?"

"You're thinking of the drugs, aren't you? That someone hurt him over drugs."

"I'm asking if you know of anyone who might have had a problem with Bo." The sheriff's gaze was gentle, so gentle and kind, Annie felt she might break beneath it.

She looked into her lap. He knew as well as she did there were folks in town who had a problem with Bo. They didn't like him walking in their neighborhoods or talking to their kids. Once, when he'd scooped a little boy out of the street who'd fallen from his bike, the mother had come screaming out of her house. She'd grabbed her son and slugged Bo on his chest, hard enough to leave a bruise. She told the police when they came that she didn't want "that weirdo's" hands on her kid. "He should be locked up," she said. Annie remembered JT saying it was a good thing the woman hadn't had a gun.

Would she have killed Bo, if she'd had the means? Annie didn't know. She guessed anybody would do anything, given the right amounts of fear, real or imagined, and sufficient provocation.

She thought of Leighton Drake. She had risked her heart with him for a few heady, hectic weeks last summer, something she had never done before, and then he'd betrayed her, threatening Bo's life in the process. But he was gone now. He'd moved back to Chicago, where he was from, in August. She met the sheriff's gaze. "There are people in this town who harass Bo, who don't want him around, and sometimes, it's gotten physical. But not so much, really, since high school."

"Okay, then. But if you think of an incident or anyone specific—"

"I'll let you know," Annie said.

"What about JT? I'd like to talk to him, too. Find out when he last saw or spoke to Bo. Do you know where I can reach him?"

"He's usually home from work around six o'clock, but I can call him now and find out his location. I should talk to him anyway and let him know what's happening." Annie paused.

"What?" Sheriff Audi found her gaze again.

She shook her head; she didn't want to say where her mind was, that it had wandered back to have another look at her sense that JT knew something. He didn't; he couldn't. He would never let her worry herself sick this way. "It's nothing," she said and scooted out of the booth.

Cooper and the sheriff followed her.

The café was mostly empty, although a few people, a dozen or so, lingered. Their faces were familiar to Annie. They were the regulars, the ones she waited on almost daily. She felt their eyes on her as she crossed the floor to get her cell phone out of her purse. She felt their concern, and she realized they knew Bo could be in danger. If she were living in a town larger than Hardys Walk, she might have wondered how the word had spread so quickly.

"What can we do to help?" One of the women who worked at the library intercepted Annie. Others joined her, making a small crowd. Madeleine came out from the kitchen with Carol.

"I need my purse, my cell phone to call JT," Annie said.

Carol said she'd get it and ducked back into the kitchen.

Sheriff Audi said he was putting out the BOLO, and then raising his voice, he addressed everyone in the café. "I think most of you know Bo Laughlin. If you've seen him since Friday, I'd like to hear about it."

There were headshakes, an exchange of worried glances, a low rumble of uneasy murmurs.

"I usually see him," Annie heard one woman say.

"It's odd not to," said another.

"I can get folks together to go and search for him, Hollis."

Annie looked at the man who had spoken. His name was Ted Canaday. He owned the sporting goods store across the street. She'd served him his lunch today, chicken salad on wheat toast, hold the pickle. He'd ordered the same thing for lunch as long as she'd worked there.

"Ted, if you want to set up a central location and ramrod a search effort, I know we'd be grateful for the help, and so would Miss Annie here." The sheriff smiled at her.

"Ted," Cooper called out. "Count me in. Whatever you need. I'll get my dad and my uncle, too."

Someone else suggested they headquarter the search effort in the community center down the street.

Carol said, "We need a photograph to make flyers."

"Annie isn't sure she has one." Cooper answered when Annie didn't.

"I've got one on my cell." Carol touched Annie's elbow. "I took it when we bought Bo those red rubber gloves. Remember? To match his muffs."

Annie nodded even as she thought she would never let that picture be used. She'd go to JT's, find another, one that wasn't silly. Other voices rose and fell, swirling around her, but she lost the individual words and their meaning in the swelling clamor of her panic. She felt sectioned off from reality. Why had she spoken to the sheriff? Bo was fine: he'd call; he'd show up. Didn't she know that? Know him? Annie touched her fingertips to her temples.

"Do you want me to call JT?" Madeleine spoke at her elbow.

"No," Annie said. "I'll just go in the kitchen so I can hear."

"It's the right thing, filing a report, letting everyone know." Madeleine seemed to have read the doubt that clouded Annie's mind.

"But what if he isn't missing? What if he's just off somewhere new, a place we haven't thought of?"

"Then we'll have something to celebrate when we find him, won't we?"

"He got into a car with a stranger, Madeleine. I've never known him to do that."

"People do all sorts of odd things on a whim."

"I'd better call JT," Annie said.

"Bo's all right." Madeleine's voice followed Annie. "We'll find him, and he'll be fine. He'll ask us why we made such a fuss."

"You're right," Annie said. "That's exactly what he'll say."

7

Jeff came back to the warehouse after lunch on Tuesday, looking grim. He'd met with a vendor, he said when Lauren asked, and they'd had words. And then he left her, going into his office, closing the door. Not a slam exactly but hard enough that she knew it would be unwise to follow him. He wouldn't welcome her intrusion, her commiseration. He was in one of his moods. Shutting her out. It made her furious and anxious in equal parts.

She went into the showroom, where she'd been cataloguing a collection of Depression glass, but she couldn't focus. She thought of calling Tara, but since Sunday, she'd left a half-dozen unreturned texts and equally as many messages. Still, she reached for her phone and dialed Tara's number. "Why don't you call me back?" she said to her sister's voice mail.

A while later, she left without telling Jeff she was going. Let him hunt for her, she thought. Let him wonder. But her exit was spoiled when her car wouldn't start. Maybe it was a blessing. At least it forced them to be together, forced his attention.

He opened the hood and jiggled a few things. He asked her to try it again, to no avail. Eventually, they called a tow truck, and once the Navigator was loaded and gone, she shouldered her purse and followed him, feeling the distance between them widen with every step. Not so long ago, she could have mapped the territory of his emotions the way she could number his ribs or chart the architecture of his shoulder blades, but it was harder now, and the fact that he was no longer as easily accessible grieved her.

Jeff got into the truck and looked over to where she stood, holding the passenger-side door open. "Are you getting in?"

She boosted herself into the cab, slamming the door, meeting his gaze. "What?" she said.

He gave his head a slight shake. "Nothing," he answered.

Liar, she thought, turning away from him, mind running loose on its circuit of worry. Then quickly, she looked back at him. "It isn't a vendor you're angry at, is it?"

"Huh?" He kept his eye on the road.

"I can't see how a vendor could piss you off this much, so it must be me. Something I've done. What is it?"

"I don't think I said it was a vendor, did I?"

"Yes, that is what you said."

"Well, I meant to say contractor. It was Wick Matson, and I didn't want to tell you—"

"Because we owe him a lot of money." Lauren was guessing, but it only made sense, given that Matson National Equipment provided Wilder and Tate with the heavy machinery they used for demolition. But even knowing the source for Jeff's anxiety, that it wasn't about her finding the Oxy after all, didn't give her much relief.

"It'll be all right."

"You don't need to protect me."

"I'm not." The streetlight made a haggard puzzle of his face. "You need time, is all, and I'm trying to give it to you."

"This is about the bank, isn't it? I'm back to square one in your mind, because I forgot we opened the account." Why had she told him? But what did that make her, if she didn't let him see how handicapped she might be—was. Still. For who knew how long? What if she never recovered all of her wits? She looked out the window, fighting tears, damned if she'd cry.

They passed several miles in silence.

She broke it. "Sell the farm. I don't care. I just want us out of this mess."

"I don't know. Maybe it's not the best idea. Like I said before, I don't know when I can get back out there. Neither does Tara. We talked about hiring someone to finish the job."

"What happened? I mean, I know you got into it about the money, but what did she say? I'm guessing Greg overheard and neither one of them liked your advice, right?"

Jeff made a sound, something derisive. He fiddled with the radio, turning it on and off.

"I told you, didn't I, that Greg does that day-trading thing? He'll probably offer to invest for her." Lauren's pulse tapped lightly in her ears. There was no *probably*. Tara was already investing with Greg. Lauren knew because he had told her last August over coffee at a café where they often went—after a meeting. So this particular secret, unlike his other one, wasn't covered by the pledge of confidentiality. Lauren was free to say whatever she liked about it, which was nothing.

"Well, that's a sucker bet, a fast way to lose everything. She better run like hell."

Lauren picked at her thumbnail. Too late now, she thought. Greg already had his hands on some of Tara's savings. Not all of it.

He had told Lauren on that August night, nearly bragging, that he wouldn't let Tara take out *all* of her savings.

Lauren was shocked. "How could you take anything from her?" she demanded. "What if you lose it?"

"I know what I'm doing," Greg countered.

"You need to give it back," Lauren said. "Now." She pressed her fingertips to her temples. "God! This is such a mess, all the things I know about you and now this."

"You won't tell her I told you, will you? About the money, I mean."

"I don't know, Greg. What you're doing isn't safe, and she can't afford to lose anything."

"Look, I'm sorry. I'd never hurt her for the world. You know how much I care about her, and you, and Jeff and your kids. You guys are like family to me."

The note of pleading in his voice made her heart ache.

By then, she'd known his background, that he'd been taken away from his parents, both addicts, who had neglected him so severely CPS became involved. From the age of six, he had been bounced from one foster home to another. At meetings, he often spoke about the yearning he had inside to belong to a family, one that would love him and that he could love in return. Lauren knew what he meant; she knew his hunger and need were bone deep.

She had sympathized with Greg that hot summer night. His pain was so like her own. But she also knew enough about addiction and its hold on the addicts who were possessed by it to be afraid. Addicts could slip; they could pick up their old ways and, out of desperation, commit unspeakable acts, and it wouldn't be only money that was on the line then, but someone's life. In this case, Tara's life. Or Lauren's, or Jeff's, and the children's lives could be at risk.

She didn't know what to do about Greg and his secrets, and since finding them out, she had avoided him. And it was confusing, because her doubts aside, she missed him. Greg was a good and loyal friend to her. The only friend to stand with her in this place, this lonely, foreign, ex-addiction place, where no one but another ex-addict could or would want to be. It was just one more in a numberless line of losses, all of them lying behind her like a row of crooked stitches.

A group of boys, Drew among them, was shooting hoops in their driveway when she and Jeff got home. Jeff parked at the curb, turned off the ignition. "We could order pizza for dinner." He didn't look at her.

"I was thinking the same thing," she said, when truthfully, she hadn't thought about dinner at all. "I have a meeting." She wasn't sure where that came from, either. She hadn't planned to go to a meeting.

"Again? Weren't you just at one a few days ago? Thursday, wasn't it?"

"I should attend at least two a week. I thought you wanted me involved."

"It takes up a lot of your time, is all." He glanced at her, and she saw something in his eyes, frustration, disappointment. Some pained mix of emotions that she couldn't bear.

"I found some Oxy tabs over the weekend in the study in a stack of old catalogues. I don't know how they got there." The words were gone before she could stop them, but she owed them to him. Owed him the truth.

His eyes widened. So much she could see flashes of white. His astonishment was palpable, and her heart fell against the wall of her chest. He hadn't known. She almost groaned aloud. Why hadn't she kept her mouth shut?

"What did you do with them?"

"I flushed them, Jeff, I swear. And I promise you, I have no clue how they got into our house, much less the study." She felt his stare, his disbelief. She said, "Gloria says I could have hidden them at some point. People at meetings have talked about it, how they'll find stuff they were using, booze or drugs or whatever, ages after they quit."

"I searched the house, though. I look through those catalogues all the time. Why didn't I find them?"

"They were pretty far down in the stack."

"How can you not remember hiding them?"

"I don't know. Maybe because of the head injury? I did have a dream Friday night that was—Oh, God, I sound so crazy."

"You didn't take them?"

"No. I wouldn't do that to you." Of course, she had done it to him, countless times.

"Maybe Gloria's right. It makes sense, I guess. But, Jesus, it makes me want to search the house all over again. It scares the shit out of me that the kids'll find it." Jeff took the keys from the ignition.

Lauren wiped shaky hands over her face.

Jeff got out of the truck, saying he would phone in the order for pizza.

Drew shouted at them, and the other guys called out greetings when they walked up the drive. Jeff lingered, horsing around with them, but Lauren only waved and went into the house, needing space, knowing Jeff needed it, too. Setting her purse down on the countertop, she gripped the sink's edge. Whoever said confession was good for the soul didn't know what they were talking about. She didn't feel one damn bit better. And Jeff was more suspicious and worried about her now than ever.

She blinked up at the ceiling. How she wished she could redo it, all of it, going back to the day she'd volunteered to climb into the church bell tower. She might have screamed from frustration if she hadn't heard Kenzie coming down the stairs. Lauren shook herself slightly, and turning, picked up the mail, smiling when Kenzie appeared, dressed in her black leotard, pink tights, and pink ballet slippers, twirling a series of piqué turns across the floor.

So like a tiny fairy, Lauren thought, heart bursting. "How was your lesson?" she asked.

"Okay." Kenzie boosted herself onto a stool next to Lauren.

"You practiced in your toe shoes?" Lauren tucked loose strands of hair from Kenzie's ponytail behind her ear.

She nodded, not smiling. She didn't smile a lot since getting braces, and when she did, she covered her mouth. Lauren deplored it; she was nearly as anxious as Kenzie for the ordeal to be over.

"It was hard, I bet," Lauren said. Miss Madden, Kenzie's dance instructor, had warned Lauren privately that the transition from demi pointe to pointe would be more difficult than Kenzie realized. Few students were prepared for the amount of work that was involved, never mind the pain that was also part of it. Only the girls who were serious bothered to persist. Lauren thought it was Miss Madden's way of culling the students who lacked the necessary passion and discipline.

"It was awful, Mommy. I fell." Kenzie admitted this in a small voice that cracked with humiliation.

"Oh, honey." Lauren put her arm across Kenzie's narrow shoulders, pulling her tight against her side. "You aren't the first, you know?"

"That's what Miss Madden said. Even Jodie told me she fell, too, when she first got her toe shoes."

"Well, there, you see?" Lauren jostled Kenzie a bit. "And just look where she is now."

Jodie was Miss Madden's star pupil, a senior in high school who had recently landed a scholarship to Juilliard.

"She's so nice," Kenzie said. "She told me if I want to, she'll work with me after class sometimes. I said I would ask you."

"Can we talk about it later? Daddy ordered pizza, and we need to make a salad."

The four of them sat down when the pizza came.

"I found a great deal on a four-wheeler on Craigslist," Drew said, stuffing half of his pizza slice into his mouth.

"What makes you think you're getting a four-wheeler, champ?" Jeff asked.

"I've got money saved."

"He thinks if he gets it, he can ride it at the farm," Kenzie said. "I told him you're selling the farm, but he didn't believe me."

"Yeah, dummy, because Aunt Tara said—"

"You talked to Tara?" Lauren asked.

"Not lately," Drew said.

"Well, you're not getting a four-wheeler, bro," Jeff said.

"Have you talked to her since you got back?" Lauren addressed Jeff.

He shook his head, chewed his pizza, drank his Miller Lite.

Watching him, Lauren was seized with fresh doubt. It wrote itself into the crevices of her mind, as dark and indelible as the blackest ink. They were talking, Jeff and Tara, behind her back. Lauren would bet the month's grocery money on it.

Get off the dope or lose your kids.

Wasn't that the ultimatum they'd given her?

It's for your own good.

How many times had Tara said that?

It's because I love you and them, she had insisted.

Lauren put aside her napkin. Even though she'd been off drugs almost a year, they were still treating her like she was some kind of lawbreaker, and entering a treatment facility and attending 12-step meetings were conditions of her parole.

"You know, you and Tara were never such huge friends before I cracked myself up," Lauren said, and she was staring at Jeff. Staring hard at him. She had a sense of the children, frozen in her peripheral vision, but she couldn't stop herself, couldn't break her glance.

"What are you talking about? Before what?" He looked perplexed.

Genuinely so.

Was it an act? Lauren held his gaze, trying to decide. But it was impossible, and she left the table, feeling his eyes, and Drew's and Kenzie's eyes, following her. Feeling trapped and as helpless as a beetle tipped onto its back, legs fruitlessly clawing the air. She heard noise, a kind of buzzing. It seemed to originate in her brain, and she touched her ears with her fingertips. Was this insanity? Could a person know the exact moment she lost her mind? She thought again of Dr. Bettinger's warning that she might continue to suffer from any number of symptoms as the result of her fall.

Or she might not.

"It depends," he'd said.

Depends. He used the word a lot. It wasn't helpful.

"You didn't do your head any favors, getting hooked on Oxy." Bettinger said that a lot, too.

. . .

Jeff thought she shouldn't go to the meeting, but when she insisted, he offered to drive her.

"I can do it," she said. "There's no reason you should go. You're exhausted." She pushed a smile.

He handed her the truck keys. "Maybe you do need a meeting." He meant because of how she'd behaved at dinner.

She said yes, but thought no. It wasn't a meeting she needed, but Greg. Greg had been at the farm. He would know what was going on with Jeff and Tara. He might not want to talk to her after the way she'd distanced herself from him, but she'd make him. She'd tell him she wasn't leaving until he did.

She was pulling into a parking space at the Methodist church when her cell phone beeped, signaling she had a message, and she closed her eyes, praying, and dreading that it would be from Tara. Instead, the message was from Kenzie. She didn't want Lauren thinking her fall during ballet practice would stop her.

I'm not afraid, Kenzie had typed.

You are my brave girl, Lauren responded, and the letters swam in her vision.

Lauren got out of the pickup, searching the half-filled rows for Greg's car and not finding it. He wasn't in the church classroom, either. It worried her. He never missed meetings. In fact, he was so religious about attendance that Lauren often teased him. He'd make God wait, if there was a meeting on the night he died. She took a seat, nodding at a few others she knew, most of them only vaguely. But that was her fault. She didn't try to know them. She didn't feel she was like them. She'd tried explaining it to Greg once, that her addiction was the result of her accident. She hadn't been looking to get high or looking for a way to escape anything, except the brutal pain. Greg had argued the reason for getting stoned didn't matter; the result was the same.

You were hooked if you couldn't get through a day, an hour, a moment of your life without it.

The meeting came to order, people got up and spoke and sat back down. Lauren kept her eye on the door and missed most of what was said. When the session ended, a few of the guys wandered outside, lighting cigarettes. Lauren went over to them and asked about Greg.

"He came by early and told us he was taking off," said one of the men.

"Taking off?" Lauren heard the question in her voice, the protest.

"Said he was going to Kansas City, didn't he?" Another man spoke.

"Yeah, something about a job."

Lauren felt as if she'd been punched. She took a step back, almost staggering; then catching herself, she walked away, quickly, ignoring the men when they called after her.

Sitting in her car, she tapped in Tara's number and when her voice mail came on, Lauren said, "I'm worried about you, I'm on my way over."

She had just clicked off when her cell rang.

"Not now," Tara said before Lauren could utter a word.

"What's wrong? Is Greg there? I'll only stay a minute."

"No, I've got some kind of stomach crap. It's going around at the office. I don't want you catching it."

"You sound funny," Lauren said, and it was true. Tara's voice was stretched as thin and taut as a wire. "Is it Greg? Is something wrong between you?"

Tara said she couldn't talk; she would call later. "When I'm better," she said, and before Lauren could answer, she was gone.

Lauren sat listening to the dead air, feeling disturbed, unsure why. After a moment, she started the truck and drove home.

The children were in bed by the time she got there. She heard the television going in the great room and went to the doorway, waiting for Jeff to see her, and she was nervous. She felt on the verge of something and started to speak, uncertain of what she intended to say, but then the news commentator said something about a man who was missing.

". . . since last Friday," the commentator said.

Lauren whipped her glance to the television screen, knowing the man's identity before the commentator said his name. "Bo Laughlin." The reporter went on, asking for anyone who might have knowledge of the young man's whereabouts to contact the Lincoln County Sheriff's Office.

"I should call and tell them I saw him on Friday," Lauren said. "Remember, I told you I nearly hit him?"

Jeff looked sharply at her. "You already called."

"I know, but that was only to ask if they'd check up on him. He wasn't missing then."

"The woman you spoke to didn't seem concerned, you said." Jeff scooted to the edge of his chair. "She yakked on and on about the salvage business."

"She did, but—"

"Well, I don't know what more you can tell the cops." He picked up the remote, switched off the set. "I'm going to bed. You coming?"

"In a minute." Lauren waited until Jeff was gone, then lowering herself to the ottoman in front of his chair, she switched on the TV again. Now the reporter was interviewing a girl. She was slightly built, with a pert, upturned nose. Her hair was cut short, not more than a cap of auburn curls, and framed her small face like layers of petals. She was wearing earmuffs, red earmuffs, and somehow Lauren knew it was Annie Beauchamp, Bo's sister. She thought she would have known even if the girl wasn't shaking from top to bottom. She looked so young and frightened, just heartbroken. Lauren's own heart constricted. She thought of Bo, that he'd told her he was on his way to get candy for his sister.

I have a dog named Freckles . . .

Lauren looked at him in her mind's eye. She saw him come out of the store and get into the car with the older, white-haired woman, the elegant woman. She looked at his hands, but they were empty. He wasn't carrying anything. He hadn't purchased the candy he'd said he was going to buy, or anything else.

She sat a moment after she turned off the television, listening to the sound of the water running in the pipes, and then, going into the kitchen, she opened her purse and slipped out her cell phone.

Making the call was the right thing to do.

8

Bo wasn't mislaid like the mate to a pair of socks or a library book. He wasn't going to turn up any minute, the way Madeleine and others said when they offered Annie their perky reassurance. No. He was gone, totally gone. Vanished. Poof. Annie knew it. From Day One, the moment when Sheriff Audi had initiated the BOLO, she'd felt Bo's absence in her bones, in the deepest recesses of her brain. But no one other than law enforcement and the media was talking about the possibilities, the dark and logical realities, that he had been hit by a car or met with foul play. There were vague hints of robbery or a drug deal gone wrong.

Annie could look at the speculation only sidelong and only for a moment. Her eyes kept filling the empty spaces with his presence. She would see him, vividly, sitting in a booth at the café or on her front steps or on the sidewalk outside the community center. She imagined him peering in the window there, wondering at all the activity—the people going in and out or seated at tables answering phones that now, halfway through Day Two since his disappearance had been reported, rang constantly.

Annie had thought, given Bo's erratic behavior, his handful of drug arrests, the police would wait at least twenty-four hours before they set up a command post and called on volunteers for help, but Sheriff Audi said Bo's case was different. Because of his mental issues, Annie thought. Because he's vulnerable and everyone cares about him, Madeleine and Carol said. But Annie couldn't take it in, that people—she'd had the idea everyone, or most everyone, was disgusted by Bo—would drop everything to assist her and her family. She didn't know how to respond. Her emotions were in turmoil. She was grateful for their help, but at the same time, her need for it humiliated and infuriated her, which made her feel ashamed.

People were only acting out of concern for her. They only meant to be kind when they plied her with reassurances and food and urged her to rest. And she was sorry to disappoint them. But she couldn't eat more than a bite or two, and she didn't even try to rest until very early on Day Three, Wednesday, during the hours after midnight—the ones her mother had called the despair hours—when, over her objections, Sheriff Audi barred her from joining yet another team of searchers, a group assigned to an area north of Hardys Walk that included a heavily wooded, rural neighborhood.

Cooper drove her back into town, to the café. Madeleine toasted grilled-cheese sandwiches for them, and Annie, with Madeleine sitting over her, managed to eat half. She was more exhausted than she'd realized, almost falling into her plate, and she didn't protest when around one in the morning, Cooper led her to his truck parked in the alley behind the community center. He assisted her into the backseat. Rufus hopped in after her, sitting on the floor, while Cooper covered her with a blanket that was soft and smelled clean, the way he did, like pine. Like the woods after a good rain. She liked the smell, she thought, drifting.

Setting Bo's earmuffs over her ears, she closed her eyes and slept hard, jerking awake a short time later when she thought she heard Bo calling her name. Annie sat up slowly to listen. Rufus sat up, too, eyeing her worriedly, as if he knew the nature of the calamity that was unfolding. After several minutes passed, when she heard nothing other than the insistent throb of her own heartbeat and the rush of her breath, she pulled Bo's earmuffs off her head.

"I can't hear him now," she whispered to Rufus. "I can't hear him at all."

She climbed down from the truck, and Rufus came with her. He trotted off to relieve himself on some nearby shrubbery, but Annie paused, lifting her chin, looking into the sky's high arch. It was too late for stars, even the moon had fled, and the air had taken on a brittle quality. It wasn't cold exactly, but there was a premonition of fall in the slight breeze, like a warning. And so far as anyone knew, Bo was in shirtsleeves and chinos, a pair of worn-out tennis shoes. He might or might not be wearing socks. Sometimes he forgot. Soon it would be cold all the time, and it would rain, and Annie couldn't stand the idea of him outside in horrible weather, all alone. It was silly. She knew that. He walked the streets in every season. The difference was that on his own turf, he knew where to find shelter, and she knew where to find him.

Putting his earmuffs back on her head, she walked down the alley toward the community center, Rufus by her side. Light glared from the metal-caged fixtures mounted above the row of shop doors. Still, she was glad for Rufus's company. In fact, she preferred it to human company. He didn't ask her continual questions about how she was doing. He didn't push food on her or beg her to rest. He never promised her it would be okay.

A group of teenagers appeared, walking toward Annie, carrying stacks of flyers, the ones Carol had helped Annie make on Monday evening. She'd found a suitable photograph of Bo in a box at JT's. She thought her mom had taken it. It showed him leaning against one of the front-porch posts, his mouth quirked into a half smile, a teasing light in his eyes. He looked so cute, as if he had a secret. He looked normal.

As ordinary as any one of these kids, who, having recognized Annie, had stopped now in front of her and stood shifting their feet, not quite meeting her eye. They didn't know any more than she did how to proceed, and Annie didn't know how to help them.

She was grateful when one of the girls, a tall brunette, wearing glasses, stepped forward. "We're going to put these up at shopping centers and malls, the ones between here and Houston. Everything around here is pretty much covered." She was unsmiling and grave, but there was an aura of excitement in her demeanor, too, as if she were launched on an adventure and thrilled to be part of it.

Annie thanked her.

"It's the least we can do," one of the boys said.

Another said, "Hang in there," and bending over, he patted Rufus and spoke to him. It was easier than talking to her, Annie thought.

"We know Bo," the brunette girl said. "He comes to all the football games, basketball, too."

"Really?" It was news to Annie that Bo went to the high school games.

"Yeah, he's like our mascot, one of our biggest cheerleaders. We love him," the girl said.

"Not everyone does," said the kid who'd been patting Rufus.

"Some people are just mean." The girl's glance darted toward Annie, and away.

Her breath went shallow. "Did someone threaten him, threaten to hurt him?"

The girl said no, looking uncomfortable. Rufus's fan, the boy, didn't answer until Annie pressed him, and then he was vague in a way that made Annie feel he wasn't being honest, that he might even be fearful. She asked his name.

"It's Sean," the girl said when he didn't answer. "Sean Hennessy. I'm Gabriella, Gabby for short." Gabby introduced the others, but

Annie wasn't listening. She was repeating Sean's name to herself so that she would remember it when she spoke to Sheriff Audi.

Gabby talked a bit more about Bo, saying how funny he was and how sweet. The other kids chimed in, awkward in their praise of Bo, more awkward in their leave-taking, and watching them go, Annie felt half-bewildered, half-irked, some frustrating combination. People kept telling her things about Bo that she didn't know. They talked as if they shared a warm, fuzzy connection with him. But weren't these volunteers the same people who called him a head case or a retard, the very ones who would turn away from Bo in alarm or disgust or stare with outright annoyance when he erupted into constant chatter or lapsed into sullen silence? Where were these caring, concerned people when he was still here?

Annie didn't know, couldn't sort it out.

The lights at the back of the community center were off when she let Rufus inside. The volunteers manning the telephones were grouped around tables at the front of the building, in the reception area that overlooked the street and the sidewalk where Annie had been interviewed by the local media on Tuesday night. She hadn't wanted to speak publicly, had only consented when everyone said it might do some good.

Nothing could have been further from the truth. The segment aired at ten o'clock, and there she was for everyone in the entire state of Texas to see, or most of the state, anyway, wearing Bo's earmuffs. She'd been wearing them so constantly, she'd forgotten them, and no one pointed it out to her. She figured it was only the seriousness of the situation that kept the immaculately dressed and perfectly coiffed blonde commentator from laughing. Watching the segment with JT later, Annie wished the earth would open and swallow her down whole, but JT had turned to her, eyes swimming with tears, and cupped her cheek in his rough palm. The gesture was so rare, so singular, and unexpected, she forgot herself. It embarrassed them both when she barreled into his arms.

Feelings were hard for him. On Monday afternoon, when she called to tell him Sheriff Audi was writing up Bo's missing person's report, JT had taken one sharp breath, and then he'd said he was on his way, that the police would need help setting up a command post. Annie had been surprised at how quickly he'd reacted. It had been a few years since she'd seen him operate in rescue mode. It was as if a long-forgotten switch had been flipped.

Within an hour of hearing about Bo, JT rounded up some of the guys from his crew, and together, they installed extra telephones at the community center. Then he worked with the sheriff's department, coordinating the task of arranging for a number to be designated as a tip line. He'd organized the search teams, too, and he was out somewhere now with one of them, waiting for dawn's first light. Annie knew from seeing him in action before that he wouldn't stop. Not until Bo was found.

Rufus spotted Cooper and deserted her, and without him to bolster her courage, Annie hung back, on the verge of retreat, but then Cooper's gaze found her. He lifted his arm as if he meant her to stay, and the look on his face, some curious mix of delight and concern, compelled her to wait while he crossed the room toward her. In addition to Rufus, there was a woman with him, and before anything was said, Annie knew it was Cooper's mother.

The woman took Annie's hands, both of them.

Cooper made the introductions.

"It's nice to meet you, Mrs. Gant," Annie said.

"Please, call me Peggy." She searched Annie's eyes, and like everyone else, her commiseration was palpable, so heartfelt and true, that Annie was undone by it. She had to look away, to harden her throat against the push of her tears, an unwelcome return of the anger she wasn't entitled to. But, honestly, how could Cooper have done this, brought his mother to meet her under these circumstances? Why couldn't he see how it would embarrass her?

Something of her turmoil must have shown on her face, because Cooper's mother let go of Annie's hands and pulled her into her embrace. She was tall and solidly built, and she smelled faintly of chicken soup with an underscore of something floral. It was nice, the way she smelled. Annie wanted to lean against her, to give in to what was an overwhelming need for reassurance, but she was too afraid of losing control and stood stiffly erect while Cooper's mother rubbed her back, murmuring a host of things, all promising a happy ending.

"We'll find him, honey. You wait and see. Pat is out there now. So many of your neighbors are. Come daylight, I'm sure the entire town will be back out hunting for him."

Pat, Annie thought ruefully. Cooper's dad, who had fixed her car, who was still waiting for his money.

Peggy said she'd brought a potful of chicken soup, which explained her soothing smell, but when she offered it, Annie's teeth clenched. She couldn't breathe, couldn't take another moment of Cooper's mother's solicitude, and broke free of her embrace, mumbling an apology, somehow feeling even more humiliated and angry—at Cooper, at his mother and father, the circumstances, God, whatever. It was unreasonable, and Annie regretted it. She was trembling when Rufus, who was sitting next to her, leaned against her, and her hand, as if it knew the way by now and belonged there, lowered to his head.

"I think you've stolen my dog," Cooper commented mildly.

"His heart, for sure," Cooper's mother said. Peggy seemed unruffled, if she was even aware of the chaos of Annie's feelings. "The soup's in the kitchen whenever you want it," she said. "I know it's not daylight yet, but chicken soup is good anytime and so good for the nerves. Good for everything."

Annie thanked her. She said "Maybe later" and "It was nice meeting you," and she took a step, putting distance between them. She knew it was rude, turning her back on Cooper's mother, but she couldn't stop herself.

Cooper caught her arm.

"Let us help you," he said.

"That's very kind," Annie said, "but there's really nothing you can do." She looked over his shoulder at Peggy and was relieved to see her talking to someone else.

Carol came to Annie's side. "You're supposed to be resting."

"Can you talk sense to her?" Cooper asked. "She won't listen to a word I say."

Carol slid her arm over Annie's shoulders.

"I don't know where to be," Annie said in a low voice. "I feel like I should be walking the streets, pounding on doors, asking if anyone has seen Bo, or hunting the roadsides. Then when I'm doing that, I think I should be at home or at JT's, in case Bo comes there."

"Hollis has that covered," Carol said. "Deputies are driving by both places regularly."

"Annie?"

She turned to Madeleine, who looked exhausted. "You should go home," she told the older woman.

Carol agreed. "I'll drive you."

Madeleine shushed them both. "I'm fine. Stop fussing. We've had a call, or I should say, they got a tip down at the sheriff's office."

"What sort of tip?" Cooper asked.

Annie quelled an urge to put her hands over her ears.

"A man thinks he saw Bo walking along the interstate east of town yesterday evening."

"How far east?" Carol wanted to know.

"Outside the original search grid, maybe just the other side of Marshall? Hollis didn't say, exactly. But he did say he thought the tip was worth investigating. They're going to interview the man now."

Annie rubbed her eyes. There had been dozens of sightings reported to the hotline since Monday, maybe hundreds by now. Every one had proved worthless. It was the same with Bo's cell phone. Tracing that had proved useless, too. According to the records law enforcement obtained from Bo's provider, his last call was to Annie more than a week ago, the same day he'd come to the café and they'd had tea. If he'd used the phone since, there wasn't documentation of it.

Madeleine was saying something about dogs. Search-and-rescue dogs, Annie realized, and her breath hitched. Weren't dogs brought in as a last resort? When most everyone figured the lost person was dead? Weren't those dogs sometimes called cadaver dogs?

Cooper looked at Annie. "They'll need something that belonged to Bo, something that will give the dogs his scent."

Annie pulled Bo's earmuffs from where she'd been wearing them around her neck. "Will these work?" She was reluctant to give them up, even for a good reason. She wondered if she would get them back. She wondered if she put them over her ears right now, would she finally hear Bo. Would he tell her where he was?

Cooper took them from her. "I don't know, since you've been wearing them. Maybe these and something else. A shirt or something?"

"I'll go home," Annie said, "see what I can find."

"I'll drive you," Cooper said.

But Annie said no, she had her own car. "You've done enough." She went in search of her purse.

Cooper followed her. "You aren't in any condition to drive."

"And you are? Have you slept?"

"You're missing the point," Cooper said. "I'm not as emotionally strung out."

"I didn't ask for this." She meant his concern.

He misunderstood. "No one asks for stuff like this."

She averted her gaze.

He cupped her elbow. "Annie, let me drive you."

"All right," she said, and she thought she agreed because she was too weary to argue further. But probably, mixed in with that, was a wish not to be alone, and she was annoyed at herself for it. It didn't pay to rely on anyone, to need them, because eventually they left. They always left. Or they betrayed you, like Leighton, and then they left.

Cooper drove through town, along the quiet streets, past still-darkened houses, where porch lights burned at random, surrounded by the shadows of doomed moths. Annie imagined the papery whisper of their wings, beating and futile. They flew at the light, heedless of the risk, the way Bo walked the streets, without regard for the danger. Stopping him was no more possible than stopping the moths. Hadn't she tried, a hundred, a thousand times? Would it have worked if she had tried once more? Had she given up on Bo too soon?

She directed Cooper into the driveway that led to her tiny bungalow, and when he started to get out of the car, she asked him to wait. He settled back and said, "Okay," but he looked unhappy.

So much so that she said, "I'm sorry," but then letting herself into the house, she wondered what she was sorry for. She wondered what might have happened between her and Cooper if the circumstances were ordinary. Probably nothing. Guys made her nervous. Other than Leighton Drake, she'd never had more than a fleeting relationship with maybe two or three of them. She hadn't even had a date to her senior prom.

She went quickly through her living room and into the tiny room that Bo shared with her sewing machine when he stayed with her. The narrow twin bed was made; there was nothing out of place, a sure sign he hadn't been there. He was messy, and once he was gone again, she would set about picking up after him, usually muttering to herself, things like she ought not to have to put up with it, him and his stuff he left everywhere, and why couldn't he at least toss his dirty clothes into the hamper?

She went around the foot of the bed, not out of hope that she would find some unwashed article of his clothing, but because she was thorough, and there it was, the twisted wad of green knit. Annie yanked on it, recognizing it was a T-shirt of Bo's, laden with his scent, and relief flooded her. She sat on the end of the bed and spread the shirt out across her knees, smoothing the creases. It was one of Bo's favorites, dark green, lettered in a pale shade of gold with a quote from his idol, Henry David Thoreau, that read: *The moment my legs begin to move, my thoughts begin to flow.*

Annie's mother had bought it. She had thought it was perfect. She had thought in another time, a simpler world, maybe Bo would have only been considered eccentric, like Thoreau was in his day.

"Annie?"

She looked up as Cooper crossed the room and sat beside her.

"He tested off the charts in some ways," she said. "Reading comprehension and writing, especially. When he was little, they said his IQ was really high. One hundred thirty-five, I think."

Cooper kept his silence.

"He wanted to take me to my senior prom, but I said no, because by then he was starting to get weird and people thought I was weird, too. By association," Annie added. "All through school, I blamed him for why I never had a date or any friends." A sound broke from her chest. She bit it back, balling the shirt in her fists.

Cooper slid his hand over hers. She felt his palm, warm against the bones of her knuckles. He was close enough to her that she felt the warmth of his breath stirring the hair at her temple, and when she turned to him, he kissed her. It wasn't a demanding kiss, or she would have pulled away. It wasn't passionate but tender and filled with mercy. It was a kiss that commiserated, if that was possible. And it was more than that, more than words she knew to describe it, and then it was over.

He lifted his mouth from hers, searching her gaze, and she was afraid he could see the naked longing in her eyes to burrow into him, to let him hold her.

She ducked her chin, running her fingers around the cup of her ear. "I can't do this now," she said softly.

"They're waiting for this." Cooper touched Bo's shirt. "We should go."

Annie led the way from the room. She didn't know Cooper's feelings, whether he hadn't heard her or if he was giving her space. She felt disconcerted, somehow irked and torn with longing all at once. She didn't need this, she thought. Didn't need Cooper Gant. She got into his truck, and she waited for Rufus to push his nose between the seats, then remembered they'd left him at the community center. She missed him.

Cooper got into the driver's seat and switched on the ignition. He looked at her. "Is that your phone?" he said.

She found her purse and fished out her phone. "There's a message," she said, tapping the screen. "Oh, my God!"

"What?" Cooper was backing down the drive, not looking at her.

"It's a text from Bo."

"What?" Cooper hit the brake.

"It says he's at the library in Houston. Downtown. He rode there with Ms. M."

"Who's Ms. M?"

"I don't know. I thought his phone was dead. How could it send a message?"

Cooper said, "We should call Hollis."

But Annie said no. She had a sick feeling in her stomach. "We have to go there."

"To the library? It's four in the morning. I think we need to let the police know—"

"No," Annie repeated. "We can't wait for them. We don't have time."

9

Two years ago, when Lauren found the small, two-story country church on a bright, chilly day the week before Christmas, she'd been driving to her grandparents' farm. She hadn't taken the usual route but instead wound her way along a network of tar-drizzled, sun-dazzled rural roads—ranch roads—that uncurled through the woods. She marked the little church from the corner of her eye as she passed it, and stopping, she backed up some fifty feet to have a longer look, feeling somehow drawn to the place. In retrospect it would seem eerie, given all the church would take from her. But the day she found it, she was intrigued.

It was close to the road's edge and surrounded by a crooked lacework of wrought-iron fence. The gnarled canopy of an ancient live oak bowed over the small building, as if it meant to lift it into its embrace. The effect was magical, a habitation for fairies despite the evidence of dilapidation: white clapboard that was rotting, a roof that sagged. The four Queen Anne–style windows Lauren could see were cracked and broken, puzzles rendered in jeweled colors of stained glass. *What a shame*, her mind whispered.

The gate screeched, piercing the silence when she opened it, and she winced. A paper taped to the padlocked entry doors indicated the property was scheduled for demolition, giving a date and a number to contact. Lauren took down the notice, folded it, and tucked it into her coat pocket. She stood back a bit, looking up at the steeple, catching her first sight of the bell behind the louvered enclosure. Even then, she knew she would be the one to go up there, to determine what would be necessary to dismantle the tower and bring down the old bell. Her heart leapt at the prospect.

She thought Jeff would say the job was too small, and he did, but once he saw how much she wanted to do it, he made time on the schedule, lined up the crew and the equipment, mostly hand tools. Lauren wanted to preserve as much of the church's architectural history as she could.

It took a couple of weeks to make the arrangements, locate the property owner, halt the demolition, and gain the proper permits for deconstruction. In the meantime, an old parishioner Lauren spoke to, a woman in her eighties, said her grandfather had built the church and his brother had fashioned the furniture, but then the nearby farms had fallen on hard times and were sold, and most of the congregants moved away.

Standing outside on the day they were to start work, remembering the old woman, Lauren thought how she would like to take her a souvenir and wondered what it should be. She was still thinking about that when she climbed the stairs and then the ladder that led into the steeple. The light filtering through the rotting louvers glistened like opals; the dust-laden air smelled musty, reminding Lauren of the attic at the farm. She called down to Jeff that she was within sight of the bell, and it was right after that, when the bat flew at her, startling her, that she fell.

Like a bird shot from the sky, she plummeted to the floor of the church narthex, landing with a wet-sounding thwack—poetically it would seem—dead center inside yet another church treasure, a marble-tiled wreath of white lilies. Jeff, who had stepped out of sight into the sanctuary, said later that when her body hit the floor, the sound it made reminded him of the summer day when, as a kid, he'd dropped a ripe watermelon off the back of a truck. He told the ER doctor that when he first knelt beside her, he thought Lauren was dead.

But she was only broken, cracked up worse than Humpty Dumpty.

She would never clearly recall the hours she spent in the emergency room or in surgery. Jeff told her later she hadn't been expected to live. He said he prayed for her, an act she found hard to believe. She'd never known Jeff to pray. She had a faint memory of him pacing beside her bed, saying how terrified he was of raising their kids alone, but she didn't know if it was real. Even when she was fully wakened from a medically induced coma, when Dr. Bettinger spoke to her about the damage to her brain and her body, she couldn't take it in. She thought she was dreaming.

But it wasn't as if she could pretend it was someone else who was strung up like a joint of beef on a spit. The metal rod attached to a contraption above her bed was skewered through her knee, not the knee of another patient. Bettinger explained it was intended to stabilize her smashed pelvic and hip bones, giving them an opportunity to knit themselves together in some fashion that might once again support her.

But understanding of that came later. Initially, Lauren's single awareness was of pain. Pain and Jeff. The touch of his work-roughened fingertips across her brow, the calluses on his palms when he cupped her cheek. His mouth at her ear murmured a nonsense of words meant to comfort, to pull her through. He basted her cracked lips with an ocean of soothing balm. Sometimes as she lay immobilized, trapped and grunting like an animal in her agony, he held her hand. The nurses marveled at his devotion. *Isn't it something?* they whispered.

But devotion borne out of a sense of duty was not the same as devotion that rose, helpless and unbidden, as the extant and unstoppable side effect of love. While Jeff's devotion in the days and weeks following the accident had been unflagging, what else could he have done? Given the gravity of her injuries, how would it have looked if he were to desert her?

But he must have wanted to. He must have looked at her broken, damaged body and been sickened and overwhelmed at the enormity of her need. What sort of wife could she be to him? What did she have to offer when she could barely walk or lift a hand to help herself? It was nearly four months before they had sex again, and even then, every moment was fraught with their mutual anxiety that he would somehow reinjure her or cause her fresh pain.

Still, he never spoke of leaving her, not until almost a year after her fall when her use of the Oxy got out of control, when it was only fair. But suppose now that the worst was behind them, he continued to stay out of obligation, for the sake of appearance? Because playing the hero came naturally to him? Suppose love had nothing to do with it?

Lauren glanced sidelong at him, where he sat at the granite-topped island in their kitchen, sipping coffee. He'd lost weight in the past two years; she could see the blades of his cheekbones. The shadows under his eyes stood out against the fresh-shaven pallor of his skin. He was different since her accident, altered in ways she didn't know, struggling with burdens he refused to share, and in all honesty, no matter how she protested, maybe she didn't want the weight of them. Maybe she couldn't stand up to the truth if she knew it. Maybe he would get fed up one day and walk out because of all she'd cost him, all she'd put him through. The idea sat in her head as ugly as it was regretful.

Was it trustworthy?

Who knew?

Her mind was so full of tricks.

She turned her attention to the breakfast dishes, finished loading them into the dishwasher. Drew and Kenzie had already caught the bus for school, and she wondered why Jeff was still here. Ordinarily, he left before they did.

"I've got a meeting with Kaiser at nine," he said. "When are you going to be ready?"

Ben Kaiser, Lauren remembered, the owner of the Waller-Land building. Jeff was counting on its demolition to make their fourth quarter. But she was drawing a blank in regard to a meeting with the building's owner. "You're waiting on me?"

"Well, yeah." Jeff seemed faintly amused. "You don't have your car?"

She blinked. She had no clue what he was talking about and felt an inkling of alarm mixed with despair.

"It wouldn't start after work last night?" Jeff prompted. "We had it towed to the dealership?"

"I rode home with you." Lauren spoke through her hands that she'd tented over her mouth, as the memory, in all its vivid audacity, swaggered out of some mental closet, taking its own sweet time. She turned from Jeff, wanting to hide her distress.

"It's all right," Jeff said, and it angered her. It so obviously wasn't.

She rinsed the dishcloth. "You don't have to wait," she told him, lifting her voice over the sound of the running water. "I'll call the dealership and have them deliver the car if it's ready. I have things to do here anyway."

"Suit yourself." Jeff shrugged into his jacket and pulled his truck keys from his pocket, kissed her, lightly, perfunctorily—it was their usual ritual even in the worst of times—and catching her gaze, searching her eyes, he said, "I'll see you later?" Translated, what he really wanted to know was whether this was going to be one of *those* days. The sort of day when she and everyone else would be better off if she stayed home.

He would probably prefer it. What use was she with only half a brain? Jeff must wonder.

The door closed behind him.

A moment later when the landline rang, Lauren answered it without checking the Caller ID, and she was greeted by a man's voice, calling her by name. When he identified himself as Detective Jim Cosgrove and said he was with the Lincoln County Sheriff's Office, specifically the criminal-investigation division, her heart started to pound as if in anticipation of bad news.

"I understand you called last Friday, asking for a welfare check on a young man. Bo Laughlin. Is that correct?"

"Yes," Lauren answered, and although she realized it wasn't a member of her family who was in jeopardy, her anxiety wouldn't settle.

"My partner and I are in the area. We'd like to stop by and ask you a few questions about your encounter with Mr. Laughlin."

Lauren sensed he wasn't asking. "No one's found him yet?"

"No, ma'am. We'd like to talk to you," he repeated.

"When?"

"Now, if it's convenient."

Lauren walked quickly from the kitchen and down the hall to the front door, where she could look out to the street, and there they were. Two men in a plain dark-brown sedan. She could see the passenger, Detective Cosgrove, she guessed, had a phone pressed to his ear, waiting for her answer.

She flung the door wide, wanting to catch his attention, wanting him to see that she wasn't intimidated, even though she was. "Come right in," she said into the phone. He met her gaze through the passenger window, and she thought she saw one corner of his mouth lift, a fraction of a smile.

She led them into the formal living room, a room she disliked. It was uncomfortably furnished for one thing, and set apart from the rest of the house, seeming far removed from its heart, which was the combined kitchen/great-room area. Lauren had never known what to do with the space and had lately thought of making it into a room for herself. An idea had germinated recently that she might write about her experience with antiques and salvage. She didn't plan a lot of text, rather she would tell the story through photographs of rooms she'd helped her clients create using old, rescued furniture and architectural remnants. She wanted Tara to help her. It would be a great project for them. A sister project. Now she wasn't sure Tara was even speaking to her.

Lauren asked the officers if they would like coffee. They declined. Detective Cosgrove, the evident spokesperson, opened a notepad and set it on his knee. He and his partner looked a bit uncomfortable with their respective woolen-suited bulks wedged into the narrow-armed embrace of the two matching pink silk-upholstered wingback chairs Lauren had installed across from a small brocade sofa. Perching on the edge of one of the sofa's cushions, she wondered why she had brought the chairs home, how she could have ever thought they were stylish, much less serviceable.

"I was going to call you," she said, "after I heard about Bo's disappearance on the news last night." She hadn't managed it after all. Before the call could go through, Kenzie had wakened, crying out from a bad dream, and Lauren had gone to her, forgetting her intention.

"Can you tell me what you were doing in the area where you spoke to Mr. Laughlin last Friday? You did speak to him, right?"

Lauren said she had and repeated the gist of their conversation.

"We don't advise that motorists approach unknown pedestrians as a rule." Cosgrove straightened his knee and brought it back.

"I know," she said, "but I nearly hit him." She added in defense of herself, "I wanted to be sure he was all right."

Cosgrove's look seemed commiserating.

"He was so close to the edge of the road." Lauren flattened her palm on her chest, feeling her breath shallow in memory of her alarm. "Anyway, it isn't something I would do ordinarily, but—I've seen him before, around town, walking. Do you know anything about him? Why he—? Is there something wrong with him? He mentioned his sister, Annie, but does he have parents, other family?" She looked down, distressed suddenly, and fiddling with her wedding rings, she apologized. "It's none of my business."

Cosgrove didn't confirm or deny it, and neither did his partner.

"I would stop for a hurt animal, you know? Why not a person?" Lauren felt compelled to say this.

"Was anyone else with you at the time, Mrs. Wilder?"

Cosgrove shot her a look from under his brow, one Lauren couldn't interpret. It gave her an odd feeling. "No," she answered.

"Can you describe what he was wearing?"

"Gray pants, chinos," Lauren answered, "and a blue-plaid cotton shirt. Short-sleeved and buttoned to the neck. And tennis shoes. They were dark-colored, navy or black, maybe. He was very neat, neat as a pin," she said.

"The car you saw him get into, you say it was a Cadillac, but could it have been a Lincoln, a Town Car?" Cosgrove's partner, something Willis—Lauren hadn't registered his first name—spoke for the first time.

Lauren looked at him. He was older than Cosgrove, and unlike Cosgrove, who was wiry and thin, Detective Willis was fat. His meaty cheeks fell in folds to his neck. A thick scallop of flesh lapped his belt. Lauren couldn't imagine how, if the occasion arose, he would chase down a criminal. Answering him, she said she was pretty hopeless when it came to identifying cars. "It was a sedan, long and black. I know that for sure."

Cosgrove jotted a note and looked up at her. "Did he get into the car willingly? Was there anyone around him? Did anyone else get in the car?"

"Not that I saw."

"Did you get in the car, Mrs. Wilder?"

Lauren jerked her gaze to Willis. "No! Why would you ask—?"

"No reason." Willis patted the air. "So, there were no other passengers then, only the woman driving?"

"That's right," Lauren answered. "He looked happy, not as if he was in any danger or afraid in any way. I thought he must know her."

When Cosgrove asked, Lauren gave him a description of the woman. "She was older." Lauren frowned into the middle distance, trying to reassemble the woman's image. It was important to be accurate. "She kept her hands on the steering wheel, and she bent over a little, watching Bo get into the car. She was laughing with him. I mostly saw the back of her head, her white hair. She wore it up in a French twist with a comb, a tortoiseshell comb."

"Tortoise what—?" Cosgrove was out of his depth.

Lauren smiled. "It's a decorative comb to help keep your hair in place. It's all shades of mottled brown like a turtle's shell."

"Huh." Cosgrove made another note.

"We could get her to work with a sketch artist," Willis suggested.

"Yeah. We'll see," Cosgrove said.

"What about the license plate?" Willis switched his glance to Lauren. "Did you see whether it was local or out of state?"

She started to shake her head, but then she realized she knew the answer. "It was a Texas plate, the one with the bluebonnets on it. I've always wanted one, but the extra charge seems like an extravagance." She smiled again.

Cosgrove did, too.

"Do you remember any of the letters or numbers?" Willis asked.

Lauren said she didn't. She apologized again. "I wish I could be more help. Do you think—I mean, it isn't possible this woman kidnapped him, is it?"

"We don't really know what happened at this point, Mrs. Wilder. But if you think of anything else, please give us a call." Cosgrove passed her his business card and after flipping closed his notepad, he stood up. Willis followed suit.

"Of course." Lauren stood up, too. "But I can't imagine anything I know could be useful." She led the way to the front door.

"You'd be surprised," Cosgrove said. "Sometimes the smallest detail can be the whole answer."

"You're actually the last person to have spoken to him," Willis said.

"That we've found," Cosgrove added.

"Yeah." Willis confirmed it, staring hard at Lauren.

She didn't like him, the way he seemed to imply something vaguely accusatory, as if he were insinuating she knew more about Bo Laughlin's disappearance than she was saying. She took in a breath, preparing to deny it, but then she caught herself and bit back her speech, some instinct warning her how foolish it would sound. Standing aside, she allowed the officers passage through the front door onto the porch. "His family must be out of their minds with worry."

"A lot of folks are concerned for him," Cosgrove said. "More than half the town's population is either manning phones at the community center or out searching for him."

"I hope nothing bad has happened to him." Lauren felt stricken, as if she should have done more. "If only someone had come when I called on Friday," she began.

Willis interrupted her. "An officer went by the store, Mrs. Wilder. Laughlin was gone by the time he got there."

"I see," Lauren said.

"Thanks for your time." Detective Willis followed Cosgrove down the steps.

"There's one other thing." She spoke even as the memory surfaced.

Willis paused, turning to squint at her.

"Bo showed me a roll of cash. There was a rubber band around it. I said he should put it away. Someone could rob him, hurt him." Lauren was thinking of Bo's vulnerability.

"You see any evidence of drugs?" Willis asked. "Anything that would make you suspect he had them in his possession or that he was on something? Were you on something?"

"No!" She stared at him, unnerved by his query. "Why are you asking me that?"

"Just looking for an opinion, Mrs. Wilder," he said.

But there was something in his expression, a canniness that said otherwise. It said he and probably all of law enforcement in the county knew her history and assumed that because of it, she had knowledge, dealings in that world. "I don't have one," she told Willis, coldly.

He nodded. He was steps away when he stopped again. "You said you were alone on Friday. Where was your husband?"

"At work. Why are you asking?" She didn't give Willis time to answer. "I've been cleared to drive. You can ask my doctor. It's all right as long as I keep to a familiar route and don't go too far." She spoke in defense of herself, feeling like a child called on to explain or face punishment, and in the moment of silence that followed, she waited for them to challenge her regarding her legal right to drive or the accuracy of her statements concerning her meeting with Bo, but they did neither.

They only thanked her again, and Cosgrove repeated his request that if she did remember anything else, he'd appreciate a call.

"I have your card." Lauren brandished it.

He touched an imaginary hat brim, got into the patrol car, and Willis drove away.

Watching the taillights wink and then disappear around the corner, Lauren began to tremble. *Drugs.* The word appeared in her mind. The detectives had come here because of drugs and because they thought she was unbalanced, a brain-damaged druggie who couldn't be relied on or trusted. They had the idea she had traded Bo that rubber-banded wad of cash for OxyContin. Was that right? The wonder and doubt, the invitation to panic hovered like smoke in Lauren's mind. She went into the house, through the kitchen to the breakfast nook, and dropped into a chair at the table, dropped her face into her hands. Her heartbeat felt light and too rapid in her chest. It was that word, the very word *drugs* that had the power to so thoroughly unhinge her. Greg said some people would never believe she wasn't still using. In meetings, he and others talked about how that was especially true if you relapsed. Greg had fallen off the proverbial wagon twice in three of the past four and a half years he'd been sober.

In fact, that could explain what was going on with him now. Lauren lowered her hands. Maybe he hadn't gone to Kansas City. Why would he go that far to find work? Maybe that was only the lie he'd told to cover up that he was using again. She sat back in her chair.

Suppose Tara knew—and that, and not a stomach virus, was what was ailing her? She would be heartsick, of course, and it made sense that she wouldn't want to talk about it. But she would get past that, and in a few days, she'd call. She would confess the trouble, and she and Lauren would talk. They always did, eventually.

It has nothing to do with you, Lauren would say. Addicts relapse. They fall back into compulsion. A person can be drug-free for any number of years—five, fifteen, twenty-five years—and then, boom, in the wink of an eye, in the time it takes to swallow a pill or shoot up, roll the dice, or down a drink, they're back at it. Nothing but want, a huge ache, a bottomless hole looking for a way to get filled.

I live in fear of this. Lauren imagined how freeing it would feel to say this, to name what was her second-to-worst fear to her sister.

Her very worst fear was that she'd lose her children.

She was pulling her keys from her purse when her cell phone rang. She glanced at the Caller ID window. *Jeff.*

"Did you get your car back?" he asked when she answered.

Lauren closed her eyes. *God!* Where was her mind? The Navigator wasn't here. She knew that, didn't she know?

"Look, I'm really under the gun here. The Waller-Land demo is scheduled to start day after tomorrow, and I can't find the permits, plus the truck with all the shit from the Anderson barn job just showed up."

"I think I saw the permits and the contract on the desk in the study. I'll look," Lauren said. "What about the trailer load of stuff you brought back from the farm? It's there, too, right?"

"It's a fucking mess, Lauren. You have no idea. When can you get here?"

"Jeff? Are you all right?"

"Maybe we need to talk."

"Okaaay." She drew the word out, uncertain, half-alarmed.

"You ever think maybe we should sell everything and go, just get the hell out from under all of it—the goddamn debt, all the obligations—"

"The business? You would sell the business?"

"Hold on a sec."

Lauren could hear him talking to someone. The UPS guy from the sound of it.

He came back on the line. "You still there?"

"Are you really considering selling Wilder and Tate?"

"We could move to some no-name island in the Caribbean—if only that would fix it."

"Fix what?"

He laughed, but the sound wasn't funny. "You must be kidding, right?"

"Jeff? What is going on?"

"Trust me, you don't want to know."

She groaned. "Do you have any idea how tired I am of hearing that? We're in this together. The property, our life, assets, debts—all of it has my name all over it, too." She waited, and when he didn't respond, she said, "Did it ever occur to you that I might have some ideas about ways to help?"

"Like what?"

"Like we could see an attorney, file bankruptcy."

"Oh, hell no, Lauren." He paused. "You know what? Never mind. I think I've got it handled. For now anyway."

"Fine, but you want to know what scares me?" Lauren's voice shook with her aggravation and the sense of some dark foreboding. "That you're going to kill yourself, and then where will the children and I be?"

"That's not going to happen."

"Really? Can you guarantee it? Because at the rate you're going—"

"Can we change the subject?"

"Fine." She matched his clipped tone. She wasn't any happier with him than he was with her. "The police were here."

"What? What the hell?"

"They asked me about Bo Laughlin." *They brought up drugs.* Lauren wanted to say this, too. But she was afraid of the effect it would have. Jeff was already wired. And the fact that she couldn't talk freely to him was disconcerting, so much so that she felt a sharp pain, as if she'd stepped off the curb and come down hard on her ankle.

"You didn't call them, did you?"

"No. They called me. Evidently, I was one of the last people to talk to him."

"Jesus, this is all I need."

"A boy is missing," Lauren said.

"I understand that, and I'm sorry, but he isn't your responsibility. You can't get involved."

"Can't?"

"I mean I'm up to my ass here, and I could really use your help. I thought it was what you wanted, to be treated like a partner."

She didn't answer.

"Look, you've already done everything possible to help, right?"

Lauren thought about it. Had she? "The detective said there's a huge search effort going on. They've set up a command post at the community center in town."

"That's great, Lauren, but speaking for myself, I've got enough on my plate, trying to help my own family."

Another silence fell, one she didn't feel like breaking.

"You aren't considering going there? Volunteering?"

"What if I am?"

"We should talk."

"About Bo?"

"About our situation. Our *partnership*."

"So talk," she said without hope or conviction.

"Not on the phone." He hesitated. "Please don't go into town. Come here instead, okay? I need you."

He was asking, sincerely asking, and she answered she would be there as quickly as she could. And maybe, in the moment, she meant it.

But perversely, after the dealership finally delivered the Navigator around lunchtime, instead of heading to the warehouse, she drove to the community center. Her interview with the detectives worried her. Willis's mention of drugs, his seeming inference that she might have been complicit in some deal with Bo, that she might have handed him cash in exchange for Oxy, had gotten under her skin. She kept going over her encounter with him, and nowhere in her recollection was there anything of the sort. She would remember if she'd traded him money for the Oxy. She wasn't that far gone. The voice in her brain was insistent on this point, cycling through its litany of reassurance even as it dished up the whole question of the Oxy tabs she'd found in the study later, on the same day she'd met Bo.

How could she explain that to Cosgrove or Willis if they asked? What would she say?

10

Bo wasn't at the library. At four on Wednesday morning, there was no one there other than a homeless man who muttered, "Piss off," when Cooper disturbed him.

"It was worth a shot," Cooper said as they walked back to his truck, and Annie was grateful when he didn't seem to require a response from her. As if he accepted that coming to the library at such an insane hour, expecting to find Bo, was a reasonable idea.

It wouldn't be for anyone else. But what defined normal behavior for most people didn't work for Bo. Even as a young child, he'd done things, acted in ways that were difficult to classify, that seemed nuts but might as easily have been hallmarks of some off-the-chart, oddball intelligence. She remembered a time when he'd counted things, canned goods in the pantry, squares of toilet tissue, the individual pieces of kibble in Freckles's dog dish. He'd driven them crazy, dragging things out of cabinets and closets, stringing them across the kitchen table or the floor to numerate them: one, two three . . . a hundred one, a hundred two.

He arranged the canned goods in reverse alphabetical order. Using selected letters from each label, he created a secret code, then a poem, then two paragraphs that told a story. It was bizarre and funny and brilliant. Then it was over. The obsession passed. He was imaginative, creative, and curious, her mother said. Exceptionally so. Annie's mom had used that description a lot when she talked about Bo.

She looked at Cooper now, and said, "Bo can be delusional. I don't mean from taking drugs," she added quickly, and from the glance Cooper gave her, she saw he wasn't sure how to respond. No one ever knew, which was why she didn't like talking about Bo. She looked down at her hands, picking her thumbnail. "He might have dreamed he was going to the library with someone named Ms. M. It happens sometimes, but it isn't a dream to him."

"He thinks it's real."

"Yeah." Annie's assent came on a sigh that was part plea, part protest.

"Is he . . . ?" Cooper began and then stopped.

Annie heard his doubt, his wish not to pry, his care in addressing her, and her heart opened. And her guard that had been firmly in place since Leighton left fell, allowing in a warm rush of emotion against her will. She said, "People think when you have delusions or hallucinations that it automatically means you're on something or you're schizophrenic, maybe even violent."

"I can't see Bo being violent," Cooper said.

"No," Annie said. "But not that long ago, I couldn't have imagined he'd prefer living on the street, either." She looked out the window, loosening her glance, letting it travel beyond the interstate's edge to the gas stations, mini-marts, and business parks they passed, the forest of signs, the tangled webbing of power lines, all the commercial litter that was backlit now in the dirty golden glow of the oncoming day.

Cooper checked the rearview and changed lanes, leaving a space. She could continue talking or not as she chose.

"It always feels like an invasion," she heard herself say, and the rest followed, spilling out of her in a lamentable torrent. "Whenever I talk about Bo, I feel this wall of defense come up. It's all the labels. People attach so much weight to them. They conceive an image based on a word, and Bo becomes that. He's schizo or bipolar or a druggie or whatever. No one can act naturally around him. They're afraid of him or they're sorry for him."

Annie pushed her hands down her thighs and thought how she was talking too much. She thought how Cooper had that effect on her. She didn't know if it was a good thing. Somehow it felt good and bad all at once. She didn't know how to feel when he didn't respond, either, but then she felt the warmth from his palm when he covered her hand with his own. And she let it be there.

She didn't move.

• • •

Sheriff Audi wasn't at the community center when Annie and Cooper got back. Another deputy was watching the door for Annie's arrival, and when she handed him Bo's shirt, he was brusque, unhappy with the delay. The dog handlers were waiting, he said.

She apologized and explained about the text from Bo, and even as the deputy interrupted her, advising her that she ought to have contacted the sheriff's department before taking matters into her own hands, she was talking over him. "I didn't want to take the time in case Bo was there; he could leave. I know it sounds crazy. Obviously the library's closed, but Bo's message said he was there."

The deputy asked to see her phone, and she handed it to him.

Cooper said, "I'm wondering if the delivery of the message was delayed. I think that happens sometimes, doesn't it?"

"Yeah." The deputy tapped the screen, studying the data that appeared. "This message was actually sent on Friday. Friday afternoon at 1:32." He held it so that Annie could see, pointing out the date.

"Why didn't I get it on Friday?"

"A glitch in the server would be my guess." The deputy shrugged.

Cooper said, "So Bo might actually have been in Houston at the library last Friday, or at least it was his intention."

Or Ms. M and the library trip could be a figment of Bo's imagination, Annie thought. She could have said it, that often what Bo wrote down or said was only as real as the moment he conceived of it. She could have said that pinning him down was like catching smoke. Most of the time. But not always. Not everything Bo did was irrational.

"We'll send someone to talk to those folks down there, show his photo around. Maybe someone will remember seeing him." The deputy returned Annie's phone to her.

"Don't you have his cell records?" Annie said. "There must be a record of this text, right? Someone should have already gone there."

"Could be it was overlooked. In any case, it's Wednesday now." The deputy paused, giving Annie time to see it, that if Bo had been there, he was long gone. "It's frustrating, I know," the deputy said.

No, Annie thought. You really don't.

He kept her gaze. "I guess you don't know who Ms. M is."

He wasn't asking, but Annie answered no as if he were. She nodded at the shirt the deputy held in his hand. "I want to go with you when you take that to the dog team."

"That's not a good idea," Cooper said, and the deputy agreed.

"Why not?" she asked, and then she was annoyed—at herself for asking and at them for treating her like a child. "It isn't as if I haven't already been out there," she reminded them.

"Yes, but we've got plenty of people, trained personnel now," the deputy said. "We do this for a living, Miss Beauchamp. Trust me, if your brother's out there, we'll find him."

Not alive. They didn't expect to find Bo alive; that's why they refused to let her go there. The intuition rose quick and merciless, riveting Annie's attention, loosening her knees along with her hope, and she slammed her mind shut against it. She looked after the deputy, then called out, "Wait," and when he turned, she said, "I talked to some high school kids last night. They were taking flyers into Houston, and one of the boys, Sean Hennessy, acted as if he might know something."

"Like what?" the deputy asked, flicking his glance at Cooper.

Annie frowned, thinking about it. "I don't know, really. The kids were talking about everyone at the high school loving Bo, but Sean said not everyone did. I know when Bo was in school, there were kids who made fun of him."

"Anybody do more than run their mouth? Did it ever get physical?"

"Sometimes."

"How does Bo react to that?" The deputy stepped toward her.

"If he gets pushed hard enough, he'll push back." Annie realized it scared her. If Bo was hurt, if something awful had happened to him, he might have brought it on himself.

The deputy wrote down Sean Hennessy's name. He said a detective named Cosgrove was going out to the high school. "I'll pass this along." He tucked the notepad into his pocket and took his leave.

Annie pulled out her cell and called JT to ask if the initial *M* meant anything to him, leaving a message when he didn't answer.

"I bet he's with the dogs," Cooper said, "or else he's gone to question the guy who called in the tip."

"He's going to kill himself," Annie said.

"Maybe I can find him, see if I can talk him into coming back here to get some rest."

"I doubt you can." She kept Cooper's gaze.

"What?"

"JT's certified SAR, did you know?"

"As in search and rescue, you mean."

"Yes. He's a certified EMT, too. Certified everything rescue, actually. He used to belong to a team of professionals. They were always getting called out." Annie remembered the nights when the phone would ring, waking her from sound sleep, and the hurried whispers and quiet rustling that came afterward as her mom and JT gathered his gear together. She hadn't realized then the toll it took on him, but her mother had worried about it. Her mother had said JT felt things too deeply. He felt the need to make things right, to perform miracles, and maybe, a while back, that had been true.

"A team like EquuSearch?" Cooper prompted.

"Not as big as that or as famous. It's an organization based here in Lincoln County. They're called Emergency One."

"I've heard of them," Cooper said. "Met a few of them, looking for Bo."

Annie said she had, too, and after a beat, she said, "I doubt JT ever thought he'd be looking for his own son."

"No," Cooper agreed. "It's not like I know JT that well," he added after a pause, "but it doesn't surprise me. That he's SAR, I mean."

Annie wondered what Cooper had picked up on. Something similar to what her mother had seen in JT. Something Annie was only beginning to see.

"You said *used to*. When did he quit?"

"Around four years ago."

The call, what turned out to be the final call JT would respond to, came during the daylight hours, on a rainy Saturday. Annie and Bo were playing rummy on the back porch. She was winning a fourth hand, and Bo was pouting. He always pouted when he was losing. She could see the two of them in her mind's eye, and she could hear JT's voice in the background, rising and growing sharper as he talked into his cell phone. "Slow down," he said, and he said it again. Then, "I can't understand you . . ."

Annie found Cooper's glance. "It was the wife of one of his coworkers, who got into trouble. He asked JT to help, and JT went even though he had to drive all the way into Louisiana."

Cooper wanted to know what happened, and Annie felt the warmth of color faintly stain her cheeks. "It's kind of bizarre. They were camping east of Natchitoches, in the Kisatchie National Forest—the husband and wife, and they had . . . had . . . you know . . ."

"Oh, right." Cooper nodded his understanding, saving Annie the trouble of having to say it, that the couple had had sex. It would have been too intimate, at least for her. Annie liked Cooper for understanding, for respecting her feelings. She liked his smile, the faint teasing light in his eyes.

She cleared her throat and said, "Yes. Anyway, they argued at some point after that, really badly argued, I mean. So badly, she took off. She wasn't wearing any shoes or a stitch of clothing."

"You're kidding."

"I told you it was crazy."

"Her husband let her go?"

"Yep. He was mad and figured once she got cold and soaked, she'd come back, but she didn't, and by the time the guy called JT, it had been a couple of hours, plus it was over a three-hour drive for JT to get there. Even the other search-and-rescue people were delayed because of the weather."

"The rain must have washed out any trail she might have left anyway, and if she was naked with no shoes—anything might have happened to her."

"It was all so ridiculous and tragic." Annie found Cooper's glance. "It took a lot away from JT when he didn't find her. Mom said it was because he made the mistake of promising the guy he would, when he knew better. But they were close friends as well as coworkers, plus the couple had two little kids."

"Jesus. That's terrible."

"I know. JT was in bad shape for a while after that, not eating right or sleeping. He took off from work so much he nearly got fired. I don't know how my mom put up with it, but she was so patient, and after a while, he started to pull out of it." Annie looked off. She wouldn't go into the rest, how when her mom died, JT had pretty much given up again, spending most of his spare time sitting in front of the TV. Until last Friday anyway.

"It sounds as if he wanted a miracle to happen," Cooper said.

"It's sort of the same now." Annie met Cooper's glance. *What if there's no miracle here, either?* She couldn't bring herself to ask, but she could tell by Cooper's expression that he saw the question hanging in the frightened shadows of her eyes.

He plowed a hand over his head. "What about you?" he said. "Can I talk you into going home? I'll drive you."

"No, thank you," Annie said. "I'm going to the café to start the baking. These people need to eat." She gestured at the volunteers, the ones standing around in small groups, the others who sat waiting behind phones that were mostly silent at this early hour.

Cooper seemed to know it would be of no use to argue. He walked out with her, Rufus at their heels, and when she headed up the alley toward the café, he ordered Rufus to go with her.

Annie went to her knees and embraced the dog's neck. "Thank you," she said, meeting Cooper's gaze. "I can use his company."

"You call me if you need anything," he said, backing away. "Take good care of her, Doofus," he ordered the dog.

Annie got to her feet. The tug of her smile was unexpected, and touching her mouth, she was somehow reminded of Cooper's kiss. When he returned her smile, she saw in his eyes that he remembered, too. She knew if she made even the slightest move toward

him, he would come to her, and she was pierced with sudden longing. Her permission was what he waited for, all he needed. The
understanding of this was clear, and it hovered between them, and
then it was gone, and a moment later, Cooper was gone, too, walking quickly away to his truck.

Annie watched him go, then with Rufus at her heels, she went
into the café.

Inside the larder, she took stock of the shelves and found the
ingredients she needed to make loaves of orange-cranberry bread
and several dozen sausage kolaches. By the time she was pulling
baked goods from the oven, the flour-clouded air was tinged pink
with morning light and redolent with the smell of breakfast. Setting
the kolaches on racks to cool, she put together the batter for a double batch of pumpkin muffins, and she was spooning it into greased
muffin tins when she glanced up and saw Hollis Audi. The sheriff's
tall, rangy frame filled the doorway, blocking the light, throwing his
face into shadow, making it impossible to read his expression. But
he had his hat in his hands, and something about that, a tremor in
his fingers perhaps, caused Annie to go very still. A glob of muffin
batter dropped unheeded from the spoon she held, half of it falling
onto the tin, half not.

"Is he dead?" she asked.

"No. I don't know. Aw, Jesus, Annie, they found a body. Down
in Houston. Victim of a hit-and-run. Nobody knows who it is, but
it might be Bo. We can't know for sure until someone makes an
identification."

The sheriff came toward her as if he meant to comfort her, but
she let go of the spoon, letting it clatter onto the countertop, putting up her hands, warding him off. She would shatter if he touched
her, and she would not trade her composure for his sympathy.

Sheriff Audi stopped, looking disoriented, as if he had no idea
how to proceed. "I tried calling JT," he said.

"Oh, no, you can't tell him a thing like this over the phone." Annie met the sheriff's gaze. "What if it isn't Bo? I think I should go and see before anyone says anything to JT."

"You want to go to the morgue?" The sheriff eyed her doubtfully.

"Yes. Can you take me?" She didn't think she could drive herself.

"You're sure?"

She wasn't, but she nodded, untying her apron. She asked him to give her a minute and went into the washroom where she splashed cold water on her face and ran a comb through her hair. When she came out, she said she was ready, but that was probably a lie.

"My car's in front of the community center," the sheriff said when she reappeared.

"That's fine. I need to walk Rufus down there anyway." She beckoned to the dog, and he sat upright, alertly watching her. She beckoned to him again, and he came instantly.

Twenty minutes later, as she and the sheriff were leaving the center, Cooper drove up beside the patrol car. "You called him?" Annie asked the sheriff.

He looked sheepish.

"I'm coming with you." Cooper got into the backseat.

"What about Rufus?"

"My mom will take him home with her."

Annie wasn't happy to have Cooper along, but whatever breath she might have had to protest was lost to the clamor of her panic. She had never seen a dead body before, other than on television. She was spared the viewing of her mother's body. There had been no doubt as to her mom's identity for one thing, but then the coroner and the funeral director had gently suggested the family might want to remember the pretty woman Annie's mother was when she was living. Annie didn't know if it was better not to have seen, to be left to wonder about the extent of her mother's injuries.

She hadn't suffered, the coroner said. Death was instantaneous. He'd said that, too, as if that made it all right.

11

It was early on Wednesday afternoon when Lauren got into town, and traffic was light as it usually was on any ordinary weekday at that hour. What was unusual was the number of cars parked along Prescott, the street running in front of the community center. The adjacent streets were parked up, too. Lauren finally found a space three blocks down from the center, in front of Kim's Needle and Book Nook. Ordinarily, the shop door would have been standing open, Kim would have been inside, and Lauren would have waved to her as she passed by. But today, the door was closed and the lights were off, and while Lauren was aware of the window display that combined a number of fabric pumpkins with groupings of children's books featuring an assortment of witches and other hobgoblins, what arrested her eye was the flyer posted prominently in the window's center.

"MISSING!" The red-lettered word seemed to shout from the page.

Lauren looked up the street in the direction she was headed and saw there were flyers pinned up everywhere, wrapping the light poles, papering every window. She counted three mounted in a row in the window of Shear Heaven, the beauty salon where she got her hair cut. The salon itself, like Kim's shop, was dark. No one was working. Had they closed because of Bo? Was everyone out looking for him? It seemed wonderful and terrible all at once that the town would drop everything and pull together to find this young man.

But where were we before? Lauren wondered. Which ones of us ever stopped for him, thought about him, thought of asking what he might need—before he disappeared? Why did it always take a calamity to get people moving, to make them care, make them do the right thing?

The flyer posted on the community center door was larger than the others, poster-size, and Lauren paused to study it. The photo of Bo in the center showed him leaning against a porch post, smiling with such open-faced happiness at whoever was taking the picture that Lauren thought he must love the person with the camera very much. She touched the crown of his head, smoothed the tip of her finger down the line of his cheek. He looked so bright, so endearing and likable. But the intensity, the vulnerability she'd seen in him when she'd spoken to him last Friday was there in the photo, too, and it made her heart ache.

She ran her eye down the bulleted list of statistics: *Birth date: May 6, 1991; Height: 5'11"; Weight: 155 pounds; Build: Slender.* A paragraph following the list noted he had wavy brown hair and light blue eyes and that he was last seen on Friday, wearing the exact clothing and in the exact location Lauren had described earlier for Detective Cosgrove and his partner.

Lauren paused, her hand on the door, wondering if she could handle running into them again. She looked back down the street in the direction of her car. It would be easy enough to walk away, but she didn't.

Pushing open the door, she stood inside it, scanning the crowd, and while she didn't see Cosgrove or Willis, there were a lot of other people, more than she'd expected, including several she recognized, answering phones or gathered, talking, in loose knots. But the hum of voices was quiet, the wrong sort of quiet. The hair on Lauren's neck rose. Had they found him, then?

Spotting Madeleine Finch across the room, she walked over to her. The usual greetings would have seemed out of place; she didn't bother with them. "I came to see if I could help," she said. "Am I too late?"

Madeleine lifted her hand—in helplessness, pleading?—Lauren didn't know. She was trembling, though. Even her head wobbled on her neck like an overly heavy flower on its stem.

"Maybe you should sit down." Lauren cupped Madeleine's elbow and slid her hand down her forearm, feeling the rigidity of bone through the looser tissue of her flesh. She hadn't seen Madeleine in a while. It might have been longer than a year, Lauren guessed. She couldn't remember. She and Tara had used to come to the café for lunch quite often in the days when they were still working together. They'd always commented on how spry Madeleine was, close to eighty and still full of pepper. But she looked exhausted now.

"Why don't I take you home?" Lauren suggested.

"No," Madeleine said. "It's very kind of you, but I can't leave."

A woman came to Madeleine's side. "She's as stubborn as the rest of us."

"Carol, right?" Lauren recognized her. "I was just out at your farm."

"Len said he waited on you."

Lauren smiled. On another day, she and Carol might have chatted. Lauren might have said how hospitable Len was, that he'd offered her tea and a mini croissant. They didn't run in the same circle; Carol and Len weren't aware of Lauren's fall from grace. They might have carried on talking as if Lauren were her old self. But this wasn't the day for idle conversation. "This is such an agonizing situation," she said instead. "I can't imagine how the family is holding up."

Carol and Madeleine exchanged a look that worried Lauren.

"Do you know Annie, Bo's sister?" Carol asked. "She left with Sheriff Audi a while ago. He's taking her to the morgue in Houston."

"Oh, no," Lauren said.

"A young man was found dead in the street last night on the north side of the city," Madeleine said. "Word is that someone hit him and left him there. He's the right age, wearing similar clothing . . ." She broke off.

Now it was Carol who took Madeleine's arm, who told her she needed to sit down. "You need a cookie, too, and a cup of tea, something in your stomach. And no arguing," she added. She looked at Lauren. "Would you like to join us?"

Lauren thanked her, declining the invitation, head swimming with the memory of how close she had come to hitting Bo herself.

"What sort of person leaves someone to die in the street?"

It was a woman behind Lauren who asked. More than asked, demanded, Lauren thought.

"Some kind of monster." A second woman answered in a voice that was as hard and affronted as the first woman's.

"Well," said the first woman, "if they catch the driver, I hope they kill him."

"Not me," the second woman answered. "I hope they lock him up in prison for the rest of his life, where he has to wake up every day and remember what he did, you know?"

Lauren didn't know which punishment was right. She only knew that neither one would bring Bo back.

12

You won't have to see him," the sheriff said as if he could discern Annie's thoughts, the thready pulse of her fear. "The actual body, I mean."

Annie looked over at him.

"They'll show you a picture of the face, or if that's not . . . They'll try to find an identifying mark, something else that'll . . ." The sheriff lifted his hand, letting it hover above the steering wheel, obviously flustered.

Annie didn't need to hear the words he couldn't bring himself to say. She understood that if the victim's face was battered beyond recognition, the way she imagined her mother's face had been, they would hunt for some other distinguishing mark to photograph. She felt Cooper's hand on her shoulder, and she wanted to turn to him, to look into his eyes. She wanted to climb over the seat and into his lap. She wanted to tell Sheriff Audi to stop. To say I can't do this. But she didn't move. She kept thinking of JT, that a father shouldn't have to see his son dead.

"Sometimes, when nothing else is available, they match dental records," the sheriff said.

Annie wouldn't ever remember whether anything was said after that, and she wouldn't recall very much about the actual morgue visit, either, other than a handful of details: the waxed sheen of the floors through an endless network of corridors, the sparse furnishings of the room she and the sheriff and Cooper were eventually led to, the flat black hands on a wall clock that jerked with the passing sweep of each minute.

A man joined them eventually, introducing himself, inviting them to sit. She wouldn't ever recall his name or his face. She didn't look at him but at his shirt cuffs. They were pin-striped and just visible beyond the hemmed sleeves of his starched white lab coat. In particular, she noticed his wrists, the space where they joined his forearms. The knobs of bone there seemed large, excessively so. The man, possibly a lab technician although she'd never know, slid photos out of an envelope and set them in a row, directing her attention to them, but she only wanted to study his wrists.

Cooper, sitting next to her, laid his hand on her arm, looking from her to the photos and back at her, and his glance was meaningful, somehow urgent. She kept his gaze, aware of the ringing in her ears, of her blood passing, thick and logy, through her veins. Cooper nodded once at her, and she took strength from that, from him, enough so that she was able to turn her attention to the photos. There were three altogether, and in each one, the face was peaceful. There wasn't a flaw, not a mark on it.

He looks like he's sleeping. Did she actually say it or only think it? Or was it merely that she'd heard it a hundred times on television? It was another detail that would elude her.

Looking up at no one in particular, Annie said, "It's not him."

"You're sure, Miss Beauchamp?" the tech asked.

She was, she said.

"It's not," the sheriff said.

"No," Cooper said, and Annie realized he and the sheriff had known before her the man in the photographs wasn't Bo. That was why Cooper had been so insistent that she look. He'd wanted her to know it, too, as quickly as possible. She imagined Cooper expected her to feel relief, but she was uncertain of what she felt.

Sheriff Audi scooped the photos into a pile and handed them to the tech. "Thank you," he said.

"Thank you for coming." The tech returned the photos to their envelope. "Good luck with the search." He looked at Annie. "I hope you find your brother."

She looked at the envelope. "I hope you find his family," she said. "It's harder, not knowing."

But she wondered, riding back to Hardys Walk, if that was true. Maybe it was better this way. At least when you didn't know for sure, you could invent whatever story you wanted, to explain the circumstances, like Bo was buried in the stacks of a library in another town, having forgotten the world, or he'd hopped a train that was headed to California.

She had Sheriff Audi drop her off at the café. Facing the mess she'd left there was preferable to facing the folks at the community center. Many of them teared up at the sight of her, as if her very presence brought them pain. She didn't know what to do with that or their kindness, the scope of their sacrifice. She didn't know the answers to their questions.

She picked up the bowl of pumpkin-muffin batter, and giving it a stir, decided she might as well finish spooning it into the tin. Who knew? Maybe the muffins would turn out. She was surprised and somehow gratified when she pulled them from the oven to see they were fine. After they cooled, she stowed them under a glass dome and set to work washing up the small mountain of bowls, pans, and utensils she'd used. She was hanging the kitchen towel when a man said her name: "Ms. Beauchamp?"

Her back was to him, and she wheeled.

He apologized for scaring her, flipped open a badge. "I'm Detective Jim Cosgrove," he said, "with the Lincoln County Sheriff's Office? I wonder if you have a minute?"

Annie was still clutching the towel, and she twisted it now in her hands, searching his gaze for some sign of what he might have come to tell her. She nodded at him, mute in her alarm. He wore a suit instead of a uniform, but his civilian clothes only made him seem more intimidating.

"Is there someplace we can sit down?"

Cosgrove's apparent concern flustered Annie, and instead of answering him, she asked whether he'd like a muffin. "They're fresh," she said.

Cosgrove declined.

She went past him into the café, sliding into a booth.

Cosgrove sat opposite her.

"Do you—? Have you found him?"

"No," he said kindly. "Nothing like that. I need to ask you a few questions, is all."

"I've told Sheriff Audi everything I know."

"Yeah, but I'd like to hear directly from you, you know, things like who his friends are, where he likes to hang out, whether you ever knew him to use or sell drugs."

Annie made a sound at once rueful and annoyed. "I knew this would happen."

"What?" Cosgrove asked.

She leveled her glance at him. "Bo's disappearance has got nothing to do with drugs, okay? He's not taking drugs now, or selling them."

Cosgrove kept her gaze, and she squirmed slightly under his regard. She had the sense that making her nervous was his intention. "I know he's taken drugs in the past, but he stopped, last summer."

"What happened last summer?"

She hadn't told Sheriff Audi when he asked, but she had to say it now, Annie thought, no matter how it pained her, in case it meant anything at all. "I dated a man, Leighton Drake."

Something flickered across Cosgrove's expression.

He knows, Annie thought, and looked at her hands. Why should it surprise her? Probably everyone in the whole town knew what Leighton was, except her. She'd learned the hard way. "He wasn't who I thought," she said, wishing Cosgrove would let it go at that.

He didn't. "What do you mean?"

It irritated her that he would make her say it, what he already knew. "He's a drug dealer. Bo told me he was when Leighton first asked me out, but I didn't pay attention. Not until Bo made me go with him to Leighton's condo, and there it was—the proof." Annie remembered her first sight of Leighton's inventory. The stacks of small cartons—packed with everything from marijuana to pharmaceuticals, amphetamines, cocaine, and even heroin—had been stored alongside neatly rubber-banded bundles of cash, so much cash she had not believed her eyes. Her brain kept telling her it was a mistake. Leighton had said he sold pharmaceuticals, all right, but legally.

"Where in the condo was it?"

"Under the stairs. He made a place there and painted it so you'd never notice. I didn't."

"How did you pull that off, though? Finding the drugs without Drake knowing?"

"We waited until he was out of town and used the extra key he kept hidden outside to go in. I broke it off with him after that. He didn't take it well. He made threats against Bo, called him names, idiot, retard—" Annie stopped, not wanting to say the rest.

Her ignorance about Leighton felt as huge and terrible now as ever. It angered her the way she had fallen for him, the way she'd let all his talk of her prettiness, her sweet innocence sway her. She'd treasured the tokens he'd left her along with a generous tip on the table at the café after she'd served him: a single rose, a heart-shaped charm, a tiny violet suspended in a bubble of glass. Her heart, her unknowing, unschooled heart, had thrilled to every masterful move. The first time they made love, Leighton had entered her with such reverence and tenderness, she'd been mesmerized. He had said she was unique, a rare and delicate flower; he had said there was no other woman like her. It was laughable, really, and she was a fool.

"Did you contact the police?"

Annie looked at Cosgrove. He knew she hadn't. "I was afraid of what he'd do if I did. Anyway, he left town, went back to Chicago, I heard."

"Maybe not."

"He's not here?" Annie sat forward.

"I think you'd be smart to keep an eye out."

"Has he done something to Bo? Is that what you think?"

"There's no evidence of that. But there's a history between them. Aside from you, I mean, and the truth is we're not sure of Drake's whereabouts."

Annie pushed out a breath, biting her lips. What had she done, bringing that man into her life and Bo's?

Cosgrove took out his phone, thumbed it, then held it out to her. "You recognize this guy?"

Annie looked at the photo on the tiny screen, her glance registering a man in his thirties with a strong jaw and a haunted look about his deep-set eyes. She shook her head. "I've never seen him. Who is he?"

"His name's Greg Honey. You sure you didn't meet him when you were going out with Drake?"

"He's a friend of Leighton's?" She hadn't met many of Leighton's friends. They'd stayed mostly to themselves, which made sense now.

"More like an associate. Honey's a sometime dealer, but unlike Drake, he's a user, too—heroin mostly."

"Bo doesn't like needles."

Cosgrove fanned his fingers, as if that was of no consequence, or maybe he was like a lot of people who thought if you'd try one drug, you'd try them all.

"Why are you asking me about him?" She nodded at the cell phone.

"They know each other, all three of them, your brother, Drake, and Honey." Cosgrove pocketed his phone, bent his weight on his elbows. "And here's the thing—they're all missing."

"I told you, Bo isn't involved with drugs anymore."

"What makes you so sure of that, Ms. Beauchamp?"

"When I was dating Leighton, Bo was scared I'd start using. It made him realize how much he'd put me through, worrying over him. So he quit."

"Like that." Cosgrove snapped his fingers.

"I knew it wouldn't make sense to you."

Cosgrove took out a business card and pushed it across the table toward her. "If you think of anything else—" he began.

"You heard about the text Bo sent me on Friday, the one where he said he was with someone he referred to as Ms. M?"

"Yeah. It's not much use, though, having only an initial to go on." Cosgrove stood up.

So did Annie.

"We're following up on that kid, Sean Hennessy, too," the detective added, but with so little enthusiasm Annie knew he didn't think that lead was much use, either.

She said, "You think something terrible has happened to Bo, don't you? Something to do with drugs."

Cosgrove pushed a finger alongside his nose. "We'll be in touch, Ms. Beauchamp. You call now, you hear, if you need anything or think of anything."

She didn't answer, and he left her there to watch him go, holding his card in her hands.

She was sitting in the booth and the business card was on the table when Cooper came in with Rufus a while later.

"Come here, old doggie," she said, and bending over him, she buried her face in the thick fur at the back of his neck, feeling his joyful wiggle. When she straightened, he went under the table to lie at her feet. Cooper sat across from her, and she felt his regard, felt him waiting, giving her the chance to speak first.

"A detective was here, asking me questions." She pushed the card over to Cooper.

He studied it. "What sort of questions?"

But Annie didn't want to go into it. "Have you ever watched *The First 48*?" She named the television show that chronicled real crimes committed in cities across America from the point of commission through the first two days and nights of investigation. That harrowing, hysterical, fraught-with-hope, and torn-with-despair passage of time that, once it was gone, if there was no resolution, meant the chances of arresting a perpetrator or finding a missing person unharmed were practically nil.

Cooper said he had.

Annie said, "It's been five days since anyone saw Bo."

Cooper kept her gaze; there was nothing he could say.

"Sheriff Audi said they'll probably be closing the command center later today or tonight."

"I heard that," Cooper said. "Most of the volunteers won't quit, though."

"They can't keep at it forever. They have jobs and families, obligations and lives of their own." Annie looked into her lap.

"Detective Cosgrove is like Sheriff Audi. He thinks Bo was involved with drugs, too."

"But you don't?"

"It's possible," Annie admitted, and then, despite her misgivings, she went on, telling Cooper more than she'd ever expected to or wanted to about her relationship with Leighton, the threat it had posed and might still. She felt her face burning, but she was unable to stop.

And when she was done, Cooper said he was sorry for what she'd gone through. He seemed to Annie to be as flustered and uncomfortable as she was. "There are fresh pumpkin muffins," she said. "I'll get them." She left the booth, but before she could get away entirely, Cooper caught her hand and, locking her gaze, searched her eyes.

"You haven't done anything wrong," he told her.

She nodded, slipping her hand from his grasp, afraid she would cry. She was back in a few minutes, and Cooper helped her unload the tray she'd laden with muffins and mugs of strong coffee.

She sat down again, indicating the sugar shaker. He shook his head.

Annie slid her feet a little nearer Rufus's sleeping form, close enough to feel his warmth through her shoes, taking comfort in it. She stirred sugar into her mug.

"I heard you say Bo is your stepbrother."

"Yeah. My mom and JT met when JT moved here from Morro Bay, California, after his mom died when he was five."

"That's a long way to come with a little kid. Do they have other family here?" Cooper helped himself to a muffin and took a bite.

"There isn't any other family that I know of. I think they were looking for a change, a fresh start," Annie said. She was distracted, watching Cooper, worried the muffins were awful.

But then he groaned in a good way, closing his eyes. "These are so good." He was practically smacking his lips in his pleasure.

Annie's gratification, her delight at his enjoyment of the food she had made from scratch, stole through her, a momentary benediction.

Cooper helped himself to another.

Annie said, "JT's first wife was sick for quite a while, almost from the day Bo was born." She paused to think about it, how ironic it was that Bo's mother's death had spared her having to live through this current anguish. Annie's own mother had escaped the nightmare, too. *Lucky for them.* The words were heated, a whisper that sawed across her brain.

She looked at Cooper. "You know Bo's earmuffs?"

Cooper nodded.

"He had them on the first time I met him. He said his mom talked to him from heaven through them. He was so little." Annie's throat narrowed at the memory.

"Was it cancer?"

"Brain." She touched her temple.

Cooper grimaced. "He remembers her?"

"He remembers going to see her in the hospital and crawling into her bed. She told him all kinds of things, that they'd go to Disneyland when she was well, and the zoo. They'd swim in the ocean. She said they'd travel to every country in the world. It seems sort of cruel—" Annie's voice caught, and she stopped.

Cooper said, "Maybe she thought she would beat it."

"Maybe." Annie toyed with her napkin. "From what Bo said, she read to him a lot, but she'd fall asleep a lot of the time, too. From the medication, I guess. Anyway, he missed out on how the stories ended, so Mom and I read them to him. He loved *The Wind in the Willows* and the *Just So Stories*, anything about animals." The threat of tears was serious now, and she pressed her fingertips to her eyes. "Sorry."

"No," Cooper said, and he went on talking, saying something about how close he was to his own mother, that he couldn't imagine what he would do without her, and Annie thought he was trying to soothe and distract her.

He wiped his mouth. "I'm the kid the other kids called a mama's boy, but I've never cared much what anyone thought about it." A smile, half-abashed, tilted over his mouth.

Annie smiled, too. She liked that he was close to his mother, that he was man enough to admit it.

His gaze held hers. "I'm so sorry about your mom, Annie. You lost her way too soon."

"It's hard without her. She was my best friend; I could tell her anything." Annie closed her hands around her coffee mug. "All my life, until I was ten, it was just the two of us, then Bo and JT came . . ." Annie paused, remembering the crowded house, the lack of privacy, having to share things. Not only her mother. The bathroom, her toys and books, the television remote control. "I wish I'd been a better daughter, a better sister. I wish I'd taken better care of Bo." She looked at Cooper, then away. The memory of Leighton, her confession, hovered in the air between them, but maybe it was only her guilty conscience.

He cupped his hands around hers. "It isn't your fault, Annie, no matter what's happened to Bo. He's a grown man."

"In his body, not so much in his mind."

"But even you have talked about how independent and stubborn—"

"You don't know anything about him or me." She pulled her hands from under his and scooted out of the booth. She couldn't listen to him anymore, taking her ill-advised confessions and turning them into some sort of an excuse, a justification.

"Maybe not, but I'd like to if you'd let me." His voice followed her, quiet and steady; the words were an offering.

Annie stopped, shoulders loosening, chin lowering, as if someone had pulled a pin. She was drawn to him, to the strength she felt in him; she couldn't deny it, and she wondered in that instant what it would be like to accept, to say yes to him. But even as her heart grabbed like a thief at the possibility, she knew she didn't deserve the relief of leaning on Cooper, or the happiness he might bring into her life, not while Bo was missing.

"Annie?"

She lifted her head.

"Someday you're going to have to trust somebody again, or you'll always be alone."

She might have answered that he wasn't telling her anything she didn't already know. But she didn't want to encourage him. It wouldn't have been fair to him. Lifting her chin, she wiped her face and walked away, through the kitchen and out the alley door.

She heard Rufus, the click of his nails on the tile floor, following her, and then she heard Cooper.

"Come on back, boy," he said. "She doesn't need you."

• • •

Annie was shaken and meant to go home after she left Cooper. She had some idea that she'd shower and put on clean clothes, maybe take everyone's advice and lie down for a bit. Instead, for reasons she would never fathom, she detoured by the community center, the one place she dreaded being above all others. She was talking to Mary Evans, one of the librarians, when she happened to look up to find her mother looking back at her. At least for one mind-numbing, heart-gladdening moment, Annie thought the woman who was staring intently at her was her mother.

The impression was strong, garnered more from a wish for it to be so than the handful of similarities; the woman's size and stance bore a likeness to Annie's mother's, as did her hair coloring and style. Her complexion was as flawless as fine porcelain, the way Annie's mother's had been, too, and her eyes were the same gentle shade of green. Even the way the woman tucked her hair behind one ear, which had signaled Annie's mother's anxiety, was reminiscent, and Annie felt a wave of longing so hard and fierce, it loosened her knees. She put out her hand, almost flailing, foundering.

The woman took it. "What is it?" she asked. "How can I help?"

Annie couldn't speak. It was as if her voice had fallen down a well.

"Come and sit down." The woman led Annie to a nearby chair. Settling beside her, she introduced herself. "I'm Lauren Wilder."

Annie started to repeat her own name, but Lauren said she knew and offered an apology that slid into a rueful groan. "That sounds ridiculous. When I think of all you're dealing with."

"No, I—" Annie broke off in confusion. There was too much she couldn't say, not to a stranger. *You are so like my mother. I miss her so much.*

Lauren tried again. "I—I heard about the awful ordeal you went through this morning."

The trip to the morgue, Annie thought. Of course, she would have heard about it. Annie raised her glance to Lauren's, then let it fall away. It was hard to look at her, this woman who for one soul-riveting moment of utter joy had been her mother. It felt awful that she wasn't, like the cruelest joke, the sort where Annie struggled to get the punch line, and once she did, she felt aggrieved, as if her mother had been taken from her all over again.

"It wasn't him, thank God," she told Lauren, and she was on the verge of standing, of excusing herself, but some impulse made her turn back to Lauren. "I think I'd know, don't you?" She was seeking more than Lauren's opinion. "I mean if Bo was—" She couldn't say the word *dead*. "If something that awful had happened, I'd feel it, wouldn't I?" It was so unlike her to reach out in this way, so against her natural reticence to open herself to a stranger. She felt her face warm.

"When my daughter was six," Lauren said, "she broke her arm on the playground at school, and I knew something had happened before the school called. I wasn't surprised. I think such things happen when you love someone. There's a special connection."

"My mom used to say the same thing," Annie said.

Lauren fiddled with the strap of her purse. "I have to tell you something." She searched Annie's gaze in a way that made her heart constrict. "I feel just awful about it, too. I should have come before now."

Annie was at sea. "I don't understand."

"I saw Bo and spoke to him," Lauren said. "Last Friday," she added.

13

L auren apologized, this time for not having come forward sooner, as if any number of apologies made a difference. The horrible fact was that, no matter what she said or did, Bo would still be just as gone, and precious time when her information might have helped would still be lost. She thought of Tara. What would she do if her sister vanished? If one day Tara disappeared into thin air without a trace? The sense of what Annie must be going through emptied Lauren's mind. She wanted to do something for her. At the very least, she would have covered the trembling knot of Annie's hands with her own had she not been afraid Annie might take offense. She was small, much smaller than she had appeared on the television last night, a tiny slice of a girl, and as delicately boned as a wren, one that would fly if Lauren touched her, if Lauren even looked as if she might.

"I had turned the wrong way, or I never would have seen him," Lauren began, and she went on, describing her meeting with Bo. It wasn't until she mentioned the dog, Freckles, that Annie interrupted her.

"We don't have him anymore," she said. "He died six years ago."

"Oh, Bo seemed—that is, I thought—"

"I know." Annie looked away. "He gets confused sometimes."

"I should have insisted on getting your phone number from him."

"No, don't blame yourself. He wouldn't have waited for me."

"He did seem to have a plan."

Annie made a face. "He probably did. He kind of has this one-track mind. He'll even write down what he's going to do in a little notepad he carries. He could have written down the name of the woman you saw him drive away with. You didn't see it, the notepad?"

"No." Lauren thought a moment to be sure.

"I feel as if I should know who that woman is," Annie said, "but then I'm finding out Bo has all sorts of friends I know nothing about."

"A calamity has that effect," Lauren said. "Things come to light—" She stopped.

Annie looked curiously at her.

What about drugs? You think he could have been on something? Were you on something? Detective Willis spoke in Lauren's mind; she saw his face, that wily look he'd given her, as if he was on to her and knew her for the liar she was. She thought of the roll of bills Bo had shown her. She thought of telling Annie about it, but she might not know the police associated her brother with drugs, and if she didn't, Lauren didn't want to be the one to tell her. Neither did she want to implicate herself or speak of her own addiction. It was painful enough talking about her downfall at 12-step, where she was accepted, where forgiveness was automatic. Annie wouldn't be so forgiving, Lauren thought, and the realization filled her with regret. What a mistake she'd made, coming here.

"It's hard to keep secrets when someone's in danger." Annie broke the silence, and her tone, her expression when Lauren met her gaze seemed freighted with some odd significance. Panic tapped at Lauren's temples. A thought rose: that it was foolish to imagine she and Bo would have engaged in a drug deal in broad daylight on one of the busiest street corners in town. And further, even if she had bought drugs from Bo, what would that have to do with his disappearance hours later?

She jumped now, hearing someone—Madeleine, it turned out—say Annie's name. Lost in the swirl of her anxiety, Lauren hadn't heard the older woman approach.

Lauren stood up, and so did Annie.

"I thought Carol took you home." Annie's tone was lightly scolding.

"She tried, but I want to stay. See to the food," Madeleine added, and it sounded more like an excuse than an explanation.

It sounded, Lauren thought, as if Madeleine was afraid Annie would discover what seemed obvious: that Madeleine stayed for Annie's sake. Lauren sensed that if Annie would let her, Madeleine would have the girl in her arms in a heartbeat, that she would like nothing better. And it was surprising, because Lauren had always thought of Madeleine as aloof, even austere. Not at all the mothering type.

According to the talk around town, she'd never been married. Rumor had it that she'd been engaged a long time ago, but her fiancé had died suddenly from a rare heart defect. Who knew if it was true? Madeleine had never felt compelled to confirm or deny the story. She kept to herself, and while she might appear aloof, she wasn't unkind. Far from it. Everyone local knew if there was a need, Madeleine Finch would move heaven and earth to fill it.

She cooked meals and delivered them to people when they were ill, and employed others, like Bo, when they were down on their luck. A few years ago, when Tara was home recovering from an emergency appendectomy, Madeleine brought over her famous eggplant casserole because it was what Tara ordered most often when she and Lauren had lunch at the café.

Annie was talking about a text message she'd gotten from Bo, that it had been delayed, that it had mentioned a woman named Ms. M. "Does it ring any bells?" she asked Madeleine.

The older woman said it didn't.

"Could he have meant you?" Lauren asked.

"Oh, I don't think so. He calls me Ms. Finch, or sometimes Ms. Birdie." Madeleine flushed pink as if it pleased her, Bo calling her Ms. Birdie.

Annie said she hadn't considered the *M* might be the letter of a first name.

They looked at each other, taking a moment to think about it, the letter *M* and the possibility it might be related to a first name as easily as it could be to a last. Their shared silence was pocked with a dissonant clamor of ringing telephones, a low rumble of voices.

"I don't think the police care who she is," Annie said. "The detective I talked to, Jim Cosgrove, told me they don't have enough of a description to find her."

"Detective Cosgrove talked to you?" Lauren worked to keep the flare of fresh apprehension from showing in her voice.

Annie's look was curious.

"I talked to him, too. He and his partner came by my house this morning." Lauren paused, making herself breathe. She wanted badly to ask if her name had come up when Annie talked with Cosgrove. She wanted to know if Willis had been present. Instead, she said, "I think they came because I'm the last person they know of to see Bo."

"Can someone put these up?" A woman approached, carrying an armload of flyers. "Somehow we missed both sides of Prescott Street from here north to Oak Hill."

Madeleine reached for them, but Annie intercepted her. "You go and rest. I'll take these."

"I'll go with you," Lauren said, and it was sheer impulse. "I'd like to help."

Annie thanked her. "I need to run to the restroom first." She handed Lauren the stack of flyers.

Watching her go, Madeleine said, "That child has seen way too much trouble, more than most people get in their lifetime." She sounded almost angry, as if she took Annie's trouble personally, and she went on, not leaving Lauren time for a reply. "Her daddy walked out when she was a baby. She lost her mom a couple of years ago, and now this. JT does his best, but mostly he's just going through the motions, putting one foot in front of the other. He's a good man, but he hasn't got a clue what to do with a girl, much less one as sensitive and stubborn as Annie. Or Bo. JT never has known what to do about Bo, either."

And no wonder, Lauren thought. Raising a child was hard enough when they were mentally whole and there were two parents.

"It hurts him, the way Bo is," Madeleine said, and her voice tremored. "I see it every time JT looks at the boy. But being hurt over what ails a child never does any good."

"No," Lauren murmured. She wondered if Madeleine had been interviewed by the police, but couldn't bring herself to ask.

"Annie's mother is the one who looked after Bo; she looked after all of them. She kept them together, and ever since she passed, that little family's been like a boat adrift without a rudder. It just cuts me to the bone—" Madeleine's voice broke completely.

She was so obviously flustered at her loss of control that Lauren reached out, putting her hand on Madeleine's arm, and it occurred to her that if Madeleine was without a family of her own, it wasn't by choice. Lauren understood then that Bo and Annie were the closest Madeleine had ever come to mothering anyone. She saw it so plainly: Madeleine's utter despair, her loneliness and longing, and it saddened her. "What can I do?" she asked.

Madeleine brought her hands to her face, and Lauren looked away, giving her privacy, a space to gather herself. She took only moments, and then she said briskly that money was needed. "For a reward," she explained. "Annie's against it. She doesn't like asking anyone for anything, much less their money. But I keep telling her sometimes money is the only way people will talk."

Lauren's cell phone rang, and she pulled it from her purse, checking the ID. *Jeff.* She tucked the phone into her jacket pocket, feeling bad about it, but the situation here was so dire. She felt compelled to stay, to do what she could, and he would only argue.

Madeleine mentioned renting a billboard along I-45, the interstate that cut through town. "We could put Bo's photo and a phone number on it so folks could call in tips. A lot of people drive that freeway."

"What about organizing an auction to raise money?" Lauren spoke as the plan took mental shape. "We've held them at Wilder and Tate before. We have things we could donate, and we could ask others to contribute items, too. They don't have to be antiques." She would call Tara, Lauren thought. Tara knew people, important people, through the public relations manager she worked for. Her boss had connections all over Houston, all over Texas. Lauren could imagine what Tara would say, that at least he was good for something. She and Lauren would laugh. "What about Sunday?" Lauren offered the day and then bit her lip. Did she honestly think she could arrange such an event so quickly, in three days? Was she nuts? What if Jeff didn't go for it?

"It's kind of you to offer," Madeleine said. "You do realize we could go to all the trouble to organize an event and Bo could show up."

"So much the better. It would become a celebration then, wouldn't it?"

Catching sight of Annie, Madeleine said, "Maybe we should wait until we know for sure what we're going to do, before we say anything to her."

Lauren would have disagreed or at least questioned Madeleine's reluctance to advise Annie of their plans, but the young woman rejoined them too quickly. Slipping her wallet into her jacket pocket alongside her cell phone, Lauren asked if Madeleine would mind taking charge of her purse. Carrying the flyers, Annie led the way out of the community center, and she and Lauren headed north, taping posters to the light poles and inside the windows of the shops they passed. They handed flyers to the folks on the sidewalk. By now, Annie's face was familiar to them from the news, and they spoke to her in that way, asking how she was, as if the question could have a reasonable answer, one that wasn't readily apparent. It annoyed Lauren. There was a look in their eyes she didn't like, some mix of complacency and relief that this terrible thing that had happened wasn't theirs.

No, no. Blessedly for them, they had dodged the calamity bullet this time.

Good for you! Lauren wanted to say to them. *Aren't you the lucky ones?*

By the time she and Annie finished walking both sides of the three blocks that comprised the downtown area, Annie was white-faced and shivering, and Lauren was like Madeleine, consumed with a heated desire to protect Annie, to pull her close and say, *Never mind them.*

Instead she kept the polite distance of the near strangers they were between them and asked, "Are you cold?" even though both of them knew what ailed Annie wasn't the weather.

She answered she was fine, looking not at Lauren but far beyond her, at some unknown point on the horizon.

The sound of Lauren's cell phone jarred her, and she tugged it into view, just far enough to check the ID. *Jeff. Again.* She ought to answer; he'd be worried. But, as if her mind had other ideas, she thumbed the "Off" button and stuffed the phone back into her jacket pocket. She didn't want to leave Annie, not just yet, and realizing they were close to Uncommon Grounds, Hardys Walk's answer to Starbucks—so close, in fact, that the air was fragrant with mingled aromas of coffee and sugary Danish—she said, "Let's have something warm to drink. My treat."

Annie said no. "It may sound awful, but I can't face one more person. They're so sorry for me. They ask so many questions. I know they want to help, but all I want is to find Bo. If only I could know—" She broke off, clamping her jaw so tightly the muscle at its corner pulsed.

"We could sit outside. It's warm enough in the sun, don't you think?" Lauren pressed, speaking quickly, her gaze taking in the comfortably furnished patio area that fronted the coffeehouse, then coming back to rest on Annie. She was surprised and gratified when, after a moment, Annie agreed. "You go and sit down," Lauren told her. "I'll bring you something. What would you like? What's your favorite?"

"Hot chocolate. With extra whipped cream?" Annie's smile, self-conscious and fleeting, tilted the corners of her mouth.

Lauren nodded, and her heart swelled with a ridiculous amount of happiness that she could perform this small service for someone who badly needed it. Inside the coffee shop, she ordered Annie's hot chocolate and a pumpkin-spice latte for herself, and on a whim, asked for an assortment of scones, too, enough for a half-dozen people. She was embarrassed when she rejoined Annie and unloaded the bulging sack of its contents; she was equally thrilled when Annie helped herself to an iced cranberry scone and took a bite and then another.

When she caught Lauren watching, she blushed. "Thank you," she said, popping the last of it into her mouth and dusting her hands. "It was delicious. I know I should eat a regular meal, but it's hard."

"Then don't. Just eat what tastes good."

Annie smiled, and Lauren knew she'd given the right answer. She thought how she would never have said that to Drew or Kenzie. With them, it was always lecture, lecture, lecture. Maybe she should stop. Maybe it was okay once in a while to have pancakes for dinner, as Drew often suggested. Hadn't she seen it on a bumper sticker, the admonition: "Eat Dessert First"?

Annie folded her paper napkin in half and then in half again. She ran the tip of her index finger along the crease. "People think I should be relieved it wasn't Bo at the morgue, but I don't know if I am."

"I don't see how it could be a relief to see anyone in that place."

"I feel terrible for the man's family, but I envy them, too. At least they know where he is and what happened to him. And if they find whoever hit him—" Annie didn't finish, but Lauren didn't need her to.

Justice. Annie meant they would have justice. Maybe closure, Lauren thought, if such a thing existed.

Annie put her empty cup and napkin into the paper sack. "I haven't been the best big sister."

"Me, either," Lauren said.

"You have a brother?"

"Sister." *I think she and my husband are plotting a way for him to leave me and take my kids.* The thought popped up in Lauren's mind, an ugly surprise. She set her teeth against it. Where had it come from?

"I always wanted a sister," Annie said. "Are you close?"

"Maybe not as close as we once were." Lauren wasn't sure where that came from, either, and she was grateful when Annie didn't pursue it. But then, after a moment, as if Annie had asked the nature of the difficulty, Lauren said, "Tara and I inherited a family business, but after I married, we merged it with my husband's business. It was fine until last year. Tara got into trouble financially, and she had to sell her share to my husband and me, and ever since then, she— we—" Lauren faltered to a stop and looked out into the thin blue air. What a lie it was, using the buyout, accusing it, accusing Tara of being the one who had changed, who had caused the ten thousand tiny fault lines that were cracking beneath them and breaking apart the ground of their relationship. While there were lingering hurt feelings over the buyout, the real trouble hadn't started until the moment Lauren began doping herself in secret. "We're still working through it," she said.

Annie nodded, and they shared a silence.

Lauren broke it. "Madeleine told me about your dad and mom, that you lost them. I hope it's okay. I was so sorry to hear."

"I don't really remember my dad, but my mom was my best friend." Annie took a breath.

Lauren sipped her latte, which had grown cold.

"My mom died in a car accident two years ago."

"Oh, both my parents did, too. It's awful, isn't it? The suddenness is such a shock."

"Madeleine really helped me. I'm not sure I would have come through it without her."

Thinking of Margaret, Lauren said she understood.

"People think they know her because of the way she comes across, kind of unfriendly. But just because you're alone and you keep to yourself doesn't mean you're a snob or that you don't have feelings, that you aren't capable of love."

A pause as light and awkward as a newly fledged bird perched between them. Lauren didn't know what to do about it. Annie spoke before she could decide. "It was my fault," she said.

Lauren looked at her.

"Mama wouldn't have been in the car on the freeway at two o'clock in the morning if I hadn't called her to come and get me." Annie ran her fingertip along the table's edge, keeping her eye on it. "I've never said that to anyone—that I was to blame."

"Can you explain? Do you want to?"

"You'll hate me."

"No. We all make mistakes." Lauren waited a beat, then added, "You have no idea."

"There was a party in Houston. I don't usually go to parties. They make me nervous. I never know what to say, especially to guys, and I don't usually drink." Annie extended her arms on the tabletop.

Her cheeks were flushed, but otherwise she was very pale. She looked to Lauren as if she were suffering more from a fever than embarrassment, and Lauren quelled a fresh motherly impulse to pull Annie's face around and flatten her palm against Annie's brow. She so badly wanted to wrap this tiny slip of a girl into her embrace and promise her everything would be all right. But no one could make that guarantee, least of all Lauren.

"For some reason, I decided to go that night," Annie said. "I drove myself there in my mama's car, and I drank. I broke every one of my rules."

"You tried to drive home afterward?" Lauren thought she understood.

"I wish I had. Then maybe I'd be the one dead and not my mom, and Bo wouldn't be missing, because she took better care of him than me." Annie wiped her hands down her face. "I knew I was too drunk to drive, and I called her to come and get me. She had to borrow our neighbor's car since I had her car, and this semi driver rear-ended her and pushed her—pushed her right off the 610 Loop onto 59. They said—said he passed out at the wheel. If I hadn't called her—if I'd found another way home—"

Lauren touched Annie's arm but nothing more. Sometimes appearance was all that remained of your dignity.

"Mama didn't ask any questions or lecture me when I called her. She told me to wait, and she'd come. She said she loved me, and she was glad I didn't try to drive." Annie bit her lip.

Lauren offered a clean napkin, and Annie dabbed her eyes.

"She said I did the right thing, that she was proud of me. Can you believe it? She was proud of me?"

Lauren found Annie's gaze and held it the width of two heartbeats, three, five.

"My daughter, Kenzie—" she finally said. "She's eleven now, but I hope I can be as calm as your mom if she calls me in a situation like that."

Annie blew her nose. "Thank you," she said.

"I didn't do anything," Lauren said.

Annie looked at her. "You didn't try to talk me out of blaming myself."

Lauren made a face. "What I hear is that forgiving yourself takes time, but if it counts for anything, I don't think your mom would like it, that you blame yourself."

"No, she wouldn't." Annie stuffed the napkin into the sack with the rest of their trash. "I've imagined the worst, you know? When it comes to Bo, I mean."

Lauren said it was human to do that. She said, "Your mind can run away with you."

Annie said, "I think Bo's dad—I think JT knows something."

"Oh, well . . ." Lauren felt unsure of herself. Everyone knew things.

"It's just a feeling. Probably crazy. Like you said, your mind plays tricks sometimes." Annie looked off. "Bo's a grown man. He could have left of his own free will, you know? Ms. M could be someone who means something to him, someone he never told me or JT about. What if everyone has gone to all this trouble, and Bo just decided to leave town with her?"

"He had money," Lauren had to say it, at least that much. "He showed it to me."

Annie made a face and said she figured he did. "It's a bad habit of his, taking out his cash."

Where had Bo gotten it? Did Annie know? Lauren looked into the middle distance.

"He isn't stupid; that's the thing. He's not retarded the way some people think. In fact, in some ways, he's really kind of—"

Lauren interrupted, "The white-haired woman had a dog!"

Annie frowned.

"Bo was laughing when he got into her car, not at her but at the dog in the backseat. I just remembered." Lauren touched her temple. How could she have forgotten something so important?

"He might go with someone who had a dog, even if they were a stranger." Annie was apprehensive. "You're sure?"

Lauren nodded. "It was a brown-and-white dog. Medium size, I think. Short fur. There was a black blaze down his nose. His eyes—" She paused.

"What about his eyes?"

"They were blue. The dog turned its face and looked at me out the window when I passed. The eyes were blue." Lauren was sure of it.

Annie stood up and carried their trash to the receptacle. "We should go back to the center and find Detective Cosgrove or Sheriff Audi. The police should know. It might help them find her."

"I'm so sorry," Lauren said. It shook her that she'd forgotten. There wasn't an excuse for it. It wasn't fueled by emotion or related to her family but completely independent of them.

Annie said it was okay, but her expression was marked with something that suggested aggravation, disbelief, some mix of the two. At least that was how Lauren interpreted it, but then she was angry at herself and more than a little frightened. She felt disoriented.

"I have trouble with my memory sometimes." Lauren fell into step beside Annie, and when she caught her questioning glance, she said, "I fell a couple of years ago and took kind of a hard knock on my head."

It was obvious from Annie's expression that she didn't know what to say, and Lauren felt terrible about her discomfort. She felt she had to explain now. "I was helping my husband take down an old church. I fell from the bell tower, a couple of stories. I was in a coma for a bit. I don't like talking about it." It was all Lauren wanted to say, but somehow it wasn't enough; she felt she owed Annie more, so she gave her the rest, leaving out her struggle with the Oxy.

"It sounds as if you're lucky to be alive," Annie said when Lauren finished.

"I've heard that before." Lauren followed Annie through the community center door.

"There's Sheriff Audi." Annie directed Lauren's attention to the man in a uniform across the room, talking to Madeleine.

Once Annie introduced Lauren to the sheriff, it took only a few minutes for her to repeat the story of her Friday-morning encounter with Bo, this time including the details about the dog. As Detective Cosgrove had done, Sheriff Audi wrote down everything Lauren said in a small notebook.

He looked up. "You didn't mention a breed. Do you know it?"

"The blue eyes make me think it was an Aussie. Australian sheepdog," she said at the sheriff's questioning glance. She and Tara had an Aussie named Blue when they were growing up. "It might have been some other kind, though, a mixed breed of some sort."

"But you're sure about the eye color? Sure the dog was brown-and-white and medium size?"

Lauren looked away. Was she? Would she testify to it in a court of law? Swear it on a stack of Bibles? Should she explain about her memory that was as shot full of holes as an old, moth-eaten quilt? Would that make her seem like less of a hapless idiot? She looked back at the sheriff. "You know, I only saw the dog for a few seconds."

He nodded, putting away his notebook.

Lauren turned on her phone, and it immediately rang. Without looking, she knew it was Jeff and excused herself, saying, "I have to take this."

"Would you like me to get your purse for you?" Madeleine asked.

"Oh, yes, would you, please?"

"I might want to talk with you again," Sheriff Audi said.

Lauren nodded distractedly, taking her purse when Madeleine brought it, talking over Jeff—he tended to shout when he was worried—telling him she was on her way, that he should calm down. She realized too late it was the wrong thing to say.

"Calm down?" His voice was a sharp bark. "I'm out of my mind here! You said at eleven this morning you were coming in. Now it's after four in the afternoon! I've been calling and calling—your cell, the landline at the house. When I called the dealership, they said they brought you a loaner so you could get to work. Jesus, Lauren! How can you do this?"

"I'm sorry . . ." Her head felt light, and she touched her temple.

"Lauren? Sweetheart, are you all right?"

It was hearing him call her sweetheart that made her throat close. Suddenly, she longed for him. "Oh, Jeff, I don't know. I—I only came by the community center to see if there was something I could do to help find Bo. I—I lost track of time."

She quick-stepped toward the entry. A man arriving from outside the door at the same time pulled it open, allowing her to pass, and when their eyes caught, despite how her mind was caught up in its own web of anxiety, she was moved by the aura of grim exhaustion that seemed to emanate from him. She nodded her thanks, trying to place him, why he looked familiar. It came to her once the door closed behind him, that the man was Bo's dad, JT. She'd seen him with Annie on the news last night, pleading for anyone with information about his son to call the police or the hotline.

Yet earlier, when Annie mentioned JT, she had sounded suspicious of him in a way that made Lauren think JT might somehow be involved in Bo's disappearance. She stopped to look through the center's plate-glass window, following JT as he crossed the room to join Annie and the sheriff. JT put his arm around Annie, and they seemed to sag against each other. Lauren's heart constricted. It was such a terrible situation. She felt awful for leaving—

But Jeff was talking, saying something about the loaner again, that she needed to get it back to the dealership. "You need to pick up your car before the service department closes."

"But I already have my car." Lauren was thoroughly confused. "Someone, a guy named Danny, brought it to the house, around noon. There must be some mistake." She searched ahead for a sign of the Navigator's dark roof, expecting to see it, waiting to see it.

Except she didn't.

The SUV wasn't where she'd left it.

A gray Nissan Altima was parked in its place.

"Oh, no . . ." The protest, not much over a whisper, slipped out. Tiny prickles of alarm burst under her skin.

"Lauren?"

"It's not here."

"Where are you?"

"In front of Kim's shop on Prescott, where I parked." Lauren shut her eyes tightly and opened them again as if that might make the car appear. Poof. Like magic, the Altima would become the Navigator. But it didn't happen. She backed away a step, gaze whipping from side to side. Maybe she had parked in a different space nearby. Her feet followed the thought, half running first to one end of the block, then to the other before she paused again in front of Kim's shop, scanning the opposite side of the street.

But there was no SUV within her view that resembled hers even remotely.

"Oh, God, Jeff. It's been stolen!"

"No, Lauren," Jeff said reasonably, calmly, patiently. "It isn't stolen. It's at the dealership. You're driving an Altima, a gray Nissan Altima. A 2011, I think they said. Do you see it there?"

"Yes, but how—? This isn't right. I distinctly remember driving the Navigator here. I gave Danny a tip for bringing it to me."

"Well, that may be true, but according to a guy I talked to in the service department, Danny or whoever it was brought you the Altima as a loaner after you called them and said you had to get to work."

They waited through a heartbeat of silence.

"You don't remember that," Jeff said.

It was a statement, not a question, and his tone was flat with disappointment, an edge of disgust. She'd let him down—again.

Finally, he told her to go back to the community center. "I'll have someone from the dealership bring your Navigator. They can switch it out with the Altima." He said he would come, too. He was reassuring and kind, and he called her sweetheart again.

But this time she wasn't moved by the endearment. "Okay, but I'm going to the dealership. I want to talk to Danny myself, and I'd like you to be there."

"All right," Jeff said. "After you get your Navigator back, if you still want to, we'll go talk to him."

"You're damn right we will!" Lauren rarely cursed, but she was scared and furious, and sick of doubting and defending herself. It made her feel mean.

"We'll go to the dealership," she repeated, "and then we'll go to the police. Because this is some kind of sick joke." She took a moment, seeing the plausibility. "That's what this is, Jeff. Some kind of prank."

He didn't argue; he said she should wait for him, and Lauren took strength from that. She thought he accepted her theory, that he thought it was plausible, too.

14

JT came up to where Annie stood with the sheriff. She felt his arm come around her, felt his weight as if he might need her for support, and she was glad for it, for his presence and the relief of someone to hold her up, too, even if only for a moment. She told him about her visit to the morgue. It upset him that she'd gone.

"I should have been the one to go," he said to the sheriff.

"I tried to call you," he said. "You were out of range or your cell was dead."

"I volunteered," Annie said, and she could still feel the impossibility of saying the words *morgue* and *body* in relation to Bo over the telephone to JT.

JT pulled her closer to his side, and she turned her head, pressing her face into the soft spot beneath his shoulder, where she smelled the weariness of days spent in the same clothes, a fainter memory of his aftershave, the underscore of something sad, like despair. She thought of the gap that had existed between them for most of their years together, closed now by the zipper of calamity. Their unlikely bond was its dark gift, she thought. Tragedy's incongruous treasure. And she was grateful for it. She thought, until Bo came home, JT was all the family she had in this world. "It wasn't Bo," she said, straightening. "That's the good thing."

JT made a noise, something between a groan and a word of assent, and lowered his head, pinching the bridge of his nose, and he stood that way long enough for Annie to wonder if he was crying. Long enough for her to think that if he was, he had a right to his tears. But when he looked up, he was smiling. Not a real smile. Maybe it was intended to reassure her. She didn't know, couldn't quite interpret its meaning, really. It seemed grotesque, when the rest of his expression was so bloodshot and gray with exhaustion, the terrible grind of anxiety. But what bothered her more was his refusal to look at her. If their glances happened to catch, he jerked his away. She remembered when he left search and rescue—a job that had been a huge and vital part of his life, a job he'd done thoroughly and well—he'd acted the same way. Evasive, furtive. Too quiet.

What's wrong? Annie's mother had asked repeatedly. *Nothing,* JT had answered. *No need to worry,* he'd said. It was the wife of one of his coworkers who ultimately told Annie's mom that JT had quit, and when her mom confronted him, he excused himself, saying he didn't want to burden her. He'd already piled enough on her plate bringing Bo into her life. Something like that.

He always wanted to be the good guy, the rescuer, the fixer. If he knew something about Bo now, something bad, he'd keep it from Annie, forever if he could. He'd feel he was protecting her, saving her. And it annoyed and alarmed her, the thing he might know. She didn't need saving. What she needed from him was the truth.

He shrugged off his backpack. Annie had watched him unload the pack and check over his equipment: bottled water, a basic first aid kit, a small saw, a utility knife, a couple of heat sheets—the list wasn't so very different from what you'd take if you were going camping—before reloading it on Monday near midnight. He still knew the drill. That's what JT had said to her right after he said he wouldn't quit until Bo was found. He'd stopped short of promising. Annie guessed he wouldn't make that mistake again.

"How long since you slept, man?" the sheriff asked him. "You should go home."

JT answered he was fine, and by the way he said it, Annie could tell he had no intention of going anywhere except back out to look for Bo. In fact, despite his obvious fatigue, there was an eagerness about him, an animation that had been missing for a long while. It was as if the search for Bo had restored meaning and direction to his life. Yet another backhanded gift of calamity, Annie thought.

She said, "Before you go, I need to talk to you."

"What about?"

She looked at the sheriff, then back at JT. "I talked to a detective earlier, and he brought up Leighton."

"The drug dealer?"

JT knew about him because Annie had told him last summer when the relationship ended. She'd been worried for herself and Bo. "Detective Cosgrove said they don't know where he is."

"Christ." JT looked at the sheriff. "He's not in Chicago?"

"We're still checking. There's a BOLO out."

"I knew we should have reported that son of a bitch to the cops."

Annie had talked JT out of it. *He's gone*, she'd said. *That's the end of it.* She'd pointed out that Bo had stopped using drugs. *Leave it alone*, she'd begged. And JT had listened to her.

"There's another guy we're looking for, an associate of Drake's. Greg Honey?" Sheriff Audi was addressing JT. "Does the name ring any bells?"

JT said no. He didn't recognize the man in the photo the sheriff showed him.

"You think Bo could be messed up with drugs again, JT?" the sheriff asked. "You see any sign of that lately?"

JT said he hadn't. "But that doesn't mean anything," he added, and Annie's heart sank.

Madeleine joined them and after looking JT over, she said, "You need to eat something."

He shouldered his pack. "Thanks, but I'm not hungry."

"Nonsense," Madeleine said. "Do you suppose you'll be any good to that boy if you drop from starvation? Either of you?" She divided her glance between Annie and JT. "There's plenty of hot food right here in the kitchen." She went over the menu, mentioning Cooper's mother's chicken soup, Annie's baked goods, the variety of casseroles, salads, and desserts others had donated. "Plus there are sandwiches," she added. "C'mon, I'll fix you a plate. You, too, young lady. You'll feel better with some decent food in your stomach."

JT caught Annie's glance. "If I'm getting my arm twisted, so are you."

But Annie said "No, thank you" and "Maybe later," and she wasn't that surprised when neither Madeleine nor JT argued. They were too tired to fuss at her.

Annie's gaze followed them as they crossed the room. Madeleine disappeared into the hallway that led to the kitchen, but JT was stopped repeatedly. Some folks, the nicer, more polite ones, only wanted to offer commiseration, but others wanted news, facts, details. Watching, Annie felt pangs of distress, knowing JT found the attention as difficult to handle as she did. She would have joined him if she hadn't heard the door to the community center open and glanced around to see Lauren coming through it, looking white-faced and shaken. A man was with her, an exceptionally tall, strongly built, good-looking man. They were having a very animated discussion.

"Lauren?" Annie went to meet her. "What's wrong?"

"Oh, Annie, I don't want you troubled with it. My husband and I just need to talk to Sheriff Audi a moment."

"No, we really don't," said the husband.

Annie glanced at him, and when their eyes met, his veered away.

"Lauren's a bit wound up, is all." He put his arm across her shoulders as if he meant to turn her and guide her back outside.

She balked, holding her ground. "Of course I am. My car's gone. Stolen."

"Oh, no," Annie said. "Are you sure?" She didn't know why she questioned it. Lauren was clearly upset. So was her husband, but not in quite the same way. Annie's eyes collided with his again, and she realized he was embarrassed. She imagined if she asked he would say he wished he was anywhere but here. She could sympathize. As small and petty and awful as it was to admit it, sometimes Bo embarrassed her, too.

"She's been through a lot recently," Lauren's husband said, and Annie knew he was referring to Lauren's accident. His voice was rough with the history of it, the recollection of anguished hours spent pacing the floor while his wife, the mother of his children, was in the ICU, hovering between life and death.

"Don't make excuses for me, Jeff."

Lauren didn't speak the words so much as bite them off, and Annie reached out to her, touching her forearm, saying, "It's okay," when it clearly wasn't.

"Is there something I can help with?" The sheriff joined them.

"My car's been stolen," Lauren said. "I think this guy, Danny, from the dealership where it was taken for repairs, took it."

But her husband said no, it was a misunderstanding. He introduced himself. "I'm Jeff Wilder," he said, and he shook hands with Annie and then the sheriff. "I think Lauren is a bit confused. Her Navigator was taken to the dealership yesterday for repairs, but today when it wasn't ready in time for her to go to work, they brought her a loaner, a Nissan Altima. She's not much of a car person. She gets the makes and models mixed up all the time."

"Oh, for God's sake, Jeff, even brain-damaged, I think I know the difference between a sedan and an SUV." Lauren was visibly shaking.

No one spoke. Jeff looked at the ceiling. The sheriff plowed his hand over his head.

"Where's the key to the Altima?" Lauren asked, making it sound like a demand. "Not in my purse." She fumbled it into her hands, and there was something sad and desperate about the way she pawed through it. "Here are the Navigator keys." She dangled them. "But there aren't any others."

Jeff shot a fast-fading smile in Annie's and the sheriff's direction. His eyes were freighted with emotion. He seemed to beg their indulgence, their understanding. He turned his attention to his wife and her purse. "The keys to the loaner must be in there."

Lauren dropped to her knees and after dumping the contents onto the floor, she scrabbled through them.

Annie squatted beside her. "Did you check your jacket?"

Lauren sat back, feeling in her jacket pockets, face flooded with hope that came as quickly as it went.

"Maybe you locked them in the car?" Jeff might have been addressing a child, one who was overly tired and on the verge of collapse.

Or he might have been speaking to someone who had been very ill, Annie thought, as Lauren had been. Judging from Jeff's demeanor, his weary patience, it seemed he'd been down this road with her, or one like it, many times before.

Lauren said no in a way that seemed more a denial than a protest.

When she turned her gaze to Annie's, her eyes were filled with pleading. They clung to Annie's own eyes as if Annie couldn't possibly know the scope of the disaster that was taking shape. She helped Lauren repack her purse. They got to their feet, and Annie was glad when Jeff tucked Lauren close to his side.

"Let's go and see," he suggested.

"At least, then you'll know," Annie said when Lauren looked at her.

"I'm really sorry about your brother," Jeff said.

Annie thanked him.

"I don't guess you've heard anything." He shifted his glance from Annie to the sheriff.

"We're looking at several possibilities," Audi said.

The pause, no more than a heartbeat of silence, felt awkward to Annie, and she would have spoken if the sheriff hadn't.

"You were out of town on Friday, the day your wife saw Bo?" He was asking Jeff, who looked taken aback, Annie thought, but then, she was mystified by the sheriff's question, too.

"I didn't leave until that afternoon," Jeff answered. "Why?"

"Well, when the detectives interviewed your wife this morning, she said you don't like her driving by herself, but she was alone on Friday and for the rest of the weekend. You didn't come back until Sunday. She could have driven anywhere. Isn't that right?"

"Yes, but her doctor cleared it, so—" Jeff shrugged.

"Stopping like that, for a pedestrian, it could be dangerous."

"I'm standing right here," Lauren said strongly, "and I'm not deaf. I didn't go anywhere other than to the warehouse and home . . . and the farm, the Fishers' farm," she added, but she was frowning as if there might be other places, destinations that eluded her.

Annie couldn't imagine it, how it would feel to lose the whole thread of your days, where you'd gone, what you'd done.

"It's all right now," Jeff said, hugging Lauren more firmly. "We'll get it sorted out. Don't worry."

"But this isn't—I just don't see how I could have—" Lauren twisted out of Jeff's embrace, and looking from the sheriff to Annie, she said, "I'm sorry."

"It's okay," Annie said, because there was nothing else anyone could say. She followed them. "Lauren? Will you let me know—" She stopped, suddenly unsure of what she wanted.

But Lauren's gaze softened in nearly the exact way Annie's mother's gaze used to, and Lauren did what her mother would have done—she pulled Annie into her embrace and held on to her. "I'll be back," she said, and her voice slipped and caught. "I'll do whatever it takes to help you find Bo, okay? Don't worry about this with the car. It's nothing. I'm fine, truly."

Annie nodded, watching Lauren go, feeling anxious for her. It wasn't nothing. It was weird. It wouldn't be so terrible if Lauren had only misplaced her car. Annie had done that a time or two, for long enough that she'd considered reporting it stolen, but if Jeff was right, if Lauren had driven another car, one the dealership had loaned her—

Well, as Lauren herself had asked, how could you forget something like that?

15

Jeff went ahead of her, striding down Prescott Street toward Kim's Needle and Book Nook, a man on a mission, and Lauren let him. She felt sick with frustration and dread. What was next? Would she forget where she lived? Her children's faces? Where she'd left them? Would Jeff take her car keys now? Her license? Would she lose her freedom entirely?

Her head filled with white noise.

He stepped off the curb where the Altima and not the Navigator was parked, and walking to the driver's side, he bent to look in the window. Lauren knew what he would say before he straightened and said it, that the keys were there.

"In the ignition." He sounded rueful, apologetic.

"That doesn't prove I drove it." She clung to the last of her conviction.

"Well, there's also a scarf on the seat. I think it's the one that belonged to your mom."

"No," she said.

"Come and see for yourself," he said.

"How would it get there? I didn't bring it with me. I don't wear it with this jacket." She joined Jeff, reluctantly, looking from him to the car. Not directly, because she couldn't bear catching even the smallest sight of the scarf her mother had brought home one year from Paris. French women had worn scarves for years, her elegant mother had said, winding the length of vintage pale-pink-and-cream silk around Lauren's neck. "It's the height of haute couture." She'd been laughing. "There, my darling." She had turned Lauren so that she could see herself in the mirror. "Beautiful, no? A runway model should have such a stunning look."

"I don't remember bringing it with me," Lauren said now. "I almost never wear it." It was fragile. Her mother had said it was from the forties.

"Maybe you missed her. You get it out sometimes when you do."

Lauren looked up at Jeff. His eyes were soft with commiseration. He circled her shoulders with his arm, pulling her against him, kissing her temple.

She turned her face into his chest. "I don't remember driving this car. How could I not remember?"

An SUV pulled to a stop behind the Altima, blocking it. Lauren recognized her Navigator, but the red-haired man who hopped out wasn't Danny. He was older, a complete stranger to her, and she was relieved. The last person she wanted to see now was Danny, after the accusations she'd made against him. He hadn't heard them; still, it shook her how willing she'd been to blame him rather than admit the truth, which was that she was incompetent.

"You the Wilders?" the red-haired man asked.

"Yeah," Jeff said. "I hope you brought an extra set of keys for the loaner."

"Got 'em right here." He pulled them from his pocket.

Jeff asked him to unlock the door. He retrieved Lauren's mother's scarf and gave it to her. He thanked the guy for bringing Lauren's

SUV, and handing the man a twenty-dollar bill, he said, "I'm really sorry for the trouble."

"Hey, it's no problem. I know how it is. My wife was pretty shaky when she got out of the hospital, too."

Lauren stared at Jeff, cheeks burning with fresh mortification and something hotter, like rage. She felt it pulsing behind her eyes. "What did you tell him?" she demanded after the guy drove off in the Altima. "That I was nuts?"

"No. I only said you had an accident a while back. It's nothing to be ashamed of, Lauren. Why do you always take it so personally? Let people help you. Let me help you. It's all I want to do."

"It will never be different, will it? You'll never get past it. Every mistake I make, every time I forget, you'll automatically assume I'm incompetent or strung out. No matter what I do, you'll always be watching, checking—" Her voice broke, and she hated it, the loss of control, how it further cemented what seemed apparent, the fact that she was coming apart.

"You think you're the only one feeling like this fucking nightmare is never going to end?" Jeff glared at her. "What do you want me to say? That this was some kind of joke and you really didn't drive a loaner into town? No matter what I say, I'm going to be accused of meaning something else." He walked away, walked back. "You know what your problem is, Lauren? You overthink everything." He punched his skull above his ears with his forefingers. "You're in your head too much. It's making you paranoid."

"How am I supposed to trust what you tell me to my face when you're going behind my back, telling people I'm nuts? Huh?" Lauren pushed her hair behind her ears, wiped her eyes, pinched her nose. "How do you think it makes me feel to stand by and listen while you make up excuses to cover up your wife's crazy behavior? Ha ha ha." Her voice shot high, a falsetto mockery. "Poor Lauren doesn't know the difference between the makes and models of cars. Poor Lauren, doesn't know if she's driving a car, much less what kind."

"Jesus." Jeff rolled his gaze skyward. "This is why I can't talk to you."

"That's all right, because I'm done." Lauren wanted to end this. If it went on any longer, she thought she might punch Jeff. They would erupt, explode, brawl in the street. And it wasn't as if she didn't know her anger was unreasonable. She did. But she still couldn't help it.

"What does that mean?"

"Nothing. Can I have my keys, please?" she asked sweetly.

He handed them to her. "You sure you can drive yourself?"

She shot him a look.

"Okay, okay." He backed off, hands raised. "I've got to go back to the warehouse and finish up. I shouldn't be long. You want me to stop and get something for dinner? Hamburgers, maybe?"

"That's fine," she said, and when he said he'd see her at home, she nodded, but on reaching the freeway, instead of turning north toward their subdivision, she turned south and headed into Houston.

Why go home? What was the point of trying so hard to be the sane, sober Lauren when, so clearly, she wasn't that woman anymore? When it was so obvious that the new Lauren couldn't distinguish reality from delusion.

16

"How well do you know her?" Sheriff Audi watched Lauren follow Jeff down Prescott.

"We only met today. She reminds me of my mother," Annie added after a beat. She was still disconcerted by the resemblance, the way it had seemed to loosen her tongue, making her confide things about herself and her life that she'd ordinarily never admit to anyone, least of all a stranger.

"They do favor each other," the sheriff said.

Annie looked at him. "You knew my mom?"

"She came to see me a few times. She was concerned about your brother and asked if we would keep an eye out for him."

Annie wasn't surprised. Her mother had solicited help with Bo from so many people, including Annie, and in the end, they'd all failed him.

"Sometimes even when you do the best you can, it's not good enough."

Annie looked at Sheriff Audi and wondered if he was reading her mind. Or maybe he was thinking of his own failures. "What about the dog Lauren saw in the car with Bo?" she asked. "Couldn't the vets around town be contacted to see if any of them recognize the description? They might even know the woman or the car."

"Might be worth a shot," the sheriff said, but without conviction.

If pressed, he'd talk about his limited resources. He would say as much as he might wish it, Lincoln County didn't have the big-city manpower of, say, Harris or Dallas or Tarrant County. He would reassure Annie he was doing his best. How many times had she heard him spout the party line on the local news and never paid attention because it hadn't concerned her.

But there was nothing to prevent her from contacting the local vets with a description of the dog, was there?

"Doesn't seem like her memory is too good." The sheriff was looking out at the street, in the direction that Lauren had disappeared.

"She told me she fell and sustained a bad head injury. She still feels kind of disabled, I think." Even as Annie said this, it didn't jibe. Lauren had seemed so pragmatic and steady, so down to earth—so like Annie's memory of her mom. But the Lauren who had dropped to her knees to grope through the contents of her purse for keys to a vehicle she hadn't known she'd driven had been tenuous and frightened. *Unbalanced.* The word appeared in Annie's mind. Like Bo could be, Annie thought, but not in the same way.

The sheriff said he knew about the accident. "It's a crazy business she and her husband are in, taking down those old buildings. Anything can happen." He started for the door.

Annie caught his elbow. "What about the dog?"

"I don't know as I'd put a lot of stock in anything Mrs. Wilder said, Annie, you know?"

"But she described the woman to a T. It's the same description Cooper gave."

"He didn't report seeing a dog."

190

"No, but maybe he forgot, too, or the dog could have been lying down."

"I'll look into it, okay?"

"Fine," Annie said, and she smiled as if she believed him, as if she didn't recognize the dismissal in his eyes. Like the deputy earlier, the sheriff didn't believe Bo was alive, either. His urgency was gone. Even his shoulders seemed to have rounded with his sympathy and regret. It was only a matter of hours before the search would be called off, the command center shut down and the whole calamity forgotten. It panicked and angered her. She wanted to call Sheriff Audi on it, to say *How dare you?*, even as she fought an urge to plead with him not to give up.

He cupped her upper arm with his big palm and said, "Hang in there," and she bore that, too, and once he took his leave, she went to find JT. But when she got to the kitchen, only Madeleine was there, washing dishes. "He left a few minutes ago," she answered when Annie asked.

Picking up a towel, Annie joined her at the sink. "Did he go home?"

"No. He's as stubborn as you are."

"Look who's talking," Annie said.

Madeleine let the water out of the sink. "I'll go home if you will," she said.

"Okay," Annie said. "If that's what it takes."

Madeleine looked at Annie, not believing her. "You promise? Because you've worn yourself out, and there are plenty of other folks who are doing everything that can be done."

Annie promised even as she thought there could never be enough people.

"It only takes one to find him." Madeleine stated a fact.

"It'll be dark again soon." Annie stated her own fact, one that happened to be her worst dread. It was true what people said. Terror was more easily managed in the light of day. At night, it ran away with you; it seized your mind, conjuring every worst-case, missing-person scenario you'd ever had the misfortune of hearing about. There were hours, the ones after midnight especially—her mother's despair hours—when Annie believed she couldn't take one more breath without breaking from the fear.

Abruptly, Madeleine brought her open palms down hard on the sink's edge, and Annie flinched. "What is it?"

But Madeleine only shook her head. "Nothing. Just tired and worried sick, like you."

No, Annie thought. There was something more complicated than simple fatigue working in Madeleine's eyes. Something like anguish, maybe. Or remorse? Annie couldn't sort it out. She thought she was the cause, what she'd said about it being dark soon, and she apologized.

Madeleine wasn't having it. "You have nothing to be sorry for."

She loosened her grip on the sink's edge, and Annie saw that her hands were trembling. They were old hands; the backs were covered in the thinnest tissue of flesh and networked in a delicate lace of blue veins. Their fragility made Madeleine seem vulnerable somehow, in a way Annie had never imagined before. She wanted to reach out to Madeleine, but she knew better. There were boundaries, lines of reserve between them that had never been crossed. Annie thought they were there because that was how Madeleine wanted it.

The older woman sniffed. "Such a lot of foolishness." She wiped her forehead with the back of her wrist, turned on the tap and rinsed the sink, then wrung out the dishcloth, and her motions were as crisp and businesslike as the edges of her personality, the parts of herself she would let people see. But who knew what underlay that? Who could know the mysteries of another's heart?

Annie cleaned the counters, dried a dozen coffee mugs, and set them on a tray. She made a fresh pot of coffee in case someone wanted it, although it being the dinner hour, the center was mostly deserted.

"Would you like to come home with me?" Madeleine spoke in a rush.

Annie looked at her, startled.

She was flushed pink, diffident, stammering. "You—you'll be alone otherwise."

"That's very kind of you," Annie began.

"Never mind. I don't know why I asked."

Annie started to protest or apologize again, she didn't know which, but Madeleine held up her hand. "Let's say no more about it."

"All right," Annie said, but she was disconcerted. She slipped into her jacket, shouldered her purse, and together they walked out the back door of the community center and into the alley, where they'd left their cars. The sun was gone, the air chilled. The prospect of the coming night pressed down hard on Annie's shoulders. She thought of Bo's bare ankles. She thought of the man in the lab coat at the morgue, his blistered-looking, bone-white wrists.

"You're welcome to come anytime." Madeleine paused near the battered, rear bumper of Annie's BMW. "To my house, I mean. Bo comes sometimes. Did you know?"

Annie hadn't known. "He never told me."

"He asked me not to tell you." Madeleine pulled her keys from her purse. "He likes to sit in the garden. I've been teaching him the difference between the perennials and the weeds."

"Huh." Annie was flustered. The number of Bo's secrets kept mounting.

"He'll make a good gardener one day. I told him I'm happy to pay him for his trouble. You, too. We could talk about it once this is over, the three of us." Madeleine cast out the suggestion, not looking at Annie, and she seemed to brace herself, as if for rejection.

Not that Annie knew how to reply or even what Madeleine was offering. Extra income? A larger role in their lives, that included financial support? A place for Bo to find shelter? Had Madeleine and Bo discussed this? Anything was possible, Annie guessed. She thought of asking for further clarity and couldn't; she couldn't think of one thing to say, and after another moment or two, Madeleine seemed to draw herself up. She retreated a step and said, "All right then" and "Good night," and turning, went toward her car.

Annie watched her go, still unable to find her tongue, the breath for speech. *Wait.* The syllable sat mired in confusion at the back of her throat. She looked up at nothing, upset with herself. She'd hurt Madeleine's feelings, letting her go without a word. Was it so far-fetched that Bo would find solace in Madeleine's garden, that he would find a friend in her, that she would care for him and consequently care for Annie, too? Was it such a mystery that Bo kept aspects of his life private? Annie didn't tell him everything, either.

Where are you? She might have been asking the sky, its vast empty arc.

Annie started her car. The question felt eternal; it felt branded into the wall of her brain.

On her way home, she ran what had become a familiar circuit since Friday, going by the library first. But Bo wasn't there, and no one had seen him. She shouted his name through the train switch-yard and, in response, heard only the lingering resonance of her own voice, the whish of an errant breeze. She called for him softly along the pathways of Greenlove Park, where he liked to lie in the grass under a particular wide-canopied bur oak and write in his notepad. There was no answer there, either, other than a cricket's uncertain song.

She drove home, but once there, she couldn't stand the silence, the emptiness. She needed her mother, and all that was left of her was at JT's. So Annie went there, and for all the sense it made, as she entered the house, she was filled with a hope that was as unreasoning as it was foolish. Because a quick search of the rooms turned up nothing. Bo was no more present in this house than he was in her own, no more present in either place than her mother.

There was nothing of them left other than Annie's memory of them, and that was fading, slipping from her mind like water through her fingers. The remembrance of their voices, the sound of their laughter, their fragrances—mixed notes of morning toast and spring flowers, laundry soap and sunshine; some wonderful smell that made Annie feel safe, made her feel she was home—all of it was going now, hour by helpless hour, becoming as ephemeral and distant as an echo.

Wandering back into the kitchen, her eye caught on the answering-machine light that was blinking on the telephone at her elbow, the landline JT insisted on keeping because phones were his business, his profession. She hadn't noticed it before, and watching it now, she was somehow mesmerized. No one called the landline anymore; no one who would leave a message anyway. It wasn't her phone; who called, the messages they left weren't her responsibility or even her business, but she picked up the receiver anyway and dialed into the system. The canned voice announced there was one new message, and retrieving it, she heard a human voice, a woman's voice, sounding hesitant and somehow agitated, introduce herself as Constance McMurray from Rose Hill in Morro Bay, California. She was calling for JT or Sandy Laughlin, she said.

Sandy? Annie's heart paused. Sandy was her mother's name.

Constance McMurray described her need to speak to either Mr. or Mrs. Laughlin as most urgent. "Please return my call as soon as possible," she said.

In anticipation, Annie yanked open a kitchen drawer, found a pen and a scrap of paper and jotted down the number where Constance McMurray said she could be reached. The message ended; the machine voice came back, advising Annie what she could do now, but she only stared at the telephone, unable to choose among the options that were offered: save, delete, listen again. She cradled the receiver when the machine started to repeat her choices, and picking up the note she'd made, she studied the name and telephone number.

The memories were too hard for us. That was how JT had explained moving himself and Bo across the country after Bo's mother died. Annie looked at her note again. Rose Hill sounded like the name of a cemetery.

She went into the den and turned on the computer, an old IBM PC, a relic leftover from her and Bo's school days. The desk where it sat was big enough that they'd often done their homework at it together, one on either side. When the home page appeared on the screen, she typed in *Rose Hill,* a plus sign, and *Morro Bay* in the search bar and clicked "Return." Her fingertips registered the faint stickiness of the keys, raising a memory from the floor of her mind of the day that Bo, in a childish fit, overturned her Dr. Pepper on the keyboard. She'd been working on an essay for her sophomore English Lit class, something loosely based on Jonathan Swift's, "A Modest Proposal," and Bo had been doing stupid tricks with a yo-yo he'd gotten for his birthday, needling her. *Lookit, lookit!* His voice was like a dart in her ear. *Shut up!* She ordered. *Get out of here, you little nerd*, she said.

In one half second, he upended her soda can. *Who's the nerd now?*

His long-ago taunt, rough with an edge of something very like tears, rattled off the walls of Annie's brain.

Why hadn't she given him the attention he'd craved? Two minutes, maybe less. Would it have been so hard? She remembered spending nearly an hour drying out the keyboard and feeling lucky and relieved to find it still worked.

She remembered she never would have passed algebra that year or geometry the next without Bo's help.

Rose Hill Community Center was the first entry on the search page, and from the sketchy verbiage that was included there, Annie gathered it wasn't a cemetery but a mental-health facility. A knot tightened in her stomach. She clicked through to the home page, dotted with photographs, many of them showing people— amazingly normal-looking people—engaged in a variety of ordinary activities. Some were of groups seated in a circle, chatting or playing instruments. There was a shot of a youngish man lying beneath a tree on a grassy knoll, reading a book. Rose Hill's landscape was vintage university fare. Ivy-covered walls included a couple of turrets. It was bizarre, really, the resemblance that the hospital, or whatever it was, bore to a college campus or a quaint out-of-the-way hotel. The information Annie read made it sound like a spa, a haven, a retreat for the agitated and emotionally distressed. It talked about restoring wellness of mind, body, and spirit. She kept looking for the place to sign up.

Bo, who had been diagnosed at one time or another with nearly every mental aberration this center treated—schizophrenia, schizo-affective disorder, bipolar disorder, and the catchall, *other, often hard-to-place psychosocial profiles*—had never looked as carefree as the people shown in the photographs. He was clean, obsessively clean, and his clothes were clean, but he was stiff in them. He moved in them like the Tin Man from *The Wizard of Oz*. He bent to the right as if the string on that side was pulled too tight; he talked to himself. His cheeks were hollows, and his eyes burned as if with fever for which no one, not even the most gifted therapist, had found a source or a cure. Scrolling back through the pages, studying the photos, Annie felt dismay, the sourer taint of derision.

She couldn't picture Bo in any of them.

Annie got her cell phone and bringing it back to the den, she sat down in front of the computer again and dialed the contact number Constance McMurray had left in her message, noting that, except for the last four digits, it was the same as the main number for Rose Hill.

"Constance McMurray," the woman answered, sounding breezy, as breezy and carefree as the website models.

Annie mentioned the message.

"Oh, yes." The woman was instantly grave. "I'm afraid I don't have good news, Mrs. Laughlin."

"Is Bo there? Is he all right?" Annie didn't bother correcting Constance McMurray's misapprehension about her identity, and she would wonder later how it might have altered the conversation if she had. She would think Mrs. McMurray probably would not have been so forthcoming.

"Bo? No, he isn't here. I'm calling about Lydia, Bo's mother, Mrs. Laughlin. Since I spoke to your husband last week, her condition has been downgraded to critical."

"His mother?" Annie frowned. She was on the verge of saying, *His mother's dead; both our mothers are dead,* but Constance didn't leave enough of a pause, and Annie didn't have breath for speech anyway.

"She's in acute renal failure, not responding to treatment. I'm afraid she's—well, her prognosis isn't good. As I explained to Mr. Laughlin before, she came to us too late this time. She's receiving the best of care, of course. She's as comfortable as we can make her, but the doctors aren't encouraging. Will you tell Mr. Laughlin that if he's changed his mind about Bo seeing his mother a final time, he should come quickly?"

"Are you sure you have the right—?" Annie stood up. "I mean—that is, I thought—" *Dead.* Bo's mother was dead. JT had said she was. Annie's mother had said she was. Bo listened to her through his earmuffs—

"Mrs. Laughlin?" Constance McMurray prompted.

"No, I'm her daughter. My mom—Sandy died two years ago."

"Oh. Oh dear, I didn't know. Mr. Laughlin never said—I'm afraid they—I mean, Mr. or Mrs. Laughlin—are the only ones authorized to receive information about Lydia."

"Bo is missing, Mrs. McMurray. Did you know?" Annie wasn't sure why she chose that question to ask rather than any one of the overwhelming number of other questions she might have asked.

"What do you mean, he's missing?"

"He disappeared last Friday. The police are looking for him. Does he know his mother is still alive?" *Was I the only one who was lied to?*

"Well, I don't know if I should—"

"Look, if he knew, there's a chance he's there or trying to get there."

"Well, honestly, I don't believe he did know. I think when they moved from here, Mr. Laughlin decided the boy would be better off if he was told his mother had died. Because of her condition, you know. She was hardly capable of—"

"What was—is—her condition, Mrs. McMurray? I mean, besides kidney failure?"

"I shouldn't—" She faltered. "But given the circumstances—" She hesitated again, and then, seeming to cast aside her reservations, she said, "Lydia was first brought to us by her parents years ago when she was in her twenties and diagnosed with paranoid schizophrenia. She's been in and out of treatment here at Rose Hill and at various other treatment facilities in the area and other locations ever since."

"Is that where it comes from? Why Bo is—? You know he was diagnosed, not with *paranoid* schizophrenia, but—" Annie stopped, uncertain how to continue.

"My understanding is Bo's issues have never been as severe," Constance McMurray said.

"Why would JT not want him to know his mother was alive? It seems cruel." *Did it?* Had she said it aloud? *Cruel* was such a harsh word, a judgmental word. She'd never known JT to be cruel, which only made the situation all the more confusing.

"I really can't say any more without the proper—"

"Mrs. McMurray, any information you can give me may help the police find Bo." Annie paced into the kitchen, looking out the door for JT's truck. The knot in her stomach was a small, heated coal, fueling the chaotic stew of her emotion, a blistering lash of words . . . all the things she would say to JT when she saw him.

Constance McMurray was explaining Lydia's situation, but Annie only caught parts of what she said, that Lydia lived on the street when she wasn't in treatment or in jail, that she could be violent, that, like Bo, she was prone to self-medicate with alcohol and whatever drugs she could find. That all of her history was bearing down on her now with enough force to destroy her.

Annie asked about Lydia's parents.

"Her mother's in end-stage Alzheimer's. Her father died a few years ago. Massive coronary. I knew them through the years. They did what they could for their daughter, as much as parents can do. It's a very trying and difficult situation when someone you love is afflicted in this way. They tend to not want to take their medication or to attend counseling sessions or do any of the things necessary to help themselves."

"Yes," Annie murmured, because she had experience, and because there was nothing else to offer other than the acknowledgment of a reality that was as grievous as it was inexorable. She thought of the people pictured on Rose Hill's website. She doubted Bo's mother resembled a single one of them.

"I'm sorry," Mrs. McMurray said, "but I really have to go. If you'll let Mr. Laughlin know I called—"

"If Bo comes there—"

"Of course, I'll contact you immediately."

"You mentioned you spoke to JT last week?" Annie asked.

"Yes."

"What day? Do you recall?"

"Tuesday," Constance McMurray answered. "I remember it because Lydia was much improved. Her vital signs stabilized; even her mind was clear. She was still weak, but we were optimistic, mistakenly, as it turns out. Anyway, she asked us to contact Mr. Laughlin, and I placed the call for her. She wanted him to bring Bo to see her. I think she knew—"

"You're sure it was Tuesday?" *I could tell you something.* Bo's words from last Wednesday circled Annie's brain. *But just listen,* he'd said, *I heard talking* . . . Why hadn't she paid attention? He'd been agitated and upset, not from a sugar overload or because he just got that way sometimes, no. He'd learned his mother was alive. Somehow, he'd overheard JT on the phone, talking to her, and he'd put it together. What a shock it must have been. He would have been desperate to go to her. Annie knew, because that was how she'd feel if someone told her that her mother was alive. She would want to go to her. Nothing would stop her.

She looked at him again in her mind's eye, seated across the table from her, pouring packet after packet of sugar into his tea, scattering grains across the table and onto the floor in his haste and his anxiety. He'd come to the café to tell her his mother was alive. If she'd given him the slightest encouragement, he would have said he wanted to see her; he'd have asked Annie for help getting there. He might even have wanted her to go with him. She didn't doubt that had been his intention. Just as she didn't doubt that if, instead of lecturing him about his diet, she'd asked him what was bothering him, it would have changed everything, and the enormity of her mistake took her breath.

She didn't explain the reason for her urgency when she called JT and summoned him home, and when he appeared, she didn't apologize, either, for scaring him half to death. She was too hurt, panicked, and angry to take much notice or care of his feelings. While he stood in the doorway to the den, she paced in front of him, letting him have it. He'd lied, she told him. "How could you?" she asked.

He took his head in his hands, clearly stricken.

Annie's heart didn't soften at the way he stumbled to his recliner, where he didn't sit down so much as collapse into it. His frailty only riled her further. "She's his mother, JT! And all this time, all these years, you lied to him and to me! You and Mama. I just don't believe it—"

"You don't understand. Lydia's mental condition—"

"No." Annie stabbed her finger in JT's direction. "Don't blame her. You took Bo away from her. You took them away from each other. My God, he was only five years old. You broke his heart! He was still crying for her when you married Mom and moved in here. You know he wore those stupid earmuffs just to hear her voice." Annie crossed her arms, chest heaving, indignant. "I guess you thought you were doing what was best, as usual."

He didn't answer. He was so pale, so ragged and done in. The slump of his shoulders, the way he sat with his chin lowered nearly to his chest . . . Now, with her anger abating, Annie did ache for him. She wanted to go to him and comfort him. She was angry with him but no more angry than she was with herself. And the place he was in, its very untenableness, sapped her of any remaining fury.

She waited while he wiped his hands down his face. She saw the effort it took for him to gather himself.

"I came home from work one time—" He began slowly, voice halting and rough with some mix of apology and pain. "Bo was around four, and I was working nights then—and his mother wasn't there. The kitchen was a wreck, eggs broken on the counter and the floor, flour everywhere. Back door open, stove going, TV blasting, but no Lydia and no sign of Bo, either. Scared the shit out of me. I was yelling my head off, running through the rooms like a madman. Finally, I realized if Bo was there, he was probably scared, so I stopped shouting and got real quiet, and he came out of his closet. He couldn't tell me much, but from the little he did say, I knew Lydia went off her rocker, a full-blown episode. She's schizophrenic, but she's got bipolar tendencies, too. And when she drinks or does meth or any of that shit—" JT didn't finish.

Wordless, Annie sat on the edge of the ottoman.

"I was scared to leave him with her after that. Her parents tried to help." JT found Annie's glance. "They're well-off. Did Constance tell you that?"

Annie shook her head.

"They set up a trust fund for Lydia. That's how come she gets the star treatment. At least, whenever her folks could manhandle her into Rose Hill or any of the other places they packed her off to. Once, they took her to some treatment center in Switzerland, stayed there with her six months. Didn't do shit for her. Her dad's dead now, though, and her mom's not in great shape."

Annie said she knew.

JT smoothed his palms down his thighs. "They never liked me. I wasn't a professional man, a college man. He said I didn't know what I was letting myself in for, like he was helping me out, which was bullshit. It pissed me off, but I should have listened to him because I knew Lydia wasn't right. From the beginning, there were signs. But I loved her, you know?" JT's voice caught.

Annie's throat closed.

"Every time I look at Bo, I think I caused it. I went along when Lydia wanted a baby, when I knew there was a better-than-average chance he'd lose his mind at some point, just like his mother."

"He's not like her, JT." Annie came to her feet. "He's not nearly as—not even close," she finished, and now her voice was shaky.

"Your mom wanted to tell you the truth, but I thought it'd only put a burden on you or you'd think Bo was better off knowing and tell him yourself. Your mama argued that you should both know—well, she went back and forth, really. She wanted to protect you. I did, too. That's the hell of it with folks like Bo and his mother. Half the time—most of the time—you can't figure out what's right. It'll drive you insane right along with them. It nearly has me, more than once."

"Bo remembers seeing her in the hospital. He remembers her reading aloud to him."

"Yeah. The times she ended up in treatment before we were divorced, I took him to see her. That was when I still thought things might work out, that we'd still be a family. I had this crazy idea they would get her on the right meds or she'd just get well—presto! I thought seeing Bo, being around him would make the difference. It did for a while. But he wasn't out of diapers when she started taking off. She'd up and go for days. We wouldn't know where. The last time, when she was gone for nearly two weeks, her dad found her on the street. She was going with men, you know, to get money for a fix. I filed for divorce after that. Her folks paid for the attorney and all the court costs. They paid for me to move here with Bo. Texas was their idea."

"But didn't they want Bo close by, where they could see him?"

JT brought his gaze to Annie's, and it surprised her when he defended them, when he asked her not to blame them. "Lydia's their only child. They'd already been through a lifetime of crazy bullshit with her. They just couldn't face watching it happen to their only grandchild."

"But to saddle Bo with that, before they even knew—" Annie interrupted herself. "He's never said anything to me about any of this."

"I don't think he remembers much about that time," JT said. "Or maybe he doesn't want to."

Annie thought about it, how she wasn't much different. She tended to push the hard stuff out of mental view, too, the same way she stuffed her overdue bills into a drawer, as if that would make them disappear.

But her mother had never avoided anything; she hadn't kept secrets. In fact, she'd always said she was opposed to them, that a secret was like an untended splinter, festering below the surface, and the longer it stayed there, the more trouble it caused when it came out. Clearly she'd made an exception. Maybe more than one.

The revelation surfaced in Annie's mind, along with the understanding that her mother had shared things with JT, hopes and fears, doubts and concerns, that she'd never shared with Annie, and it pained her. It occurred to her that her mother had loved JT, and she'd never thought of that before. It was one of the realities she'd consigned to a drawer in her mind. She didn't want to share her mom with him, and she had made sure he knew it.

She looked covertly at him, feeling the vestiges of the old resentment, a child's jealousy, and a newer warmth of dawning shame, wishing she could change the past. Wishing for the courage to say so, to make amends, but even as she hunted for the words, she couldn't pluck a single one from the tangle of her emotions. Suppose he didn't know what she meant?

"Did you call Sheriff Audi?" JT asked.

Annie said she had. "They're checking the terminals, but I don't think he expects to find out anything. He's got it in his mind that wherever Bo is, it's related to drugs."

"Well, he did have all that money," JT said. "That's what worries me. Where did it come from?"

"Madeleine. I told you. She paid him."

"But she said he had more than that. Even that woman, Lauren, said what Bo showed her was a pretty big roll of bills."

"So what are you thinking?"

"You know how stubborn Bo is. If he wanted to get to his mama bad enough, he'd find a way. He'd do whatever he needed to raise the cash."

"Sell drugs, you mean." Annie held JT's gaze. "What if he tried to contact Leighton? If Leighton hurt him—" She broke off. She would never forgive herself.

"What if overhearing me talk about his mother is what caused him to leave?"

The silence that fell was heavy with blame, the futility of second guesses.

"Why didn't he just ask me?" JT spoke to the ceiling.

"He was probably scared," Annie said, "or mad, or maybe he didn't know if it was real. He's been listening to her through his earmuffs for so long." She sat down at the desk. "I saw him right after that, at the café, and I knew he was upset. Why didn't I ask him what was wrong? He would have told me. You know how he is; you have to ask."

"It's not your fault," JT said.

Annie fingered a stack of mail. "He's so easily confused," she said. "Anything outside his own neighborhood and routine just— Morro Bay, JT—it's so far." She locked his gaze. "Anything might have happened by now. Even if he got there safely, how will he manage getting to the hospital? Does he even know which one his mother is in? Shouldn't we go there?"

"To California? It'd be like looking for a needle in a haystack. We have to let the cops do their job."

He was placating her, Annie thought. JT was trying to get her to accept that whatever had happened to Bo, it was something that involved drugs.

An exhausted pause hung around them like a shroud.

"They closed the command center," Annie said.

"Yeah, but folks are still looking, and Audi swore he wasn't giving up. He knows I won't. Not until we bring Bo home."

Tears seared the backs of Annie's eyelids. If only Bo could hear his dad; if only he knew how much JT loved him. If only JT could have expressed it before, but regret now was as useless as blame. "You should go to bed, get some rest," she said.

"I'm fine right here." JT settled his head against the back of the recliner and closed his eyes. "You'll stay? You need sleep, too."

"I'll stay," she said, because neither one could face the rest of this night alone. She flipped off the lights, and going into Bo's old room instead of her own, she lay down on his narrow bed, pulling the throw at its foot over her. But after only moments, she flung the small blanket aside and got up. There was another throw in JT's bedroom, and carrying it into the den, she covered him with it. He mumbled what sounded like thanks and something else she didn't catch, and she waited a moment before leaving him again, but he said nothing more.

Back in Bo's bed, Annie pulled the small blanket to her chin, clutching its edge, wide-eyed. She kept thinking of the white-haired woman, of what she might know, the answer she might have. She felt wired and alert, as if she were the one endangered. It seemed to her the entire world was in jeopardy, and it amazed her how the night went on, impervious. The wind sighed through the trees, loosening the shadows in the room, making the house creak like old bones as it settled. Pretty soon, Annie heard JT's breath fall into ragged snores, and she curled on her side. Once she had complained to her mother about his snoring, that it was loud enough to raise the roof. *How am I supposed to sleep through that racket?* she'd demanded. Now it was a comfort to her, hearing it, and she was glad for JT, that he was finally getting some rest, however brief.

• • •

As Wednesday night gave way to Thursday morning, Annie did little more than toss and turn, and finally, giving up on the notion of sleep altogether, she rose at four and dressed quietly. JT was still snoring softly when she left the house and drove through the darkened streets to the café. It was her usual routine, flipping the lights on in the kitchen, pulling the ingredients from the walk-in pantry, sifting quantities of flour, measuring out cups full of butter, spoonsful of spices, and she gave herself to it, losing herself in the rhythm of mixing and kneading. Madeleine came at five thirty and tied on her apron, and if she was surprised to find Annie there, she didn't remark on it. Neither did Carol, when she arrived a while later. Not one of them talked beyond what was necessary to get breakfast going, and at seven, when Madeleine unlocked the café's doors, several of the regulars walked in, and they were subdued, too.

Annie couldn't face them and stayed in the kitchen, making herself useful by washing dishes, Bo's old job, until the breakfast crowd thinned.

"You don't have to be here," Madeleine said when the last diner left. "We can manage."

But Annie had no place else to be. She sat with Madeleine and Carol over coffee and told them about Bo's mother, that she was alive, that he might have gone there. They agreed it made sense.

"I don't believe that business about the drugs, though," Madeleine said.

"I'm lighting a candle," Carol said.

They took their empty mugs to the sink, and Annie asked Madeleine if she could use the computer in the office. "Just until the lunch crowd picks up."

"Honey," she said, "you take as long as you need. Carol and I can manage."

Carol nodded, exchanging a look with Madeleine that on any other day might have caught Annie's attention, but her registration of such details now wasn't more than subliminal. She was grateful when they didn't question her. The last thing she needed was one more person telling her how futile it was to search for the white-haired woman through the ownership of a blue-eyed dog.

She was startled a bit later by a light tapping on the door frame, and looking up, her eyes collided with Lauren Wilder's.

"Madeleine told me you were in here," Lauren said. "I hope you don't mind."

"No, it's fine," Annie said, although she wasn't sure. "Did you find your car?"

Lauren said she had and abruptly averted her gaze, pointing her face into the late-morning light that slanted through the window, as if to signal she couldn't say more without losing her composure.

She looked awful, Annie thought. Parched and bruised, like a ruined flower. She looked . . . *haunted*. The word appeared in Annie's mind, and she could understand how that might be. She knew what it was like, having to fight to hold yourself together. "I'm glad," Annie said and left it at that.

"Is it true they closed down the command post?"

"It costs a lot of money to run something like that. Anyway, people have to get on with their lives."

"I suppose I can understand that, but I meant what I said yesterday about helping you. You can't give up, you know? Because sometimes, even when everything looks really hopeless, it can work out. If you just give it . . ." Lauren didn't finish.

But she didn't need to. Annie knew what she meant, that you could never give up when a horrible nightmare involved someone you loved. You couldn't go home from that. You couldn't just take up your life. "Thank you," Annie said when she could speak. "I'm trying to find the dog." She picked up the list of area veterinarians she had made. "The one with blue eyes you described."

"Any luck?" Lauren asked, setting down her purse.

"I've gotten about a quarter of the way through. Some of the practices have blue-eyed dogs as patients, but so far, none of the owners are white-haired women."

"Want to tear the list in half?" Lauren pulled her cell phone from her purse. "We'll split the vets that are left, get through them in no time."

The surge of Annie's gratitude caught her off guard. She covered her face with her hands, and when she could, she looked up at Lauren. Their eyes locked and what passed between them was visceral, as physical as the warmest of handshakes, as tender as an embrace.

17

Her arm hung over the side of the mattress, fingertips dipping toward the floor. That's what wakened Lauren early on Thursday morning. The weight of her arm, throbbing and dead with sleep. Her head, too, hung over the bedside, and she pulled it back, along with her arm, curling into herself, turtle-like. Awareness rose, gritty and harsh. Dry. Her mouth was dry, her tongue a stone. And she hurt. Everywhere. As if she'd been battered. Was she dreaming? Ill? Tentatively, she straightened her knees, almost moaning with the effort.

Her feet—what was on her feet?

Her eyes hitched open. She sat up, heedless of how the room tilted, a ship in a rough sea, and flung away the bed linen, staring at her feet in some mix of alarm and dread and utter disbelief. Mud caked her toes; it clung to her bare soles, along with odd bits of leaves and grass. There was mud smeared on the sheets. And her shirt, the one she'd worn yesterday. She still had it on. Where were her jeans? Maneuvering carefully, she stood up, loosening a jolt of pain so raw, she almost cried out. Tears stung her eyes, and her hand fell to her hip, the one she'd smashed in her fall from the church bell tower. *What had she done to herself?*

She took a step, and the room swam in her vision, making her wobble. She groped for a handhold and found the nightstand's edge. She thought of calling for help, but then bit her lip. It was barely six according to the clock. Besides, she knew what any member of her family would think if they were to catch her in this sorry shape. But it wasn't true; it couldn't be true.

She hadn't taken Oxy.

Had she?

Reaching the bathroom, she flipped on the light, and when she saw them, the four tablets in the small plastic sleeve, sitting in plain view on the vanity, she whimpered, shutting her eyes against them. But they were still there when she looked again, mocking and ruthless. Accusatory.

She snatched up the packet, spilled the tabs across her palm, turned them over with the tip of her index finger. They were yellow 40s, the same as before, but this time she didn't remember anything about getting them. She didn't have so much as the vestige of a dream to go on. Closing her fist around them, she brought them to her chest, squeezing her eyes shut, trying to find her breath or sense—or the way to wake up now, please—and she jumped violently when Jeff said her name.

"Lauren?"

She peered at him, trying to read his expression, seeing clearly that he knew. "I—I'm so sorry. I don't know what happened." She looked away, fighting tears, an urge to fall to her knees. Possibly she would beg, if begging would make a difference. She would do whatever it took. The thoughts, her terror, tumbled hollowly through her mind. *My children* . . .

"What do you remember? The last thing."

His tone was neutral, not expressive of any emotion she could name. She wanted to answer him properly, and she thought hard, raising a jumble of impressions from yesterday: the detectives,

Willis and Cosgrove, seated in those ridiculous pink chairs in her unused living room, asking her questions about Bo Laughlin. Annie Beauchamp's eyes, aching with loss when she spoke of the car accident that had taken her mother . . . Madeleine Finch's idea to do a fund-raiser to collect money for a reward for information leading to Bo's whereabouts . . .

. . . her SUV that she had believed to her core was stolen, that had turned out not to be stolen after all.

Lauren groped her way to the Jacuzzi and sat on its wide edge.

"I came home with dinner, and you weren't here. The kids said they hadn't seen you, and you hadn't called. When I tried your cell, you didn't answer. I filled up your voice mail. You never responded. I thought about calling the cops, but I knew you wouldn't want that. It would only piss you off—after yesterday. I mean, you seemed pretty shook up that the detectives came to the house, you know? And then the way that sheriff was looking at you . . ."

Lauren glanced at Jeff. "What are you saying?"

"Nothing, really. It's kind of crazy, that's all. You being the last one to see that kid, Bo, then a couple of days later there's this mix-up with your car."

"The two things aren't related." Lauren heard how she sounded, indignant, offended. Was it how an innocent person would sound? Or a guilty one? She put her face in her hands.

"No, but I didn't think you'd want to draw more attention from law enforcement, right? If you'd still been gone this morning, I'd have had to contact them. I'm just glad it didn't come to that." Jeff's voice was so quiet, it was almost surreal.

Lauren was confused by it. "Why aren't you yelling at me? I would be if I were you."

"What good would it do?" he asked.

She shook her head.

"I must have dozed off, waiting for you, and when I woke up around two this morning and you still weren't home, I went outside and found you passed out in the yard. The sprinklers had kicked on. That's why you're muddy."

"Where did I say I'd been?"

"Houston, some bar near White Oak Bayou. You said some guys there hooked you up."

Lauren closed her eyes again, feeling sick. She knew the location. It was a dive, a dank hole in a graffiti-scratched brick wall. She'd been there a few times after Bettinger cut off her legal drug supply. One of the nurse's aides at rehab had told her about it when she showed up for a session, looking as rough as she felt. He'd taken pity on her and scribbled out an address that even she knew was located in one of the worst neighborhoods in Houston. Every time she went there, she took her life in her hands. Every time she swallowed the Oxy, she knew she could die.

She nearly had died once from an overdose. She would have if Kenzie hadn't come home from school and found her. In the front yard, facedown, barely breathing. Lauren knew from Jeff's account that Kenzie had been terrified. Still, she'd had the presence of mind to work through the steps, at first trying to rouse Lauren, and when that hadn't worked, she'd gone into the house and dialed 911. The operator there had called for an ambulance, then instructed Kenzie on what to do until help arrived.

"Roll your mom on her side," the operator said. "Tilt back her head and lift her chin to keep her airway clear."

It was unbearable to imagine a child, her own daughter, being put through such an ordeal. What kid gets coached, schooled in what to do if they find their mother passed out and drugged to the gills? Remembering now, Lauren bent over her knees, almost choking on the evil tar of self-loathing that rose into her throat. She would never outlive the guilt; she didn't deserve to, and here she

was, at it again. Swiftly, she went to the toilet, dropped the tablets—
plastic and all—into the bowl, and flushed them away.

When she came back, Jeff slid his hands under her elbows and
drew her into his embrace.

"I—I sort of remember going there, but I don't remember taking anything," she said. "A—a glass of wine—I drank a glass of
wine, or maybe two."

"You had a bit more than that, I think," Jeff said.

Lauren stepped out of his embrace. Finding a tissue, she blew
her nose. She seldom drank anymore. Since the accident, alcohol
affected her differently, and its impact on her was only intensified
if she was taking Oxy. In fact, she had been warned not to drink at
all when she was on it.

"I'm surprised you didn't call Gloria," Jeff said.

"I thought about it." Lauren shrugged. It had seemed pointless. Gloria would have insisted on meeting; she would have given
Lauren the speech about waiting through the next minute, and the
next, and the next, until the whole abomination of her terrible, gut-
ripping desire to lose herself passed. Yesterday, standing in the street,
holding her mother's scarf, the evidence of her deluded behavior in
her hands, Lauren hadn't believed that sobriety was anything she
could want, much less sustain. She didn't know if she believed in it
now. After almost a year attending 12-step meetings, she still didn't
know where to find that conviction, the way out of her bouts with
despair. "It was selfish," she said. "Selfish of me to put you and the
children through that. I'm so sorry." Her voice was rough with her
unfallen tears, but she had no right to let them go, no right to a
release of any kind.

"You shouldn't have been driving," Jeff said.

"No," she said, and she turned from him to lean on the sink's
edge while the awful question of what she might have done coiled

in her brain like a snake, tongue darting, ready to strike her down with any number of sordid revelations.

"The kids need to get up. They'll be late for school. Do you want me to take care of them?"

"No, I'll do it as soon as I take a shower. There's time." Lauren lifted her glance to the mirror and, wincing at her image, looked quickly away. "I'll make waffles. They'll be thrilled." BTA Lauren had made waffles. Maybe if she copied her, if she faked those motherly, nurturing things she had done often enough, the knack of being her would come back.

She looked again in the mirror and found Jeff's gaze there. He looked so worried, so undone. Turning to him, Lauren cupped his cheek. "Just let me get a shower. Then I'll make breakfast, okay? I just need to be with you and the kids."

He wasn't convinced.

"Look, you can hide the car keys at night if you want. I'll go to more meetings. I won't drink again, ever, because maybe that's all this is, a bad reaction to the wine." Even she knew better.

"Maybe you should talk to Dr. Bettinger."

"Yes." She brightened, feeling eager. "It's almost time for my checkup anyway."

Jeff said, "Okay then. If you're sure you don't need me, I have a couple of calls to make. We're starting preliminary work on the Waller-Land building."

"Today? Oh, of course, today. What am I saying?" Her smile felt foolish, wrong. "Go," she urged, brightly.

He held her gaze a moment and then left, and she leaned, stiff-armed, on the vanity. What if she'd had a wreck last night and killed someone? What if she'd gone home with one of the men she vaguely remembered drinking with? What if a neighbor or the children had seen her passed out on the lawn?

After her shower, she woke them, first, Kenzie, who was easily roused, and then Drew, who was not. Back in the kitchen, she started breakfast, layering bacon into a frying pan, turning on a low fire underneath it. But then, getting out her cell phone, she called Tara, needing her sister, the sound of her voice, her reassurance. "Can you have lunch later?" Lauren asked when Tara answered. "I'll meet you at that tearoom near your office. What's the name of it?"

"I can't." Tara declined so quickly that Lauren was taken aback.

"What's wrong?" she asked, but then, remembering Greg, she thought she knew, and she waited to hear that Tara had found out he was gone or back on heroin or both.

Instead, Tara said she wasn't at the office but home in bed, still not feeling good. "It's some nasty intestinal bug."

She was lying, Lauren thought. It was Greg that ailed her. Tara just didn't want to admit it, that she'd lost another man, another relationship.

"I could bring you some 7UP." Lauren named the soft drink their mother had given them to settle their stomachs when they were kids.

"That's sweet of you, but I don't want you catching this."

"Okay," Lauren said, "but you can talk to me, you know."

There was a beat of silence, and Lauren got the sense that Tara was fighting not to cry. "I'm okay," she said, but her voice was strained. "I will be, I guess."

"Has he called?"

"Who?"

"Greg," Lauren said. "Have you talked to him?"

"Have you?"

"Not lately." Lauren paused. "There'll be other guys, you know."

"Oh, Lauren, if only that could fix it." Her voice hitched.

Lauren felt her own tears rise. "It'll be okay, TeeRee—"

"Has he been at meetings? Greg, I mean?"

Lauren said she hadn't gone to any meetings this week, and she was explaining about Bo, that she was helping in the search for him when Tara broke in.

"I can't talk about this now."

"About what?"

"Greg. I don't want to talk about Greg."

Lauren was nonplussed. "Okay," she said.

"Why did you want to have lunch, anyway? What's wrong?"

Lauren thought about saying it was nothing; she thought about saying the everything that it was. But suddenly, she had as little desire to talk about last night as Tara did to talk about Greg. Her antics, her backsliding were only symptoms of the real trouble anyway. "I don't trust, TeeRee. I have no faith in people. You, Jeff. I'm going to drive everyone who loves me away if I don't stop feeling like this, doubting everyone, being suspicious of them."

"People don't like their love and loyalty questioned. They don't like to be—" Tara interrupted herself. "Whatever it is you think Jeff is planning—divorcing you, taking the children—it's just not true. It's nuts for you to think either of us would do that."

"You did say—"

"Yes, but that was when you were still using, and you've stopped now."

"My mind isn't the same, though. I don't feel like me, the me I used to be. I'm scared—and lately, I feel so crazy. Crazier, I guess."

"Have you called Bettinger?"

"I'm going to."

"Maybe you need a shrink instead. I don't mean that in a bad way—"

"I know. Oh, God, the bacon's burning. I've got to go!" It was true. Lauren dropped her phone on the counter and shut off the gas flame under the frying pan. *How did it happen?* a punishing voice in her brain wanted to know. *You were standing right here*, it said.

It was the last of it, the last of the bacon. There wasn't any more, and she set about salvaging the burned batch, prying the charred centers of the strips from the bottom of the pan, then carefully pressing the curled ends into the still-hot drippings to brown. Grim now, focused on simply serving her children their breakfast, she whipped up the waffle batter. It was a sudden longing for something lovely that sent her outside to collect a few roses from the heavenly scented antique shrub, Souvenir de la Malmaison, that bloomed near the back door. The thorn that pricked the tender webbing of flesh between her thumb and the base of her index finger drew blood and a renewed threat of tears that disgusted her. She had put the flowers into a small vase and set it on the kitchen island, and she was dishing up the waffles and overdone bacon, when Kenzie and Drew slid onto their stools. They exchanged a glance, one that said louder than words, *What's up with her?*

Before the accident, Drew would have smarted off about the bacon; Kenzie would have turned up her pert nose and said she wasn't having any. But these days, they never said such things. They never gave a moment's trouble, and Lauren deplored it—how nice they were, how careful of her feelings. She'd heard Jeff admonish them: Don't talk back to Mom. Don't fight with each other. Don't yell in the house, slam the door, run the stairs. *Don't, don't, don't.* Ever since she'd come home from rehab, the family walked on eggshells.

She wanted her regular, mouthy kids back, the ones who could be brats, who could shove and sass each other, who could argue and laugh and shout uproariously. She wanted the loud clatter of their feet on the wood floors, their incessant nattering and arguing.

"I heated the syrup, so be careful," she said.

"Where's Dad?" Drew cut a huge bite of waffle, poking it into his mouth.

"On the phone." Lauren brought her mug of coffee to the island and sat down across from her children.

"Mommy, are you okay?"

Lauren could have cried on seeing the gravity of her daughter's expression. The worry etched onto her sweet brow belonged to someone older, a person with a world of trouble on her shoulders, not an eleven-year-old child. "I'm fine, honey," she said, and it was an effort to lift her voice and the vestige of a smile above the well of sorrow that felt permanently wedged under the floor of her heart. No matter how clean and sober she got, the past was there. She'd never be able to undo it.

"You don't look fine," Kenzie said.

"You've got that mug in a death grip," Drew pointed out.

Lauren loosened her grasp, feeling the blood flow into her cramped fingers. She settled her breath. Still, she jumped at the squeal of brakes that announced the school bus.

Kenzie scrambled off her stool, grabbing her backpack.

"Don't forget your lunch." Lauren retrieved a small pink nylon tote she'd packed earlier with yogurt, a banana, and Wheat Thins— Kenzie was already conscious of her weight—from the kitchen counter and handed it to her.

"You're picking us up after school, right? Me and Amanda? We have ballet, and it's your turn to drive."

"I'll be there," Lauren promised.

"You won't forget?"

"Three twenty, right?" Lauren smoothed Kenzie's brow.

She nodded, but her gaze was somber and riddled with apprehension.

Lauren reached for her, hoping to reassure her, but just then Drew called to her from outside, and she wheeled from Lauren's grasp, bolting through the back door and running down the driveway, Lauren following in her wake.

When Kenzie reached the bus door, she paused and looked back, and Lauren smiled and waved, the way she always did. Maybe her smile felt more adamant and her wave foolishly large and of longer duration, but never mind. The important thing was that she was there for Drew and Kenzie—for all the neighborhood—to see she was a sober and responsible parent. And no matter what else happened today, she would be at the school this afternoon, front and center, first car in the line.

She was rinsing the syrup from the breakfast plates when Jeff came into the kitchen, carrying his briefcase. "There are waffles left-over," she said. "I can heat one up for you."

"I wish, but no time. Can I have a rain check?"

"Maybe." She was glad for his easy manner. "I put the Waller-Land folder in your briefcase."

"I saw it, thanks," he said. "I damn sure don't need an inspector on my ass today. Kaiser's nervous enough as it is."

"He didn't seem nervous to me."

"Well, I guess you haven't seen him since we found the asbestos."

"Asbestos?" Lauren hadn't remembered the inspector finding asbestos in the building. She hated for Jeff to work around it.

"Yeah. I had to tell him you can't just shovel that shit into a landfill, you know? He wasn't too happy."

"I thought it was marginal—" Lauren was guessing, pretending she knew. It wasn't necessary. Jeff was on to the kids.

"You're picking Kenzie and Amanda up for ballet, right?" He shrugged into his jacket.

"I told her I was." Affront rode in Lauren's voice. She couldn't help it.

"Hey," Jeff said, "don't shoot the messenger. She asked me, okay? She's worried. You know."

Lauren looked down at the towel, fighting the thrust of her resentment. It was as if she was the child and Kenzie the mother.

"Do you want to ride with me?" Jeff asked. "I'll wait."

She looked at him. "I don't need a babysitter."

"I didn't mean—"

She cut him off. "I'm going into town first anyway. I want to see how Annie's doing, if she's had any news."

"No! Lauren, for God's sake. You were there all day yesterday. You made yourself—"

Crazy. She wondered why he didn't say it.

"That isn't why I went off the deep end—" Lauren clamped her jaw. She didn't want to talk about the mix-up with the car. She didn't want to even think about it. "I'll be at work as quickly as I can, Jeff. I promise."

"The search effort's being shut down."

"But the police are still looking. Annie, other people—no one's giving up."

"Don't do this, okay?" he said. "Don't get yourself involved in this other family's business any further." He waited, and when she didn't respond, he brushed by her without another word or the rote kiss.

Lauren readied herself in anticipation of hearing the door slam, but he closed it behind him so gently she heard almost nothing at all, and it seemed all the more ominous that he should be so upset with her and yet make so little noise in leaving her.

She turned to stare at it, wondering what he might do, what he could be planning.

After a moment, she pulled her cell phone from her purse, dialed Tara's number, and walked to the window, twitching the curtain to one side, watching Jeff back his truck down the driveway while Tara's phone rang four times, five, then six before rolling to voice mail.

Tara had probably turned off her phone and was sleeping, Lauren thought.

"If you'd like to leave a message . . ." the canned voice said.

"I don't know what to do," she said in response. "I'm scared," she told the waiting silence, and she listened for a moment to the blood in her ears, the ticking of her pulse.

"Where are you?" she whispered.

18

They'd been calling veterinarians for close to a half hour on Thursday morning when Annie caught the lilt of what sounded like cautious excitement in Lauren's voice. Their eyes connected. Lauren held up a finger even as she continued speaking. "Yes, that sounds like the woman we're looking for," she said, then, "Would it be possible for you to give me her name and phone number?"

The reply caused Lauren to frown. Annie held her breath.

"I understand your policy of not handing out personal information, but in this case, I wonder if you can make an exception. The young man who's missing was seen getting into her car."

Pause.

"Yes, actually I am with the police. I suppose we could get a court order." Lauren shrugged at Annie, making a face that seemed to say *Whatever it takes*.

Annie smiled, mouthing, *Yes!*

And when Lauren wheeled her chair around, picked up a pen and began writing, Annie went to look over her shoulder, watching as Lauren wrote down a name: Charlotte Meany and an address, and next to that she wrote a number, seventy-eight. Charlotte

Meany's age? Annie was guessing. *Meany*, she thought, looking at the *M. Ms. M.*

Lauren added another number, a phone number this time, and finding Annie's gaze again, she grinned, thanking her contact profusely. Annie nearly laughed out loud, hearing Lauren use the words *civic duty* and *helpfulness in an ongoing police investigation.*

"I'll probably be arrested," she said, ending the call, "but we got it!" She held her note out to Annie.

"You really think it's her?" Annie studied the details.

"Janie, the girl I spoke to, knows the lady and her dog. They're neighbors, if you can believe the luck. Charlotte lives about a half mile down the road from her, and her dog's named Blue Sky. She even knows who Bo is. She's seen him with Charlotte a few times."

"Are you kidding?"

Lauren said she wasn't, and when she pointed out that Meany started with the initial *M*, the same initial Bo included in his last-known text message, Annie said, "It could be a coincidence."

"Maybe, but we won't know until we talk to her." Lauren took her car keys from her purse and pulled it onto her shoulder. "Shall we go?"

"Now?" Annie was unsure, not about going to see Charlotte Meany but about going with Lauren. Who wasn't her mother no matter how much she reminded Annie of her mother. Who wasn't anyone Annie knew at all. Who only hours ago had seemed very unstable.

"Something tells me we're better off not to give her any warning."

Annie didn't say anything.

"You aren't thinking we should tell the police, are you? They never took this lead seriously before, why would they now?"

"Let me tell Madeleine and Carol where we're going." Maybe it was stupid to go along with Lauren, but the lead she'd found was all Annie had.

. . .

Cedar Cliff was northeast of Hardys Walk and small at less than half the size, and while the interstate bisected the heart of Hardys Walk, Cedar Cliff was miles from the highway, tucked into a pocket of the piney woods like a half-forgotten souvenir.

"We could be in the middle of nowhere," Annie said after they'd gone several miles in silence down a narrow, gravel-edged ranch road. Bare-branched trees overhead cast bony shadows that danced like throngs of skeletons on the pavement. The effect was eerie, isolating.

Lauren said if Annie thought this was nowhere, she ought to see the farm.

"You have a farm?" Annie asked.

"My sister and I inherited it from our grandparents. It's not far from here, actually, but talk about the boonies. It makes Cedar Cliff look like Houston. Well, not quite." She smiled. "We're trying to clear the place out now so we can sell it. It's so remote, not much to do." She paused, then added, "We'll miss it. At least I will. Tara, too."

They drove another few miles before Annie mentioned Bo, that he might have gone to California to see his mother.

Lauren glanced at Annie in consternation. "That's so far. What makes you think he would attempt a trip like that?"

Annie told Lauren what she'd found out, beginning with the phone message from Constance McMurray and her revelation that Bo's mother was alive. "Even my own mother knew, and it's hard for me to believe because I thought we told each other everything."

"She might have been trying to protect you and Bo."

"That's what JT said, but having things out in the open, in the light of day—telling the truth, no matter how hard it is—" Annie broke off, picking at her thumbnail, feeling some combination of hurt and confusion along with the warmth of Lauren's concern, her presence—that seemed so normal and ordinary. So motherly. "It's what my mom preached," Annie said, "but I guess it's not what she lived by. She didn't walk her talk."

Lauren didn't respond for so long that Annie thought she wouldn't, but then she said, "It's easy to say the words, to say what you should or shouldn't do, or the way you should be or not . . ."

It sounded as if Lauren was speaking in more than generalities. "JT said they went back and forth." Annie offered this in the face of her silence.

"Well, it's difficult when a parent is unstable, especially if drugs are involved."

Something sharp and raw in Lauren's tone drew Annie's glance, raised the rate of her pulse.

The canned voice of the GPS announced the need for a left turn, and Lauren did as instructed even as she said, "Can this be right?"

They bumped along a rutted single lane that was more serpentine path through a heavy mixed growth of oaks, towering pines, sweet gums, the occasional oak or redbud, and bright-berried yaupons. Annie was glad they weren't in her old BMW.

Lauren said, "Let's hope Charlotte Meany isn't waiting for us with a shotgun."

Annie's laugh was strained. It was Texas after all, where folks had strong ideas about their right to bear arms, especially in the boonies. They'd shoot their gun at somebody for no more reason than the look in their eye. They'd shoot their gun to celebrate good news or just because they felt like it, and sometimes that thoughtless shooting killed somebody.

The house came into view, a small white bungalow with a deep, columned porch across the front. It looked old but well maintained.

"That's the car I saw Bo getting into," Lauren said. "I remember the license plate."

Annie looked at the carport, at the black Lincoln parked there. The specialty tag was adorned with a spray of bluebonnets, the Texas state flower. She traded a glance with Lauren, excitement and trepidation brimming in the air between them.

It was her, the woman Lauren had seen. Annie knew it the instant Charlotte Meany opened the front door in answer to Lauren's knock. Not because of the older woman's white, white hair that was swept into the exact French twist Lauren had described nor even because of the blue-eyed dog that stood beside her, a tail-wagging but otherwise quiet companion. No. Annie knew this was the woman because of the sharp intake of Lauren's breath.

"May I help you?" the woman asked.

"Yes, I think you certainly may," Lauren said. "You're Charlotte Meany, is that right?"

The woman gave a tentative nod, as if she wasn't sure of her identity, or maybe she wasn't sure she wanted to own it. In fact, she looked bewildered, even a little frightened, but Annie only registered these details subliminally.

"You know my brother, Bo Laughlin, don't you." Annie wasn't asking. "You know he's disappeared, that the police are looking for him."

"You aren't friends of my daughter's?" Charlotte looked from Annie to Lauren. "She didn't send you?"

Lauren said no. "We came to ask you about Bo."

"You'd better come in, then," Charlotte Meany said, and she was grave, very grave, in a way that made Annie's heart slide hard against her ribs.

Charlotte opened the screen door.

The dog stepped out.

"Hey," Lauren said, smiling down at him.

"This is Blue Sky," Charlotte said. "Sky for short. Go on, boy, it's all right," she told him, and they watched him go down the steps, out into the yard. Annie thought how she would like to follow him; she thought how much Bo would have liked him.

She and Lauren followed Charlotte into a small front room that was cluttered with furniture: a silk-upholstered love seat was pushed against one wall, and an assortment of chairs was clustered around a low table of some vintage style Annie couldn't name. But she thought the chairs were French. There were so many that she decided, as she picked her way among them, Charlotte must collect them. All of them were old; some had arms and some didn't, but all were gracefully made, with turned legs and touches of gilt paint gone chippy with age. Most were cushioned in needlepoint bouquets of faded flowers. It wasn't a look Annie would have for herself, but she could admire it. She sat gingerly on the edge of the love seat.

"I was just going to make myself a cup of tea," Charlotte said. "Would you like some?"

"Where is my brother?" Annie said. "What have you done with him?"

"What? Nothing. I've done nothing with him." Charlotte looked alarmed; she darted a glance at Lauren.

"I think a cup of tea would be lovely," Lauren said soothingly, keeping her glance on Charlotte. "If it's no trouble. It was a bit of a drive up here from Hardys Walk. I was just telling Annie on our way that my grandparents' farm isn't far."

"Oh?" Charlotte answered. "Whereabouts is it?"

Annie understood what Lauren was doing, making small talk, but she longed to run through this house, to throw her glance against every wall, fling open every closet door.

"I'll just be a minute." Charlotte left through an arched doorway that Annie assumed led to the kitchen. "Make yourselves at home," she called over her shoulder.

Lauren settled between the gilt arms of one of the small parlor chairs and looked meaningfully at Annie, commanding her attention, her silence. They could hear Charlotte moving around, the soft clink of cutlery and china, a brief shriek from the kettle before it was lifted from the burner. Now there was the gurgle of water as it was poured into a teapot.

When Charlotte reappeared in the doorway, Lauren rose quickly to retrieve the tray she carried.

"If you'll just set it there." Charlotte indicated the low table in front of Annie's knees.

Lauren did as she asked. "Would you like me to pour?"

"No, dear. I can do it." Charlotte settled into another of the gilt-armed chairs, one that was adjacent to Lauren's. "I'm old, not helpless nor hapless. Not that you mean to imply that," she added, cutting off Lauren's protest.

There was a suggestion of apology in Charlotte's tone of voice, but Annie caught a bitter note, too, as if Charlotte had been regularly saddled with those very labels and had grown tired of it.

"It's almost too beautiful to touch." Lauren was looking at the tray.

Feasting her eyes, Annie thought. It was a beautiful presentation, laden with delicate cups and saucers, a sugar bowl and creamer, and what Annie thought was a pink Depression-glass plate arrayed with perhaps a dozen crisp-edged cookies. There were even cloth napkins, tiny embroidered squares edged in a fine webbing of lace.

Lauren was clearly enchanted by the sight. From the look of her, she was as filled with delight as any child at a party, and in that moment, Annie, unreasonably, ridiculously, almost hated her.

Charlotte thanked Lauren, and they went on like two old hens at a gabfest, talking about china, German, Bavarian, French, oohing and aahing over its artistry, and when they got around to discussing the beauty and intricacy of table linen, Lauren unfolded her napkin and examined it as if it were a freshly unearthed and exceedingly fragile treasure.

"Have a cookie, dear." Charlotte Meany held out the plate for Annie.

"Where is my brother?" she asked, and this time, she minded her tone, keeping it soft.

Lauren set down her cup. "I did see you with Bo last Friday, I believe," she said gently to Charlotte. "Am I right? Wasn't it you I saw driving the car he got into, the one parked under the carport outside?"

Charlotte closed her eyes, briefly revealing lids that were shaded in pale lavender and as lined and translucent as worn tissue. She set down her cup with a sigh. "I know I should have called the police, but in my defense, I really don't know anything helpful."

"My brother was in your car. You took him somewhere, and you didn't think you should tell the police?" Panic made Annie sound disbelieving and harsh. "Where is he? What did you do to him?"

"Where did you take him?" Lauren asked, and by contrast, her tone was calm and deliberately kind, and Annie knew the reason why, yet it only further provoked her. An urge to scream at both women seared her brain, and she clenched her teeth against it.

You can snare more bees with honey than you can with vinegar. Annie's mother's voice drifted through her brain.

"We bought sandwiches and went to Hermann Park and had a picnic. Afterward, we walked Sky around and then went to the library."

"In Houston?"

"Yes. As long as it's not too hot or too cold, Sky doesn't mind staying in the car. Bo loves going down there to that library. There are so many books, and he likes to count them. He likes to ride the elevator, too. Sometimes we find a quiet corner and read aloud to each other—poetry, mostly."

Annie listened to Charlotte in amazement. "He texted me he was there with you. He called you Ms. M."

"There aren't many young folks who are as respectful as Bo," Charlotte said.

"Afterward, where did you go?" Lauren asked.

"We came here. I brought him here." Charlotte looked only at Lauren, almost as if the sight of Annie caused her pain, and she seemed afraid now, more than she had before. "It's our usual routine. One Friday a month, I pick him up in Hardys Walk, at the little store. We go to the library afterward, usually there in Hardys Walk. Then we have lunch and come here."

"Really." Lauren spoke conversationally, stirring her tea.

"Bo loves Henry David Thoreau, but I imagine you know that." Charlotte glanced now at Annie and away. "I love Thoreau, too. Bo can quote whole passages."

"You said you brought him here last Friday? And then what did you do?" Lauren lifted her cup as if there were all the time in the world to wait for Charlotte's answer.

When there wasn't. When as far as Annie was concerned they were out of time. "How long have you known him? How long has this been going on, that you pick him up and take him places? Why do you? What is he to you?" The questions shot off her tongue, sounding like accusations, making Charlotte blink.

Making her head wobble on her neck.

On a level deeper than emotion, Annie knew she was wrong to attack Charlotte; she knew the old woman felt threatened and confused by her, and she regretted it, but there wasn't time for regret, either. "Please, please, tell me what you know."

Charlotte poked at her hair, her fingers trembling over the cusp of her ear, then to the tortoiseshell comb that fastened her French twist. "We met at the library there in Hardys Walk a few months ago and got to talking. I asked him what he did for a living, and he said he didn't do much, that he wanted to work, but not very many people would hire him. When I asked why, he said it was because they thought he was crazy, a—a psycho. That was the word he used. It broke my heart, that sweet boy—"

"I can imagine," Lauren said, and she sat easily with the ensuing pause.

Somehow Annie managed to keep still, too, gripping her elbows in her opposite fists, thinking of people's cruelty, how it hurt Bo, in ways most people couldn't imagine and didn't care about. Only Madeleine had ever taken a chance and offered him a real job.

"I was so upset for him, and once I got home, all I could think about was how I could help him, and I decided I would ask him to work for me, doing little jobs, like weeding the flower gardens and such." Charlotte stopped; she fiddled with her napkin. "I understand how he feels. It isn't the same, but when you get old, people haven't any patience or compassion if you're forgetful or if you get confused or repeat yourself. Even one's own family . . ." She trailed off. "I'm sorry. What was I saying?"

"That you brought Bo here last Friday," Lauren reminded her softly.

"I paid him." Charlotte sounded almost defensive. "Ten dollars an hour. He was worth every penny, too. He's a hard worker, a bit skittish maybe, but he always gets the job done, and he was regular. As regular as rain in April."

"What work did you have for him?"

The look Lauren shot Annie belied her conversational tone. She was wound as tightly as Annie. She just wasn't letting Charlotte see it.

"He was going to replace a board on the porch that's rotting. My daughter says I'm clumsy enough without—But you don't want to hear about her." Charlotte grimaced as if she didn't want to hear about her daughter, either. "Anyway, last Friday, Bo was different. He was fine at first, at the library talking and laughing like always, but after he gathered all the tools and the lumber he needed to do the work, something changed. He couldn't settle. He kept pacing. He kept saying he needed to go to the bus station, that he needed to get to California. He wanted me to take him. To the bus, I mean. He said his mother was ill and—"

"Did you? Did you take him to the bus station?" Annie bent forward.

"No, dear. That's just the thing. I said I would. Of course, I wanted to help. I told him to wait by the car, I would get my keys, but when I went outside, he was gone. I called and called for him. I even walked to the end of the drive. It's such a long way. Well, you know. You drove up here. I was so worn out, I nearly couldn't make it back."

"You don't know where he went?" Lauren asked.

"Maybe the highway? Maybe I was too slow, and he thought he could catch a ride there. But you know how he is, he walks everywhere, just like Thoreau. It's admirable, really."

"By now, he could be anywhere, with anyone." Annie pulled her cell phone from her purse. "I'll call Sheriff Audi and tell him Bo was here. I don't think any of the search teams came this far north."

"But shouldn't we alert the local police?" Lauren asked. "Someone around here might have seen Bo and reported it."

Annie looked at her. "We could take them a flyer. Maybe put some up in town. I have a few with me."

"I know the sheriff in town. His name is—it's—" Charlotte frowned a moment and then brushed the air with her hands as if it were of no consequence that she couldn't remember. She stood up, saying she had his card somewhere, that he came to see her sometimes, and something about her daughter. "They're good friends. I think she's asked him to keep an eye on me. It's ridiculous, of course. I manage perfectly well on my own."

The sense of Charlotte's injury lingered in the air even after she left the room.

"His name is Caleb Neely," she said when she returned. She handed a business card to Lauren. "I would have called him myself if I had known Bo was missing, but I almost never watch television."

Lauren thanked her.

Charlotte saw them out.

Sky was lying on the front porch, and when he saw them, he got up and followed Lauren down the steps.

Annie turned to Charlotte. "I'm sorry I was rude."

"I'm sorry I didn't tell the police right away," Charlotte said.

"Was Bo all right when you saw him on Friday? Was he acting normally? Or as normal as he gets?"

"He was himself, dear. Sweet and kind, if a bit agitated." Charlotte studied Annie's face. "I consider Bo my friend, you know? We're not so different, he and I. My mind slips because I'm old, and he's—well, sometimes his connections—" Charlotte's voice caught, and she put her hand to her throat. "He's very kind to me," she added. "He's just a lovely young man."

Annie's throat closed; her heart softened, and when Charlotte, seeing this evidence of understanding, of commiseration, reached out a hand, Annie felt the tremor of her fingertips on her wrist, as delicate as the dance of a sparrow's foot. She thought how much Charlotte was like Madeleine in her care of Bo.

"You'll let me know when you find him, that he's safe?" Charlotte asked.

"Yes," Annie said, and she would have turned away, but something came into Charlotte's gaze, a clarity and a certainty that Annie hadn't seen before, and it kept her in place.

"You will find him," Charlotte said. "I'm convinced of it. I don't often let on to strangers, but it's true I have a sense about such things. I've had it ever since I was yay high." She flattened her palm at a height near her hip.

Alive? Is he alive? Annie wanted to ask, but she wouldn't. She wasn't sure she believed in what Charlotte was suggesting, and in any case, she didn't think she could bear to know Charlotte's answer.

"There's something else," Charlotte called after them.

They turned.

"He was carrying cash. A good deal of it in a rubber band. He showed it to me."

"Did he say, or do you know, how much it was?" Annie asked.

"He counted it at my kitchen table; he had two one-hundred-dollar bills, five twenties, a ten and three ones. And some change."

"Did he say where he got it?" Annie shaded her eyes.

"He'd done some work for a man. He didn't give a name."

Annie's heart sank.

"It's bad news, Bo having that much money?" Lauren nosed the SUV down the drive.

"His dad and I—the police, everyone seems to think Bo is involved with drugs." Annie pushed her hands over her face, over her ears. She blew out a mouthful of air. "I just don't want to believe it, but if he had over three hundred dollars—I don't know how else he'd get that much money." She looked at Lauren. "I haven't ever bought a bus ticket, but I bet he has enough to get to California."

"Yes, probably," Lauren answered, but she seemed abruptly distracted, upset. Annie was on the verge of asking if she was all right when she said, "After my accident, while I was in physical therapy and still in a lot of pain, I—somehow I became dependent on my pain medication. I—my problem was bad enough that I got the drug—OxyContin, illegally. I'm off it now and in 12-step, nearly a year—" Lauren stopped.

"I'm not sure why you're telling me this." Annie said the only thing she could think of.

"Because the detectives, Willis especially, seem to think I bought Oxy from Bo last Friday." Lauren glanced at Annie. "They didn't tell you?"

"I've only spoken to Detective Cosgrove." Annie shifted her gaze, not wanting Lauren to see her consternation and assume Annie was judging her. She wasn't. She was remembering yesterday, that when Lauren came back to the center with Jeff to report her car stolen, Sheriff Audi had made a real point of establishing that she was alone the weekend of Bo's disappearance. He'd inferred Lauren could have been anywhere, doing anything. Annie didn't want to see the correlation now between that and Lauren's admission to having a drug habit, but it was impossible not to. "Did you buy drugs from Bo?"

"No!" Lauren was offended. "He wasn't on anything, either. At least when I saw him, he was clear-eyed and articulate. He was fine. Fine," she insisted.

Annie stared out at the roadside scruff. She couldn't decide if Lauren was defending Bo or excusing him. Maybe she was lying for him. Didn't people on drugs stick together? A sense of foreboding filled her. She regretted having accepted Lauren's help, and yet without it, would she have found Charlotte? And if she had, could she have managed to get the information Lauren had?

Annie looked at Lauren. "I'm not very good with pain, either," she said, and it was the closest she could come to saying she understood.

· · ·

The heart of Cedar Cliff was small enough that it could be taken in with the sweep of one glance. The dozen or so storefronts arranged around the town square were mostly shuttered and wore a sour look, like a group of old men dressed in moth-eaten suits who complained of their backs and the loss of bygone days. Lauren parked in front of the old bank building where Charlotte had said they would find the sheriff's office, and she held the door for Annie. Once inside, they paused, blinking in the sudden gloom.

Dust, unsettled by their entry, spun idly in the tarnished, late-afternoon light.

"Can I help?"

Annie peered in the direction of the woman's voice and picked out her silhouette from the shadows in the corner, where she sat at a desk behind an old-fashioned railing. "Maybe we aren't in the right place." She suddenly had doubts, not that she knew what a sheriff's office should look like, but this place was so deserted and quiet, and the woman who addressed them was reading a book, of all things—as if there were nothing pressing or urgent or criminal that required her attention.

Annie explained who she was, that Bo Laughlin was her brother and they had information for the sheriff.

The woman came to life. "I've heard about him on the news. I'm so sorry. Oh my goodness—" She was flustered now, shutting the book without marking her place. "Caleb?"

A man in a uniform, obviously Caleb Neely, the sheriff Charlotte had said they should speak to, came to the doorway. Annie had expected someone older, a man Sheriff Audi's age. Sheriff Neely didn't appear to be much older than Annie.

In a matter of minutes, introductions were made, and once Annie explained why she was there, she and Lauren were seated in the sheriff's office.

He sat down, too, and when he asked why she thought Bo was in the area, Annie explained about finding Charlotte and what they'd learned about Charlotte's connection to Bo.

"So," the sheriff said when Annie paused, "he does odd jobs for Charlotte, but how did they meet? It seems odd, them knowing each other."

Annie explained that, too, with increasing frustration. "Look, Sheriff, he was upset about his mother when he left Charlotte's house; he might have gotten disoriented. He could be lost. He could have hurt himself. Anything might have happened."

"Well, more likely, he caught a ride—"

"No. Bo wouldn't get into a car with a stranger." Annie repeated what she'd known all along. Charlotte Meany, as it turned out, was no stranger to Bo.

"Maybe not under ordinary circumstances," the sheriff agreed, "but according to you, he was desperate to see his mama."

"He had a lot of cash, Sheriff." Lauren spoke for the first time. "I saw it myself, and Charlotte confirmed it was over three hundred dollars. Someone could have robbed him."

Sheriff Neely didn't answer. Annie heard the shift of his feet under his desk, and the sound suggested impatience to her. She got the sense that the sheriff wished her gone, as gone as Bo. Her jaw tightened. "You have to do something, Sheriff Neely, get people together to look for him."

He sighed, audibly, wearily. "I'd like to help," he fixed Annie with a regretful gaze, "but we're a small department with limited resources. There are four officers total, including me, and two of the guys are part-timers. And don't even get me started about the budgetary constraints."

"I didn't come here to talk about your budget," Annie said, and she would have said more that was heated and angry, but the sheriff cut her off, saying sharply that he knew Charlotte Meany and she wasn't reliable. "You can't trust what she told you."

"Are you saying she's a liar?" Lauren asked.

She sounded incensed, as if the sheriff had accused her of being untrustworthy. She probably got that a lot herself, Annie thought. They were all three alike in that respect, Bo and Charlotte and Lauren. No one put much stock in anything they said.

"No, I'm saying she's elderly, and like a lot of folks her age, she has trouble with her memory." The sheriff touched his temple. "Her daughter, Diane, wants her to sell the house and go into an assisted living facility. She's afraid Charlotte's going to injure herself. She for sure shouldn't be driving anymore. The state took her license over a year ago."

"No, Sheriff, here's what's for sure." Annie bent forward. "She drove my brother from Hardys Walk to her house almost a week ago, and he hasn't been seen since. That's what's for sure."

The sheriff's mouth flattened.

Annie brought her palm down on the desktop. "You can't just dismiss—"

"Wait." Lauren cut in, holding Annie's gaze for a single reassuring moment before addressing the sheriff. "It's true Bo could have found a ride with someone, but that someone might live here in Cedar Cliff. They could have information about where they took him, what shape he was in, what he might have talked about. It could help find him."

"They would have come forward by now," Sheriff Neely said.

"Charlotte didn't," Lauren countered.

The sheriff looked reluctant, as if he didn't want to see the logic in what Lauren was saying. He looked as if he was too tired to move, and it infuriated Annie.

"Don't you even care?" she demanded. The ensuing pause rang with her indignation. She could hear the heave of her breath. Even her heartbeat was loud in her ears.

"Is that your wife and baby?" Lauren asked.

Small talk? Annie stared at Lauren. She was making small talk again? In some disbelief, Annie followed Lauren's gaze to the credenza behind the sheriff's desk, where a framed photograph showed a woman sitting in what was clearly a hospital bed, holding a newborn. The woman's mouth was curled into an exhausted yet triumphant smile.

"Yeah," the sheriff answered. "That's the last time he slept, I think. It was taken a month ago," he added.

"Your first?" Lauren asked.

He nodded. "I wasn't prepared. I mean, everyone says how they're up day and night, but my God, I don't think he's slept more than ten minutes since we got him home. My wife spends all her time worried sick there's something terrible the matter with him."

"It gets easier. In another month or so, you'll be wondering how you could have ever imagined your life was full before your son was born."

"I hope you're right."

"I hope you'll consider putting together a search effort for Bo," Lauren said smoothly. "He's Annie's brother but also somebody's son. As a father yourself, you can imagine how it would feel if your son were to disappear without a trace."

Annie held her breath.

The sheriff took his time before saying, "All right," grudgingly.

Annie wanted to whoop. She glanced at Lauren, who was serene. Who looked as if nothing ever ruffled her composure or ever had. And somehow now, Annie doubted the scene she'd witnessed last night, Lauren down on her knees, plowing through the contents of her purse, shaking and distressed. That woman and this one couldn't be the same.

"We've brought flyers with Bo's photograph on them," Lauren said.

Annie extracted one from the folder on her lap and pushed it across the desk.

The sheriff picked it up, studying it. He switched his glance to hers. "I doubt he's still in the area, if he was ever here, but I'll see if we can get some folks together to have a look around. We'll start at Charlotte's place, either side of the highway there." He indicated the flyer. "Can I keep this? Do you have extras you can spare?"

Annie handed him half of what she'd brought.

"You want to post them around town, go ahead. Talk to people, if you want to, and let me know if you hear anything."

"Thank you," Annie said.

He stood up.

Annie and Lauren did, too.

"Leave your contact information with Darlene," the sheriff said. "She'll need it for her report."

Lauren's cell phone rang, and she took it from her purse. "I need to get this," she said. "Will you excuse me?"

Once she'd left, Annie addressed the sheriff. "Maybe you should question Charlotte Meany yourself."

"Yeah, I intend to talk to her, but what're you saying? She give you some reason to believe she wasn't being truthful?"

Annie hesitated. "When I said anything might have happened—" she began and stopped.

"Go on," the sheriff said.

"Suppose Bo was injured doing something at her house?" Annie was unsure how to go on. The implications were enormous. But it plagued her, the idea that he might have been hurt working for Charlotte, and because she was old, probably senile and frightened, she'd covered it up. It seemed outlandish, but so were a lot of things in life.

"I'll talk to her." The sheriff seemed to catch the gist of Annie's concern.

She thanked him as if she believed him, but she knew what he was thinking: that mounting a search for Bo this far north of Hardys Walk, nearly a week after the last sighting of him, was crazy. As crazy as Annie herself or Charlotte Meany. Or maybe he was thinking of his crying baby or his budget constraints. She stopped by Darlene's desk and gave her the information for her report, because beneath the weight of doubt, Annie harbored a glimmer of hope that something might come of it.

"If you give me a flyer," Darlene said, "I'll make copies. I can get some folks together to help get them up."

Annie thanked her, too, and while her gratitude was immense and heartfelt, it was burdened with resentment at her helplessness, at her overwhelming need, at the yawning and still-growing debt she owed to virtual strangers. *Sometimes it's harder to receive a gift than it is to give one.* Her mother had said that. Her mother had said some debts couldn't be paid back, only forward.

Darlene said, "You and your brother are in my prayers."

"Thank you." Annie said it again, and she tried not to mind the intensity of Darlene's gaze, how filled with longing it was for every last detail, the more personal in nature, the better. People craved tragedy, Annie thought, as long as it wasn't their own. They were like skeletons at the feast, and she was the main course.

She went outside. It was late in the afternoon now, but the day was still warm for early October, and the light was as golden as freshly gathered honey.

"Annie?"

She turned, smiling at Lauren, grateful to her. "It worked so perfectly, what you said to Sheriff Neely. I don't think he would ever have agreed—" But now, seeing the fear that was back in Lauren's eyes, her look of utter despair, Annie took Lauren's hands. "What's wrong?"

"Oh, Annie," she said, "what have I done?"

19

Somehow Lauren found her way out of Cedar Cliff, and when she got to the interstate, as she waited in the lane that would take her onto the southbound ramp back to Hardys Walk, she considered not returning there. Looking north, she imagined herself on that ramp instead. She would disappear like Bo, go somewhere far away to lose what was left of her mind alone, without an audience and the continual demand to explain herself and her actions.

Behind her a horn bleated, and she jumped, gunning through the intersection, breath shallow, panic racing through her veins like dark ink. She gripped the steering wheel. Jeff's voice bounced off the walls of her skull: *How could you have forgotten? Your own daughter?*

Just yesterday, she'd been torn with worry over the possibility. Now it had come to pass.

Lauren tried to focus on driving, her destination. She was almost positive Mercy General was on the southbound feeder, a little north of Hardys Walk. *God, please let me be remembering right!* The prayer sat behind her eyes. She thought she'd been there at least once before with Drew when he broke his arm several years ago, playing flag football. Kenzie had never been in a hospital, though, since she was born. She would be so afraid, and Lauren hated that. And yet she'd let this happen. It was her fault.

Are you fucked up? Is that it? You're fucked up again, aren't you, while our daughter's lying in an emergency room.

Jeff's words, his accusation, made an endless loop in her brain, caustic, wearing. But he yelled when he was scared. She'd yell at him, too, if he were responsible. God, how she hated this. She felt as if she were trapped in a fun house, full of eerie sounds, warped mirrors, and dead ends. She wondered if Jeff would believe her assuming he gave her a chance to tell him the truth, that she'd lost track of time.

That was Annie's excuse made on Lauren's behalf. She'd blamed herself. "It's because of me; you forgot because you were helping me. I'm so sorry."

She'd looked so worried, on the verge of tears, when Lauren drove off alone. Annie had said she would call JT, that he would come and get search teams organized. He would watch out for her, Lauren thought, and be sure she got home safely. At least that much was a relief.

She found a parking space at the hospital near the emergency-room entrance and switched off the ignition, but then she could only sit staring at the building. Its gray hulk loomed over her like a nightmare. The weather had changed, and the sky peered down, a cloudy eye. Moody, judging. How could she go inside? She gripped the steering wheel and lowered her head to her hands. But then after a moment, she was out of the car like a shot and through the double doors. Her half-running steps rang in the empty corridor. A nurse looked up at her approach.

"My daughter's here," Lauren said. "Mackenzie Wilder? She was in a car accident—"

"Lauren?"

She wheeled at the sound of Jeff's voice. "How is she? Where is she? I need to see her."

Jeff took her elbow, steering her away from the nurses' station, and he was calm now, and Lauren was grateful for that.

"She's going to be fine," he said. "She has a cut across her forehead." With the tip of his finger, Jeff drew a line that bisected his eyebrow, coming way too near the outside corner of his eye. "It took fifteen stitches to close it."

"Her head—what about her head?"

"It's fine, nothing like what happened to you." Jeff knew the source for Lauren's anxiety immediately. "There's not a sign of a concussion, much less the brain trauma you went through."

"Thank God." Lauren felt suddenly weak, as if her legs might give way. She stiffened her knees.

"They want to keep her overnight, though, in case."

"I'll stay with her."

"She doesn't want to see you."

"What? Of course she does." *But no.* She could see Jeff wasn't being cruel. The truth was in his eyes, in a shadow that lay deeper than his anger. Deeper even than his affront, his disbelief, his conviction that, as a mother, she was unfit. What Lauren saw in his eyes was pity. Jeff pitied her. He was sorry for her that her own daughter was rejecting her.

She couldn't speak for the longest moment, and when she found her voice, she said, "But I would never hurt her. I love her. You know that."

"She's mad as hell at you, Lauren."

Lauren lifted her chin. She had seen the cubicle Jeff had come out of, and she went past him, heading toward it. She heard him say her name and "Don't. Don't hurt yourself this way." But she had to see her daughter, to know Kenzie's rejection for herself.

She pulled aside the curtain screening Kenzie from her view, and even as she locked eyes with her daughter, Lauren confronted the terrible damage to Kenzie's face, the slim red seam that cleaved her sweet brow—that missed her left eye by the merest fraction. Lauren's knees weakened again even as she stepped toward the bed. She wanted Kenzie in her arms, wanted, desperately, to hold her and offer comfort, to murmur a thousand apologies into the silken fall of her hair.

But Kenzie raised her hands, warding Lauren off. "Go away," she said. "I don't want you here."

"Honey, I'm so sorry."

"That's what you always say. You're always sorry, but then you drug yourself and you're back to stupid. Back to not remembering anything. Not even your own family. You like your damn pills better. Everybody knows it. All the kids at school. Sarah Jane Farmer's parents say she can't be friends with me anymore because you're a druggie. Did you know that?"

"No!" Lauren was horrified. "Why didn't you tell me?"

"There's this girl Drew likes? But her folks won't let her go near him because of you. You embarrass me, Mommy. You make me sick. I told the nurse you were dead; that's why she called Daddy instead of you." Kenzie turned her face away, her small chest heaving, jaw trembling.

Lauren's heart broke. She was aware of Jeff, drawing her away, tugging her out of the cubicle, and she turned to him, needing his arms around her, his strength to hold her up, but he kept his distance. Guiding her to a waiting area, he sat her down, put a cup of coffee into her hands, and stood looking down at her. "Give her some time," he said.

"I'm not taking drugs," Lauren said. "You saw—I flushed them."

No response.

"I was with Annie. We found the woman Bo was last seen with. She lives near Cedar Cliff. I drove Annie there to talk to her, then we went to the sheriff—"

"Jesus Christ, Lauren." He backed off a step.

"Annie had no other way to get there, Jeff. Her car isn't reliable."

"I don't understand you—this obsession you have with these people, some guy that's missing, some fucking stranger." He paused. "I'm sorry. I don't mean that. I feel bad for the family, too. But you and our kids are my family. You come first with me no matter what."

"I know—"

"I'm working my ass off . . . trying to keep us together. What is going on with you?"

She bowed her head, picking at her thumbnail.

"The contract and permits for Waller-Land? They aren't in my briefcase."

She jerked her glance to Jeff's. "They are. I put the folder in there. You said you saw it."

"It's there, but it's empty."

"Did the inspector come by?"

"No, we got lucky. I can't risk it, though, working without the permit. I was on my way home to look for the paperwork when the hospital called."

"I don't know what happened." Lauren was truly at sea. She clearly recalled gathering the pages and slotting them into a folder—she wasn't quite sure when—Wednesday before she'd gone into town? She didn't know, but she had put the file in Jeff's briefcase. She could still feel the heft of it as she'd lifted it onto the desk in the study. He was wrong, she thought, and when she got her hands on the briefcase, she'd prove it.

Wiping her face, she asked about Amanda and her mom, assuming the girls had called Suzanne when Lauren didn't show up.

Lauren thought Suzanne had been driving, but Jeff said no, that the driver was a kid named Steve.

"He's a friend of Drew's, according to Kenzie. I talked to his parents a while ago when they came to pick him up. He wasn't hurt, but the paramedics transported him anyway just to be safe. His folks weren't too happy. He was driving his mom's car, and they're saying it's totaled. His dad said the kid just got his license a week ago. He wasn't supposed to be driving anywhere except to school and back home."

"But where was Suzanne?"

Jeff's eyes widened. *Where were you?* That was the question, and it sat between them, no less radiant in its condemnation for remaining unspoken.

Lauren was surprised when he sat down, but he was careful to take the chair on the other side of a small built-in table, not that he'd have offered to comfort her. But then, she didn't deserve his concern, his tenderness.

"I don't know where Suzanne was. Kenzie said Amanda tried calling her, but she must have been out of pocket. Meanwhile, Steve showed up. Amanda wouldn't get in the car with him, but Kenzie thought it was all right because she'd seen him hanging out with Drew. She was pissed at you, Lauren. You know how she hates being late for ballet."

Lauren set down the paper cup filled with machine-dispensed coffee, sharply enough that some slopped over the rim, burning her knuckles. She was angry, suddenly, unreasonably, at all the wrong people: Kenzie and Jeff, Suzanne. It made no sense to her when she knew she alone was responsible.

If Jeff was aware of her emotional upheaval, he gave no sign. He was always so calm and self-contained. Grounded in a way that she envied and resented. How was it that relationships—love—could be so twisted with contradiction?

"Kenzie's had it, Lauren." Jeff looked at her.

She looked at the floor.

"She's sick of making excuses to all her friends for the craziness." Jeff twirled the tips of his index fingers near his ears. "Sick of trying to play it off that her mom isn't a junkie. I can't blame her. Can you? After everything she's gone through on your account?"

Lauren was afraid to move. Her heart was beating too fast, and she was dizzy. Too dizzy and weak. She opened her mouth, intending to ask Jeff for help, a nurse, a doctor. "I haven't taken anything, Jeff," she heard herself say instead. "I don't know how Oxy keeps ending up in the house, in my possession when I have no recollection . . ." Lauren could see he wasn't going to brainstorm possibilities, other than the one that was obvious. To him, at least.

"You saw me flush it." She repeated the single fact she knew for sure.

"How do I know you don't have more?"

"I don't."

"Show me."

Grabbing her purse, Lauren upended the contents onto the tabletop between them, passing her hand over her wallet, her car keys, a coin purse, tissues, lip gloss, two pens, a compact mirror—a plastic envelope that contained two yellow tablets. She recoiled, looking openmouthed at Jeff.

He gazed back at her and the mercy in his eyes was tempered with fresh pity.

"I don't know how these got here," she said.

"I don't, either." He stood up.

She gathered the contents of her purse, shoving them inside it, all but the Oxy tablets. Those, she left on the table. "Kenzie shouldn't be alone," she said. "I'm her mother. I should be with her."

"Go home," Jeff said, and his voice, his eyes were weary. "Just go home," he repeated.

. . .

But Lauren didn't go home. She went to Dr. Bettinger's office. He wasn't in, but his nurse Shelly was, and Lauren was almost relieved. Shelly was easier to talk to; she didn't lecture.

"I'm a mess," Lauren said.

"What's going on?" Shelly asked.

Lauren didn't answer; she was afraid if she spoke, she would cry. What if Shelly was like Jeff and didn't believe her?

As if Shelly could read her distress, she took Lauren's elbow and drew her into an exam room. "Sit down," she said, indicating the paper-topped bed. "Now tell me," she instructed, settling onto a stool.

Somehow Shelly's air of calm, the sense she gave Lauren that she had all the time in the world, made it easier to talk about it— where Kenzie was and how she'd come to be there. "She thinks I forgot to pick her up because I'm using again. I can't stand it, her thinking that." Lauren pressed her knuckled fist to her mouth, willing away the tears.

"Well, a blood test will settle the question," Shelly said. She left the room, and when she came back with everything she needed to take a sample, Lauren looked at it in dismay.

"I drank a lot of wine last night," she said. "I know I shouldn't," she added, and she felt like a teenager who'd been trapped into admitting she'd raided her parents' liquor cabinet.

Shelly inserted the needle. "Walking—some kind of exercise or meditation would be better," she said.

Lauren closed her eyes, and immediately, the vision of her condition this morning when she'd wakened, filthy and aching, seared the backs of her eyelids. Heat rose from her shirt collar, warming her face. She couldn't speak of it to Shelly, the possibility that more than the wine was involved; it wasn't as if she needed to know the entire scope of Lauren's fear to make a proper diagnosis anyway. Humiliation wasn't relevant to the question.

"It seems as if you're having a particularly rough time lately." Shelly removed the needle. Her voice, her motions were efficient, matter-of-fact, and yet Lauren sensed her kindness, too.

"I thought I would be so much better by now," Lauren said. "It's been almost two years."

"You know there's no timetable, that you may never recover in a way that's completely familiar. When so much damage is done, the brain is forced to heal in whatever way it can. It makes new connections. It changes things." Shelly capped the vial that held Lauren's blood. "It'll be a few days before we get the results."

"You'll call?"

"Yes, of course."

Lauren rolled down her sleeve. "I know I'm not right, but I know how I feel when I take Oxy, and how I feel now isn't like that."

"Well"—Shelly bent to look into Lauren's eyes—"if it's any comfort, you don't exhibit any of the signs. Your reflexes are fine and so are your pupils. You're lucid; your speech is clear." She straightened. "You'll make an appointment to see Dr. Bettinger before you go? He's out until week after next, but we'll work you in ASAP after that."

Lauren said she would. She didn't mention Tara's suggestion that maybe, rather than Bettinger, Lauren needed to see a shrink.

She went to Tara's house after she left the medical center, where Jeff said he had taken Drew earlier when he couldn't find Lauren.

Tara's car was in the driveway, and Lauren parked behind it. Her hand shook, reaching to switch off the ignition, and she realized she was afraid to see her own sister, her own son. How had it happened? How had her family members, the ones she loved and trusted most in the world, become her fearful enemies? Or was this another game her brain had invented, another mental trick? Would that stupid accident and her even more stupid drug use cost her everything before they were done with her? She tipped her head to the seatback, closing her eyes.

All the king's horses and all the king's men couldn't put Humpty together again . . .

The fragment from the nursery rhyme ran across her brain.

A sharp rapping on the driver's-side window made her jump. Her gaze jerked toward the sound, and she flinched, for a split second not recognizing the woman whose face loomed at her.

"Tara?"

Their eyes locked through the glass.

"You can't come inside." Tara waved her arm, a wild, go-away gesture.

"Tara, for heaven's sake. Drew's here. Of course I'm coming inside." Lauren started to open the door.

"No!" Tara pushed it closed, nearly catching Lauren's foot.

"What is wrong with you?" Lauren shouted through the glass, and now her glance registered certain details about Tara's appearance: her hair that normally fell in shiny waves to her shoulders was oily-looking and unkempt and gathered into a messy ponytail. The old T-shirt she wore had stains on the front. Vomit? Was Tara that ill? With Drew in the house, exposed to whatever it was? "Let me out," Lauren said, putting her shoulder against the door. "Whatever you've got, I don't want Drew coming down with it."

"I'm not sick. It isn't that. It's one hell of a lot worse."

"Is it Greg, then?" Lauren fumbled with the keys, hunting the one for the ignition. She would get the window down at least. But before she could manage it, Tara yanked open the car door.

"Do you know where he is? Have you heard from him?"

So it was about Greg. "I haven't, TeeRee, and I'm really sorry if he's back on heroin again, but it's not your fault. It's not even personal. There's more to his story than you know."

"Oh God, Lauren, shut up! Just shut up!" Tara backed away, clapping her hands over her ears, turning in a circle.

Lauren's stomach twisted in sympathy, but then she heard Tara say something about Jeff, that he'd called. Lauren thought she heard Tara say they'd discussed Lauren. *Your latest stunt,* Tara said. Lauren was convinced that was how Tara phrased it, that she'd used the word *stunt.* She was certain, too, of Tara's judgment, her derision, and her heart was impaled on a spike of rage so hot, she pressed her fist to her chest. She was out of the car nearly before she could register moving, grabbing Tara's shoulder, spinning her around. "You're not getting away with it, do you hear me?"

Tara only stared, mute. She looked terrified.

"Don't play the innocent with me," Lauren warned. "I'm not that stupid or so far gone that I can't—" She broke off, and the sense of it, of what was really going on crystallized in her mind. "You're having an affair with Jeff."

"Oh, for God's sake—"

"It won't work, you know, having me declared unfit, or whatever it is you're planning."

"This is nuts, even for you. He barely tolerates me, and you know it."

Lauren stared at Tara.

"C'mon, Lauren. He thinks I'm the original dumb blonde, the one all the jokes are made about. He thought that about me the first time he met me, and I didn't think much of him, either. Still don't."

Lauren backed up a step. "Really? I'm amazed." It was only in the smallest corner of her mind that she was aware of how she'd jumped from condemning Jeff to defending him. "I thought you would put all that behind you, especially since he's the one who got you out of all your financial trouble. You would have lost your house if it weren't for him. You'd have nothing saved for retirement."

"Hah!" Tara's laugh was ugly. "As if he didn't get what he wanted for the favor—my share of our parents' business, the one our daddy started. It's what he wanted all along. He'd love it if I'd just disappear. Forever. For all I know, he feels the same way about you."

"That isn't true."

In the tightly coiled silence, Lauren could feel her blood pounding in her temples. "Where is this coming from, TeeRee?" she asked finally. "You came to us, remember? You suggested the buyout. Jeff even tried to talk you out of it. If I remember right, he said you should let this house go, that there'd always be the opportunity to buy another, but losing your share of the business Mama and Daddy built—" Lauren's throat closed. She swallowed. "I don't understand why you're saying all these terrible things."

Tara didn't answer, and Lauren couldn't interpret her expression. Maybe it was how your sister looked if she was sleeping with your husband and determined to deny it. "Talk to me," she insisted. "Tell me the truth."

No response.

Tara remained as still as a trapped mouse, staring into the distance, as if she hadn't heard Lauren or had forgotten her presence, and in the moment Lauren had to observe Tara, she was struck anew at how utterly diminished Tara appeared. And an idea surfaced, that it wasn't a stomach virus Tara was suffering from, but something much worse, something awful like cancer—of the breast, pancreas, bone. Panic broke through Lauren's veins. She opened her hand, a plea, an appeal. "You're really sick, aren't you?"

"Oh, Jesus, Lauren, no. Just go." She came at Lauren, taking one step, two, and the movement was hostile, menacing, as it was meant to be.

It shocked Lauren even as it confused and angered her. What game was this? "Let me tell you something, Tara. You aren't taking my children. Do you understand? You and Jeff can have each other—"

"Are we back to that?" Tara laughed, a single, harsh syllable. "You're insane."

"Probably," Lauren said. "But you're not giving me anything else to blame for the irrational way you're acting, so I want us to be clear that I'll fight you and Jeff with everything I have in me. I will die before I let you take Drew and Kenzie away from me. Do you understand? I will make your and Jeff's lives a living hell."

"Go ahead." Tara thrust up her chin, but her voice was oddly flat. "My life's not worth shit nowadays anyway."

Lauren was nonplussed. "Are you lying about being sick, then? I mean really sick. Are you? Please, tell me."

"You don't want to know, and you can believe *me* about that." Tara's stare was needle sharp and unrelenting.

Lauren felt pierced by it; she felt she might cry out from the pain of it.

"Go home, Lauren." Tara repeated Jeff's admonition.

"No," Lauren said, brushing by her. "Not until I get my son."

"You'll only upset him. He doesn't want to see you."

Lauren wheeled. "Why are you doing this? I'm your sister. Why are you lying?"

"She isn't lying, Mom."

Lauren spun around. Drew was on the porch in his sock feet, a practice she frowned on. Noting it was automatic, as was registering that the jeans he had on, a pair she'd bought him just weeks ago, were already too short. She saw that his hair was rumpled, and she recognized the look on his face, the knotted corners of his mouth, the flash in his eyes that signified he was ready to do battle. His boundaries were drawn, and he dared her to cross them. *Jeff*, she thought. Jeff had poisoned Drew's mind, too. "I don't know what Dad told you—"

"He said you're back on the Oxy."

"I'm not, Drew. I promise."

"C'mon, Mom! He said you told him you found it in the study, and you said you flushed it, but the way you've been acting, I don't believe it. Like last night—what was that? You were outside passed out when the sprinklers were going. Dad said you didn't even know your name. Then today you forgot Kenzie. You never used to do stuff like that, not until you got on dope. It's your fault she got hurt."

A sound came; Lauren felt it more than she heard it, the small, protesting cry that broke from her chest. She covered her mouth with her hands, taking a step toward Drew. She had the idea, and it was wrong, she knew it was, given the mutiny in his eyes, that she would comfort him, reassure him as if she were his BTA mother and not the person he now detested and for whom he had lost all respect. Or maybe she took the step toward him because—just as it had been with Kenzie—her body refused to register his antipathy for her, and when he said, "Stay away from me," even though she'd almost expected to hear this very thing from him, she was stunned, and her ears rang as if he'd slapped her.

Nearby, the sound of a car door slamming exploded into the taut, wounding silence, and a bird cried, a harsh mockery of notes. A blue jay, Lauren thought incongruously. Why, when they were capable of producing a full-throated and lovely song, did blue jays seem to prefer making this more raucous noise? She'd never known. It was a mystery to her.

Lauren gathered herself; she straightened her spine. "You need to get your things and come home with me," she said, addressing Drew, and she managed to summon at least the shadow of her customary authority. "Now," she said when he didn't move.

"I'm not letting you drive me anywhere when you're trashed, Mom."

Lauren thought of saying that her blood was being tested, that the result would prove she was drug-free. But that was only her word. He'd never accept it. He'd have it his way, no matter what she did anyway. They both knew it, knew she couldn't bodily drag him off the porch and down the drive to the car. He was already an inch taller and outweighed her by forty pounds. He showed every sign of being as big a man as his dad. Drew's size pleased her as did Kenzie's slender, fine-boned stature and delicate beauty. Lauren realized she took credit for her children's appearances; she felt validated by their good looks, their glowing health. She didn't know if that was bad or good. She didn't know if it was bad or good to feel that without her children, she might lose herself; she might even die.

"Lauren?" Tara spoke from behind her.

Her hand shot out. "Stay out of it," she said without looking at her sister. She found Drew's gaze again. "I'll leave you here, since it's what you want. But when Kenzie is released tomorrow and your dad brings her home, you're coming home, too. Do you understand me?"

He didn't answer, and it infuriated her, but it was useless to argue. Drew and Jeff and Tara had closed ranks against her. Even Kenzie had turned her back. They were acting in concert, shutting Lauren out. Her sense that this was true both heated her blood and chilled it.

She turned on her heel and went to her car. She would not let them see how deeply they had wounded her.

"I'm sorry," Tara called after her, and her voice was plaintive, broken. It was very like the voice she had used when they were children and she wanted Lauren's forgiveness for breaking some valued possession of Lauren's, for ruining it.

Lauren paused outside her SUV and glanced back at her sister, wondering if she had lost Tara forever.

"It's not anything you think," she said. "As bad as that is, I almost wish it was, but it isn't."

Tara's regret seemed genuine, as if she were truly convinced of Lauren's misunderstanding, or else it was a trick, one more in the bag of them Tara and Jeff were holding. Still, something in Tara's demeanor gave Lauren pause, and for a moment, she considered hashing it out with Tara, making her explain herself, but she was suddenly tired of it all, the drama, the riddles. Tired of trying to prove she wasn't on anything. Tired of trying to sort out what was real and what wasn't. The truth shouldn't be so hard.

She set her foot on the Navigator's running board, and thinking aloud, she addressed Tara. "You'll bring Drew home tomorrow when Kenzie is released." Lauren wasn't asking. "We're going to sit down and clear the air."

"No, don't argue," she said when Tara opened her mouth. "We can't go on this way. We'll lose everything, our family. Is that what you want?"

Tara looked away, adding weight to Lauren's unease, raising the fine hairs on her arms, the nape of her neck. She glanced toward Tara's front porch, but Drew had disappeared.

"Don't worry," Tara said. "He's not staying here. I told Jeff he can't. It's just not possible."

"No, it isn't," Lauren agreed, and then she waited, unsure why, what she hoped for—a glimpse of the little girl she had mothered? But Tara's eyes were empty in a way that alarmed Lauren even as she felt crushed with sorrow, and fighting the hot bite of tears, she turned from Tara, damned if she would let her sister see her cry.

• • •

It was almost dark when she pulled into her driveway. The only light came from the fixture mounted high on the garage, illuminating

Drew's basketball hoop, the apron of scuffed concrete in front of it. Lauren sat for a moment, listening to the engine tick as it cooled. Her hip ached, and she felt leaden with exhaustion. Curling her fingers over the steering wheel, she bent her head to her knuckled grip. Her eyes burned when she closed them. She thought of Annie.

What might have happened by now? Lauren found her phone, but her call went straight to Annie's voice mail. Lauren didn't leave a message.

She went into the house, flipping on the light in the mudroom, dropping her keys and purse on the chest, and when her purse tipped off the edge and fell to the floor, she left it there, intent on reaching the study. But even as she hunted through the litter on the desk and searched the drawers and the credenza and the contents of the wastebasket, she knew she wouldn't find the permits or the contract, and she didn't. Because Jeff was wrong. They were exactly where she had said, in a folder, in his briefcase.

She felt some measure of satisfaction, returning to the kitchen, and she thought of calling him, but something held her back. He would find them on his own if she waited, and no words from her would be necessary. He'd apologize. He never had trouble saying he was sorry. And in the end, she had more to be sorry for than he ever would.

Near ten o'clock, Lauren tried eating a bowl of Drew's cereal, the Honey Nut Cheerios he loved, but after a few bites she poured what was left down the drain. She called the hospital, and when she told the nurse she was Mackenzie Wilder's mother and that she was calling to check on her daughter, the nurse reported, briskly, that Kenzie was fine, that her *father* was taking wonderful care of her. It was the nurse's emphasis on the single word *father* that defined for Lauren, in a way no torrent of words could, her every parental failure and shortcoming. What decent mother, one who professes to care deeply for her children the way Lauren did, forgets her own daughter, even for a moment?

Lauren set the landline receiver back on the base, and because she couldn't rest, she paced through the house, twitching the drapes closed in the great room, pausing to glance again into the study. She went upstairs and looked into the children's rooms. Kenzie's room was tidy, but the floor in Drew's room was strewn with his belongings. Lauren began gathering his dirty clothes, something she ordinarily didn't do. She tossed socks and jeans, a pair of baggy shorts and a couple of T-shirts into the laundry basket. She held up a short-sleeve shirt by its collar, not recognizing it. It was soft, some kind of faux-silk blend; the pattern was a tropical wash of greens and blues, not Drew's usual low-key style. She thought he must have bought it the last time they'd gone to the mall. She remembered he'd asked if he could take off on his own, meet her and Kenzie later. It occurred to her that he was taking longer to dress before school, too, and recently hadn't Jeff told her he'd caught Drew shaving?

Lauren sat on the edge of Drew's bed, sliding her palm over the shirt. She had no memory of him wearing it, but he must have. His scent rose out of the folds, a mix of Jeff's purloined aftershave, overtones of growing boy, minty chewing gum, the faint tang of sun and sweat. Her son needed her, but she wasn't there for him. If, on any given day recently, he had gone missing like Bo Laughlin, she doubted she would have been able to tell the police what he'd been wearing. She hadn't been paying attention.

There's this girl Drew likes? But her folks won't let her go near him because of you. Kenzie's accusation drifted into Lauren's brain and hung there like smoke.

Lauren embarrassed her, Kenzie had said; Lauren made her and Drew sick.

Shame bent her over her knees, and then with its pulse hammering her temples, it sent her back downstairs to the bedroom she and Jeff shared. Crossing to the bathroom, she paused outside the door. She had avoided it until now, afraid she would find that more Oxy had appeared there. Afraid if it had, she would take it, down it like the elixir of hope, of deliverance and redemption it had become to her in the aftermath of the accident.

Margaret had insisted then that Lauren was brave. And months later, when the family confronted Lauren about the Oxy, Margaret was there, too, but while the rest of them—Jeff, Tara, Kenzie, and Drew—went on and on about how badly Lauren had wrecked their lives, Margaret stayed in the background. Only after the family left Lauren alone to consider their ultimatum, *Get help, or we'll take the children*, did Margaret come forward, and again holding Lauren close, she'd whispered, "You'll get through this."

"How?" Lauren asked. "My family hates me."

"No, they're afraid for you. You've always been the strong one."

"Not since I fell. I hurt, and my brain doesn't work right, and I'm scared it never will again, scared all the time."

"You raised Tara, for heaven's sake. You ran your mother and father's business. You were barely twenty. Do you remember?"

It was true. After her parents died, Lauren had done those things. But this was different, she told Margaret. "I can't fight the pain alone anymore. I'm too tired."

"You aren't alone, sweet. I'm here, and I'll be here to remind you every day, every hour if need be, of just how brave you are. All right?"

But it wasn't all right, because Margaret wasn't here. She had died of leukemia a few short weeks after Lauren's intervention. Lauren hadn't even known she was sick. At Margaret's funeral, one of her sons had said she hadn't wanted to worry Lauren. She had believed she would beat the disease anyway.

Lauren stood motionless in the bathroom doorway now, remembering.

So much for faith, for bravery and blind courage.

• • •

It was after midnight before she could make herself cross the threshold and enter the bathroom, and she was marginally relieved when she saw nothing incriminating or alarming there, not until she went into her closet and found the documents. The permits and contract for the Waller-Land job were on a shelf, slotted between a couple of her handbags, as if she'd tucked them there while hunting something to wear. Or maybe she had thought she would change purses? She picked up the papers, leafing through them, hands shaking, frowning, trying to remember. Three pages stapled together that she didn't immediately recognize turned out to be an asbestos-notification form. Lauren carried the folder out of her closet and sat down on the edge of the Jacuzzi. Jeff had mentioned finding asbestos in the building. It meant the bid would have to be renegotiated, if it hadn't been already. The presence of hazardous waste would add a substantial amount to their fee. Precautions would have to be taken; a proper means of disposal would need to be arranged. There were transportation issues. All of it was government regulated and subject to enforcement by law. It was a huge headache. Lauren knew this, but she didn't remember this paperwork or any discussion about it. Yet flipping to the last page, she saw that she had signed the form along with a notary, someone named Elizabeth McQueen at Cornerstone Bank.

Lauren felt as if she were drowning. A sound raked her backbone, her ribs, something like a howl of confusion, protest. She clenched her jaw against it.

From a distance, she heard the tinny sound of her cell phone ringing, and she thought of not answering. But what if it was Jeff, calling to tell her Kenzie had taken a turn for the worse? Or Tara, calling to say something terrible had happened to Drew?

But it wasn't either of them.

Instead, it was Annie Beauchamp.

"Lauren," she said in a small, quavering voice, "we found Bo."

20

No one had to tell Annie it was over. She knew even before JT texted her. *Come back to town*, his message read. He hadn't wanted her joining a search team in Cedar Cliff in the first place, but she had said it was either that or she'd go look for Bo alone. "You're as hardheaded as your mama was," JT had muttered. He'd gone with a different team, some guys Sheriff Neely knew who had dogs. Annie went with a group led by the sheriff.

It was before dawn and still dark enough that they were using flashlights to walk a heavily wooded area around ten miles north of Charlotte Meany's house when Annie felt something go through her, a sensation of dread that was physical, like an electrical charge. It was sharp enough to stop her in her tracks and make her look around. The other team members were huddled in a knot, all looking back at her. Then her cell phone beeped with JT's message, and reading it, she knew.

Sheriff Neely drove her back to Cedar Cliff in his patrol car. She was sure he had all the details, but he didn't say much. None of the search-team members did. She doubted they wanted the responsibility of giving her the terrible news. Or maybe JT had asked them not to.

There were a half dozen or more people standing around the sheriff's office when she arrived, but Annie had eyes only for JT. She knew the worst of it from his face, the ruin of his expression. She went to him, and his arms came around her. She pressed her face against him, smelling him, the bitter tang of his grief, the heavier musk of exhaustion and surrender that rose through the layers of his clothing, his flannel shirt and nylon jacket. She felt him rest his chin on the top of her head.

"Somebody murdered him, Annie."

She froze on hearing the reality framed in words. Her breath stopped. Even her heart paused.

"They shot him and tossed him alongside an old ranch road like he was nothing. Yesterday's trash."

"No." She shook her head against JT's chest.

He tightened his embrace. "He was rolled up in an old rug. That's the part I don't get. Who would do that? Take the rug right off their floor?"

"Can we see him? Where is he now?" Annie backed out of JT's embrace.

"Folks?" Sheriff Neely was there at her elbow. "Why don't we go into my office?" He asked Darlene to bring them coffee.

"How about a sandwich?" she said.

But JT shook his head. So did Annie. Her brain felt swimmy. She wondered if she was dreaming and resisted an urge to see if her feet were touching the floor. Her throat ached. She put her hand there briefly, then lowering it, she was surprised to feel something wet and cold nuzzle the cup of her palm. She looked down into Rufus's warm brown eyes. Somehow the sight of him comforted her. She kept her hand on his head, and searching the room, found Cooper standing near the building's entrance, hands in his jean pockets, watching her. Against her will, her heart leapt. He seemed to be asking for permission to approach, and even as a voice in her head said no, she nodded.

"I'm so, so sorry, Annie." He waited to speak until he was close enough to her that she could feel his breath on her face. Something inside her, some internal resolve, began to loosen.

Tears brimmed her eyes.

He thumbed them away and gathered her into his arms. And she let him. It was his kindness, his unremitting strength that was her final undoing. Her tears flowed, and she seemed incapable of making any effort to restrain them. They scalded her cheeks, soaking his shirt. She was aware of him murmuring softly to her, but if there were any words, she couldn't pick them out. Her ear against his chest caught the vibration of his voice, the sure and steady rhythm of his heartbeat, and the sounds soothed her. Gradually her tears abated, and she straightened, feeling shaky and self-conscious. But the undertow of her grief hadn't dissolved. She took the tissue Cooper produced from somewhere and wiped her face.

Rufus came and sat beside her, and she patted his ears absently, grateful for the weight of his warmth when he leaned against her leg. She looked at Cooper. "How did you know?"

"Sheriff Audi. JT called him after he heard from you yesterday. I was with the team that found Bo."

"You were? When did you come here? I didn't see you."

"I didn't want to bother you."

Because of the last time they'd spoken, Annie thought. At the café, after the trip to the morgue, when she'd told him he didn't know anything about her life or Bo's. She'd been rude—out of pride, out of the need to protect herself.

Someday you're going to have to trust somebody again, or you'll always be alone. Cooper's prediction from that day passed through her mind. She caught his gaze. "Were you the one . . ." *who found Bo?* She didn't say the words, but Cooper didn't need them.

"No," he said. "One of the deputies, Roger something. He's standing over there." He pointed out a man in uniform, talking to Darlene. "I was in the vicinity, though, close enough that I heard him call out that he had something."

"Where?"

"Around twenty miles or so northwest of here. We were pretty far off the highway, on a ranch road, I think. Something private like that. Hard to tell in the dark, you know?"

"What would Bo have been doing there?"

"You need to speak with Sheriff Neely." Cooper nodded in the direction of the sheriff's office.

Following his gaze, Annie saw that JT was already there, sitting in one of the straight-backed chairs in front of Sheriff Neely's desk, the same one Lauren had sat in yesterday. The chair Annie had sat in was empty, waiting for her.

Cooper took her elbow as if he meant to guide her there, but she said, "No, I can't do this now," and leaving him, she walked rapidly across the room and out of the building, and once outside, she bent at the waist, gulping the chilly new-morning air, drawing it into her lungs breath by breath as if she were starving for oxygen. Gradually, the tight bands that circled her chest eased, and she straightened, but she wasn't free of it. The nightmare, the god-awful thing that had happened to Bo, that thing that involved the word *murder*.

She sat on a bench, and pulling her cell phone from her pocket, she called Lauren's number, not pausing to think of the hour. When Lauren answered, Annie said her name, "Lauren?" and then "We found Bo."

"Oh." The syllable slipped out on an audible puff of air.

"He's dead," Annie said. "Someone shot him."

"What? No!" Lauren protested.

A silence fell that lasted several moments, fanning out between them, as useless as a bird's broken wing.

"Oh, Annie." Lauren finally broke it. "I'm so sorry. Where are you? I'll come. You shouldn't be alone."

Annie closed her eyes, thinking how her mother would have said the same thing. Thinking of how much Lauren reminded her of her mother. But maybe she only imagined the resemblance. Maybe she wanted her mother so badly she was willing to forget her doubts about Lauren, her sense that for all her seeming kindness and compassion, she was unstable.

Annie said she wasn't alone, that JT was with her. She didn't mention Cooper. "I'm still in Cedar Cliff at the sheriff's office," she said, and then stopped before she could say she'd run out of the building, run out on Cooper and JT, because she was a wimp, a fraidycat, too scared to hear the details. She wasn't aware of the pause until Lauren broke it.

"Annie? Do the police know who did it?"

Annie realized she hadn't even thought about who the murderer was. "He was wrapped in a rug and left beside the road like trash," she repeated what JT had said. "They think he was killed somewhere else, that whoever did it was trying to cover it up."

"But why? Who would do such a thing?"

Annie explained about Leighton, how she hadn't known he was a drug dealer until Bo showed her the proof. She described her shock. "I never saw so much money, except maybe in a bank vault."

"What happened?" Lauren asked.

"Leighton found out, and he threatened—what if he did this?" Annie bent sharply over her knees.

"Annie, Annie, no. Don't get ahead of yourself. Okay? Would Bo have—would he have had a reason to be with a guy who was dealing drugs?"

"I don't know. Maybe he thought he needed more money than he had to go to California. Bo would have been desperate to go there; he'd have done anything."

"But what are you saying? That he sold drugs and that's where the cash he had came from?"

"Nothing's for sure. Detective Cosgrove did say they can't find Leighton or this other guy who's a drug dealer, too. Leighton's partner, I guess, Greg Honey. Evidently Bo knows—knew both of them. I should go—"

"Greg Honey? Bo knew Greg?"

There was something in Lauren's voice, an underscore of alarm that made Annie say, "Do you know him?"

The silence lasted a beat too long.

Annie straightened. "Lauren?"

"I have to go. I'm so sorry." She spoke in a rush. "Take—take care, okay?" A moment passed, brittle with regret, or so it seemed. "God, I'm so sorry." Lauren said it again, and this time, it sounded like a prayer.

21

Lauren left for Tara's without phoning Jeff. She wanted to call him; if he wasn't so pissed at her, she probably would have, but she was afraid he would dismiss her suspicion as crazy, that Tara was hiding Greg, and try to talk her out of going or, worse, warn Tara she was coming. She couldn't take that chance, not while Drew was in the house with them.

The house was dark when she pulled into the driveway behind Tara's car. There wasn't any sign of the Jeep Greg drove, but maybe he hadn't driven himself there. Maybe Tara had picked him up. Anything was possible. Lauren eased out of the Navigator, closing but not latching the door. An errant breeze skittered through the bare-branched canopy of the sweet gum tree near the drive. Eerie shadows trembled over the lawn. She looked again at the house; the windows across the front glittered in the streetlight, like glassy eyes.

A murderer was behind those windows, inside that house, sitting with her son and her sister. He might even now be watching her, waiting for her, waiting to see what she would do. The possibility raised the hair on Lauren's head. She felt light-headed. Fear uncurled from her stomach.

Call the police. The voice in her head was strident. She had Detective Cosgrove's card, but then she remembered it was in her purse, left at home, with its contents spilled all over the floor of the mudroom. She'd only grabbed her keys when she left after speaking to Annie. She'd not even brought her cell phone. Everything had left her mind the moment Annie said Bo knew Greg. Because Lauren knew Greg, too, knew his history and what he was capable of. She'd listened to him describe his nature, its capacity for violence, in a meeting. She brushed her hands over her face. If only she'd known of the association before, she could have prevented this. Prevented a lot of things. Now Tara and Drew were in danger.

Lauren walked up the steps, onto the front porch. Tara didn't keep a key to the door anywhere outside that Lauren knew of, nor did she think she would find any of the windows unlocked, but she tried them anyway, without luck. And when the outside light came on, she wheeled, heart pounding. The front door jerked open.

"What are you doing?" Tara said in a loud whisper. She thrust open the screen, leaning around it.

Lauren saw that her hair was still caught in the same messy ponytail, and she was wearing the same filthy T-shirt and sweats she'd had on earlier.

"Where is Greg?" Lauren whispered, too.

"Greg?"

"Is he sleeping?"

Tara only gaped at her, and Lauren felt a jolt of fear-fueled annoyance. "Don't play games with me. This is serious. You have to get Drew now as quietly as you can and come with me. We'll call the police—"

"What in the hell are you talking about now, Lauren?" Tara came out, letting go of the screen door.

Lauren tried to catch it before it slammed. "Drew!" she said.

"He isn't here. I told you he wasn't staying with me. He's at Gabe's."

Lauren was perplexed. Still, she said, "Thank God." She took Tara's elbow. "We'll go to my house. We can call Detective Cosgrove from there."

Tara shook free. "If I call anyone, it's going to be the men in the white coats."

"You're determined to protect him, is that it?"

"I have no idea what you're talking about. I'm not protecting anyone. I don't know where Greg is. I told you that before."

"Let me see." Lauren whipped open the screen door and then paused, waiting for Tara to stop her.

But she didn't. "Go on," she said, "since you're so determined. Search the place."

Lauren's pulse pounded in her ears, and every instinct said it was crazy to be here in the house with a man who might possibly be armed, who was most certainly dangerous. Tara followed on her heels as Lauren went from room to room.

"You've got no sense about men," Lauren said, pausing in the guest-bedroom doorway, switching on the light. The room was neat as a pin.

Tara laughed. "And you do, I guess."

"He's a drug addict, Tee."

"So are you."

"Yeah." Lauren went to the master bedroom. While the bed there, Tara's bed, was made up, it was rumpled. She switched her glance to Tara, locking eyes with her. "But Greg's using again, and I'm not."

"Is that why you're here? You're going to turn him in?"

"He might have killed someone," Lauren said. "The boy they've been looking for all week, Bo Laughlin."

"You're insane. Why are you saying that? I thought Greg was your friend—your 12-step mentor. You're always telling me how much he's helped you, that he's the only one who understands." Tara gestured, making a broad arc with her arm. "The rest of us are idiots, out to get you, ruin your marriage, and take your kids. But Greg? He's perfect."

Lauren looked away, undone in the face of Tara's sarcasm, by the reminder of her fallibility. She tried to remember what had brought her here, what progression of thought. Because Tara was right, Greg had been there with her through the darkest period of her life. Now she was ready to condemn him? Based on what? The fact that he and Bo knew each other? She didn't know where to go from here. She wanted to back down from whatever this was that had begun to feel like a challenge, yet something—pride, she thought unhappily—propelled her to walk through the rest of the house, the living and dining rooms, the kitchen. The sound of her footsteps, and Tara's, rang in Lauren's ears.

They reached the small foyer.

"He isn't here, believe me," Tara said.

"I'd like to," Lauren said. But driving home, she thought of all the places in Tara's house she hadn't looked. Places big enough to hide a man. She thought her sister might have lied to her, and her heart felt hollow and cold with fear.

22

Annie sat a moment, holding her cell phone, but her confusion about Lauren, the abrupt way she'd ended their conversation, wasn't something she felt equal to sorting out by herself. She didn't want to go back inside the sheriff's office, either, but she had no choice. Crossing the reception area, skirting the groups of volunteers, she felt their eyes following her, felt their collective sympathy and their pity, and clenched her jaw. When he saw her, JT half rose, asking where she'd been. Distress and fear made a muddy turmoil of his expression. He looked shell-shocked, like a man coming off a battlefield. One who was hunting for a place to lie down.

"How will I tell his mother?" he asked, and his gaze clung to Annie's.

She was nonplussed. Did he mean Bo's mother who was dying?

"Come and sit down." Cooper got up, offering her his chair.

Annie didn't want to, but she went to it, sitting awkwardly, fighting aggravation and the fresh bite of tears both at once. She wanted to tell Cooper to go, that she didn't need him. What was he doing here, anyway?

"The sheriff had some questions for me," Cooper said as if he'd read her mind.

Because he'd been with the team that found Bo, Annie guessed. She wouldn't meet Cooper's eyes and looked at his hands instead. They were mapped with scars. From working with the metal, she decided. She thought how much she would like to see his art, and then she was appalled. How could she think of such a thing now?

"JT was just telling me about your brother's mental state, his drug use—" the sheriff began.

"He wasn't on anything, not recently," Annie said.

"He might have been." JT caught Annie's glance.

She shook her head.

"You didn't want to believe he'd get into a car with a stranger, either," JT said.

"And I was right about that. He knew Charlotte; he worked for her."

"But you didn't know that about him, did you? The same as you don't know whether he was using or selling drugs and that's what got him killed."

Annie opened her mouth to argue.

JT cut her off. "You never wanted to see the pain he was in. You and your mama, always thinking you could fix him when there is no fixing that—what was wrong with him. Not ever." JT flattened his palm, using it to cut the air like a knife.

No one spoke. The sheriff crossed his arms over his chest. Cooper leaned against the wall. Annie pushed her palms down her thighs.

"He knew, don't you see?" JT spoke softly. "Bo knew he wasn't right, could never be the man he might have been if—if—shit—this whole thing makes me sick. Sick in my heart!" He pounded his chest with his fist, jerked to his feet.

Annie felt his glare. She was aware of Rufus getting up, of Cooper beckoning the dog to his side, but she didn't look at any one of the three men or the dog. She couldn't. It was taking every ounce of her self-control not to cry, not to scream. What she might scream or at whom, she couldn't have said.

"Doesn't matter what any autopsy says or what dope they find in his system or even who pulled the fucking trigger on the gun and shot him." JT's voice was rough and loud with his grief. "It was how he wasn't whole—it was that little part of him that knew, that was aware he'd never be a whole man. Never be smart enough to love a woman, earn a living, father a kid. That's what killed him!"

Rufus whined, and Annie jumped when JT slammed his fist into his palm. "Can't you see? It would be like being paralyzed from the neck down and you can't do shit about it, but every day, you got to wake up and face it. How many years could you do it? Huh?" He divided his hot, angry gaze among them. "How goddamn many?"

Now in the hard, frozen silence, JT sat down again and bent his elbows on his knees and dropped his face into his hands.

Annie could have reached across the gap between them; she could have put her hand on his arm, comforted him in some way, but she didn't. She didn't know why. She was as sickened by what had happened as he was, but she was angry, too. JT was right about her mom. She had searched out ways to help Bo, tried every one, no matter how wacky—everything from macrobiotic diets to herbal supplements to acupuncture. But Annie hadn't gone along. In fact, she'd argued with her mom about it. JT knew that. He wasn't any better than her mother, though, with his stupid idea that Bo had been miserable. But none of them had truly understood him, Annie thought.

Why am I not okay the way I am? Bo had asked her once, and remembering now broke her heart all over again.

"I know this is real hard for you folks." The sheriff's voice brought an end to the bruised silence, and Annie was grateful. She gave him her full attention.

He said, "If we want to get whoever did this, we need to know everything we can about Bo, his friends, habits, what he did every day, and who with."

The sheriff looked at Annie. "You were in a relationship with Leighton Drake."

"Yes," Annie said, and she went on without prompting, recounting the details that repetition had stripped of emotion. She might have been speaking of someone else, their stupidity and not her own.

"So," the sheriff said after a pause, "during the time you were going out with Drake, did you ever meet a man named Greg Honey?"

"No," Annie answered, "but Lauren Wilder may know him."

"Your friend who came in with you yesterday?" Sheriff Neely leaned back in his chair. "What makes you think that?"

"I was on the phone with her just now, and when I mentioned Greg might be involved, she ended the conversation. It was weird. But then, she's kind of weird," Annie added and felt bad. Who was she to judge?

"When you say *weird*, what do you mean exactly?" The sheriff leaned forward on his elbows.

"Nothing, really. She's had a rough time." Annie explained about the accident and, reluctantly, about Lauren's addiction to pain meds. "I don't believe she got anything from Bo, though, or that she's on anything now." But even as Annie said this, she thought being on something might explain a lot about Lauren's moods, her unpredictability. She said, "You should talk to Detective Cosgrove. He interviewed her. Sheriff Audi talked to her, too."

"Oh?" The sheriff set down his pen.

"She was one of the last people to see Bo alive."

"Huh." Sheriff Neely leaned back in his chair. "Well, I know Jimmy Cosgrove. We've worked on some stuff together in the past."

"What about these assholes, Drake and Honey?" JT asked. "What're the odds you'll find them?"

"BOLOs for both men were issued a few days ago, back when Lincoln County wanted to question them in regard to Bo's disappearance. Those'll continue."

"That's it?" JT sounded unhappy.

"Unless you can think of anyone else we need to look at?"

"I might know of someone," Cooper said, and Annie stared at him, openmouthed.

23

After she came home from Tara's, Lauren paced around the island in the kitchen, holding on to her phone, debating. She wanted to talk to Jeff. If only he weren't so furious at her, if she could get him past it . . . *I should have been there for Kenzie*, she would say. *Our daughter should have come first before Annie's brother and his disappearance.* But that wasn't the crucial thing anymore. That's what she had to make Jeff understand. Even Bo's death, as tragic as it was, wasn't the issue. Not now that a member of Lauren and Jeff's own family was involved, however peripherally. There could be legal ramifications for Tara if she was covering for Greg. They had to do something, talk sense to her before she did something really stupid, like running away with Greg. Lauren closed her eyes in the face of that unnerving prospect.

Jeff had to see it, that Greg's involvement put a different, more urgent light on the situation.

Sitting on a stool at the island, Lauren switched on her phone, noting the time, after two in the morning. It was against her better judgment when she dialed Jeff's number. She imagined him folded uncomfortably in a chair, dozing, at Kenzie's bedside. She hoped someone had put a blanket over him. She thought, I should be there in that chair. Her eye fell on the Waller-Land folder full of the documents Jeff had needed on the job site and been without because of her foggy brain, her preoccupation with someone else's calamity. She'd let him down not once but time and again. She thought how often she complained that he didn't treat her as an equal partner in the business, but how could he? *I have got to get better*, she thought.

Her call rolled to his voice mail.

"I shouldn't have called so late," she said, "but something has happened." She paused, hesitant now to bring up Tara, to put her first. "Never mind. It can wait. Please call me when you've spoken to Kenzie's doctor. I'll wait here at home, or should I go to the warehouse?" She paused again when she heard how she was rambling. "Just call me, okay?" *I love you.* She started to add that, but something stopped her, the sense of her vulnerability, she guessed. The fear of his rejection. An underscore of resentment that she clung to in the more damaged part of her brain, the part that still struggled with feeling weak and inferior.

She fell asleep at the bar, head pillowed on her arms. The sound of Jeff's truck in the driveway woke her. She was disoriented, blinking wildly at the daylight streaming through the uncurtained kitchen window. She jumped when the truck door slammed, her elbow hitting the Waller-Land file folder, and grabbing it, she set it on the counter behind her, not completely out of view. She would have to confess her mistake, but there were other issues she and Jeff had to discuss first.

She heard him come in, heard the thunk of his briefcase hitting the mudroom floor, the clatter as he emptied his pockets into the tray on top of the chest.

He opened the door to the kitchen and spotting her, said, "You're up."

"I never went to bed." She looked past him at Kenzie, standing in his shadow. The thick padding of gauze that slanted across the corner of her left eye didn't quite hide all the bruising, and Lauren felt sickened at the sight of it. It was her fault, she thought, this damage to her daughter's face. She half rose. "I'm so sorry, Kenzie. I know I let you down, but it won't happen again. Okay? I mean it."

Without a word, Kenzie left her dad's shadow and went swiftly from the kitchen. Lauren heard her light footsteps on the stairs. She wasn't open to her mother's protestations. That door had closed, and why not? How many chances could a kid give to her mother?

Lauren looked at Jeff. "I thought you were taking her to Tara's."

"I am, but I've got a meeting with Kaiser, and I need a shower first."

"Did Drew get to school? He's not at Tara's."

"Gabe's dad took them. I had to wait for the doctor."

"What did he say? Is Kenzie okay?"

"She's fine. Everything tested normal, brain function, reflexes, all of it. But she can't do PE or ballet or anything too physical for a week."

"Oh, she's not going to like that. Where is her dance gear anyway? Did you get it? Her tote?" Lauren was suddenly worried it was lost, left behind in the wrecked car or at the hospital. She thought of Kenzie's new toe shoes that were packed inside it along with her tights and leotard. The toe shoes were still so new, so untried. Kenzie had attached the long pale silk ribbons herself, tacking each of them with a tiny, hidden stitch. She had used pale pink yarn to darn the toes. When she had brought them to Lauren to see her work, her eyes had shone.

"It's in the truck," Jeff said.

"I'll get it."

"No, she wants to go to Tara's."

"Well, she can't," Lauren said. "Tara's in no shape to look after her."

"It's just for a couple of hours. I talked to Tara. She's feeling better. It's fine."

"I went over there last night. Did she tell you? After I found out from Annie Beauchamp that the police think Greg may be involved in her brother's death."

"Really? Why do they think that?"

"Something to do with drugs, Annie said. I think Greg must be back using again. What do you think? I mean, how was he at the farm?"

Jeff shrugged. "He seemed fine, but you're the one who's always saying what good fakers addicts are."

It was true; Lauren did say that. Heroin addicts were especially good at hiding their habit. Unless you knew what to look for, you might never know. "He wasn't at the Tuesday meeting, and some of the guys said he'd left town for a job, but I don't believe it."

"The cops have any idea where he is?"

"I don't think so, but if Tara's protecting him, and she's caught, she'll be in trouble for helping him. It scares me, Jeff, what she might be involved in if she's with him."

"Lauren, I'm sorry, but I don't have time for this. I've got to meet Kaiser." He started across the kitchen.

She followed him up the stairs. "You can't put our daughter into this situation."

"Jesus, can you just let me get a shower first?"

Lauren stopped and watched him disappear into their bedroom. Within minutes, she heard the water running. She was outside Kenzie's closed door and knocked softly. No answer. Resting her forehead against it, she felt exhaustion overwhelm her. It weighted her shoulders, dragged at her spine. "I'm so sorry," she said. "Will you open the door and let me talk to you?"

Nothing.

"I'm not on anything, Kenzie, I swear it. I've even gone for a blood test that will prove it."

No answer.

Lauren went back downstairs and out the back door, walking straight to Jeff's truck. She would get Kenzie's tote, wash her tights and leotard and whatever else was inside it. She would make cookies, chocolate chip, Kenzie's favorite. The smells of fresh laundry and baking would permeate the house. Somehow, Kenzie would be lured downstairs; somehow, Lauren would reach her, reach through her fear—because that's what this was, Lauren was sure of it—and find her daughter. They'd find each other and come to an understanding.

That's what Lauren was thinking when she came through the back door into the mudroom with Kenzie's tote and saw it, the notepad with the pale green cover, one small enough to fit in a man's shirt pocket. It was on the floor in front of the big entryway chest, the catchall place, where she kicked off her shoes and set down her purse, where Jeff dropped his briefcase and emptied his pockets and the kids left their backpacks. Setting Kenzie's tote on the dryer, she bent down to pick the notepad up, but then, on seeing the name that was printed on the front, on the line that was there for that purpose—*Bo Laughlin*—she recoiled, as if it were some horrible bug, one that might attack her.

She would never be sure how much time passed before she heard Jeff calling her name. He appeared in the doorway, and she snatched up the notepad, holding it out to him. "Where did this come from?"

"What is it?"

"Bo Laughlin's notepad. Annie told me he carried one, that he wrote things down in it."

"Where did you find it?"

Lauren saw that he was watching her with trepidation.

"Right here, on the floor." In the same place where her purse had fallen last night. She remembered scooping the contents back inside it and setting it back on the chest. It was there now, and she looked at it, then back at the notepad. "Where could it have come from?" She asked Jeff as if he should know.

But his face was full of doubt and pity. "Maybe Bo gave it to you last Friday when you spoke to him? Or is it possible you've met with him since then?"

"No. I—" Lauren rubbed her brow. Her head ached, and so did her back and hip. And she was so tired.

Jeff took a step toward her, and then another, and it seemed to Lauren he was moving almost imperceptibly. She might have been an injured animal and he her rescuer—familiar roles for them both. She raised her gaze.

The silence thinned, becoming taut.

"You can tell me anything. You know that, right?" He spoke softly to her.

"You think I did something to him?" Why was she saying that?

"I don't know, sweetheart."

"Daddy?"

Lauren looked past Jeff at their daughter, framed in the doorway.

"It's all right," Jeff told her. "Get your tote, and I'll take you to Aunt Tara's."

"What's wrong with her now?" Kenzie came to Jeff's side, eyeing her mother warily, and somehow, with the two of them staring at her, Lauren felt intimidated, and she tried to mentally shoulder the feeling away, not wanting it. Not wanting to believe in it. But that would mean she was imagining it the way she'd begun to imagine so many things. She gave her head a brief shake.

She said her daughter's name. "Kenzie?"

"You need help, Mommy."

"Mommy will be fine." Jeff was calm. Reaching for Kenzie's tote, he handed it to her.

She sidled toward the back door.

"No, Jeff." Lauren blocked Kenzie's path. "Let her stay with me, please. What if she's not safe at Tara's?"

"She'll be okay," Jeff said.

"At least let me call Suzanne and see if Kenzie can stay there until you can pick her up." Even as Lauren said this, she wondered how she could ask Suzanne for a favor after yesterday, after leaving their daughters stranded. How would she explain it?

But Kenzie said no. "I want to go now, Mom."

Lauren looked down at her, and she knew holding Kenzie would be the same as trying to hold a small bird.

Jeff found her gaze. "I'll come back as quickly as I can get everything settled with Kaiser, okay?"

"How long?"

"An hour, tops."

He came to her and kissed her lightly. Lauren smelled his aftershave, something that always reminded her of lemongrass and wind. She loved it and could never remember the name. She clutched his shirtfront, bunching it in both hands. "Don't leave me. Please," she whispered against his chest. "I'm so scared."

"I won't be gone long, I promise. It'll be all right." He set her gently apart from him.

And then he was gone.

But the notepad, Bo Laughlin's notepad, was here in her hand.

How had it come to be in her possession? Panic clawed out of her stomach, ballooning against her rib cage.

She carried the notepad into the kitchen and setting it on the island, picked up her coffee mug, dumped the contents into the sink, and rinsed it. She cleaned the coffeemaker, wiped down the countertops. But she could not forget it.

Bo's notepad.

Maybe if she read what he'd written. She lifted the cover, enough that she registered pencil smudges, and rifling the pages, she saw darker strokes that seemed angular and hurried, illegible, but here and there a word emerged: parakeet, flowering, harbinger. On one page he had written: *The path of least resistance leads to crooked rivers and crooked men.*

Lauren thought she recognized it as a quote from Thoreau. She remembered Charlotte Meany—Ms. M—saying Bo had an affinity for him. But farther on, the pages were filled with more gibberish, entire lines where Bo had scratched only numbers. She let the cover fall and crossed her arms, cupping her shoulders, keeping her eye on the little notebook as if it might leap from the spot where it lay. Blood hammered through her heart like heavy footsteps.

What should be done with it?

Throw it away . . .

The sense of this, what amounted to an order, hovered in her mind. But there was only one answer, one right thing to do, and if she did not know this consciously, she did know it where it counted, in her bones, in the center of her soul.

24

"L auren Wilder is here," Carol said. "She wants to talk to you."

Annie set the last glass in the dishwasher and closed the door.

"I can say you aren't here," Carol said. "You really shouldn't be," she added gently.

"No, it's fine." Annie untied her apron and hanging it on the hook near the door, went into the dining area. Breakfast was over. There was no one else in the café but Lauren.

She looked awful, Annie thought. She looked as if she might bolt from the building or break into pieces, and when she spoke, when she said, "Oh, Annie. I'm so sorry," her voice trembled. "How are you? How's Bo's dad?"

Annie slid onto the bench opposite her. "The doctor gave JT something to sleep," she said for no particular reason she knew. Her head was full of doubt. Why was Lauren here? Was it some sort of game? Was she crazy after all?

"But not you?" Lauren searched Annie's gaze, and there was real caring there, a genuine and tender concern. It was Annie's mother's gaze. But maybe every mother could summon that depth of feeling at will. Maybe every mother lied when it suited her agenda.

Annie looked down. "I didn't want to take anything." She didn't say it was because she was afraid. She wasn't sure of what. Maybe that something worse might happen while she slept. And no one needed to tell her how silly it was, although Cooper had tried.

"Have the police arrested anyone? Do they know who did it?"

Annie thought about the two youngish guys, the possible suspects Cooper had mentioned when they were in Sheriff Neely's office in Cedar Cliff. Cooper said he'd been on an overpass, hooking up a woman's car to his tow truck a few weeks ago, and looking down into the intersection below, he'd happened to see "these jerks," Cooper had called them, "messing with Bo." They pushed him, taunted him. Bo threw a rock, hitting one of them in the face. Cooper would have called 911, he said, but the police pulled up just then. The last thing Cooper heard, though, was one of the jerks shouting that he'd *fucking kill the retard* if he ever saw him again. It was nothing new. Annie didn't see the sense in repeating it. The police had dismissed the lead anyway. They were focused on the drug angle.

"There's nothing solid yet," Annie said. She looked through the window. Across the street the door to Canaday's Sporting Goods Store stood open to the cool fall breeze. This morning, Ted had come in for breakfast. When Annie waited on him, he'd said how badly he felt, that Bo's death was just horrible and senseless. He'd had tears in his eyes, left his breakfast sandwich uneaten. She felt terrible for him, for everyone who had worked so hard to find Bo. She looked at Lauren. "You know Greg Honey." She wasn't asking.

"Yes," Lauren said. "He's my sister's boyfriend."

"Why didn't you tell me last night? The police are looking for him. Do you know where he is? How to get in touch with him?"

"I don't. I thought he might be at my sister's, so I went there and looked through the house. He wasn't there. I don't think she knows anything—"

"So you aren't sure."

"No."

"Is that why you came here now, to tell me about your sister? Because you should be telling the police."

Lauren let out a long breath. She swiped her hair behind her ears. "I know, but there are issues with my family—"

"Why are you here, Lauren?" Annie was snappish, out of patience. She couldn't help it. *Don't tell me your troubles,* she wanted to say. *I have to bury my brother, but not until the coroner gets through slicing him up.*

Lauren wasn't paying attention; she was fishing for something in her purse, and when she brought out a small notepad, Annie recognized it, and her heart stalled.

"Where did you get this?" She took it from Lauren, examining it, lifting the cover, running her fingertip over Bo's name, tracing the loops, the smudged angles of letters and numbers, mostly nonsense. Looking up, she was startled to find Lauren in tears, visibly shaking, and it seemed ominous. It seemed to confirm that Annie was right to have doubts about her.

"It's a simple question," she said.

Lauren started to answer, but then the café door opened, and Cooper walked in with Rufus. The dog trotted over immediately, wanting Annie's attention, but she couldn't give it. "This is Lauren Wilder," she said meaningfully to Cooper.

His eyes widened.

"It turns out she does know Greg Honey. Her sister's dating him."

Cooper sat down.

"She's brought me Bo's notepad." Annie turned back to Lauren, locking her gaze. "She was just going to tell me where she got it, weren't you, Lauren?"

"I found it on the floor of the mudroom at my house this morning." Lauren paused to gather herself, mopping her face with a tissue, settling her breath. "I asked my husband about it, but neither of us knows how it got there."

"Well, one of you must," Cooper said.

Lauren's gaze fell.

"Lauren?" Her name out of Annie's mouth was a warning. "What else happened when you got out of your car last Friday and talked to Bo? Did you buy drugs from him?"

"No! It was broad daylight. Do you think I would take such a risk? Believe me, when I was on Oxy, I was smarter than that."

"Maybe you arranged to meet him later, then." Annie's pulse was thrumming. She bent forward. "What happened to him?"

"I don't know. I swear I didn't see him again after Friday."

"Then how did his notepad get in your house?"

"Jeff thinks Bo gave it to me."

"What do you think?" Cooper asked.

"Bo wouldn't give his notepad to anyone." But even as Annie said this, she could hear JT saying she didn't know Bo as well as she thought she did, that all along she'd had ideas about Bo and how he would act that had turned out to be wrong.

"Maybe I'm crazy," Lauren said.

Annie gave a short, brutal laugh.

Cooper said, "Is it possible you got the notepad from Greg Honey?"

"Oh," Lauren said, and it was as if Cooper's idea surprised her. "I don't think so. I haven't seen him, either."

But she didn't look any more certain of that than of anything else she'd claimed as fact.

"You know more than you're saying." Annie was convinced of it. She'd witnessed unbalanced behavior in Bo. She knew how misled you could be by your wish to believe in people like him and

Lauren, who were kind, who appeared to be sensitive and in need of protection. Desire was a fierce thing. It could blind you to all kinds of truth.

Lauren frowned as if she was trying to work out Annie's meaning.

"You've told so many stories," Annie said, and Lauren turned her glance away. "You saw who murdered Bo, didn't you?" The horrible certainty growing in Annie's mind drove her voice higher. Cooper put a placating hand on her arm. That didn't stop her. "You were with Greg Honey when he shot him, weren't you? Or maybe you shot him yourself, and this is some kind of game."

"But why would I hurt Bo? What motive would I have?"

"Drugs," Annie said as if one word could sum it up. And she could have cried out over the pointlessness of it. Annie couldn't think of anything stupider to die over. She waited for Lauren to say something, defend herself, explain. But she only stared blankly at Annie, and there was terror in her silence. Her eyes were wild, her face as pale as old frost. Looking at her, Annie thought: *This is what it's like when a person breaks down, when they cross the border from sanity to insanity.*

"I—I have to go." Lauren clutched her purse to her chest. "My children—"

"Why don't we go and talk to the police." Cooper's tone was gently persuasive.

But Lauren shook her head and slid out of the booth.

"It will look better if you go to them on your own," Annie said. When she spoke, Lauren was near the door and she paused on the threshold, but only for a moment. Then she went out, and the door closed behind her with a sigh.

25

Walking swiftly to her car, Lauren got inside it and locked the door. Thoughts loomed, erroneous, jumbled—one, that she could die. That people did die in the aftermath of a terrible shock. It wasn't an old wives' tale or an urban myth. It happened.

God! The name, whether prayer or curse, burst into her brain. She grabbed the steering wheel, letting her head fall to her curled fists, feeling the bite of her knuckles.

What was happening to her? What in the hell was going on?

Could Greg have shot Bo in a drug deal? Had she been there? Could *she* have done it? But she had never even held a gun, much less shot one—had she? She wasn't violent. She could lose her temper, with her kids, with Jeff, at herself, at life. But didn't everyone? She wasn't insane. *She wasn't.*

But since the fall, her brain wasn't reliable. And she was an addict, one with holes in her memory. That much was true and shameful, and it haunted Lauren. She would never forgive herself for the damage she had caused as a result of getting hooked on the Oxy, and she knew there was much about that time that she didn't remember and never would.

But could she forget killing someone?

If her brain didn't remember, wouldn't her heart? Her hands? Wouldn't the knowledge run in her blood, lodge in the pores of her skin, the marrow of her bones? Wouldn't some living part of her remember robbing the life of another?

A sound broke from deep inside her, something harsh that hurt her chest, and she clamped her teeth against it, starting the Navigator, backing into the street, then jerking to a stop when a horn blared. Her rearview mirror framed the driver's red face, the stab of his raised middle finger. She waited until he passed, then waited even longer, because she realized she had no idea what to do now, where to go.

Talk to the police, Cooper had advised.

It'll look better if you go to them on your own, Annie had said.

She thought of Jeff, remembering his promise to return to her. Quickly, he'd said. *An hour, tops.* It was longer than that now, more than two hours. Pulling her cell phone from her purse, she tried calling him, leaving a message when he didn't answer. Clicking off, she didn't know what she'd said. She wondered if it would make sense. He would be worried, she thought.

She thought of her children, how angry they were with her, how it was quite possible they hated her, her own babies that she had brought into the world. Lauren could feel their small shapes in her arms, the imprint of their soles when she'd pressed their tiny feet against her mouth. Her heart ached for them, for how she knew she didn't deserve them, and for the way she understood now that neither her regret nor her atonement would ever be enough to regain their trust, much less their love and respect. But if she could face the truth, no matter how horrible and twisted, it might make a difference— at least to her. She found Detective Cosgrove's contact card and set it on the console.

There would be no turning back after she called him, and she couldn't be certain once she told him about the notepad what the outcome would be. He would arrest her, she guessed. And oddly, the thought didn't scare her. It seemed inevitable. She would have to make arrangements for her children; she didn't want them at Tara's right now. With Jeff out of pocket, there was only one option, and picking up her phone, Lauren dialed Suzanne's number before she could second-guess herself. In her former life, they had talked or texted or e-mailed nearly every day. Now she was filled with dread. She couldn't be sure Suzanne would agree to help her . . . Lauren, the nutcase, the dope fiend, the one who left little girls waiting, alone and vulnerable.

Suppose Suzanne ignored her call? Or hung up on her?

"Lauren?"

Her breath froze. "Yes," she said. "It's me." And she rushed on, words tripping over each other—that she was sorry for the misunderstanding yesterday, she didn't know what happened, well, she did, but it was dumb. Hearing herself, she paused. "Is Amanda all right?"

"She was more worried than anything. She didn't want Kenzie going with Steve."

"Amanda was right not to."

"She's not as devoted to her ballet lessons as Kenzie," Suzanne said, and Lauren thought she heard traces of the old affection in Suzanne's voice. "How is Kenzie? Amanda said they kept her in the hospital overnight."

"Yes, but she's out now. She's at Tara's." Lauren hesitated. She ran her fingertip along the lower arc of the steering wheel. "I'm really sorry, Suze. Not only for yesterday but for so much more. I can't imagine what you must think."

"If you're asking, what I think is how much it hurts me that you won't talk to me."

"I'm not sure what you mean," Lauren said.

"You've shut me out. I wanted to help you, to be there for you, but for a long time now you've acted as if we're nothing more than acquaintances."

Lauren was dumbfounded. "I thought you didn't—I mean after everything, the drugs—you know—I—"

"My sister is an alcoholic. I've gone to 12-step meetings with her, the open meetings. I've gone to Al-Anon, too. I couldn't ever judge you, Lauren. I would think you of all people would know that about me."

"Oh, Suzy, I guess I—I was just—I've been so ashamed of myself, you know?" Lauren's voice slipped and caught. She almost couldn't breathe around the tears that were jammed in her throat.

"You go to 12-step. You know what they say about shame and guilt."

"We're not supposed to go there." Lauren paused. "It's hard, Suzy."

"Yeah. I can imagine. And this is not an excuse, okay? But it's not like you were looking to get high. It was the pain. I never saw anyone in as much agony as you were after your accident. God, I still don't know how you got through it. I admire you, Lauren, in so many ways. I'm not sure I would have had the strength you do."

Lauren tipped her head against the seatback. She felt the tears come, felt them sliding down her cheeks, along the line of her jaw. She couldn't stop them any more than she could stop the wave of love and gratitude for Suzanne's kindness that swept through her.

"Lauren?"

She cleared her throat, swiped at the tears and under her nose. "I never meant for you to be hurt."

"I guess I should have tried harder."

"No," Lauren said. "It was me. I have hated myself so much."

"You have to stop that now. Okay? Can you?"

"I need your help, Suze."

"Oh?"

A weight of caution rode in the syllable, and Lauren regretted it, but she went on; she had no choice. "Kenzie is at Tara's, and I wonder if you could pick her up and keep her with you, maybe all night. I'm not sure."

"What's going on?"

"Tara's been sick. I don't want Kenzie catching whatever it was."

"That isn't the whole story."

"No. Look, I've got no right to ask you to bear with me, but can you?"

It wasn't so much that Suzanne didn't answer as that she seemed to be waiting for the more that Lauren couldn't say.

"I would tell you, except I don't know myself." Lauren cut herself off with a groan. "I know how it sounds."

"I'll pick Kenzie up," Suzanne said after a pause. "Does Tara know I'm coming? Should I call her?"

"I will," Lauren said. "Thank you, Suzy, more than I can say."

"I hope one day we can talk again the way we used to."

"Me, too," Lauren said. "You have no idea how much I've missed you. I feel so badly for how wrong I've been, and you're right. I should have known better." Ready tears packed her throat again, and she swallowed them, fiercely. There wasn't time now for despair or regret.

After she hung up with Suzanne, she made one more call to Pat, Gabe's mother, and asked if Drew could come home with Gabe after school. She hadn't wanted to load the responsibility for Drew on Suzanne, too. Pat seemed a little confused.

"The boys have an overnight planned here already," she said. "I've been cooking up a storm. You know how they eat."

Lauren closed her eyes. Had she known this? Or had Jeff forgotten to tell her?

"How is Kenzie? We heard she was in an accident."

"She's fine, out of the hospital. She was lucky." *Lucky?* The observer in Lauren's mind sneered.

Pat said they would take good care of Drew, and Lauren thanked her, and after saying good-bye, before she could lose her nerve, she called Detective Cosgrove. "I need to see you," she said when he picked up.

"I'm in your neighborhood," he told her.

Her heart jumped. But it seemed reasonable, didn't it? He was waiting for her, waiting to arrest her. She might have asked if that was the case, but instead she said she would meet him at the house. "I'll be there in twenty minutes," she added.

Before leaving the parking space, she made two more calls, another to Jeff and a second to Tara. Neither of them answered, and Lauren fought a fresh wave of paranoia that rose in her mind, threatening her resolve. She said nothing to Jeff's voice mail, but reaching Tara's, she explained that Suzanne would be picking Kenzie up. It bothered her, not talking directly to Tara, but it was the best she could do for right now. Backing into the street, she thought at least the kids wouldn't be there to see it, if she was handcuffed.

Cosgrove and Willis were waiting for her in the driveway, standing outside their plain brown sedan. Jeff's truck wasn't there, and relief that, like the kids, he wouldn't have to witness her arrest warred with apprehension. Something about his absence wasn't right, but she had no time to dwell on what it might be, caught up as she was in greeting the detectives, shaking their hands—oh, they were so congenial—and leading them into her house. She bypassed the formal living room this time, ushering them into the great room instead.

She had the notion that she didn't want to be arrested in a room with pink silk-upholstered chairs, and it was laughable that she would choose that detail to be concerned over.

Cosgrove and Willis sat on the leather sectional, and she settled on an ottoman across from them. The oversized coffee table between them had been a dining table until floodwater had damaged the bottom of its turned legs. Lauren had found it in the South of France while on a buying trip there, and she'd had it shipped to the warehouse, where Jeff had cut down the legs. She braced her hand on it now, steadied by the solid feel of the wood, and the sense of its survival, despite its traumatic history.

"I guess you're probably aware from the news that Bo Laughlin's body was found late last night." Cosgrove wasn't asking.

Lauren nodded, not correcting his assumption about her having heard it on the news.

"Do you know where your husband is?"

Lauren looked at Willis in surprise. "At work, I think."

"He isn't there, Mrs. Wilder, if you mean the warehouse." The hint of derision in Willis's tone seemed to celebrate the fact that he knew something Lauren did not.

"He might be on the job site. He's taking down the old Waller-Land building. He was meeting Ben Kaiser, the owner, there."

"Huh." Willis was full of himself. "Getting kind of late to still be on the job, isn't it?"

His attitude irked Lauren, but more than that, she was astonished and a little alarmed that the detectives had been searching for Jeff. "Why are you looking for him?" Lauren addressed Cosgrove.

He said, "You wanted to talk to me?"

"Yes. I found something of Bo's, a—a notepad."

"Where?"

"In the mudroom, on the floor. I think it fell out of my purse."

"You think? Is there some other way it could have gotten into your mudroom?" Cosgrove regarded her, brows raised.

Panic forked like summer lightning through her veins. "No," she answered. "Not that I can think of."

"What are you saying, Mrs. Wilder?" Willis asked.

"I don't know. I don't remember how it came into my possession."

"Where is it now?"

Lauren looked at Detective Cosgrove. "I gave it to his sister. Annie has it. I wanted to return it to her. I wasn't sure what to do with it or what it meant. I mean, my having it. You know I have trouble with my memory. Driving here, I was thinking if I were to undergo hypnosis, I might remember how I got it."

"Do you recognize this rug?" Willis opened a notebook and taking out a photograph, slid it across the coffee table toward her.

Lauren picked the photo up; her heart's pulse was no more than a whisper in her ears. "Where did you get this?"

"Have you seen the rug?" Willis was out of patience.

"Yes," she answered, and her manner was as curt.

The area rug had been a cornerstone of her childhood. Photos of her and Tara first crawling, then walking on it proliferated the family albums. They both loved it, not only for its beauty but also for its romantic history. It was from Kashmir, having been brought from there by their father and presented to their grandparents on the occasion of his marriage to their mother. Made of hand-knotted silk in rich shades of rose and green and soft blue, with touches of brown and gold, the pattern was a fantasy of birds, flitting through the wide-spreading canopy of a plane tree.

For the whole of her life, as far back as Lauren could remember, the rug had graced the floor of her grandparents' parlor at the farm—until she had sent it to be cleaned a year ago. When the cleaning company brought it back to the farm, she'd had them stow it in the dining room, and she'd left it rolled there, intending to talk to Tara about it, knowing they would have to decide between them who should have it.

"Mrs. Wilder?" Willis's tone bore an edge.

She met his gaze. "Where did you get this?" she insisted.

"It's a crime-scene photo," Willis said. "One of the techs took it after they unrolled Laughlin's body out of it."

Lauren stared at him, trying to sort out his meaning, to put the words *crime scene* together with the picture of her grandparents' rug. "That can't be true." She said the only reasonable thing.

"Oh, it's true, all right, Mrs. Wilder." Willis nodded, and he was cocky; he was celebrating. He had all the answers.

How Lauren hated him, a man she scarcely knew. She imagined slapping him across his fat face. She could feel the sting of his flesh on her palm, the way such an assault would jar her arm, and she relished the sensation. "I don't understand any of this," she said. "How did you know to ask me about the rug?"

Cosgrove ignored her question. "Your husband was at your grandparents' farm last weekend, wasn't he, along with your sister and Greg Honey?"

"Yes, but I don't see what that has to do with—"

"Were you there, Mrs. Wilder?" Willis asked.

"No. I told you before—" She paused, trying to remember, if she actually had told them about the headache that had kept her home.

"Told us what?" Cosgrove wanted to know.

"Maybe it was Sheriff Audi I told—I had a headache and didn't go."

"You were here alone, then? At home all weekend, after your meeting with Laughlin?"

"It wasn't a meeting. I told you, I only stopped to see if he needed help."

"Oh, right." Willis smiled. "I remember now. She's the Good Samaritan, isn't she Jimmy?"

"Why are you here?" Lauren was tired of the game. "If you're going to arrest me, just do it."

"We aren't ready to arrest anyone yet, Mrs. Wilder," Cosgrove said.

"No," Willis cut in, "but I'd sure like to know why she thinks she'd be the one. Wouldn't you, Jimmy?"

Cosgrove didn't respond, but neither did he take his eyes off Lauren.

She felt the brunt of their gazes, watchful, expectant. As if they were waiting for her to say something incriminating. It was like any number of things she'd seen on TV, on one of the crime shows or the ID channel, and something she had gleaned from watching all those shows warned her not to say more. She cupped her elbows.

Cosgrove scootched a bit to the front of the sofa, and he smiled, but it was window dressing. "When was the last time you talked to your sister?"

Lauren's heart dipped. "Tara?" It was all she could manage.

"Look," Willis said, "you need to tell us what you know."

"Should I get a lawyer?"

"Why?" Willis asked. "Have you done something criminal?"

Had she? She couldn't think, couldn't find air for speech. Her mind felt broken. She felt as if she had been handed a puzzle with dozens of pieces and a set time to work it. The clock was ticking, the task impossible. The silence filled up with the noise in her head.

Cosgrove and Willis kept talking to her, asking the same questions again and yet one more time: *When did you last speak to your husband? Your sister? What did you do the weekend they were at the farm? Where did you go? Did you ever see Greg Honey and Bo Laughlin together? Did you spend time with Greg Honey and Bo Laughlin? Did your husband? Have you or your husband ever used or sold drugs? What about Greg Honey? Ever know him to use or sell drugs?*

She answered but only for herself, explaining how she'd become addicted. She told them where she'd bought her illegal Oxy, and it wasn't from Bo. She didn't elaborate, and they didn't ask her to. She felt as if they already knew everything she was telling them.

"Do you own a handgun? Does anyone in your family?"

Lauren stared at Willis. "No. I mean as far as Jeff and Tara are concerned—they don't have a gun. We don't like them, as a family."

"What about Greg Honey? Does he own a handgun?"

"I don't know. I doubt it. He's not the type." She stopped to consider. *But no.* She had no right, no responsibility to tell the police, of all people, the thing Greg had discussed in confidence at a 12-step meeting. His legal history would be a matter of record anyway. Let the cops find it out on their own. She would bet money they already had.

"What do you know about this?" Willis opened the folder again, taking out a set of papers, stapled at the top.

Lauren didn't need a closer look to see that it was the asbestos-notification form, what looked like a copy, but she took it from him, flipping to the last page to find that her signature and that of the notary, Elizabeth McQueen, was still there. She looked at it more closely this time. And what she saw stopped her breath. She locked eyes with Willis. *I don't know anything about this.* That's what she wanted to say. She could imagine his sneer if she did. "Is this a crime-scene photo, too?" Her sarcasm tasted flat.

Not even Willis was amused. "Is that your signature?"

She studied it again. "It is, but something about it isn't—"

"Isn't—?" Cosgrove prompted.

"It looks like my handwriting, but I don't think it is."

Willis snorted and slapped his knee.

"Are you saying it's forged?"

Lauren met Cosgrove's glance. "Exactly what are *you* saying, Detective? What does this form have to do with drugs or Bo or the rug you found him wrapped in?"

"What would you say if I were to tell you that there's little to no asbestos in the Waller-Land building, yet your company, Wilder and Tate, collected some two hundred thousand dollars in cash from Mr. Kaiser for its removal, just this morning, in fact."

"I don't believe you." She didn't really know what she believed, did she?

"Really? You signed the permit. That's your signature."

"I don't know that it is," Lauren said, and she wondered how she managed to speak, her mouth was so dry. She wondered if Jeff had asked for another survey, a second opinion. It wasn't unheard of. She should remember. God, how she hated this, the way her mind dragged. *Pick up, pick up . . .*

"Are you familiar with Cornerstone Bank? Isn't it true you have an account there?"

She looked at Willis. "Yes. I mean, I've never been there, but—"

"So you don't have an account there? Which is it, Mrs. Wilder?" Willis was smiling now.

Cosgrove said, "When we visited the bank earlier and talked to Paul Thibideaux—he's an old college buddy of your husband's, isn't he?—anyway, he's the vice president there at Cornerstone now, and he told us Jeff made a deposit today into your account, an amount that almost exactly matches the sum that was collected from Mr. Kaiser under the table, so to speak, to take away the phantom asbestos along with the rest of his building."

"Are you saying that Jeff collected money from Mr. Kaiser for work that doesn't need doing?"

"I think that's about right." Cosgrove kept his glance level.

"In other words, Mrs. Wilder, the whole thing with the asbestos was a scam."

Lauren looked at Willis. "That's ridiculous. I don't know where you get your information—"

"You signed the form that indicates you were acting as the property owner's—that would be Mr. Kaiser—acting as his agent. Its existence is a matter of record, most notably Ms. McQueen's, the notary's, record. In addition, she made copies, one of which you're holding."

Willis waited.

Lauren said nothing.

"Come on, Mrs. Wilder. You signed the thing. Don't play dumb now. You must have known."

"I didn't." Lauren knew how it sounded.

"The money was deposited into your account." It was Cosgrove's turn to intimidate her.

"The joint account—" Lauren began.

"No," Cosgrove said. "It's only in your name. Mr. Thibideaux verified that. Your husband can sign checks and make deposits, that sort of thing, but his position is secondary, per your request."

Lauren touched her temples. "None of this makes any sense."

"Let me ask you this." Cosgrove inched forward, bracing his elbows on his knees. "Do you know anyone by the name of Wick Matson?"

"Wick? He's a heavy-equipment contractor we—well, Jeff—"

"When was the last time you saw him or spoke to him?"

"I don't know. Jeff had lunch with him last Tuesday."

"You didn't eat with them?" Willis asked.

"No." She remembered Jeff's dark mood when he'd come back that day, the same day she'd had car trouble. He'd gone into his office and closed the door, shutting her out. "What is going on? I don't understand." A sensation of hysteria rose quickly from the floor of her stomach; she felt it loosening her grip, the hold she had on her self-control. She thought when Cosgrove and Willis stood up, they were going to dangle a set of handcuffs in her face and place her under arrest.

But they didn't.

They turned to go.

Lauren escorted them to the front door and saw them through it.

When Cosgrove paused outside on the porch, so did her heart, but he only told her she should let them know if she heard from Greg Honey.

Willis spoke up. "Also, you'd be wise not to leave town, Mrs. Wilder," he said, and he saluted.

As soon as she shut the door, Lauren went into the kitchen, picked up her cell phone, and dialed Jeff's number. It went straight to voice mail. She tried again with the same result. "Where are you?" she asked after the beep. Clicking off, she put her fingertips over her ears and dragged them back through her hair. "What is happening?" she whispered.

It was when she picked up her phone again, intending to call Tara, that she noticed she had a text message from her and one from Jeff. She read Jeff's first: *Ran into some trbl w/Kaiser. Call u when I can. Love you.*

Liar, Lauren thought.

Tara's note read: *K at A's. No problem. Talk tomorrow.*

Lauren stared at the tiny screen a moment, and then she typed a response to Tara's message: *The police were here. I'm coming over— now!* and in answer to Jeff's text, she wrote: *Cops were here. I know about trbl. We need to talk! I'll be at Tara's,* and it was hard to see clearly enough to type through the haze of her fear-fueled fury. But she was glad for the anger, for how it burned through her panic and cleared her mind.

26

She had her keys and her cell phone in hand, ready to walk out the door, when Tara texted back: *Police???!!! Why? What did they want? Where is Jeff? Do you know? He's not answ'ing his phone. OMG!* And something about the message, beyond the words and their import, jolted Lauren beyond anything that had gone before. It took every ounce of her will to go from the house to the car, and even as she walked, she could feel the world, the one that was known to her and beloved, the one she had sought to recover, crumbling once more beneath her feet.

She went by Wilder and Tate first, praying to find Jeff's truck there, but the parking lot was empty, the warehouse locked up tight. She thought of driving out to the Waller-Land building and decided it made better sense to go to Tara's first. Driving there, her head felt hollow and her pulse ticked, a clock marking time.

Could she be hallucinating?

If only she were dreaming, it would be such a relief, like running warm water over her hands when they were chilled.

As if she'd been watching, Tara opened the back door before Lauren reached it. Her hands flew to her mouth, and the sound, what began as an awful sob—of grief, of outright terror—these were plain on her face—was stifled, and all that came out was a small cry.

"TeeRee, my God! What is it?" Lauren stepped over the threshold, gathering her sister into her arms, rocking her. And it wasn't that she forgot the hostility that strung itself as tightly as barbed wire between them. It was simply that love, the habit of caring, of soothing, was stronger just then and acted like a buffer.

It had been the same when, the year after their parents died, Tara, who had been all of seventeen, had come home and confessed to Lauren she was pregnant. Lauren's mouth had fallen open. She couldn't have been more shocked if Tara had taken a shovel and struck her with it across her forehead.

"We haven't even talked about sex," she had said.

"Well, you don't have to talk about it to do it," Tara said.

"How far along?" Lauren asked, but to herself she was thinking, *My God* and *What now?* and *How could you be so stupid?* Whether she meant herself for not realizing it might happen or Tara for letting it happen, she wasn't sure.

"Maybe six weeks," Tara answered, and then she began to cry, and Lauren reached for her. It was what their mother would have done, offered comfort first, a lecture later.

In the same way she had then, Lauren waited now for Tara's breath to settle before releasing her, and they went into the kitchen. Tara found a tissue, and Lauren switched on the small lamp Tara kept on the countertop.

"I'm sorry I couldn't keep the kids. I just wasn't up for it," Tara said.

"They're fine for now. It didn't seem wise to have them here anyway."

"Jeff won't pick up when I call. Do you know where he is? Will you call him?"

"Why? What is going on? The police are looking for him and Greg. You wouldn't believe the things they told me and the questions they asked. It's like they think I'm guilty of—They have a photo of the rug, Tee, the one from Grandma's house. They said Bo's body was found wrapped in it." Lauren paused, giving Tara time to speak, and when she didn't, Lauren said her name, "Tara? Come on! You're scaring me."

She blew her nose and splashed water on her face. "Let's make hot chocolate with Baileys, okay? And sit down."

"No—"

"Trust me," Tara said. "You're going to need it."

"Okay, but no Baileys for me." Lauren knew Tara was buying time, but she went along. She didn't know how they managed it, measuring the hot-cocoa mix and water, her hands and Tara's were shaking so badly.

They sat in the breakfast nook.

Tara opened two sugar packets, adding them to her cup as if the chocolate needed sweetening. She stirred her spoon round and round until Lauren thought she might scream, and darting out her hand, she clamped her fingers around Tara's wrist.

And that's when Tara said it, said, "Oh, my God, Lauren, we shot Bo. It was Greg or Jeff—one of them killed him."

27

Lauren stared at Tara. In her mind, she tried to find a way around it, the meaning of the words. Her brain had put them in the wrong order, or it had heard wrong altogether, as it was inclined to do nowadays.

Tears welled in Tara's eyes. "It was an accident. You have to believe that, okay? They didn't mean to shoot him, but you know, you can't see the road from behind the barn. They thought it was safe."

"Who? Who thought what was safe?" Lauren still wasn't buying it; there must be a way to hear that this had nothing to do with her or her family. She watched Tara's mouth. The tears that collected and pooled in the corners, dripped from her chin. They speckled the backs of her hands.

"Jeff and Greg found the gun. Grandpa's gun? Do you remember it? Jeff said it was a Colt .45. Vintage. Probably worth something."

"Vaguely," Lauren answered. He'd kept it in a box in the old Hoosier cabinet in the barn. Lauren remembered Jeff talking about the Hoosier when he'd called her on Saturday morning, the morning she'd been so worried he knew about the Oxy she'd found in the study. He'd said he'd been sorting through the tools inside the cabinet. He hadn't mentioned finding a gun.

"They wanted to shoot it. I thought it was a stupid idea." Tara wiped her face, raked back her hair, and her gestures seemed rough and hurtful. She asked if Lauren remembered the way the land behind the barn sloped to the road. "There are those limestone ledges there," she said. "That's where they set up their targets, old glass jars and cans. I was in the kitchen, opening a bottle of wine. I made a tray with cheese and crackers. I thought if I took that and the wine to them, they'd quit."

Tara left her chair and went to the kitchen window to look out. At what, Lauren didn't know. The only thing visible was Tara's own reflection, a near white, almost featureless oval, floating in a rectangle of glass as gleaming and black as oil.

"I was too late," she said. "Bo was down there dying even before I got the tray out the door. Jeff and Greg might not have even known he was there if I hadn't joined them. I'm the one who heard him. A whimpering sound. I thought it was an injured animal."

"But how, TeeRee? How did they not see?"

"You don't remember how thick the brush is along there? Even in daylight, it's almost impossible to see the road. And it was getting dark. The light was almost gone."

They shared a silence.

Lauren broke it. "Which one of them—?"

"I don't know. They were both firing the gun."

"Bo was whimpering, you said, so he was alive when you got to him?"

"I almost didn't pay attention. For a moment, I thought it was only the wind, but then I heard him say *please help me, please help me*. It was awful." Tara turned from the window. Tears welled in her eyes again; she brushed them away. "I went down the slope as fast as I could and found him. There was already blood under him, so much blood. I never saw—"

"Did anyone call 911? Did you go for help?" Lauren asked, even though she knew that if they had, she wouldn't be sitting here listening to a horror story.

"We couldn't get a signal, and then—then Jeff and Greg—they both—" Tara sat down and closing her eyes, rocked herself.

She needed a tissue, but Lauren couldn't move.

"I don't want to tell you the rest," Tara said. "I don't know how."

"You left him there. Is that it? The three of you left Bo there to die?"

"No! I tried CPR, but Jeff said I was making him bleed worse. We kept trying to get a signal, Greg and I did. I told Bo to hang on, but he couldn't—" Tara's voice broke on a little sob. Her throat worked when she swallowed.

"How have you kept this to yourself?" Lauren asked softly.

"It was Jeff, and I'm not just saying that. I know I'm not his biggest fan, but the way he acted—he was just manic and crazy, shouting at us that we weren't going to involve the police, and if I chose to, I'd be sorry."

"He threatened you?"

"More like guilted me. He said I should consider you and the kids, how if what happened got out and he went to jail, it would destroy your lives, and did I want that on my conscience."

"That doesn't sound like him, Tee."

"I know. He can be an asshole—sorry." Tara made a face. "He thinks you're still so fragile. He was in superprotective mode, I guess. It was weird and horrible, the whole thing—"

"It was an accident, though!" Lauren bent forward, disbelieving, adamant. "Hiding it only made it worse. Jeff—all of you—should have known better!"

"I did everything I could, Lauren."

313

Tara's voice, her wild-eyed gaze, were feverish, hectic, but Lauren was in no frame of mind to soothe her.

"What about Greg?" she said. "Did he go along with covering it up, too?"

"Yes, but at least he had a—an excuse, I guess you could call it."

"Because he killed another man." Lauren didn't think twice about giving away Greg's secret, the one she'd harbored since hearing him confess it during the 12-step meeting last summer. Confidentiality no longer seemed an issue.

"You knew?"

"I've been worried about you ever since I found out, but everything we say in meetings is supposed to stay in meetings."

"He said going to prison was his wake-up call, his come-to-Jesus, what made him get off heroin. He was in there five years for manslaughter."

"Did he tell you how it happened, that he was high on heroin when this guy tried to rob him, and he shot him? He said he could have walked away, but he didn't."

"You can tell he feels sick about it, though. He told us prison was hell, that he'd rather blow out his brains than go back." Tara locked Lauren's gaze. "He put the gun to his head."

"For all you know, he was high when he did that."

"No, I don't think—"

"He's slipped up before, TeeRee. Twice in three years that I know of. He was partners with some guy—another dealer that Annie, Bo's sister, dated. Leighton something. The police are looking for both of them."

"Greg took off as soon as he and Jeff—once they took away the body. I don't know where he went."

"That's the part I can't believe!" Lauren got up and, needing distance, went to stand behind her chair. "How could you roll Bo's body up in our grandma's beautiful rug?"

"It wasn't me!"

"But you let them." Lauren's voice was shrill. Rounding her chair, she sat down again.

"I couldn't stop them. If you'd been there—"

"You have to go to the police."

"No!" Tara's head popped up from her hands. "You can't, either. I wouldn't have told you if I'd thought—"

"Tara! For God's sake, a man—Bo Laughlin—is dead; his family is sick with worry. You can't let this go on. I can't believe you agreed to cover it up in the first place."

"I told you I didn't agree, and anyway, how can you of all people preach to me?"

"Really? That's how you want to play it?" Lauren took her cup to the sink, rinsed it, and shut off the tap, hard; then picking up a hand towel, she turned to Tara. "Fine. We'll do it your way. So you can consider this *your* intervention, all right? The one where I say you either go to the police or I will. Hmm? The way you said to me at my intervention that I could either get help or you—you and Jeff—would see to it for me. Remember? You threatened to take my children if I didn't do as I was told."

Tara didn't answer, but Lauren didn't really give her the chance. Things, details were coming together in her mind. She was angry now. It was difficult to be articulate, yet she tried to put words to what was only half-formed sense. "This whole entire week—" she began, stopped and started again. "The things I've been thinking, blaming myself for—scaring myself over—my God, I even thought I might have done something to Bo myself."

"I'm not following."

"Jeff went along when I thought I had brought the notepad into the house. How could he do that?" Lauren folded the towel in half, running her fingers along the crease. She ought to feel relieved, she guessed, to know beyond doubt that she'd had no part in Bo's death, but she didn't.

"What notepad?"

Lauren looked at Tara. "You lied to me last night. You weren't hiding Greg, but you knew. You knew what happened, that Bo was dead and how."

"I didn't want you involved. You've been through so much."

"You didn't want me involved? Are you kidding? We're family, Tara—you, me, Jeff, the children—" Lauren's voice, her mind faltered at the thought of them, Drew and Kenzie: What would she tell them?

"I'm sorry. I just—I don't know what I—"

"How am I supposed to trust you now?"

"I guess the same way I trust you even though you lied and lied to me when you were drugging yourself."

Lauren tossed aside the towel. "I thought Greg was back on heroin and that's why you were acting so weird. I thought he killed Bo in some drug deal and you were hiding him, and I was scared to death for you and for Drew when he was here. Then I thought maybe you had cancer or something. You knew I was worried sick about you, and all the time, you were covering up this—this terrible—"

Was it real? Did it happen the way Tara said? Did Greg and Jeff really—dear God, how would she tell Annie?

"Do you think I've slept since then? Or eaten or been able to work this entire week?"

"Do you think Annie or Bo's dad has slept or eaten?"

The silence banged down hard, a judge's gavel, an indictment. Then, abruptly, Lauren laughed, and the sound was ugly, truncated. "I planned to ask you to help me do a fund-raiser for Bo. Can you imagine? The only reason I didn't mention it is because you were sick."

Tara turned her mug in circles.

Lauren leaned, stiff-armed, on the counter. "No wonder Jeff didn't want me volunteering. God, what a fool I've been." She was remembering yesterday, at the hospital, when he'd blamed her involvement with Annie's family for the neglect of Lauren's own.

Some fucking stranger.

That was how he'd referred to Bo. And he'd known Bo was dead and where Bo's body was, the body he'd dumped on that no-name ranch road. It was monstrous, despicable. And then his act, that holier-than-thou performance at Kenzie's bedside—his perfect-father routine—

I'm working my ass off . . . trying to keep us together . . .

What is going on with you? He had asked her at the hospital. Asked her in a way that made her feel she was the ruination of *him.*

When he had killed Bo and covered it up. He had let her be targeted by the police.

Tara stepped toward her.

Lauren thrust up her hand, palm out. "You have to make this right," she said. "You and Jeff and Greg have to go to the police."

"Well, last I looked, I'm the only one still here."

Lauren sat at the table and put her head in her hands, fighting for composure, for clear-mindedness. It did no good to wonder how her sister and her husband and a man she thought of as her friend could, in so short a time, have become criminals who were wanted by the law. She looked at Tara. "Even if we can't find them, you still have to go to the police. Bo's family needs to know what happened to him. You can understand that, can't you? If you don't, I mean it, Tara, I will."

"You would turn me in, your own sister, but you wouldn't tell me Greg was a murderer?"

"The two things are not the same. There's no question now of violating anyone's right to keep their past mistakes private. I think the police know already. Maybe not all of it but something. They have the photo of the rug. They went by the warehouse, looking for Jeff. It's only a matter of time until they put it together."

"I didn't even hold the gun, much less shoot it. I don't know where they tossed it or where they took the body." Tara averted her face, jaw trembling. "I couldn't stop them—couldn't save him." She looked back at Lauren, and her eyes were fierce. "I tried! I tried to make his heart beat, make him breathe, but he—he—" She clapped her hands over her mouth.

"I'll go with you, TeeRee."

She didn't answer.

"Can't you see that you will never have peace unless you make this right? It doesn't matter what Jeff or Greg do. *You* can't live with this. I know, because I know you and how you're made. This will end up breaking you."

"I'm afraid, Sissy."

Sissy. When had Tara last called her that? After their parents died, Lauren thought, when she'd been so young and lost, and Lauren's sense of Tara then, the memory of her grief, her vulnerability was so visceral and real that Lauren couldn't stop herself from going to Tara and gathering her little sister in her arms. "We'll get through this together," she said. "I'll be right here beside you every step of the way." It was the same comfort she had offered Tara all those years ago, during the long and terrible nights when, except for Margaret, they had been so alone in the world.

They were in the Navigator, leaving Tara's house for the sheriff's office when the unmarked brown sedan pulled across the driveway, blocking their exit. Tara turned around, and Lauren watched in the rearview mirror as the detectives, Cosgrove and Willis, got out of opposite doors. Both men seemed to be waiting. Within a few moments, another car, a patrol car with its siren off and its lights flashing, came down the street, and in its wake, a second squad car appeared. Without the warning shriek of sirens, their approach seemed covert, even lethal.

Within moments, four uniformed deputies had joined the detectives. A low sound of voices ensued, accompanied by a minimum of hand gestures. Sidelong glances were directed toward the Navigator. One deputy had braced his hand on the butt of his gun.

Panic sat in Lauren's gut, as hard and cold as stone.

"Oh, God." Tara let her head fall against the seatback.

Lauren took her hand. She couldn't bring herself to say it would be all right. That was Jeff's line, and it had turned out to be a lie.

28

Two officers approached Lauren's SUV, one coming to the passenger side and the other rounding the tailgate to the driver's side.

"I need y'all to step out of the vehicle," he said when Lauren lowered her window.

"Are we under arrest?" Tara asked as she slid from the passenger seat, and the quaver in her voice made Lauren's heart falter.

"Are we?" Lauren got out of the car.

The deputy cupped her elbow. "The detectives just want to ask you some questions."

"About Bo Laughlin?" Lauren pressed.

"Yeah, that, and there are some other related matters."

What other related matters? Lauren would have asked, but the officer was walking her toward the street, where the squad cars waited, and she was frightened now, enough that she balked, causing the deputy to tighten his grip.

"Can't we ride together?" Lauren heard Tara ask, and looking around, she realized they were being led to separate patrol cars. She glanced over at the detectives, Cosgrove and Willis, who hadn't left the vicinity of their vehicle. They didn't meet her eye, and it seemed deliberate. She wanted to shout at them, to demand they tell her what was happening. But panic made it impossible to speak. Her ears rang with it. Her stomach was knotted in its huge fist. The officer who was escorting her opened the back door of his car and gestured her inside. She sat gingerly, wiping her sweaty palms down her thighs. Once he closed the door, the smell of something rancid in the air—body odor and a fainter stench of vomit mixed with something harsher, like fear—her own and that of countless others—almost gagged her. She took air in shallow dips and prayed not to faint.

She didn't speak on the ride into town and neither did the deputy, and when they arrived at the sheriff's headquarters, and he let her out of the car, she gulped air like a person saved from drowning. Inside the squat two-story building, she caught sight of Tara for a moment, long enough to see she'd been crying and needed a tissue. Lauren thought of her purse, left behind in the Navigator. She always carried a tissue. Mothers did that.

Her uniformed escort ushered her to the end of a short corridor lined with doors, stopping at the last one—the sign beside it identified it as "Interview Rm. A"—and opening the door, he said, "Have a seat, okay? Detective Cosgrove will be here shortly."

The room was small, not much larger than a good-sized, walk-in closet, and furnished with a metal table and four chairs. Lauren went to the opposite side of the table, facing the doorway.

"Can I get you anything?" the deputy asked. "Water, Coke, coffee?"

She shook her head, struck by his politeness. He was young and clean-cut. His mother would think he was handsome in his uniform. She would be proud. The thought made Lauren's throat tighten. She didn't know why. The door was nearly closed when she said, "Wait."

He popped his head into view, brows raised.

"My purse and my sister's—do you know where they are?"

"Here. At the duty desk. You can pick them up there when you're done."

"Thank you," she said.

The door closed. Lauren propped her elbows on the table. The top half of the wall to her right was mirrored. She'd seen enough television crime shows to know it was two-way, that she was likely being observed. She hugged herself, feeling self-conscious, and jumped when the door opened.

"Sorry to keep you waiting." Detective Cosgrove pulled out a chair opposite Lauren and sat down. He arranged the things he'd brought into the room on the table, a cup of coffee, a manila folder—it might have been the same one she'd seen earlier—a pen, and a notebook. She'd seen him write in that, too, when he'd come to her house.

She met his gaze.

"Thank you for coming," he said, taking a hasty sip of coffee.

"Did I have a choice?" Her anger now made it possible to breathe, to speak without stammering, something she tended to do when she was scared. Which she was. Plenty scared.

"Well—"

"Tara and I were coming here on our own. If you'd waited, we would have saved you and your department the trouble."

"That's me, always jumping the gun." He made a wry face.

"Where's your partner?"

"Willis? I don't think we need him in here. He just pisses people off."

"What is this about, Detective?" Lauren wasn't in the mood for humor.

"Why were you and your sister coming here?"

Lauren shifted her glance, but what was the point of being coy for either of them? Bringing her gaze around, Lauren said, "I think you know."

"Here's what I know, Mrs. Wilder—"

"Lauren, please call me Lauren." She didn't know why she asked for that. Maybe because the use of first names felt less intimidating.

"Lauren, then," he repeated. "If you call me Jim," he added, and he smiled as if he meant it.

Lauren felt her heart ease a bit. "You were going to tell me what you know, Jim. I interrupted."

"Yes, well, shortly after we left your house, you left and drove by Wilder and Tate, then drove to your sister's house. You were there for a little over an hour. In the course of your visit, you related to her that we'd been to your house and showed you a photograph of the area rug belonging to your grandparents—I'm assuming here, okay? Am I correct, so far?"

Lauren nodded.

"In addition, you told her you were informed that the rug was what Laughlin's body was wrapped in and that it had been traced back to you as a result of the cleaning tag that we found attached to it." He paused, looking at Lauren from under his brows. At her nod, he continued. "About then, she would have told you what happened on Saturday, a little after sunset, how Bo Laughlin came to be shot and wrapped in that rug."

"You're assuming again."

"Yeah. She would have told you what her role was and also what roles your husband and Greg Honey played in Laughlin's death. Am I right? You know the whole story?"

"It was an accident. They were shooting at targets. They didn't know Bo was there."

"So I've heard."

Lauren kept his gaze.

323

"That's what your husband, Jeff Wilder, told us, too—that it was an accident."

"When did you talk to him?"

"We picked him up after we left your house. He's here."

"Oh." The syllable came on a small puff of air, as if she'd been punched, which was how she felt. "You arrested him? For what happened to Bo? Can I see him?"

"He's not here solely on that matter, Mrs.—Lauren. There are other—well, let's just say we've been discussing a variety of subjects with Mr. Wilder, and your name keeps coming up. Maybe you should hear about that first."

"What subjects?"

Cosgrove opened his manila folder and took out pages she recognized were the asbestos-notification form. "You remember this," he said.

"Yes, but what does it have to do with Bo's death? I don't understand." Lauren's heartbeat was erratic.

Cosgrove flipped to the last page. "Earlier when we showed it to you, you seemed to think this wasn't your signature." He pointed it out.

"It's not," she said.

"You're sure? Take your time. We're in no hurry."

She looked at her name again. It was Jeff's handwriting. She'd known it before. But she hadn't wanted to know. She still didn't.

"Who do you think signed it, if you didn't?"

Sidestepping his question, she said, "You told me there wasn't any asbestos in the Waller-Land building, and that's accurate to a point. The truth is that it's there but not at a toxic level." A more complete recollection of the business dealings surrounding the Waller-Land contract had begun to stir in her mind. "The inspector who did the survey came by the office, and I remember him saying it was unusual in such an old building not to find more of a presence." Lauren felt confident of this memory. Jeff knew it, too; he'd heard the man, and she told Cosgrove he had. "It's possible that another survey was done—"

"You're talking about this inspector, here. He's the one you spoke with?"

Cosgrove indicated the section on the form that requested the inspector's name, licensing number, and employer. But the name that appeared there, Cameron Lewis, wasn't the name of the man Lauren remembered, and she said so.

"You're sure this wasn't the guy?" Cosgrove asked for the second time.

Lauren looked at him, and her annoyance must have shown on her face, because he apologized.

"It's like you said, sometimes you have trouble with your memory. Your husband told me since you took that bad fall and injured your brain so severely, you often do things and can't recall doing them. It doesn't seem like much of a stretch to imagine you would forget a name, right? Or that you might forget signing a document or a check? Or even meeting with certain people? I mean, for a while, you thought you might have had something to do with Bo Laughlin's death, am I right? At least that's a relief, huh? That notepad, for instance. Clearly, your husband brought that into the house."

"I'm not sure I know what to think or how to feel about any of this."

"Yeah, I can imagine. All of it, coming down like it has, it's got to be a shock."

Lauren could have laughed. She could have thanked him for his empathy.

He took out what looked like a folded brochure from his manila folder and handed it to her. "What do you know about this?"

She had immediate impressions of colors—aqua, brilliant turquoise, pink-tinged taupe, and foamy white—that suggested water and sand. Brighter colors depicted beach umbrellas and palm trees. *The Nautilus at Padre Island* was scrolled across the front panel above an elegant, low-slung building, and below that, in smaller print, the line read: *An exclusive golf club and resort.* She looked at the detective, mystified. "I don't know anything about it." *Was that right?* "I've only been to Padre once, and that was years ago."

"You don't have an interest in the Nautilus?"

"An interest?"

"You haven't purchased shares of ownership in the resort?"

Lauren searched her mind, scrambling for an answer, the right answer. She had the sense that Jim Cosgrove knew the right answer. There was nothing wrong with *his* brain or memory.

"Mrs. Wilder? Lauren?"

"Why am I here, Detective? Why can't I see my husband?"

"If you could just bear with me—"

"Is he under arrest? Am I? You can at least tell me that! Is Tara? Do we need a lawyer?"

"Well, of course as far as your sister and your husband are concerned, it would be up to them to ask for a lawyer in the event they were placed under arrest. But so far, you and I are just talking, trying to sort out some things we both find confusing."

"Am I free to go, then?" Lauren held Cosgrove's gaze.

"Yes, of course, if you want to, but you want the truth, right? It's important to you?"

She couldn't deny that it was.

"It's important to me, too," Cosgrove said. "I think it's a big part of why I became a cop. I like to get to the bottom of things. I like to see justice done. I don't like seeing innocent people hurt. Especially kids. Man, that gets to me."

"My kids are fine."

"Yeah, you're a good mom. Jeff made a real special point of letting me know that."

Was it sarcasm she heard in his voice? Had Jeff complained to him about her care of their children? Was this about taking them from her? She wanted to ask but couldn't find the breath or the courage.

The detective picked up his pen. "Tell me about Wick Matson. At our earlier interview, you said he was a heavy-equipment contractor. How do you know that?"

"Because I've seen his name on invoices; I've written him checks."

"Have you met him?"

She took a moment, then said no. "But I don't have a lot to do with the big commercial jobs. Anyway, I think even Jeff hasn't worked with him that long. A year, two at most." She paused again, thinking about it. It was when she'd come back to work after the accident that she learned Jeff had changed heavy-equipment suppliers. She remembered him saying something about the former contractor, that he wasn't maintaining his machinery and Wilder and Tate couldn't handle the liability if there was an accident. Insurance was a huge part of the cost of running a salvage yard. She explained this to Detective Cosgrove.

"So you don't know Matson in the capacity of real estate developer. You don't know that the Nautilus is his project? You haven't bought shares in the resort yourself or solicited others to invest in the property?"

Her heart tripped. "No."

"Your husband said you might know where Matson is."

"What? No. I have no idea why he would say such a thing." *Maybe he hadn't.* "Please let me talk to him."

Detective Cosgrove lifted another page from the folder. When he pushed it across the table toward her, Lauren saw it was from Cornerstone Bank. She recognized the logo at the top.

Cosgrove asked her to look at it.

She averted her gaze, and it was willful, a child's tactic. Even she knew it was useless.

"Paul Thibideaux—you know the VP over at Cornerstone, the one who's an old friend of your husband's—he was kind enough to have this printed out for me. It's a record of the deposits and withdrawals made to and from your account there in the last six weeks, basically from the time you opened it until today, this morning, in fact." He paused. "I'm going to need you to look at the list, Mrs. Wilder."

She did, scanning it quickly, her eye catching on what to her were enormous figures. There were deposits for anywhere from $115,000 to $136,000. The withdrawal amounts were smaller but more numerous. There was one for $22,000, another for $8,000, and three more for $12,000. "I've never used this account." She put the list down. "I only found out about it a few days ago."

"Really? Because, like I said before, according to your husband, you opened this account yourself."

"No. I—we were together when we opened it." Lauren tried again to think, to conjure any image from that experience, the one Jeff claimed they'd shared, but nothing came. Her head was so full of the white noise of her confusion, a higher dissonance of panic. What was going on? She bent forward. "If you'll let me talk to Jeff, I'm sure we can straighten all of this out." She wasn't sure of that or anything.

"Okay, I guess now's as good a time as any, but before we go, there's just one more thing I want you to see."

Lauren watched as Cosgrove reopened the folder, his manila envelope of horrors.

The photo he pushed across the table toward her, a grainy black and white, showed part of a street, the hoods of cars nosed into parking spaces. It was a moment before Lauren recognized the scene, and when the sense of it gelled, a frisson of unease tapped up her spine. "Where did you get this?"

"Do you recognize the location?"

"It's Prescott Street, outside Kim's Needle and Book Nook."

"Yeah. Do you recognize anything else? You see the SUV with the hood up? Could that be your Navigator?"

"Where did you get this?" Lauren repeated.

"There's a surveillance camera nearby. We took the still from the film footage. But we also have a couple of witnesses who saw you pull into the space."

"On Wednesday when I came into town to help with the search for Bo, they saw me driving my Navigator?"

"Yeah." His gaze was penetrating, watchful.

"There was an Altima in that space when I went back. Jeff said I drove it into town."

"But the picture, the film footage, and the witnesses say otherwise."

"But that means . . ." She trailed off. She couldn't begin to wrap her mind around the meaning.

Cosgrove slid a second photo toward her, its quality as poor as the first one. "Do you recognize the guy with his head under the hood?"

The image of the man was too blurry to distinguish more than the fact that he was doing something to the engine, tinkering with it, the way Jeff had tinkered with her Navigator on Tuesday evening when it wouldn't start. But Lauren didn't want to think about that, either. She said, "I don't know who that is."

"Well, it's your husband, Jeff Wilder. On Wednesday, while you were at the community center, he tampered with your car, pulled a few wires, then contacted the dealership, had them bring the loaner and switch it out with the Navigator."

"How do you know?"

"The evidence, film footage, witnesses." Cosgrove ticked through his list.

Lauren barely heard him. "It could be Danny, the kid who brought me the Navigator. When I went back to Kim's and didn't find it, my first thought was that he'd stolen it. Maybe I was right after all." In her excitement, she bent forward. "He took it for a joyride. Isn't that what they call it?"

Cosgrove only looked at her, and she got the sense he was waiting for her to run out of words, enthusiasm. She was loath to do either. "There's no way you can tell who that is from this picture. You can't even see—why would Jeff do that? We'd already paid for repairs once." Lauren's voice rose, as if its very tenor would make her denial true.

Cosgrove shuffled his "evidence" back into the folder and stood up. "If you're ready, I'll take you to see him now. You can ask him. He's just down the hall."

Lauren stood, too, and fought a wave of dizziness. "Is Tara with Jeff?" It made sense that they would be together if this was about taking the children. But somehow that seemed unlikely now.

Cosgrove said it was possible Tara might be detained.

"You mean arrested?"

"It depends."

Depends. Dr. Bettinger's word, Lauren thought, following the detective down the corridor, the one he used when he couldn't say for sure.

Cosgrove paused outside the door of another interview room only steps away from the one he and Lauren had left, and when he looked at her, she saw caution in his glance, as if he might be warning her to enter at her own risk.

"Ready?" he asked, and before she could say no, he turned the knob.

Jeff said, "Thank God," when he caught sight of her, and he came immediately around the table to hug her, but it wasn't a relief, having him close. It wasn't a comfort, and she stepped from his arms quickly, feeling as leery of him as she might a stranger. She couldn't help it, and yet her reaction was disconcerting to her.

"I'll get y'all some coffee," Cosgrove said, and he left before Lauren could say she didn't want any coffee, before she could say, *Don't close the door. Don't leave me alone in here.* She kept her back to Jeff.

He said her name, and she turned on him. "What is going on? The police picked Tara and me up at her house. They brought us here in separate cars. I thought it was about Bo, because you shot him. My God, Jeff—" She broke off, feeling the shock again as if it were new, fighting to withstand it. "How could you? And then you tried to hide—you left him, left him on the road. You would treat a dog better, or at least until now, I always believed you would."

He came toward her as if he might embrace her again, but she held her hand up, palm out, stopping him. "No," she said. She could not tolerate his touch now. "You're playing some kind of game with me, and I want to know what it is."

"Let's sit—"

"You brought his notepad into the house. It fell out of your pocket, or maybe you put it there deliberately, because you wanted me to think I was the one. You wanted me to believe I was involved, that I'd done something to Bo. Why would you do that? The police already knew it was you and Greg. What were you trying to accomplish?"

"Calm down, okay?"

"Calm down? Are you kidding? I've spent hours today scared to death, getting grilled by detectives about everything from Wick

Matson and some resort property to a bank account I've never used. There's so much—so many things that have happened lately. I've been so scared I was losing my mind, what little I have, but it was you, wasn't it? You were trying to make me doubt my own sanity."

"If you'll just let me—"

"Don't say I've forgotten or it's my brain injury or I'm on drugs. Don't say any of that. Don't talk to me about *my* issues, Jeff—that you discussed with Detective Cosgrove," she added, insult riding in her voice. It seemed a small thing by comparison, but it hurt her that he would talk to a virtual stranger about her.

She put her hands to her head. "This can't be real."

"Look, can we at least sit down?"

But she wouldn't, although he did, perhaps thinking she would follow suit.

"I know you're pissed, but I can explain," he said, and for one wild moment, her heart soared with a vain hope that an explanation was possible. "Will you sit down? Please?"

She pulled out the chair opposite him and sat, stiffly, jaw clenched in a mutinous knot. The room was a duplicate of the one where she had sat with Cosgrove, and she was sitting where he had, with her back to the door. The mirrored wall was on her left now, but she was only subliminally aware of her surroundings.

"Tara must have told you the shooting was an accident," Jeff said. "It was probably Honey's bullet. He couldn't get enough of shooting that goddamn gun."

"Oh, my God! Please tell me you aren't trying to lay blame—"

"It happened so quick." Jeff snapped his thumb against his middle finger. "Like that. Why the hell was the kid there, anyway? That's what I don't get."

"His name was Bo, and it doesn't matter why he was there, Jeff. It doesn't even matter that he was shot, as tragic as that is. That was an accident. Even the police know it, or they will. The terrible thing, what is so despicable, so beyond comprehension, is that you covered it up. That's why you're here, isn't it? They arrested you. I can't even imagine what it took, what was going on in your mind to do such a thing."

Jeff's face hardened. "I'll tell you what was going on. Our fucking lives were over, that's what was going on."

"I don't know what you mean. If you'd only reported it—"

"That wasn't going to change the fact that the kid was dead, and with the cops involved, one thing was going to lead to another, and the shit would hit the fan, just like it is now. That's what I was thinking."

"What shit, Jeff?"

"There's a lot you don't know." He kept her gaze, and there was something relentless in his eyes, some kind of awful anguish and desperation.

Lauren couldn't look away, although she wanted to. The blood in her veins felt like sludge, like ice.

He said, "You won't like it, but you've got to understand I had no choice."

Did he mean about the shooting? Hiding it? Lauren waited.

He plowed his hands over his head, and she had the sense he was hunting for the words to make her understanding happen. He found her gaze again. "We were going to lose the business, the house, everything if I didn't do something, and this opportunity— Wick brought the deal to me, over a year ago, before you came back to work, when you were still so—"

"What deal, Jeff?" But even as Lauren asked, she was putting it together, remembering the Nautilus resort brochure and the way Cosgrove had questioned her about it. *You don't know Matson in the capacity of real estate developer? You don't know that the Nautilus is his project? You haven't bought shares?*

"Wick has this fantastic beachfront property on the Gulf Coast near South Padre Island. His granddad left it to him. Wick wanted to develop it. Put up a swanky hotel, get somebody famous to build a golf course. He started getting investors. I was one of them. It looked solid, you know, and we made money at first. Everybody was happy. We kept getting new investors, more than we could handle really. But more important than that, Wilder and Tate was back to even again. The mortgage on our house was current. We were getting a handle on all the medical bills. You know how we had to drain the kids' college funds?"

She nodded.

"Well, I was able to start new accounts for them. I was going to tell you. I wanted to surprise you, make it into a celebration."

He paused as if he expected a response, but even if she were capable of speech, Lauren didn't know what she might have said.

"So, we were getting this dividend out of the project every month. The way it worked—the more you put in, the bigger the return. Sometimes I was getting over 18 percent. It was like taking candy from a baby." Jeff's eyes shone. There was a fine film of sweat across his brow, his upper lip. He sounded thrilled but in a feverish way.

Watching him, Lauren thought, I don't know this man. Even his appearance seemed altered. "But was it ever built, Jeff? Was it ever more than a paper dream?"

"See, that's the thing. The EPA got involved. They said the land was contaminated. Well, not the land but the water supply or some shit. Something about injection wells in the area. I never really understood it."

"That ended the project, then? The investors got their money back?"

"Not exactly," Jeff said, and he told her how Wick continued to sell shares. By then, Jeff was selling shares, too. "People would hear me talk about it, about the return on investment. They couldn't wait to give me their money."

"But how could you keep taking it? Didn't they know the resort wasn't going to be built? Didn't you tell them?"

"The deal wasn't entirely dead. Wick kept working with the EPA. He swore we'd find a way around all the government bullshit, that the Nautilus would eventually open for business."

"Oh, Jeff, how could you believe anything he said—but even so, you weren't honest with those people. You took their money under false pretenses."

"I know what you're saying, Lauren, but moralizing now? What good is it? And trust me, if we hadn't had that money coming in, we'd be on the street with the kids. Is that what you want?"

Lauren blinked up at the ceiling, hunting for sense, coherence, some familiar ground, but all she could come up with was another question. "How could you do all this without my knowing?"

"You did know. You saw all the cash running through the Cornerstone account. Where did you think it came from?"

It was the way he said it, with the conviction of absolute truth that tripped her, but only for a moment. "Oh, please." She bit off the words. "I'm not that far gone. The only thing I ever saw from that account was the e-mail they sent you about a new sign-in process. I never saw statements or knew there was any activity until Detective Cosgrove showed me a list of deposits and withdrawals. I don't even remember opening the account. I had to ask you about it. You were annoyed—"

"But you could say it was yours, that you made the deposits, wrote the checks. Your name is all over it. You're the primary."

"Why would I lie?"

"Look"—he bent toward her—"as good as the Nautilus deal was a few months back, it's not so good now. The investors haven't been paid anything for over a week, and for around five weeks before that, they've only gotten part of what's owed them. And by them, I mean us, too. Then, recently, I found out Wick's been bleeding cash out of a couple of the partnership accounts. While I've been running around like a crazy man trying to find new investors, he's been robbing me—us—"

Lauren interrupted, "Are these partnership accounts other bank accounts? Is my name on those, too?"

"No. They're accounts Wick and I opened jointly. It's complicated, Lauren. A venture like this—you have to move money around—"

"But it's not legal; nothing you're telling me is, right." Lauren searched his gaze, hunting for a sign of the Jeff she knew, the man who was too smart, and more than that, who was too honorable to be caught up in what this so clearly was, some scheme, a way to rob people. She couldn't fathom what had changed for him or inside him or where she'd been when it happened, and it sickened her. She felt like a person drowning, grasping for sense, any handhold.

His face closed against her; he didn't want to hear it—the moralizing, he'd called it. And he was right in a way. What good was it now?

"The thing is, folks are pissed," he said. "I've gotten threats."

"Threats?"

"Yeah, you don't fuck with people and their money, you know? Some of the investors want out; they want their original investment back. I don't have it, not for all of them. Plus I think somebody found out about the EPA bullshit and tipped law enforcement. These Lincoln County guys keep saying they brought me in here to question me in regard to the shooting, but they're asking a whole lot of other questions, and now they've questioned you, too."

"It's scary," Lauren murmured.

"Yeah," Jeff agreed.

They sat a moment, aware of but not looking at each other. Like strangers, Lauren thought, waiting to be clobbered by yet another calamity.

Jeff wiped his face. "It's only a matter of time until the feds get involved. The FBI, I mean. This kind of thing—it's federal because of the bank stuff."

"Oh, my God."

Jeff sat back. He blew a chestful of air out of his mouth. "I'll go to jail. It's that simple. They're saying it's fraud. I disagree with that, but even if I can beat whatever charges they trump up against me, like I said, there are people out there who'd like to see me as dead as Bo Laughlin. Do you understand? It's my life on the line here. Yours and the kids, too."

She frowned. "Why us? We didn't—"

"Think about it. Where will you be if I go to prison? They'll take everything, the house, the business. They'll sell the goddamn furniture."

"How can they? I wasn't involved."

"Doesn't matter. They'll do whatever it takes to make restitution."

"We can't lose our house, Jeff, our means of earning a living."

"I'm doing everything I can so that won't happen. This morning I got hold of some cash, enough to tide us over. Ben Kaiser gave me a couple hundred thousand when I met with him, but that's not going to buy us much time."

"For asbestos removal."

Jeff didn't confirm or deny it.

"There is no significant asbestos contamination in the Waller-Land building, is there?"

"Don't worry about Kaiser. Two hundred K is nothing to him. He'll get over eight million when he sells the property."

Lauren watched, mesmerized, as Jeff dismissed the issue with a flap of his hand.

"There isn't much time," he said to her. "So let me tell you what I've been thinking. We can either get a good attorney who might be able to get us out of this mess, or assuming I can get out of here, we can leave town and start over somewhere else. Whichever one you want."

Lauren registered the import of the alternatives Jeff was presenting, in some shocked part of her mind, and a memory surfaced of the folder containing the Waller-Land demolition paperwork—the one Jeff had insisted she hadn't put in his briefcase—along with the realization that he had probably orchestrated that so-called mistake, too. But she couldn't deal with it now. She wanted to know about the asbestos. "You faked a second notification form, didn't you? And signed my name to it."

He admitted he had, turned up his palms, and said it again, that he'd had no choice, adding, "Believe me," this time.

Lauren shifted her glance. It wasn't as if she hadn't known from the start he'd forged her signature. But when it comes to owning a terrible truth, there's a gap between knowing and not knowing; there are borders of acceptance to be negotiated. The journey is precarious, and Lauren was an unwilling traveler. She looked up at her husband, the man she'd married, who she no longer recognized. "You always have a choice, Jeff."

"Well, if there was one, I didn't see it. The business wasn't in good shape before your accident, and it wasn't getting better."

"I understand that, but we could have filed bankruptcy, cut our losses, and—"

"And let some banker or, worse, some lawyer tell me how to run my own goddamn business? I spent half my life and who knows how many hours, nights, days, weekends building Wilder and Tate into what it is—or I should say *was*. Maybe it wasn't some

Fortune 500 company, but it was a good company. It gave us and the folks who've worked for us a good living. I couldn't give it away to some bunch of bloodsucking jerks in suits, you know? Besides, the trouble was temporary. I just needed a bump, and it'd be all right. Everything would go back to normal. It's all I could think about—you and the kids, keeping you guys safe, keeping my family together. Protecting our name, our reputation."

He held her gaze, and she didn't look away.

"What was I supposed to do?"

She couldn't answer.

"You've been through so goddamn much, Lauren. I couldn't stand it." His voice cut out; the sheen of tears reddened his eyes.

Her own throat closed. "But you implicated me. How is that different from involving me?"

"I never would have, but six weeks ago when I found out what Matson was doing behind my back, I got my hands on what money I could, opened the account at Cornerstone, and dumped it in there. I put it in your name so the bastard couldn't find it and neither could the cops. I paid off some of the investors, too, you know? I wanted to make it right."

"There weren't only withdrawals made from the account, Jeff. There were deposits, some for a lot of money. Detective Cosgrove showed me."

Jeff rubbed his eyes. He glanced at her and shrugged. "Folks wanted in, and I'm talking even after they found out it might not happen. Some people just want to believe in the dream. Is that my fault?"

She didn't answer.

"It got away from me, Lauren, and that's the truth."

"Yeah, I can believe that," she said, and her voice hitched.

"But it can work, I think. If we stick together, we can walk away from this without major consequences, like prison."

"How?"

"You need to let me do the talking. Let me tell them you were Matson's primary partner in the resort deal. You got the investors, took their money, dispersed the interest payments. I'll say you didn't really know what you were doing, that Wick put pressure on you when you weren't yourself."

Lauren couldn't have been more astonished if Jeff had balled up his fist and slugged her in the stomach. "You must be joking." That was the only response she could make; he wasn't pleased with it.

"Come on, it's not such a stretch, is it? You did take drugs; they did screw with your head, and on top of that, you had a severe brain injury, and you're still recovering. Dr. Bettinger would testify to all of that, and after he does, do you really think a judge or a jury would convict you of anything? Even if they did, I doubt they'd do more than give you a slap on the wrist."

A slap on the wrist . . .

"Tara and I, even the kids, Diane at First State, Suzanne, all of us can give a ton of examples about how your mind isn't working up to par. It's better, but you're not all the way there yet. There won't be a dry eye in the courtroom."

When she didn't respond immediately, he prodded her. "What do you think?"

"I think forging my signature on those documents isn't all you've done to make me look incompetent." Her mind had snagged on his mention of the drug use. She was shaking harder now, so much that not even her voice was steady.

"I don't know what you mean."

But he did; she could see it in his eyes, the evasion, the wish to drop his gaze. But he wouldn't. He still thought there was a chance she might buy what he was selling. But the blinders had fallen all the way now, and while the view was brutally harsh, she couldn't deny what was there. "The Oxy in my purse and in the house—you put it there, didn't you? Didn't you?" she insisted when he didn't answer. "Where did you get it?"

"Remember when I searched the place after you quit? I found it stashed everywhere. You wouldn't believe—"

"You kept it?"

"It was in a safe place, where even you wouldn't think to look. It seemed like a shame to toss it. What if somebody needed it for pain?"

"Or what if you needed it to make it look as if I was drugging myself again, as if I was the scammer, the liar, and the robber. After all, everyone looks up to you, Saint Jeff, the poor guy with the brain-damaged, drug-addled wife. I don't believe you!"

"I'm not a saint, and I wanted to tell you. I did. But think about it, Lauren, if you'd known the plan, you wouldn't have sounded convincing."

"That's insane, Jeff! And people think I'm crazy?"

"Okay, but answer this—if you were asked if you took the Oxy, like in a courtroom, could you honestly say you didn't? Could you swear your memory was accurate? *Would* you swear it? Would you swear that at times, even since you've been off it, your judgment isn't still impaired, that you haven't forgotten things, important things?"

Like your own daughter.

Jeff's meaning hung between them, an accusing finger.

He went on. "Wouldn't there be reasonable doubt, enough that you couldn't be held accountable?"

"I'm surprised you didn't spike my morning coffee with it." The words were pure sarcasm, acid on her tongue.

"Are you serious? You think I'd do that after what I—all of us went through when you were on that shit? No! I never gave it to you, Lauren. Jesus—"

"But you did torment me with it. You did things to make me doubt my own sobriety and sanity."

He raised his brows.

"The Navigator?" she said.

"What about it?" he asked, as if he were in ignorance.

But the flush creeping out of his shirt collar, the visible heat of his guilt was unmistakable. Lauren felt the last of her hope go. She had wanted so badly for this at least to be an invention of law enforcement. "Why did you do it?"

He knew what she meant and shifted his gaze from her. His jaw worked. He said he didn't know and stopped. He said, "I was so fucking mad that day. Everything piled up." He gave her a look. "My stress level was off the chart even before the weekend at the farm. Then that kid got shot, and you got involved in the search. It scared the shit out of me when you said the cops had been at the house Wednesday morning. I decided right then I had to tell you—I mean, everything, the shooting, Matson, all of it. I thought when you got to work, we'd sit down. We'd work out something. I waited for you. Waited and waited. But you never showed."

She could see that it mattered that she hadn't kept her promise. She could see that if she had gone to the warehouse instead of going into town, things might have worked out differently, and the enormity of it, of how her own actions might have altered the outcome, jarred her.

"I was so fucking pissed. I knew where you were, that you'd gone to the community center, and I drove there. I was going to let you have it, but then I saw the Navigator—I'm not proud of what I did. I hope you believe that."

"What were you thinking? That it would make me look even crazier? I mean, when the shit hit the fan, as you say, and you implicated me? You could cite that whole little drama you arranged with the car, that you played out at the community center as an example of my faulty memory, my lack of judgment—my *criminal* behavior?" Lauren stood up, bitterness flooding her mind, coating the back of her mouth. She pushed the chair up to the table. "You're on your own, Jeff. I don't want any part in this, your latest scheme. I don't know what drove you to do such terrible things. I don't know the man you've become."

His face fell. His eyes reddened again. "But you do. You do know me," he insisted. "I'm still the same guy, your husband who loves you better, more than anything on earth. I'm nothing without you. When you got hurt, when I almost lost you, I was there at the hospital every second. I helped you learn to walk again, to talk again, to remember. I tied your shoes, Lauren, when you couldn't."

She gripped the chairback hard enough to whiten her knuckles.

"Look, I know I fucked up, but I can make it right. Let's just get out of this, and then you'll see."

Jeff stood and came around the corner of the table, and Lauren let him approach her. She was confused about why. There was some part of her that was still clinging to the idea that there was a way back. She knew better, but still . . . almost sixteen years together. How did you walk away?

"Remember when we were first married," he asked softly, "when everything was brand-new between us? I brought you breakfast in bed every Saturday."

"You put a rose on the tray. You would put it between your teeth and dance." Lauren's throat closed. "I loved you so much."

He didn't seem to notice that she'd used the past tense. Even Lauren was surprised.

"We can be happy like that again." His fingers brushed her temple, teased a path to the corner of her mouth. He kissed her; she felt the heat from his body, the familiar pull of desire. He was her husband, her lover, her friend, or so she had believed. She backed out of his embrace. "There is no we, Jeff, not anymore."

Behind her, the door opened, and a man dressed in a dark suit came in. He introduced himself. Lauren heard his name, Kevin something with the FBI, he said. Fraud division, he added. More men in suits entered the room. Their voices blended, grew louder, became a cacophony. She felt herself separate from the scene, watched from a high perch as Jeff was handcuffed and read his rights.

She heard him call her name, "Lauren, Lauren, please," and her heart broke.

She felt a touch on her arm. It was Jim Cosgrove, and it amazed her how glad she was to see him, nearly to the point of tears.

"I'm sorry," he said, guiding her from the room. He steered her down the corridor, back to the room where he'd initially questioned her. He indicated she should sit, and she did.

He stood at the table. "Are you all right? Can I get you anything, a glass of water?"

She nodded. Her mouth was dry. Exhaustion weighted her limbs. When the detective brought her the water, she drank thirstily, draining the cup.

Cosgrove sat down. "Better?"

"Yes. Thank you." Lauren set down the cup.

"I'm sorry we put you through that, but it was necessary. We wanted to know the extent of what your husband was involved in with Matson and Kaiser and also to make sure you hadn't played a role."

"You brought me here on purpose, to get Jeff to talk?" Lauren wanted to look around, to ask if they were on television. "Is that even legal?"

"He could have left at any time, the same as you. Even now that he's under arrest, he can choose not to talk to us."

"What will happen to him?"

"It depends on how good his lawyer is."

"Where is Tara? Can I see her?"

"She's waiting for you. When you're ready, I'll get a deputy to drive you home."

"Home? Tara can go home? She thought—we both thought— she would be arrested."

"She's free to go for now."

"What does that mean?"

"We want to verify her statement. We may need to question her again. We'll see."

Lauren dropped it. It didn't matter. *Tara could go home.*

A fresh threat of tears seared the undersides of her eyelids. She was so tired even the burden of a small relief was nearly too much.

Cosgrove walked her out to where Tara sat on a bench across from the duty desk.

"Oh, Sissy," she said, walking into Lauren's embrace. They held each other tightly for a moment.

Lauren stood back, searching Tara's eyes. "Are you okay?"

"Yes. You?"

"I think so."

The deputy came and walked them out of the building to his patrol car. It had been warm when they came in, but as the night deepened, a wind had come up. Lauren shivered. She wondered if the kids had their jackets. She wondered how she would ever tell them about their father, that they might not see him for a while and why. The deputy opened the passenger side doors of his cruiser. Tara slid into the backseat.

Lauren looked at the deputy. "I'll just ride in back with my sister, if it's okay."

He nodded.

She got in beside Tara and found her hand.

They didn't speak on the short ride to Tara's house, and once there, their conversation amounted to no more than the handful of words it took to agree that Tara should spend what was left of the night at Lauren's.

They slept in Kenzie's room, in her twin beds. Lauren couldn't face the bed she'd shared with Jeff. "I might have to get a new bed," she told Tara. And then they slept. Not long. Too much had happened, and there was so much more to go through, to sort out.

It was still dark on Saturday morning when Lauren woke and slipped down the stairs to make coffee. Tara came down a few minutes later, and while they sat at the kitchen island, Lauren told her everything Jeff had said. Sometimes she had to stop to find her breath or a tissue.

"Oh, Sissy," Tara kept saying.

"The man I talked to last night, who looked like Jeff, isn't the man I married. The Jeff I knew wasn't a liar or a thief. He'd never stolen from anyone in his life." Lauren didn't know why, but somehow the idea that Jeff had robbed people bothered her more than his implicating her or lying and twisting the truth. She wanted the investors paid back and wondered if there was a way. She wondered if she would receive threats now.

"I was one of them," Tara said. "I invested twenty thousand in that venture."

Lauren looked at her, incredulous.

"Initially I was getting anywhere from 18 to 22 percent, then a few weeks ago, it dwindled to 12, then 10, then nothing. Every time I'd ask, Jeff made an excuse. He seemed really nervous when we were at the farm. Even before—before Bo died, he was avoiding the subject, avoiding me. Now I know why."

"Why didn't you tell me, Tara? You must have known it was illegal—"

"It was Jeff. He wanted to surprise you."

"I thought he put your money into a federally secured mutual fund."

"Well, I always knew he was an asshole, kind of arrogant, a control freak. He knew it all, what was best for everyone. I never really trusted him."

"Tara, don't." Something in Lauren resisted blackening Jeff's image. It was almost as if they were speaking ill of the dead. "Don't talk like that about him around the kids, okay?"

"I won't. But don't be surprised if, one day, they don't talk like that about him around you."

Lauren didn't want to think of it, the way Drew and Kenzie would come to view their dad. She would have to be ready to hear anything from them. Hadn't she run through the gamut of emotions? Everything from anger and disgust to fear and grief?

"You were suspicious enough of him to go for a drug test," Tara said.

"Not him. Me. I was suspicious of me."

"Yeah, because he manipulated you."

"Well, the good thing is there was nothing there."

Lauren had listened to the message in her voice mail from Dr. Bettinger's nurse, Shelly, when she got up.

"You're clear," she had said. "Not a trace of anything toxic or illegal in your system."

Lauren had been so relieved, her knees weakened. She'd had to sit down. Her joy hadn't been diminished, either, when Shelly had cautioned that the negative result only meant Lauren hadn't ingested the drug, whether by her hand or another's, in the twenty-four hours prior to the blood sample being drawn. Shelly suggested that if longer-range results were wanted, Lauren could have her saliva or her hair tested. But Lauren didn't think she would.

It was over, whatever it had been—her love affair with the Oxy—she was done with it. She wanted life; she wanted to be a mother to her children, the sort they deserved, and drugs weren't part of that picture. Already, looking back, she couldn't understand that woman, the one who had chosen addiction over her family. Oddly, seeing the conflict in herself shed a small light on Jeff's actions. He had gone far off the path, too. The difference was, she had come back.

Tara turned her coffee mug in her hands.

Lauren said, "How much did you give him?"

"A good chunk of the money you guys paid me when I sold you my share of Wilder and Tate. Greg got the rest of it, and I've seen nothing from that investment, either." She drank her coffee. "I think I'm what you could technically call broke."

"Oh, Tara. I thought he was taking care of you. How could I have been so blind?"

"You wanted to believe in him. I guess I did, too."

"The Forever Sisters," Lauren said.

"Maybe we should be the Pollyanna sisters."

Lauren's smile was reflex. She said, "Detective Cosgrove told me they might question you again."

"They're going to the farm, to see if the evidence supports my statement about what happened."

"Will it?"

Tara looked up, hurt, annoyed. "Yes. I'm not lying."

"So, they'll let you off?"

"I think so. I don't know." She rubbed her upper arms briskly. "I almost wish I'd go to jail like Jeff, and like Greg will, too, if they ever catch him. It doesn't seem right, sitting here."

Lauren didn't answer.

"They had me call Greg while I was giving my statement."

"Really?"

"He didn't answer. His voice mail was full. He probably ditched the phone."

"Well, you're cooperating. That's got to count for something."

"What about the kids?" Tara asked after a moment. "What will you tell them?"

"I don't know," Lauren said. *Why didn't you consider the effect on them before?* The thought seared her brain. She would ask, but it would lead to hard words, more hostility. What good was that? "I'll have to pick them up soon," she said instead.

"It scares me that they could hear about their dad on the news. I mean if Amanda's or Gabe's parents listen to it—the early-morning programs . . ." Tara's voice trailed into doubt.

Lauren stared at her. She hadn't considered it before, the potential for media coverage, the fact that everyone in town, in the entire country, for all she knew, would soon know their names and worse about them. Sudden, furious tears packed her throat and stung her eyes. "How could Jeff do this? He's the one Drew and Kenzie lean on, the one they feel safe with. Not me. I'm the crazy druggie. I embarrass them. They hate me."

"They don't hate you. They just don't trust you right now, but they will. You have to show them you're okay. If they can see you handling it, that will reassure them."

"But what if I can't? I relied on him, too. Since the accident, all the stuff with my stupid brain."

"Your brain isn't stupid. I don't ever want to hear you say that again. You're strong, Sissy. Of the two of us, you've always been the strong one, like Mama was."

Lauren opened her mouth to argue, to say how tired she was of being told she was something she didn't know herself to be, but Tara waved her hands.

She said, "You've just forgotten, and I'm not only talking about how you gave up your life for me when Mama and Daddy died. I'm talking about the last two years, coming back from having your brain bashed in, coming off an addiction you never asked for."

"I couldn't have done it, though, without Jeff and you and the kids."

"Yes, but we didn't do it for you. We only showed you where you got off track. Coming back, that was you. All you."

"I've slipped."

"Who doesn't?"

"My head is still not straight all the time."

"But every day it gets straighter. You can do this, Sissy. You can," Tara repeated, and she reached for Lauren's hands. Tears stood in her eyes. "You'll be okay and so will Drew and Kenzie. We'll all be okay. You'll see."

• • •

"I want to see her," Tara said a little later when they were leaving the house to pick up Kenzie and Drew.

"Who?" Lauren asked. She was looking over her shoulder, marking her progress down the driveway.

"Annie Beauchamp. I want to tell her I'm sorry. I don't know if she'll listen, but I have to try."

Lauren headed in the direction of Suzanne's house, steeling herself, coming to terms with the fact that she would have to tell Suzanne—and Pat, too—at least something.

Tara said, "*Sorry* is such a useless little word."

"It's better than nothing," Lauren said. "Sometimes it's all we have."

• • •

The drive back to the house was surreal. The children sat in back, and Lauren could feel their mutinous stares, their furious questions, the threads of encroaching alarm, because they knew; kids always know. It was like riding with a lit stick of dynamite, she thought, and she could only pray to make it home before one of them exploded.

After they gathered around the kitchen island and Lauren explained how their father and Tara were involved in Bo's death, Drew shouted she was a liar.

Kenzie was mute; she looked terrified, and her injuries, the bruising on her face and the whip-thin slash too near the corner of her eye, made her seem even smaller and more vulnerable. Lauren would have gathered her into an embrace, but like Drew, she wouldn't have tolerated it.

"Who can trust you?" Drew shouted. "You're nothing but a fucking druggie. They always lie."

"Drew," Tara's protest was soft.

Lauren said, "Do you remember the weekend Dad went to the farm and you went fishing and caught the bass? You tried to call him, more than once, you said, and Aunt Tara, and they never answered. This is why. Because your dad and Greg did this thing—"

"And I knew what they'd done," Tara said.

"Dad's phone was off; that's all." Drew was adamant.

"I was there." Tara spoke softly. "It happened just the way your mom says. She isn't lying, honey. I wish she were."

Lauren was glad for Tara in that moment, that she was present and could back up the horrible things Lauren was forced to say about Jeff.

"How did the cops find out?" Drew's voice hitched.

Lauren explained about the rug with the tag attached, the one that Bo's body had been wrapped in. "Someone from a neighboring farm found it and called the police. The tag had my name and our farm's address on it."

Kenzie looked at Tara. "How come you aren't in jail like Daddy?"

"The police might still arrest me," Tara said. "I'm doing everything I can to help them now, but I should have called them when it happened. I was very wrong not to. It's what your mom would have done if she'd been there, but I was afraid."

Both Kenzie and Drew looked at Lauren; she didn't know what she saw on their faces. Wariness, she thought, mixed with confusion and outright denial.

Lauren thought how much more they had to know, and she braced herself.

"Is Daddy coming home?" Kenzie asked.

"No, honey. I don't think so, not for a while." She didn't have to say it now, that in all likelihood, they would never again be together as a family in the way they had been. She herself couldn't fathom how or what the future would be.

"If the cops don't know who shot Bo, whether it was Dad or Greg, then why did Dad get arrested?" Drew asked. "Where is Greg? Did they arrest him, too?"

"They haven't found him yet," Tara said.

"I'm afraid there's more that your dad has done that has gotten him into legal trouble," Lauren said.

"What do you mean?" Drew wanted to know.

"Well, you know it's been hard, money-wise, right? Ever since my accident, we've been struggling. Daddy got overwhelmed; he made some bad choices."

"What kind of choices?" Kenzie asked.

"Complicated ones," Lauren said, and she went on picking and choosing among the terrible facts, feeding them only the ones she thought they needed, slowly and gently, as if they were tiny sips of bitter medicine, and her heart broke, watching as their expressions changed, going from bewilderment to panic to something harder— maybe outright disbelief, maybe anger.

Drew crossed his arms on the kitchen-island countertop and buried his face in them as if the shame of what he was hearing about his father burdened his shoulders. Kenzie stared at Lauren as if she were trying to sort out the meaning of some strange dialect. Lauren wondered how much she understood.

"It sucks," Drew said when Lauren finished. "What he did is so lame."

His chin trembled, and Lauren felt an overwhelming ache of futility, watching his struggle not to cry. She could only pray he wouldn't hate Jeff, or at least that he wouldn't hate Jeff forever. She hoped one day he would be able to forgive them both, his parents, who were fools.

"He was desperate, honey. It warped his judgment. When Bo was accidentally shot, I think it just pushed him over the edge. I think he kind of lost his mind."

"Will he go to jail?" Kenzie asked.

"He's in jail now, stupid," Drew said.

"Don't call your sister names, Drew." Lauren's admonition was automatic.

"I mean prison, dummy," Kenzie said.

"We'll have to wait and see," Lauren said. "There will be a trial first, and Daddy will have a lawyer so he can tell his side."

Kenzie asked if they could go to see him.

"I'm sure we can, if you want to."

"But I don't have to?"

"No," Lauren said, "absolutely not."

"Well, I'm not going. I don't care if I never see the asshole again." Drew pushed his stool against the island and shoved his way out of the kitchen. His steps were hard on the stairs, and when he slammed his bedroom door, it felt to Lauren that the whole house shook.

29

Four days after Jeff Wilder was taken into custody, Greg Honey was arrested in Las Vegas. Sheriff Audi called JT with the news, and Annie found out when she brought JT vegetable soup and salad after her shift ended at the café. She had been bringing him meals nearly every day. She was afraid he wouldn't eat if she didn't.

"Honey shaved his head," JT said. "He had a cane, and he was sitting up front, big as fucking Dallas, in the handicapped seat of a bus bound for LA, like no one could see through that shit. What an idiot."

"What will happen now?" Annie took the heated soup out of the microwave and set it on the table in front of JT.

"They'll extradite him, bring him back here. Audi acted like he didn't know what he'd get charged with. He said they don't have all the evidence together yet. I told him he better not say the word *accident* to me or I'd go through the phone and wring his neck."

"Where are the crackers?" Annie shifted things around in the cabinet next to the sink. She was sick of it, the whole ordeal. Every indication so far was that the shooting was exactly that, a horrible, tragic accident. But Bo was gone, regardless, and nothing was going to bring him back. Let him rest in peace, she wanted to say. *Let us all rest in peace.*

But JT didn't want peace. He wanted revenge.

She sat down across from him. "I called the coroner's office. They'll release Bo's body to the funeral home tomorrow. We need to talk about final arrangements."

Because they had both heard Bo express a wish for it, they asked that he be cremated. The funeral home director suggested that since they weren't active members of a church, they might want to hold a service at the funeral home itself. There was a small chapel there for that purpose, but JT and Annie said no. It would only draw the media attention that was currently trained on Lauren Wilder's family back to their own, and neither Annie nor JT could tolerate the idea of being back in the news.

• • •

A couple of days later, after collecting Bo's ashes, they drove to the switchyard, where he had often sought refuge. Annie carried the canister, and JT walked alongside her, hands shoved into his jacket pockets. She was nervous and wished she could say how little she knew about how to do this, but he seemed so remote from her, and she was hesitant to intrude on his silence.

They threaded their way between the corroding walls of a half dozen long-out-of-service railcars, went another fifty yards or so beyond them, and finally Annie stopped at a spot where the weed-choked rails curved right before losing themselves in the blue distance. A crenellated lacework of clouds clung to the horizon, and although the sun had risen above them, the morning was chilly with a bit of wind. As if by mutual consent, Annie and JT turned their backs to it, facing east, facing the light, and when she opened the canister and tipped it, gently shaking it, they didn't look at each

355

other. Instead, they looked out, watching as the wind picked up Bo's remains, scooting them into the air above the rusty tracks and off into the tall grasses that sprouted along the rail bed. It took only moments for the last of him to be gone, to be free.

Annie's throat knotted with the urgency of her tears, and when JT put his arm around her, she turned her face into his shoulder.

• • •

Cooper was sitting on her front steps, Rufus beside him, when she got home. Rufus came to greet her on the front walk, brown eyes liquid with joy, tail wagging. She bent to pat him, to talk silly dog talk to him.

Cooper stood. "Are you okay?"

She shook her head, and when he came to her, she went into his arms, and she cried, and with her face pressed against his chest, she told him about scattering Bo's ashes.

Once she was quiet, Cooper led her to the steps. Rufus followed, and they sat down.

"I don't want your pity," Annie said, wiping her eyes.

"Who said anything about pity?"

She brought her knees close to her chest and wrapped her arms around them. It was cold. She ought to invite Cooper in, make hot tea, share a muffin. She'd brought a few home from the café, apple strudel, a recipe she'd invented.

"I might pity you," Cooper said, "if I didn't know how strong you are, but even strong people can use a shoulder now and then. They can use a friend."

"Yes." But he had her wrong, she thought. She wasn't strong. She was lost, as lost as Bo must have felt when he set off walking down that country road to his death. She had resigned herself to never knowing why he'd been there in the first place. The police hadn't been able to tell her, and if Lauren's sister, Tara, knew, she wasn't saying.

"Look, if you want me to leave you alone, all you have to do is say so."

Annie met Cooper's gaze. "You've been so kind to me, you and your family. I don't deserve it. I've been ungrateful. Mean," she added.

"You've been going through a very rough time," Cooper said.

She shook her head. "We're so different, Cooper."

He asked her what she meant, but how could she tell him that when she thought of his family, his big, happy family, when she thought of the radiating waves of doting parents, grandparents, aunts, uncles, and two dozen cousins that were included in Cooper's circle, she knew she didn't belong there? It didn't matter how much she might want to be part of such a family, yearn for it even, she knew it wouldn't work. She couldn't abandon JT to his sorrow and guilt, couldn't leave him and Bo behind her like closed chapters in a book, and what part of that grim life could she bring into a future with Cooper?

He deserved better.

Not that he'd asked to share a life with her. He had only asked for her friendship. But why go there at all? It was best this way, ended before it ever began, before she could hurt him more than she had already. She stood up. "I should let you go," she said, "before you and Rufus freeze."

Disappointment flared in his eyes, but all he said was, "All right, then" and "I guess I'll be seeing you sometime." He looked down at Rufus. "You ready, buddy?"

Rufus wagged his tail uncertainly, looking from Cooper to Annie, and the worry and dismay in his eyes nearly shattered her resolve. Swiftly, she bent and hugged him, and without another glance at him or Cooper, she left them standing on her front steps. It took every ounce of her will to close her door.

. . .

As Annie had anticipated, there was nothing in the coroner's final report to indicate Bo's death was other than accidental.

The evening after the ruling became official, Annie made lasagna and brought it to JT's house.

"You heard the news." He was grim but quiet.

Annie braced herself. "I did. It's what we expected, right?"

"Yeah, but you know what pisses me off? How every time I turn on the TV, I have to look at that asshole Wilder's mug shot. I have to listen to the hundred-and-ten ways he ripped people off, but not one of those media ghouls ever mentions the fact that he also shot my son. It's like it never happened."

No one cares.

They've all forgotten.

Annie waited for JT to say these things, too.

But he didn't. Instead, he said he'd gone for a drive earlier.

Annie looked at him.

"I went to see where Bo was killed."

"Why?"

"I needed to see where it happened, if it was true you couldn't see the road, the way the detectives said."

Annie drank her iced tea. It was what Detectives Cosgrove and Willis had reported after they'd examined the scene. They'd found it to be exactly as Tara Tate described it. Some of the cans and bottles Greg and Jeff used as targets were still standing on the ledge. There were shell casings on the ground, in a pattern consistent with target practice. They'd found the gun, too, an old Colt .45, in the woods across the road, where Tara had said Jeff tossed it.

"*Could* you see the road?" Annie asked JT.

"No," he said, and the syllable rang with his resentment.

Annie kept still.

"It tears me up, all three of them getting off like what they did was nothing. It's not right." JT dropped his fork onto his plate, making a clatter.

"Sheriff Audi didn't say they'd get off. Maybe Tara will, but Jeff and Greg are both being charged." Annie set down her fork. She wasn't hungry.

Greg Honey was still awaiting extradition, but when Annie had last spoken to Sheriff Audi, he'd said it was only a matter of days until the man would be returned to Lincoln County, where at the very least, like Jeff, he'd be charged with evading the police, hampering their investigation, and concealing evidence. There could be other charges made against them. Fines might be levied. The search for Bo had cost the county a lot in man-hours.

"Bo's death is still an active homicide investigation," Audi had said, and he'd qualified that by explaining he meant in the way that someone had taken the life of someone else.

"It's bullshit," JT said. "That Tate woman—how in the hell do you sit by and let the cops and other folks—hell one of them was her own sister—how could you let the search go on and not contact somebody?" He wiped his face with his napkin, and his hands shook.

Annie wondered if every meal would be like this, eaten in an atmosphere of bitter hostility.

JT wasn't finished. "I tell you what. I ever see one of those assholes on the street, I won't be responsible for what happens. You think if I whip out my gun and shoot one of them, they'll rule it an accident and let me off?"

"You don't even have a gun—"

"Wilder's wife," JT said.

"What about her?" Annie asked. "She hasn't done anything. She wasn't there."

"She's a dope fiend. Probably had Wilder screwing people out of their hard-earned cash to finance her habit."

"That is ridiculous, even for you!" Annie threw down her napkin.

JT looked at her in amazement.

"I can't stand this. If you're going to give yourself a heart attack, you can do it alone." Without waiting for an answer, Annie took her plate into the kitchen, set it in the sink, walked out the back door, got into her car, and drove home.

That night, unable to sleep, she sat on her front porch, huddled in her jacket, fists pushed into her pockets.

Earlier that day, at the café, Madeleine had said nearly the same thing as JT, that she wanted the three who were to blame for Bo's death to pay. She wanted them to be sentenced to serving time in prison. *Life,* she had said. A life for a life, she meant.

"It's not right, them letting Tara Tate go," Madeleine echoed JT's opinion. "It's as if the justice system in this state doesn't consider what she did criminal. It makes me so angry."

"Don't do this to yourself," Annie said. "You'll make yourself ill."

Madeleine didn't answer; she only stood there, trembling, incensed, hurt.

Taking a chance, Annie reached for her, putting her arms carefully around the old woman's shoulders, bringing her into a tentative embrace.

Madeleine had bent her face to Annie's shoulder. "I can't help it," she had said. "I loved that boy."

Annie lowered her forehead to her knees now, feeling the night chill, feeling the concrete step, hard and cold underneath her. It couldn't go on, this terrible, wounding hostility. It was as if Bo kept dying over and over.

He would hate it, she thought.

. . .

She was sweeping her front stoop on the next afternoon when she heard a car, an SUV, stop in the driveway. She looked up, and her eyes connected with Lauren's through the windshield, and the moment spun out as fragile and delicate as handblown glass. Annie couldn't move. She watched Lauren get out of the car, and when she leaned through the driver's-side window toward the passenger seat, she saw the other woman. Their voices carried on the breeze.

"I can't," said the woman.

"You wanted to come" and "It's the right thing," said Lauren.

And now Annie realized the passenger was Tara Tate, Lauren's sister.

Annie didn't know what to do. She turned to go into the house; then clutching the broomstick, she thought, no, she wouldn't run from them like a scared rabbit.

Tara got out of the car and met Lauren in front of it. Lauren kept her glance on Annie as she approached, but Tara watched her feet, shuffling along as if she were old.

"Can we talk, please?" Lauren asked, pausing at the foot of the steps.

"How did you know where I live?"

"Your address is in the book."

Annie looked off, down the street.

"Tara asked if I'd bring her to you," Lauren said.

"Why isn't she in jail like your husband?" Annie asked as if she didn't know. As Cosgrove had explained, being complicit in a crime wasn't necessarily illegal.

Tara looked up now. "I wish I were."

Annie thought she would feel the same if their positions were reversed.

"I'm so sorry," Tara said, "and I know it means nothing, changes nothing, but I wanted to tell you anyway." Her words dissolved, and for a long misshapen moment, there was only the sound of her breath, ragged with the attempt to quiet her tears.

They rimmed her chin, fell onto her crossed arms. Tara seemed unaware of them.

Annie said, "Detective Cosgrove told me you tried to save him."

Tara swiped at her eyes as if they made her mad. "I wish I'd done more."

"What? Like reported it?" Annie asked sharply.

"Yes," Tara answered.

A car passed in the street. There was a honk; the driver waved. Annie didn't wave back. She looked at Tara. "Did Bo—did he say anything?" She hated how her voice broke. How it sounded as if she were pleading. She pressed her fist to her mouth.

A sound burst from Tara's chest, liquid and hurt.

"Tell me," Annie said.

"He wanted help, that was all. He wanted someone to help him." Tara half turned as if to leave, staggering slightly.

Lauren steadied her.

Annie wiped furiously at her eyes.

"I know it doesn't matter," Tara said, "that it's no comfort to you or Bo's dad, but I will never forgive myself."

Annie had nothing, no words.

"If there were a way to undo it—" Tara's voice slipped.

Lauren pulled her closer.

Moments of silence ticked past, hot and bright as sparks.

Annie looked at Lauren. "I heard about your husband."

Lauren's mouth flattened, and there was a look of forbidding in her eyes. The subject was off-limits. *Taboo.* The word came into Annie's mind.

She set the broom against the porch post, meaning to go into the house, to close the door in their faces, but instead, she turned back. "How could you?" Walking to the edge of the stoop, she addressed Tara. "If you'd shot an animal, some varmint, you'd have had the decency to bury it." Annie clamped her jaw.

"Greg is back. He got here late last night. He's been charged. You heard, didn't you?"

Lauren offered this as a consolation prize. What did she want? Thanks? A reward?

"He and Jeff will be punished," Lauren said. "At least Detective Cosgrove told me they wouldn't just get off."

Another consolation prize, Annie thought. She wondered if Lauren wanted her husband to pay for what he'd done. What must her and her children's lives be like now, with their dad jailed and facing a whole laundry list of federal charges, including bank fraud? The media had dubbed him Bernie Madoff Junior, as if it were funny. But some folks around town, who were as mad as JT, called him a lot worse. A goddamn liar, a fucking thief. They said he was a coward. He'd been respected as a businessman, a neighbor, and a father, and deeply admired for the care he'd taken of Lauren throughout her long ordeal. Now they felt betrayed.

Annie looked at Lauren. "Nothing will bring Bo back," she said.

"No," Lauren answered.

"I always felt as if something terrible would happen to him." Annie felt compelled to say it.

"Your mind goes to the most horrible places," Lauren said. "It isn't your fault," she added.

It was what Annie's mother would have said, and it touched the painful crux of it, the bruised heart of Annie's grief. She looked away.

"You did everything you could for Bo." Lauren spoke so softly, as if she and Annie were alone, and there was nothing between them but the connection of the heart they had shared when they met. "It was his choice to live the way he did, to put himself at risk. He wanted to be independent. He wanted to be free, and you gave him that. You gave him his dignity."

Annie didn't answer; she couldn't. It was everything she needed to hear and couldn't yet believe, from the most unlikely source. "I'm going inside now," she said.

"Thank you," Tara said, and Annie nodded.

Down that same long tunnel in her mind, where there was sadness for the others who had been impacted by this senseless tragedy: Lauren's children, poor Madeleine and Charlotte Meany, other innocent and mostly innocent bystanders, there was also hope. Annie hoped things would work out for Tara; she hoped Lauren and her children would be all right, and going into the house, she thought how strange and surprising it was that she could feel as bad for them as she did for herself.

30

A nnie was kinder to me than I deserve," Tara said.

They had stopped by her house after leaving Annie's so Tara could pack some clothes, her toothbrush, the basics of what she'd need to stay with Lauren a few days. Neither of them wanted to be by themselves. Lauren wasn't sure which one of them needed the other one more. She put the socks and underwear Tara brought her into Tara's quilted tote. "It was brave what you did, facing Annie. I'm proud of you for it."

"If I were her, I think I would want to rip out my guts."

Lauren zipped the tote closed. "Come on, girlfriend. Let's go home."

Drew was at the island, eating a bowl of Honey Nut Cheerios. He greeted his aunt, but all he said to Lauren was, "When are you going to the store? There's nothing to eat."

"Soon," Lauren said.

Tara hefted her tote and went upstairs. Within moments, there was the sound of water rushing through the pipes.

Lauren asked Drew where Kenzie was, and he muttered something rude that included the words *tutu*, *fruitcake*, and *bedroom*. She stowed the milk and cereal, ridiculously pleased by his surly attitude for how it reminded her of ordinary times.

. . .

It was the week between Christmas and New Year's when the four of them held a family meeting, Tara included.

"We have to decide what to do about stuff," Lauren said.

"What stuff?" Drew asked.

"School. You can't keep doing the classwork at home forever. We have to decide if you want to start the next semester here. I know it hasn't been easy, and with Dad's trial coming up, there may be more publicity."

Lauren had been twice to the county jail to see Jeff. The first time she'd taken Kenzie at her request. It was awful. Lauren had expected Jeff to be angry. Instead, he'd been apathetic, disheveled, unshaven. His hair was sleep-matted on one side. There were deep creases on his face. Kenzie kept giving Lauren worried looks. *What is the matter with him?* She had cried when they left, and Lauren had lain awake that night, wondering which one was the real Jeff. Was it the strong, vital, confident man she remembered marrying, or had the weak, broken, defeated man been lurking in his shadow all these years? The next visiting day, Lauren went alone and told Jeff she was filing for divorce.

"I don't blame you," he said. "For any of it," he added.

He had asked her not to come back again, not to let the children come. "It's too hard, seeing you. I can't take it."

I . . . I . . . I . . . She had hardened her jaw to keep from saying it.

She'd been driving home when the quote from Thoreau that Bo had written in his notebook surfaced in her mind, the one that read: *The path of least resistance leads to crooked rivers and crooked men.* And crooked lies, she had thought. Thoreau might have added lies to the list. She had thought of all that Jeff's deceit had taken from her and the children, but by far the worst of the consequences would be his to bear. He was so twisted up inside, who knew if he would ever find his way back, if he would ever have any decent sort of life again. But as her father used to say, you make your bed one decision at a time.

"So, what do you think?" Lauren divided her glance now between Kenzie and Drew.

"We could live at the farm," Tara said. "People there might not know so much about what happened."

"Or we can stay here," Lauren said. She only thought that was possible because Suzanne and Pat had asked her to consider it.

They had come the day before Thanksgiving, loaded down with a boxed turkey dinner that included all the trimmings. Lauren had been touched to tears. She and Tara made coffee; the four of them sat down. At first, the conversation had been uncomfortable, and the worst moment came when Suzanne and Pat confessed that Jeff had approached them and their husbands about the bogus real estate investment, too. They had declined because they knew it was a scam. Lauren squirmed inside. It was everything she could do to remain seated. Finally, she apologized.

But neither of the women wanted her offering of remorse. She wasn't responsible, they said.

And it was somehow in all of that awkwardness and humiliation that a connection, however tenuous, was reestablished, and they'd been building on it ever since. Suzanne, especially, kept in touch, calling and dropping by, so consistently that Lauren finally began to believe her when she said their friendship meant the world to her. One day she made Lauren come out and walk the jogging trail through the neighborhood, something they'd done regularly in Lauren's previous life. She had reminded Lauren then of her divorce seven years ago, how horrible it was, how she had dragged around.

"For months," she said. "Do you remember? You didn't let me go. You stayed right in that cesspool with me, slogging through it. Now it's my turn. Let me help you." She took Lauren's hand and squeezed it. Lauren squeezed back, and something warm and light rose inside her. It had been a long time since she'd felt it, but she thought it might be hope.

Now, addressing Kenzie and Drew, she said, "Aunt Tara and I have talked about opening an antiques shop."

"I thought you had to sell everything," Drew said.

"Maybe," Lauren said. It depended on what her lawyer advised, whether filing bankruptcy was the logical thing to do. Regardless, she was taking every step she could to protect her assets. "But if we sell the farm instead of moving there, and if Aunt Tara sells her house, we think we'd have enough money to keep our house here and to buy inventory for the shop. It would be like your grandpa Freddie's shop."

"We thought of a name," Tara said. "Freddie Tate's, Too."

Kenzie said she liked it, and after a beat, she added, "I don't want to miss ballet," and tears came into her eyes.

"I don't want people thinking I'm a wuss like Jeff," Drew said.

Jeff? Lauren exchanged a look with Tara, who shrugged.

"Are you saying you want to stay here?" Lauren asked him.

"Me, too," Kenzie said. "Drew and I talked about it. If we move, everyone'll think it's because we're scammers, too, and we're not. *We* didn't do anything, and we're not responsible for what Jeff did."

Lauren's throat tightened. She felt Tara's hand rest lightly on her knee, as if to reassure her, to say *See, I told you they'd be all right.* It was a start, Lauren thought, a beginning they could work with.

"You're sure?" Lauren looked from Kenzie back to Drew, and when they nodded, she said, "Okay, then. Looks like we're staying."

"Aunt Tara, too?" Kenzie asked.

"If it's okay with you guys," Tara said.

"We'll have two moms," Kenzie said and grinned as if the notion made her happy.

"Some family," Drew said.

"Girls rule," Kenzie said.

"We'll see about that, dork." Drew grabbed Kenzie's arm, and when she twisted away, he chased after her. The sound of their footsteps pounded up the stairs. Something fell, a door slammed. There were two shouts of laughter, precious, *like heaven*, Lauren thought.

"I should send them outside," she said, but she didn't move.

31

JT turned down a second cup of coffee when Annie offered it. Since he'd gone back to work, he came to the café every morning on his way into Houston to have breakfast. Annie knew he did it for her because she said it reassured her to see him, to see that he was all right, that he was safe.

His anger, the lust for revenge that had driven him had eased in the weeks that Greg Honey and Jeff Wilder had been in custody. The media had picked up the story again, and they were making a lot out of the way the two men had, with cold deliberation and considerable forethought and planning, attempted to hide the shooting, causing the county thousands of dollars and man-hours in what they had known was a fruitless search.

Of course, Jeff Wilder's legal trouble went even deeper, but Annie hadn't really paid much attention to the news stories about it. She had heard that Lauren had started divorce proceedings. Sometimes she thought of calling her, but she had no idea what she would say. Maybe they would talk one day. Their paths might cross. Who knew? If she'd learned anything from the nightmare, it was that you could never tell about life, what it would do, how it might unfold.

Madeleine came from the kitchen, drying her hands, and when JT saw her, he said, "You women are going to make me fat."

"Hah," Madeleine said. "I'd love to think I could put an ounce of weight on you or Miss Annie."

"Did she tell you she's off to culinary school in Houston next week?" JT asked, and Annie's face warmed at the pride in his voice, in his eyes.

Madeleine was talking about the recommendation she'd written on Annie's behalf, and she was laughing, but looking over Annie's shoulder toward the door, she sobered suddenly.

Annie looked, too, encountering Cooper's gaze. Her heart bumped.

"Hey, Coop," JT called. "It's good to see you, man." JT went to him; the men shook hands.

Annie was mystified. She hadn't even realized they knew each other except on the most surface level. But they were chatting now like old friends. Watching them, she wondered why she'd ever been distressed about JT. Why had she felt as if they were such outsiders, so much so that she'd closed the door in Cooper's face? He was laughing at something JT said, some joke they'd shared. Something eased in Annie's heart.

JT turned, giving her a salute. "I'll see you for dinner?"

She nodded and watched him go out the door.

Cooper took a seat in a booth near the kitchen and opened a newspaper.

"Could you take his order?" Annie asked Madeleine.

"Well, I would, but Carol's in kind of a hurry, and I need to talk to her about the farm order before she goes."

"Okay." Annie smoothed her hands over her apron. If she didn't know better, she might think it was a conspiracy; she might think she was being set up. But she couldn't believe Cooper was here on purpose to see her, and he gave no indication of it, either.

When she asked what he'd have, coffee was all he said, and he barely glanced at her. Mostly, he kept his nose buried in the paper, the sports section.

She brought him a mug. "Black, right?"

He nodded, giving her another cursory glance.

She was stung by his indifference and then surprised at herself. But now, the prick of her tears annoyed her. What did she expect, after the way she'd put him off? She had what she wanted, didn't she? Her space, her privacy . . . her lonely isolated life?

She left him to his coffee and his newspaper, doing her job as if he were just another diner. She pocketed the tip the young family in the booth near the door left her after they paid for their meal. She asked the couple who were still seated at the counter's end if they needed anything more, and then, when there was nothing else left to do, she brought Cooper his check . . . taking it from her apron pocket, sliding it across the table.

And when he circled her wrist with his fingers, brought his hand up her forearm to cup her elbow, she met his gaze.

His eyes were full of questions.

She touched his temple, the fullness of his lower lip, and she smiled.

ACKNOWLEDGMENTS

In the midst of working on this book, I moved, and almost every-thing in my life changed except one: my lovely and intrepid agent, Barbara Poelle, who is there at every hour, a constant guide and tireless cheerleader. B2, you are the best. Like me, Tara Parsons, my fantastic editor at Lake Union, moved, too, and she reached out to me in a way I will never forget. Her belief in this novel and in my work and her unflagging faith mean more to me than words can say. Thank you, too, as ever, to my critique partners, Colleen Thompson, TJ Bennett, Joni Rodgers, and Wanda Dionne. Even in absentia, I hear your voices. I wouldn't be the writer I am without all our years together. Thank you to the early readers of this story, Colleen and my sister, Susan. And many thanks to Leslie McManus, who before I ever wrote down one word of this book, listened while I outlined the plot, contributing ideas of her own to consider, and all for the price of a cookie and a cup of tea. Huge thanks to my son David, who, once I did start writing, ever so patiently helped me work my way out of the many sticky fictionalized corners. And huge thanks to Jink Willis for her friendship, encouragement, incredible faith, spot-on advice, and tireless support, and to the members of both book clubs with whom I was able to connect through her.

The evenings I spent with them will always mean more than they can know. Huge thanks to my copyeditors, Jerri Corgiat Gallagher and Carrie Wicks who, together, straightened out my words, sentences, and paragraphs with so much kindness and patience, page after page. Jerri and Carrie, this book is better for your expertise. And a beautiful bouquet of gratitude and appreciation to Gabe, Dennelle, and Tyler at Amazon, and to Robert, Sara, and Crystal at BookSparks—all of you have made me feel so welcome, so much a part of the team—the village, really—that it takes to bring a book to life. Thank you for taking this book into your hearts and for all your help launching it. And last but never least, a huge shout-out to readers everywhere, because without you, what would be the point? Sending my deepest thanks to you and enough joy to circle the world.

QUESTIONS FOR DISCUSSION

1. After nearly hitting Bo with her car, Lauren stops to be sure he's all right. Would you stop for a stranger in similar circumstances? Was Lauren foolish or compassionate?

2. Lauren called the sheriff's office, asking for a welfare check on Bo. Was she interfering? Would you follow through, asking the police to check on someone you feel might be endangered?

3. Could you understand in the aftermath of Lauren's accident, the long and painful road to recovery that she endured, how she could become addicted to OxyContin? Do you feel her husband and sister were right to have conducted the intervention? Were they right to threaten her with losing her children? How would you handle it if a relative were in similar circumstances?

4. Tara keeps secrets from Lauren. What do you think of her motive for doing so? Have you ever kept a crucial secret and felt torn about it? Have you ever regretted keeping a secret?

5. Issues of trust are a recurring theme of this novel. Lauren's family has difficulty trusting her; she has difficulty believing in them and their support. Discuss the role of trust among family members. How important is it? Can a relationship survive without it? What happens if a family member is hurt in the way Lauren was? How would you handle it, if you couldn't rely on your spouse because of such an event?

6. Annie blames herself when Bo goes missing, but given that he is a diagnosed schizophrenic, do you agree that she should have been paying closer attention? How much independence should those with mental conditions be given? What do you feel Annie's responsibility to Bo was?

7. When Annie meets Lauren, she feels an instant bond because Lauren reminds her so much of her mother. Have you ever lost someone you loved only to see them again in the face of a stranger?

8. As a child, when Annie's mother remarries and Bo becomes part of their blended family, she is resentful as many children can be. Discuss blended families and how you might ease the transition if you were called on to help children deal with what they might view as an imposition.

9. Annie clearly loved and admired her mother very much, and finding out that her mother kept secrets from her was hard. Have you or would you ever keep a secret from someone you loved in order to protect them? Or is keeping everything in the open, no matter how painful, the best option? Discuss how you and your family members have handled issues of this nature.

10. Cooper's attempts to comfort Annie are rebuffed by her time and again, yet he doesn't give up. Why is that? What does he recognize in Annie that she very possibly doesn't see in herself?

A Conversation with the Author

At the beginning of *Crooked Little Lies*, Lauren Wilder is struggling to recover from both mental and physical damage she suffered in a terrible accident. She stops alongside the road to render aid to someone who is equally challenged. What was your inspiration for this story? How do you relate to Lauren?

Once when I was driving in a neighborhood where I used to live, I saw a young man walking alongside the road, just like Bo. I didn't almost hit him, but I could see how it might happen. I dismissed the thought from my mind, but several days later when I saw him again, and then seemed to see him walking roadside, even on the freeway shoulder, nearly every time I went out, I started to worry that there was something wrong. I kept feeling as if I should pull over and check and felt terrible for it every time I passed him without doing anything. It was like a war in my head: Do I stop and risk my safety if he's actually dangerous in some way, or keep going, hoping someone else will deal with the issue? Or suppose there is no issue? Finally, I called our local police department, and it turned out they were well aware of this young man. My head kept going, though, and soon there was an idea for a story.

Was the farm and what happened there part of the story from the beginning?

The two ideas were of a parallel track. The idea of what occurs at the farm in *Crooked Little Lies* was one I'd thought about off and on. How often can we be out doing something really innocent, having fun, not a care and then, boom, some horrendous event occurs, some calamity falls down on our heads, and not only that, but some action of our own brought it down on us. Now what? What are you going to do about it? And we aren't talking about a scraped knee or spilled milk here.

Were Lauren's and Annie's characters mapped out from the start? Did you have the ideas for their families in place or did they come to life as you wrote? Were there any interesting surprises?

I have to admit, Annie and her family were an author's dream, coming the way they did, almost of a piece, from the beginning. Lauren was more difficult. Maybe because she was so hurt, so fragile in the beginning. The surprise was huge. I had planned right down to the folks who would be in attendance what would happen at the farm, but when I wrote the scene, my muse took over. It didn't go down on the page the way I thought it would. But I love that, being surprised in that way.

What is your writing process? What is the part of it that is most difficult and what is the greatest joy?

I write every day. Mornings are best for me. Usually I go over the previous day's work and pick up from there. There is something about quickly skimming from the first page to the place where I've stopped that keeps the work coherent for me. But then, once I get too far in, more than fifty or seventy-five pages, say, it takes longer to read from page one. I don't do it as often. I'll try to stop myself at certain points, and then do an overall reading, but even with that, my threads are often knotted. I'll drop one and pick up another. It can make for a pretty big tangle at the end. And that's the most difficult thing, one of them. The joy is when the writing just falls out on the page, easy and fluid. Some passages will come and scarcely need a second glance. The other joy is sorting out those knotted places. One thing I find is almost nothing is wasted. Even when I toss in some detail or even a character that seems out of place, I'll find out why by the end. I'll see it and think to myself: Oh, now I know why I wrote that. To me, that's a joy.

About the Author

B arbara Taylor Sissel writes issue-oriented, upmarket women's fiction that is threaded with elements of suspense and defined by its particular emphasis on how crime affects the family. She is the author of five novels, *The Last Innocent Hour*, *The Ninth Step*, *The Volunteer*, *Evidence of Life*, and *Safe Keeping*.

Born in Honolulu, Hawaii, she was raised in various locations across the Midwest and once lived on the grounds of a first-offender prison facility, where her husband was a deputy warden. The experience—interacting with the inmates, their families, and the people who worked with them—made a profound impression and provided her with a unique insight into the circumstances of the crimes that were committed and the often-surprising ways the justice system moved to deal with them.

An avid gardener, Barbara has two sons and lives on a farm in the Texas Hill Country, outside Austin.